ML

WI

THE CORNISH LEGACY

Recent Titles by Barbara Whitnell from Severn House

DEEP WATERS
THE FRAGRANT HARBOUR
THE MILL COTTAGE

THE CORNISH LEGACY

Barbara Whitnell

severn
House

This first world edition published in Great Britain 2000 by
SEVERN HOUSE PUBLISHERS LTD of
9–15 High Street, Sutton, Surrey SM1 1DF.
This first world edition published in the USA 2001 by
SEVERN HOUSE PUBLISHERS INC of
595 Madison Avenue, New York, N.Y. 10022.

British Library Cataloguing in Publication Data

Whitnell, Barbara
    The Cornish legacy
    1. Cornwall (England) - Fiction
    2. Love stories
    I. Title
    823.9'14 [F]

    ISBN 0-7278-5683-9

Typeset by Palimpsest Book Production Ltd.,
Polmont, Stirlingshire, Scotland.
Printed and bound in Great Britain by
MPG Books Ltd., Bodmin, Cornwall.

BOOK ONE

CLARE

One

Clare Chandler, quite untypically, could not decide what to wear. Given to – indeed, noted for – making swift decisions that usually proved correct, her decisiveness had been one of the qualities that had impressed those at the top of Claremont City Trust, ensuring a rapid propulsion into the stratosphere, professionally speaking. Now, however, she surveyed the wardrobe that stretched from wall to wall in her converted warehouse overlooking the Thames, quite unable to decide between the Bella Freud number or the rather divine leather trousers with the Zulu bead belt. Or then again, there was the black Parigi, years old and worn a million times but still a favourite. She always felt comfortable in it.

"Oh, to hell with it," she said, snatching impatiently at the trousers. "It's only Duncan, after all."

It was a little worrying, this strange indecision, for she was aware that anyone in her line of business trod a tightrope where one small hint of weakness could lead to disaster. She hoped very much that the same lack of conviction hadn't been apparent during the afternoon's meeting when she'd been asked for her presentation on the Hoffman Holdings merger. She'd thought it a perfectly safe proposition yesterday; why, then, the butterflies in the stomach and the slight feeling of nausea when she had been required to nail her colours to the mast today? It wasn't like her, and she found it upsetting. Thinking about it now, she still wasn't at all certain that she had done the right thing, said the right thing . . .

"Oh, to hell with it," she said again, but wearily this time, bored with herself. The die was cast, for good or ill, and no useful purpose would be served by worrying about it. A nice, undemanding dinner with Duncan McMurtrie, whom she'd known since he was a struggling accountant and she was a very

3

green PA to Neil Fuller, fresh from Oxford and full of ambition, seemed just what was needed after a stressful day; except that there had even been something in Duncan's manner lately that seemed to say there would be decisions to be made in that quarter, too, before long. Why men could never settle for an uncomplicated—

The telephone shrilled and she threw the trousers on the bed while she answered it, still thinking of Duncan. However, the moment she heard Minnie Jago's West Country accent on the other end of the line she knew instinctively, with a sinking of the heart, that she was about to hear news she had dreaded for a long, long time.

"Is it Verity?" she asked, barely able to frame the words.

"Yes. Oh, Clare, 'tis the end, the doctor thinks. Says he doubts if she'll last mor'n a day or two. She took to her bed a couple of days ago feeling just a bit wisht, nothing much, she wouldn't let me call the doctor, but oh, she'm gone downhill that fast."

"I'll come tonight." Clare looked at her watch, no longer indecisive. "If I leave now I can be with you by about one o'clock – *damn!*" She had just remembered that having had intermittent trouble with the steering, she had left her car at the garage that very afternoon. "No, I can't do that. My car's in dock." Her mind ran over the possibilities. Could she hire? Borrow Duncan's car? Swiftly she came to a decision. "I'll catch the night train. Is – is she in any kind of pain, Minnie?"

"Doctor says no; just very weak, he says."

Clare chewed the inside of her lip, maddened at the thought of being unable to take to the road there and then.

"The train gets into Truro pretty early," she said. "Can't remember the exact time, but I'll be with you as soon as I can possibly make it. Oh Minnie, I'm so glad she's got you."

Minnie made no coherent answer to this and Clare knew she was crying; awkwardly, no doubt, the tears scrubbed from her plain, craggy face as if they were something to be ashamed of.

Immediately she had said goodbye, Clare swung into action. She phoned Duncan – no dinner after all, she said. Predictably, he argued. The train didn't go until quite late – close on midnight, if he remembered correctly from the last time she caught it. She still had to eat, and having done so, he could take her to Paddington.

4

"Well, let's eat here," she said. "I don't feel like going out. I can rustle up something and pack at the same time."

"Whatever. But don't worry about cooking. I'll take care of that. Pasta OK?"

"More than," Clare said gratefully. What a sweet, thoughtful, reliable kind of guy Duncan was, she thought as she put the phone down. He'd been a good friend, always. She could do a lot worse—

She dismissed the thought, impatient with herself once more. She hadn't stayed single until the age of thirty-six – heavens, thirty-seven in two months' time! – to settle for anything less than the best. Not doing a lot worse had never been part of her philosophy.

A call to Neil Fuller was the next thing, to explain that she would be taking a few days away from the office.

"It's your great-aunt in Cornwall? The one who brought you up? My dear, I'm so sorry." His dark brown voice was meltingly sympathetic and Clare knew exactly what expression he would have on his face. It would be the compassionate look, the one he wore when he was telling the head of some ailing firm that the bank no longer considered him a viable investment, but that they were all terribly, terribly sorry about it. There was a short pause, a moment of hesitancy. "Er – how long do you think you'll be away? There's the board meeting—"

"Neil, I just don't know what I'm going to find, or what's going to happen. I'll phone you when I get there."

"She's a good age, I seem to recall—"

"Ninety-eight. As old as the century."

"A good innings, in anyone's language."

"I know. Even so—"

"You must be there, of course. I do understand. Take as long as you like, my dear. Maybe a week—?"

"Neil, I don't know," Clare said again. "It might take longer. If she does die, there'll be all kinds of things to deal with."

It was only then that she thought of her mother, and continued to think of her after she had put down the phone. She ought to be told. Ought, at least, to be given the option of coming to Verity's bedside, even if years ago she had consciously removed herself from those that were left of her family. For years now she had limited her contact to the odd flying visit from her

villa in Majorca, an annual Christmas card or a brief phone
conversation which, delivered in her high, penetrating voice,
detailed her own social whirl without mentioning her daughter's
or aunt's well-being, except as a distinct afterthought. It was all of
two years – nearly three – since Clare had seen her in person.

Verity had loved Beatrice and had been hurt by this apparent
neglect. She hadn't said so; had never, in fact, made any adverse
comment about her, her associates, her manner or her way of
life, but even so Clare, attuned as she was to her every mood,
knew exactly how she felt. Her expressive eyes tended to give
her feelings away. On the occasion of her ninetieth birthday, eight
years earlier, Clare had expressed annoyance when no recognition
by post or phone had arrived from her mother to mark the day.

"She owes you so much," she'd said, angrily. "We both do. It
isn't right, the way she just doesn't seem to give a damn. She
could at least phone regularly and come and see you from time
to time. Majorca isn't the end of the world."

Verity had given a grunt of laughter at that. "It might as well
be," she said. And then she had sighed. "I'm not saying it isn't a
pity, or that I wouldn't love to see her. It seems such a long time
since she came home. You'd think, for your sake . . ." Her voice
trailed away, as if suddenly she had remembered the traumas that
had made past visits more of an endurance test than a pleasure
for any of them.

"In all fairness," Clare said, seeing the direction of her thoughts,
"I suppose we didn't have a lot to say to each other the last time,
did we?"

"Really?" Verity's mouth twisted with sardonic amusement. "I
think your memory's at fault. I seem to remember you had rather
too much to say."

Clare gave a rueful laugh at that. "Yes, I suppose I did. Well, I
was young and brash, full of ideas about putting the world to rights
and quite sure I knew the way to do it. What a pain I must have
been! But honestly, did you ever hear anyone spout so much clap-
trap as my sainted mother? She lives in a kind of Colonial time-
warp where anyone who doesn't belong to that wretched English
Club of hers simply isn't worth knowing. And as for her political
views – words fail me! Attila the Hun isn't in it! No, Verity, I'm
quite resigned to the fact that she and I have nothing in common,
but that's not the point. She ought to come and see you."

"I'd hate her to do so simply from a sense of duty."

"She owes you so much."

"She doesn't owe me a thing. She gave me you, didn't she? I'll always be grateful for that."

This gift, for Clare, had meant a blissful childhood by the sea in Cornwall, and a settled, secure home at Lemorrick, the house on the cliff, in place of the nomadic existence she had known with her mother, for Beatrice, buttressed against the mundane need to earn a living by the income inherited from her parents, had drifted around various British enclaves on the continent from an early age, enjoying a life of pleasure-filled futility. She had flitted from Antibes to Monte Carlo, Portofino and back to Nice and from there to Malaga where, at the age of thirty, she met Geoff Chandler, the skipper of a wealthy industrialist's yacht. He was handsome and charming but it was generally agreed, even among the happily dissolute set that constituted Beatrice's friends, that he had the morals of an alley cat. But he did look exactly like Errol Flynn and was fun to be with, so who cared?

When Beatrice found herself pregnant by him, it appeared that, after all, he possessed a few finer feelings. He loved her, he said. They would be married and he would change his ways and settle down. Beatrice was in a haze of happiness. The fact that she had money and he didn't was of no consequence, she assured her less gullible friends. They were in love, and nothing else mattered.

Geoff left the employ of the wealthy industrialist and, with Beatrice's money, bought a yacht of his own, the *Lady Bea*, which he proposed to charter. It was an enterprise that couldn't fail, he said; but it did, along with the marriage which foundered on a sea of womanising and drinking and bad faith, not to mention Geoff's realisation that Beatrice didn't have nearly so much money as he had imagined. Their union lasted no more than eighteen tempestuous months, after which he sailed away on the yacht that she had bought for him, leaving her with a year-old baby girl and a mountain of debts. She never saw him again, though much later in life Clare, through sheer curiosity and in defiance of her mother, had managed to trace him. She found a sad, emaciated wreck of a man dying of lung cancer in a London hospital, and through pity had attended his funeral three weeks later where she was one among only three other mourners. Geoff Chandler's charm, it seemed, had brought him few friends that lasted.

After his desertion, Beatrice was forced to curb the extravagances she had once enjoyed, but still contrived to wing her way round the more fashionable Mediterranean watering holes. Eventually, after a succession of casual affairs, she met a man who was not at all casual. Or handsome. Or amusing. Still, Gerald Pryde had money – serious money, which undoubtedly compensated for the fact that he was fifteen years older than Beatrice and looked even more. He was a large man with a thin, humourless mouth and a beaky nose, disadvantages that she found herself able to overlook in view of his wealth. He, it seemed, adored her. Marriage was a distinct possibility, except for the fact that he nourished a total aversion to children, even a solitary, self-contained little girl like Clare who had learned the hard way to be no trouble to anyone.

To Beatrice, the prospect of marriage to Gerald seemed on a par with sinking back into a comfortable feather bed. There would be no more money worries, no more making-do, no more striving to keep up with the rest of her set. Gerald had merely been visiting friends in St Tropez when she first met him and was himself the owner of a wonderful old house in Majorca, on a hillside above Deya. He would keep her, she immediately realised, in a manner to which she had always wanted to become accustomed.

Where Clare fitted into this scenario was less obvious, and it was inevitable that Beatrice should think of Verity as the means of disposing of the one stumbling block to a blissful solution of all her problems. Verity loved children and was frightfully good with them – look at the way she had taken Beatrice herself in when she was small! She would surely welcome the chance to look after Clare. It might not be for long, she told herself mendaciously – repeating this to Clare and to Verity, too, when the proposal was put to her. It was just a case of getting settled, she assured them. Gerald would probably come round to the idea of having a child about the place before long.

"Darling, you're just the same age as I was, when I went to Lemorrick," Beatrice had said to her apprehensive little daughter. "I know you'll have a simply lovely time. Verity will adore to have you, and you'll adore it, too. And then, of course, you can fly out to Gerald and me for your holidays. Won't that be wonderful?"

Even now, so many years after, remembrance of this caused

Clare a certain grim amusement. It had not been at all wonderful, nor could any child have thought it so. A summer spent at Gerald's Majorcan villa might sound ideal in principle, but in practice it meant days of tedium and loneliness and not-speaking-until-spoken-to, and getting into trouble for reasons she didn't understand. It wasn't many years before she begged to be allowed to stay in Cornwall for the summer, a request which her mother was only too ready to grant, for Gerald had not come round – nor, it seemed, was ever likely to. The arrangement was that Beatrice would come to Lemorrick for part of every holiday and for a while that is what happened, until such defections on his wife's part began to interfere too radically with Gerald's comfort. Both Clare and Verity continued to write to Beatrice regularly, letters that were seldom answered, but gradually the gaps between her visits grew longer until there was really no point in pretending that mother and daughter were anything but strangers to each other.

But she ought to be told about Verity. Clare dialled the number of the villa, only to hear the phone ringing on and on with, apparently, no one at home to answer. Strange, she thought. You'd think that Juanita at least would be there. Juanita was the housekeeper who lived in a couple of rooms over the garage, and invariably the phone was switched through to her at night when Gerald and Beatrice were away. Maybe it was her night off.

She was about to put the phone down when there was a click and a whirr and she heard her mother's voice on the Answerphone.

"*Buenos dias*," she began, in her oh-so-cut-glass English voice. This was presumably a gesture to Spanish culture, though it came as no surprise to Clare that she did not continue in the same language since this represented almost the sum total of her vocabulary, despite the many years she had been living in Spanish territory. All her friends were English or American, so what was the point? "You have reached the residence of Gerald and Beatrice Pryde. I am so sorry that neither of us is at home. Please leave your message after the tone and we will get back to you as soon as possible."

"Clare here. It's Monday evening, 31st October. Just to let you know that Minnie phoned earlier to say that Verity is very ill. The prospects aren't good—" Clare was conscious of a sudden quaver in her voice and took a breath to steady herself. "In fact

9

I'm afraid – I'm afraid the doctor thinks it's the end. I'm going down immediately. Thought you ought to know." For a second she hesitated. There ought to be more, she thought. Something warmer, like "Hope you're both well", or "It would be so nice if you could come over."

The awful thing was that it wouldn't. Not at all. Any sentimentality about the mother–daughter relationship had been knocked out of Clare long ago. They were simply two grown women who had nothing to say to each other – who, in fact, rubbed each other up the wrong way to an almost unbearable extent. Verity was a different matter, though.

"I know Verity would love to see you," she said at last, before putting the phone down.

But would she be capable of seeing anyone?

She felt paralysed with sadness, and wrapping her arms round herself she stood for a moment with her shoulders hunched, incapable of movement. She ought to get moving, she thought. Pack a bag. Get organised. Instead she stood staring out at the scene below her: the river, the lights, the night sky that, no matter what the hour, was never as dark here as it was at Lemorrick.

Riven in two, she thought, mocking herself for a moment, consciously dramatic. Here was the London that had been home for most of her adult life; the London that excited and exhilarated and disturbed; that seethed with people and traffic, and deals and ideas and all the stimulation that she had, for years, considered the breath of life.

But tomorrow she would be where the sea surged like coloured light over the shingly strand at Lemorrick Cove; where rocks from the granite cliffs above had tumbled down to form caves and inlets on the beach below, and rocky pools that swarmed with tiny creatures when the tide went out. And there would be seaweed, wet and shiny brown, and bladderwrack and gulls' feathers, and all the shells that any child could desire. And the air would be fresh and salty and clean.

Tomorrow she would stand in the drawing room at Lemorrick where tall windows looked eastwards towards the cove and the path that led upwards over the fields to the gate and the stile, and westward to the village of Porthallic with its little harbour that sheltered the fishing boats, and where, above it, pastel-coloured cottages climbed tier upon tier.

The house, she knew, was going to be hers. Verity had said so; had said that Beatrice wouldn't want it, had never really liked Cornwall once she had grown out of the sandcastle stage and had since lived too long in a Mediterranean climate to have any interest in this wind-swept corner of the far south-west. And it wasn't, after all, as if she needed the money. Clare, on the other hand, would cherish Lemorrick as it should be cherished.

"But not yet," Clare had said at the time. "Not for ages and ages and ages."

She still felt unready, unable to cope. Please not yet, she whispered to whoever might be listening; but almost immediately, as if the thought of Lemorrick itself had the power to console, she was conscious of a great longing for it, and a great peace despite her sadness, as if a hand had been placed upon her to smooth out the stresses and strains that were so much a part of her London life.

For a moment longer she stood, looking at the reflected lights in the river, not seeing them at all. Then she shook herself and went to pack.

As the taxi came to a halt outside the granite-grey house, she saw that Nigel Collins, the doctor who had looked after Verity ever since his father retired, was about to leave, but he got out of his car and came to her as she paid off the taxi, putting a hand on her arm.

"Clare, I'm so sorry—"

Clare stared at him, eyes wide with distress.

"I'm too late?"

"She died in the night. Quite peacefully. She just went to sleep and didn't wake up."

"Oh, Nigel, I should have been there!"

Minnie, her eyes red with weeping, came down the front steps and joined them on the drive.

"You couldn't have got here in time, no matter what, my love," she said. "You come as soon as you could."

"I should have—" Clare broke off, biting her lip. There seemed, suddenly, all kinds of things that she should have done and the knowledge that it was too late for any of them seemed too much to bear.

"Clare, you've nothing to reproach yourself with," Nigel said gently, as if divining her thoughts. He had, after all, seen the syndrome many times before. "She was always talking about you. She loved you very much, you know that."

Clare nodded, not speaking. He was right. She knew this to be true.

"I've got to go," Nigel looked at his watch. "I've a couple of urgent calls to make before surgery. Maggie will be in touch – and my father, of course. He knew Verity all his life and thought the world of her. If there's anything any of us can do—"

"Thanks, Nigel." Clare managed to smile at him. "She thought the world of you, too."

She went inside, and leaving her case and coat in the hall, went straight upstairs to Verity's room, her footsteps slowing as she approached the door. She was, she admitted to herself, a little afraid. She had never seen a dead person before.

The room, however, was so much as she had always known it that her heart slowed once more, as if acknowledging that this was simply one more aspect of normality. Its scent was the same, fresh and flowery. No one had drawn the blinds, and the pale sunlight of early morning shone through the tall bay windows, filling the room with the light that always seemed more diffused and more silvery here, as if the sea gave it its own special ambience.

Slowly she approached the wide bed where Verity lay as if asleep. She looked so natural that Clare almost expected her to open her eyes, turn her head and smile at her. The stillness, however, was absolute, not just in the figure on the bed, but, strangely, in the atmosphere. It was as if the house held its breath for a moment; as if no clocks ticked, no refrigerators hummed. Then, outside, a gull cried and the spell was broken.

Clare moved to sit beside the bed, to look for the last time at this beloved woman who had meant so much to her, for so many years. This is the way she would have wanted it, she thought. "To cease upon the midnight with no pain." And for it to happen here, in the room she had slept in most of her life, the wide expanse of sea beyond the window. Ninety-eight years! Who, in all honesty, could grieve? This is where her treasures were. The books she had loved most; the photographs on the table beside her bed.

"My best-beloveds," she had called them. Clare was among them, of course, the portrait taken all of fifteen years ago, just after graduation. Her hair had been long then and her face a little fuller. And more idealistic, she thought now with a futile pang of regret. Idealistic and innocent.

There was a portrait, too, of Beatrice, forever young and pretty, with rounded cheeks, unlined brow and soft rosebud mouth. No sign there of the desiccated woman she was to become; no warning of the constant dieting that was to turn her into an angular clothes-horse, with hard and restless eyes, her once luxuriant hair thinned by years of bleaching.

A picture of Harry, Verity's brother, occupied a silver frame. A fine young man, she had called him. And the greatest fun. In the photograph, though, Clare had always thought he looked solemn and a little severe. They were solemn times, Verity said, when she commented on it.

And then, of course, there was Jeremy. Little Jem. An enlarged photograph, this; just a snap of a little, laughing boy with a blond quiff of hair, clutching a teddy bear. Verity could never bring herself to say much about him, except that he was the son of friends who had been killed in the war. She had adopted him when he was only a few weeks old and brought him up as her own, but he had died very young, killed by a hit-and-run driver up at Howldrevel, the gloomy mansion set amid the woods above the village. It happened long before Clare was born, and nobody really knew who was to blame, though of course there was talk . . .

Verity had never made any accusations, or named names. Others did, however, and Clare knew perfectly well who was implicated by that talk. The village was, after all, a small one, full of old people with long memories. "I thought my heart was broken," Verity had said once in a confidential moment while Clare was still quite a small girl. "But hearts are tougher than that. You know what? You saved my bacon. I learned to love again when you came along."

And this Clare had accepted, without question. Verity had loved her. She had never questioned it. And yet, she thought as she looked at her now, how little I really knew this woman. I just took her for my own, with all her uniqueness, all her fun and laughter and prejudices and secrets. But what had made her the way she was? Why hadn't Clare asked while she had the chance? About Harry. About the friends who had been baby Jem's parents. About Jem himself and what had really happened that fateful day at Howldrevel. About a million and one things that she had just accepted, taken for granted.

"She left a letter for you," Minnie said when, having said her goodbyes, Clare eventually joined her beyond the green baize door that led to the kitchen. "Here, I made some coffee. Have it while it's hot."

"Thanks, Minnie."

Clare took the coffee and sat down at the table where long ago half a dozen servants had taken their meals under the stern gaze of the cook and the butler. Now there was only Minnie, and the two women who came from the village twice a week.

"I reckon she had a premonition, dear of her," Minnie went on. "Said the letter was to be kept until after she died. Writing it for days she was, a couple of weeks back. 'Tis in the rosewood box on her little writing table in the drawing room."

When she had finished her coffee, Clare went to find the letter and sat on the window seat to read it, marvelling at its length, for arthritis had affected Verity's fingers and writing had long been a laborious process for her.

> My dearest Clare,
>
> I have for some time now been conscious of time's wingèd chariot and wish to write this while I am still in my right mind (at least, as right as it's ever been!). Yet it is hard to say what I want without seeming sickeningly sentimental, which I know you would hate.
>
> Well, steel yourself, for here goes!
>
> You have been a great joy to me, my darling, from the time you came to me at the age of six until the present day. A wonderful friend. Does that sound a strange description of a great-niece, sixty years my junior? Yet I feel that friends are what we have been, and I want you to know how much I have valued that.
>
> I like to think of Lemorrick being yours and have made quite certain that it will be so when I am gone. However I fear that with all the repairs that are needed it may prove a poisoned chalice, much as we both love it.
>
> Don't feel you have to hang on to it for the sake of family or tradition. Sell it, if you wish. Or enjoy it, if that's what you want.

The second thing I wish to say is don't mourn for me. I have had a long, long life and I am very tired and ready to go. I have had great joys and great sorrows in the course of it, as you well know, and have dealt with both in the way that seemed best at the time. Not always wisely, perhaps, but I've never claimed to be infallible. Far from it!

As I look back, I am struck by the little I have done with my life. Nothing great or grand or important. Who was it who wrote of "the long littleness"? It seems, as I reflect on it now, that I have done merely what other people have expected of me, reacting to events rather than being the cause of them. I had a friend once who used to urge a thing called enlightened self-interest upon me. In my turn I now recommend it to you. Perhaps you will be better at it than I ever was.

One thing I have learned: we have one chance here below, whatever may happen hereafter, and it behoves us to make the most of it. Life goes by so fast and it is easy to let its joys go, like a handful of pearls slipping through the fingers. Without doubt I have been guilty of that at times, and I pray most earnestly that you hold fast to your pearls when you find them. Don't, I beg you, let them slip away.

Be happy, darling Clare, in whatever you choose to do with your life. Am I wrong in detecting that the rush and fret of banking is wearing a little thin? Perhaps. Or perhaps you are just tired, and need a holiday.

Well, take it. Pamper yourself. Don't let those powerful men grind you down or try to form you in their own image. You are unique and, if I have not yet made it quite clear, you are very dear to me.

There is so much more I want to say, but I write so slowly and already have taken several days over this.

One last thing. I loved your mother, too, but things took a wrong turn between us and were never wholly put right, though I can honestly say that I tried. In her mind she is convinced I have never forgiven her for past mistakes, but this is not so. She was guilty of no more and no less than any other girl of her age, and I truly believe it is she who cannot forgive herself for the grief she caused. This is what has driven the wedge between us. She was, in a way, always a perfectionist, and once the relationship between us proved less than perfect she had no time for any of it.

It saddens me that you and she have similarly drifted apart, and my dearest wish is that you should come to some rapprochement with her. You have only one mother, she has only one daughter. In many ways, you are the stronger and hold all the cards. She, I know, can seem hard, impervious to family ties, interested only in getting and spending, which she has done with considerable success. I am convinced, however, that under the surface, despite Gerald's riches, she is an unhappy woman haunted by the past, tormented by the fact that she gave up her only child. So I ask you, darling, have a little pity in your dealings with her. You have a wonderful life and a great future whereas old age is staring her in the face. It seems to me that you can afford to be generous.

My one regret is that I shall not know the end of your story, or of hers. Or perhaps I will. Who can tell?

Goodbye, my very dear Clare, and God bless you always.

Your loving Verity.

Clare leant her forehead against the cool glass of the window, glad to be alone, glad to be able, at last, to cry. Oh, she was going to miss her so much! Just knowing she was there, in the background, always ready to talk or just to listen, always interested and involved and ready to be amused.

But what on earth had her mother done to cause such grief and such guilt? Verity wrote as if Clare should know. Perhaps she imagined that she had at some time confided in her, for there was no doubt she had become forgetful over the past year or so. But nothing had ever been said, nothing explained. And was it conceivable that she and her mother could ever become close again? Was there really, despite their differences in circumstances and outlook and opinions, some kind of invisible, silver cord that held them together, willy nilly? It was hard to imagine, though it had to be admitted that she was not entirely impervious to her mother's opinion of her. Her rise up the professional ladder, her salary, her flat, her car, the size of her Christmas bonus – all of them were trophies that gave her pleasure not only because she had earned them, but because they would show Beatrice (and she could be sure that Verity would detail them in her regular letters) that her daughter was someone to be reckoncd with, someone who had done very well, thank you, without the benefit of a mother's love and attention.

And could Verity possibly be right when she said Beatrice was an unhappy woman? It had never struck Clare that this was so, but thinking of her restlessness she had to admit that it was at least a possibility.

Verity, after all, had usually been right. She was certainly right about the relationship between the two of them. It had been a friendship. They weren't just relatives thrown together, making the best of it. They had liked each other, been on the same wave-length, laughed at the same things, despite the age difference. And Clare wept once more, the reality of her loss sweeping over her.

Later that night, she rang Beatrice again but still received only a recorded message in reply. Where could they bc? They must have closed the house up, gone away somewhere for the winter. Gone on a cruise, maybe. Gerald enjoyed cruising. She tried desperately to think of any of her mother's friends that she could contact, someone who would know where they might be found. Beatrice, she remembered, talked much of a woman called Bonnie whenever they met; but Bonnie who? Try as she might, she couldn't remember. Perhaps she had never known. Well, she'd try again well before Friday, the day fixed for the funeral.

It was, perhaps, as well that there were practical arrangements to be made, for it blunted the edge of the grief that Clare could not avoid, even though she accepted Verity's contention that she had been ready to go. She had grown frail these last years, and her failing hearing had prevented her listening to the music she had once enjoyed so much. She had always loved books, too, but latterly reading tired her. Still the house without her seemed empty.

At some time in those days that preceded the funeral Clare, quite late one night, drew her bedroom curtain aside to look out at her own view of the cove. It was flooded on this occasion by the light of a moon that was almost full. The sea was gentle, its waves like rippled silk. The stars were thick in the sky, and there were pinpoints of light far out in the bay where fishing boats were at work. Nearer at hand she could see the gleam of the road that followed the line of the cove, and beyond it the darker bulk of the hilly field with its path that led to the stile. And as she looked closer, she could see that there were figures out there. Two people, hand in hand, running and stopping to melt into each other and running again. A girl and a boy, she guessed, who had gone up to the stile to see the silvery path the moon was making on the water, to hold each other and kiss and kiss again.

As she had done. She and Nick. Long ago.

She let the curtain drop. It had been a sweet and innocent thing, but it had been over for – heavens above, she thought, suddenly hit by astonishment. It was twenty years since that summer of '78 when she and Nick Courtfield had been inseparable. Nearly a lifetime ago, but still with the power to bring a pang of nostalgia. She'd never been able to hear Olivia Newton John and John Travolta singing "Summer Nights" without feeling, all over again, the utter bliss of being sixteen and in love. And remembering, too, the pain when it was over.

It had been one of the few periods in her life that Verity had seemed less than sympathetic. Normally Clare brought friends home in the sure knowledge that they would be made welcome, for Verity was the soul of hospitality. Nick Courtfield, son of the Courtfields of Howldrevel, had proved the exception. Verity had been perfectly polite but totally devoid of warmth and, in that mood, could be quite daunting.

"Why can't you be nicer to him?" Clare said reproachfully on one occasion after Nick had endured a particularly uncomfortable meal with them. "It's because of Jem, isn't it? You think Nick's father might have had something to do with his death. Everyone says so," she added hastily as Verity turned startled eyes towards her as if horrified that the conversation had taken this turn. Clare stuck to her guns. "It's not like you, Verity. Whatever you suspect his father of, it's not fair to blame Nick. He wasn't even born then."

For a moment Verity had said nothing. She seemed to be staring at Clare without seeing her, her lips clamped together; then she relaxed a little, sighed and turned away.

"Nothing was ever proved against Hugh Courtfield," she said. "I know that, of course. I've tried to be fair, but the fact remains . . ." her voice trailed away and the sentence remained uncompleted. "As for young Nick," she went on after a moment. "Well, I'm sorry if I was ungracious. I can't expect you to share my hang-ups – why should you? I have to admit that he seems a pleasant enough lad. However—" she paused and sighed once more. "It's simply that I should be extremely sorry if you were to ally yourself with that family in any way. I've known them all my life, remember."

"So you do think Sir Hugh was guilty—!"

Again Verity hesitated and conflicting expressions seemed to chase themselves across her face. "I try not to think about it at all," she said at last. "Nobody knows what happened that day in Howldrevel Woods and nobody ever will. It's simply that, as you children would say, the Courtfields have always been bad news."

"But you said Nick's grandmother was your best friend. You said you were always over at Howldrevel when she lived there."

"I was. But Frances was only a Courtfield by marriage – and a very bad marriage it was, too."

"Well, Nick and I aren't getting married. We're much too young even to think of it. We're friends, that's all."

"Good," Verity had said. But her eyes had remained clouded, for she knew Clare too well to be deceived. Her great-niece was fathoms deep in love, and she clearly feared for her and, later, was relieved when the romance came to an end.

Historically the Courtfields had made their money from tin, but this had long been a dying industry and after the war Hugh Courtfield, Nick's father, had branched out into the leisure industry, turning Howldrevel into an hotel and later expanding into other enterprises. Nick had gone into the family business soon after that summer and only shortly afterwards had met the daughter of a wealthy business associate of his father, a man who owned several London hotels. It was all so suitable, people said when he married Lorraine di Celento, for she was beautiful as well as rich. On her engagement, her picture had been featured at the front of the *Tatler* and later the wedding had been reported in its pages, since the very cream of society were among those present. Nick was, after all, heir to a baronetcy, while the di Celentos were royalty in the hotel world.

She was glad for him, Clare had assured herself, and hoped they would be happy. For herself, she had no thoughts of marriage, though there were boyfriends in plenty. There was too much she wanted to do even to think of settling down – yet somehow, on the few occasions they had met over the years, she recognised that there was still a spark between them, still a glint in the eye that was meant solely for the other. Once she had run into him by chance in London, at a book-launch honouring a celebrated Cornish author. He'd been on his own, without Lorraine who was on holiday on the Caribbean island owned by her father. They'd had dinner together, and it had been a good evening, easy, without strain, full of laughter. She'd been aware of lurking regrets that night – had thought, during dinner, how easy it would be to start something all over again. Instinct told her he felt the same, but she had reminded herself that he was married, and when he had taken her home he had said goodnight with no more than a brotherly kiss on the cheek, and she'd been glad. He wasn't the sort to stray, she told herself, and she wouldn't have liked him so much if he had been.

Even so, she wished, the night she saw the young lovers running down the hill, that he hadn't been brought quite so vividly to mind. Sleep had been elusive enough since she'd been at Lemorrick, and remembering that summer did nothing to help.

There was so much to think about: the house, the funeral, the music – what would Verity have liked best? And readings. There was a book of poetry on her little table. She must have been reading it during the last days; modern poems, by an unknown poet. What had Verity thought of them? Had she loved them? Hated them? Her opinions had always been unpredictable. Better stick to something tried and tested, perhaps. On the whole, she had liked things that gave at least a nod towards rhyming and scanning, but it would be great to know her opinion—

Not ever again, Clare thought. Maybe after Friday she would be able to accept the fact that Verity had gone. There were notices to be sent to the papers, local and national. A memorial service to be organised. Despite all Verity had said in her letter about having done nothing grand or great, her influence had been felt in many quarters. She had been known throughout the county as a public-spirited benefactor, founding the Cottage Hospital in memory of her father, donating generously to many local causes. She had, in her time, been Mayor, Magistrate, Chairman of the Women's Institute, Secretary of the Parish Council, Chairman of the Lifeboat Committee. She had distributed prizes at school speech days, opened bazaars for numerous charities and inaugurated, in a small way, a local music festival.

Such activities had left her amused and a little bewildered.

"I'm not that sort of person at all, you know," she said to Clare more than once. "I can't imagine how I got into any of it. As for standing on my hind legs and making speeches, believe me, I'm simply *terrified* on every occasion! I quake in my shoes and each time I vow that I am never, never going to do it again."

"You're a soft touch," Clare told her.

"Well—" she shrugged her shoulders. "I suppose someone has to do it and it's hard to say no. It does rather amuse me, though, when I sit listening to people singing my praises. I can't help wondering what my mother would say if she could hear them, not to mention Lady Courtfield, Hugh's grandmother. Her opinion of my morals was unprintable. She thought me without virtue of any kind."

"Really?" Clare had looked at her in amused astonishment. "What on earth had you done to deserve that?"

"Very little." There was a touch of wistfulness in Verity's smile. "Believe me, these days my so-called crimes wouldn't cause so much as a raised eyebrow, but then I was regarded as a social pariah." And though she laughed, she had then sighed and looked distracted as if the memory still brought a certain sadness.

"Do tell—" urged Clare.

"I will, one day. Right now I've got to go and pick raspberries." Or plant wallflowers, or paint a fence, or cycle down to the village to do some shopping and enjoy a gossip at the shop.

"She'm a good sort, Miss Ashland," people in the village said. "Always a smile and word, dear of her. She'm just like one o' we."

"I was sixty-seven when you came down here," she once said to Clare. "I must have seemed as old as Methuselah."

But Clare had frowned, trying to remember, and had shaken her head.

"I don't think so," she said. "Well, let's face it, anyone over thirty is ancient to a child of six. I don't think you seemed much older than any of my friends' mothers. And you did things like swimming in the cove with me, and not minding me making a mess with paint and sticky paper, which is more than a lot of them did. And other girls' mothers liked to have lots of warning of things, whereas you never mind things being sprung on you. And you used to drop everything if the fancy took you, like going for a picnic if it happened to be a lovely day. Do you remember that time on Bodmin moor—?"

"When you and the Marshall girl fell in the stream, complete with picnic? I certainly do! You were soaked to the skin."

"You spread our clothes on the grass and we ran around with nothing on. Such freedom!"

"You were very little. I remember envying you and wishing I could do the same. Maybe I should have done. There was no one there to see."

"Except the wild ponies! It was magical."

More so, perhaps, the adult Clare reflected, because of what had gone before. It seemed, looking back, that she had been born with a longing for the kind of stability that Lemorrick provided. Once her initial shyness was over, living with Verity had seemed like a new birth and she had embraced it rapturously. And now Verity had gone, and she was alone. Even her mother remained unreachable, though she had tried to contact her several more times.

Nothing seemed real, that Friday of the funeral. She felt as if she were simply sleep-walking through the day. She had expected a full church, for although Verity had outlived all her contemporaries there were plenty of others who appreciated the contribution she had made and wanted to pay their respects.

Clare's eyes had gone automatically to the Courtfield pew, but Nick wasn't there, though his parents had put in an appearance. They had come, Clare felt sure, simply for the look of the thing. It was expected of them and they would have been criticised if they had neglected to do so, though heaven knew, Sir Hugh was no stranger to criticism. He was a cold, awkward, irascible man, entirely without the common touch and highly unpopular in the village because of it. For years it had been whispered that he was involved in the death of the little Ashland boy, up in Howldrevel Woods. No smoke without fire, people said, and were scornful of the arrogance and cowardice that had prevented him from confessing his part in the tragedy.

Sir Hugh and Lady Courtfield did not come back to Lemorrick after the funeral, though a number of closer friends did so. It was expected, and Verity would have wanted it, Clare supposed, but for herself she found it an ordeal. It was an effort to keep thanking people for coming, thanking them for their condolences. She didn't feel like smiling, yet felt that she had to. She thought: if anyone says once more that Verity had a good innings, I won't be answerable for my actions; then immediately felt sad because this was one of Verity's own pet phrases, invoked when infrequently she ran out of patience. It had always amused Clare to think of her great-aunt suddenly running amok among the committees that were the usual cause of her irritation.

When, finally, everyone left, Clare and Minnie sank back in relief.

"They Courtfields didn't see fit to come," Minnie said, over the small, restorative drink that Clare had poured for each of them. "He didn't have the face, I s'pose."

"They were hardly close friends, were they?"

"Well, I know *that*! How could they be, after what happened? Still and all, it's a matter of respect."

Clare said nothing for a moment or two but sipped her drink reflectively.

"Why does everyone think he had something to do with Jem's death?" she asked at last. "Verity wouldn't talk about it and I've never heard the full story."

"Oh—" Minnie shrugged her shoulders. "'Tis all water under the bridge—"

"Except that it's not, is it? People still suspect him, even though nothing was ever proved. It hardly seems fair to the poor man."

"Poor man?" Minnie looked scornful. "Ee ent no poor man, not Sir Hugh."

"Not in terms of money, I know, but just imagine for a moment that he was entirely innocent of Jem's death. How can he have felt, all these years, with the whole village whispering about him, thinking the worst?"

Minnie's face set mulishly. "He deserve all he gets, thass what I say. I can't never forgive him for what he done to Miss Ashland, dear of her. She never got over it."

"I know that. But just suppose—" Clare, seeing Minnie's expression, broke off short and refrained from finishing the sentence or pursuing the subject further. Whatever the truth of the matter, she was unlikely to hear an unbiased account from Minnie's lips and was suddenly too weary even to try. Instead she rose to pour herself another drink.

"By the way, speaking of the Courtfields, what's Nick doing these days?" Her voice was studiously casual as she came to sit down once more.

Minnie grew more animated. "You heard his marriage broke up, I s'pose?" she said. "I wasn't surprised. That wife of his always seemed a snooty piece to me, taisy as a snake so I'm told by them as worked up Howldrevel. And there was Other Men." She folded her lips, looking self-righteously pained at this.

"I had no idea! Verity never mentioned it."

"Why would she?"

"Where is Nick living now?"

"Ee's up at Howldrevel again, so they tell me, but for how long I can't say. Talk is they'm opening another hotel in the Scillies on its own special island, and I'm told there's a new Theme Park place over to Penzance, though what a Theme Park is I'm sure I don't know. Miss Ashland says – said –" She paused, her face working a little, then swallowed hard and continued. "She told me 'twas a kind of make-believe village, with fishing boats and smugglers, but I can't see the point myself. Plenty of real places like that without building make-believe ones, if you ask me. Still, 'twill bring the money in, you can depend on that, knowing the Courtfields."

Clare brought her thoughts back from the contemplation of a newly single Nick Courtfield to point out that the family had, after all, created employment. "Which can't be bad," she said. "Cornwall needs all the jobs it can get."

Minnie looked unconvinced. "They never thought of that when they closed the mines," she said. "Never a thought for the workers then. My grandad he worked at Wheal Lily all his life, and my dad, when he was a boy. Both laid off without a thought."

Clare shot her an amused look for she had heard this complaint many times. The final closing of the Courtfield mines had taken place at least fifty years before but the way Minnie told it, you would think it was last week. Her father, far from losing his job, had in fact been taken on to work on the Howldrevel estate and his family housed in the gatehouse, but proximity to the Courtfield family had apparently done nothing to soften Minnie's attitude towards them.

"Mining had been in a bad way for years," Clare said. "The Depression just about finished it off."

"That's as may be. I never noticed the Courtfields going without."

"I don't suppose they did. Still, it can't have been an easy decision to turn Howldrevel into an hotel, can it? And credit where it's due, Minnie – they're involved in the leisure industry in a big way now. They must be by far the largest employers in the area."

Minnie sniffed again. "Thass what they said when they opened the hotel. 'Twould bring money into the village, they said. But thass nothing but a load of rubbish. Oh, they have some of the local girls up there as chambermaids, and so on. They've taken a few men on as gardeners, and Mrs Polkinhorne's girl is one of the receptionists, but for the most part they bring staff in from London. The chef's French, I'm told. And you don't see many of the guests spending money in our shops, oh dear me, no! It's down here for a luxury weekend, a round of golf, have a go with the jacuzzi and off back to London again. You know," she added, her eyes narrowed "it wouldn't surprise me a bit if they tried to get their hands on Lemorrick."

The thought had already occurred to Clare. Lemorrick would, undoubtedly, make a good hotel. It was very much smaller than Howldrevel but in a far better position and it seemed to her quite possible that the Courtfields might see it as a valuable addition to their empire. However, noting the look of distaste and outrage on Minnie's face, she realised it was not an idea to be pursued at this point.

So what was the answer? Keeping Lemorrick presented insurmountable problems; losing it was even worse. She sighed and shook her head slowly, defeated by the size of the dilemma that confronted her.

Where was all her much-vaunted decisiveness now?

Two

Neil Fuller was not pleased when Clare phoned to say she was not yet ready to come back to London.

"I'm sorry, Neil," she said. "There's a great deal to sort out down here—"

"But it's the board meeting on Friday! I must insist you're here for that. After all, this insurance deal is largely your pigeon."

Insurance deal? As if from another life, Clare dimly recalled details of the proposed take-over of Diamond Assurance by Claremont City Trust. It had, she remembered, taken up hours, if not days, of her time over the past weeks, but basically it was Neil's plan, his brain-child. He'd had his heart set on the bank branching out into insurance for as long as she had known him.

"Oh, yes," she said, a little lamely. "I'm afraid I'd forgotten—"

"*Forgotten*?" Clearly the idea astonished him.

"Only momentarily, I promise."

"I should hope so! So you'll be there?"

Still she hesitated. "Can't you do without me, Neil?"

"I most certainly cannot! Brewster and Jim Braithwaite aren't in favour, and I can't be certain of Foster's vote, either. Surely you can fly up for the day? I know you're out in the sticks, but they have heard of planes down there, I suppose?"

Clare ignored the sarcasm. "OK," she said. "I'll be there. But I have several weeks' leave owing me so I'll take it from next week—"

"That'll be no problem." Neil was smiling again. She could hear it in his voice. "You can hand all the Van der Liemen papers over to Mark for him to deal with. No one's indispensable, after all."

Ouch, thought Clare as she put the phone down. That's me put in my place. She found herself strangely unaffected, however, by the thought of Mark Wiltshire – bright, predatory, ambitious Mark – waiting in the wings to step into her shoes the moment she faltered.

A few weeks ago every hackle she possessed would have risen in protest, but now it seemed supremely unimportant.

And oh, how wearily unenthusiastic she was about this trip to London! Maybe Verity had been right. She needed a holiday, was burnt out, you could say, which perhaps explained the indecisiveness, the tiredness. Even the forgetfulness. How could she have forgotten the insurance take-over, even for a second? It wasn't like her. She had told Neil that there was much to be done down here, but in fact she felt she was living in a kind of limbo, idling away her time and doing very little. She had dealt with the few outstanding bills and had written letters notifying various agencies of Verity's death. She had dealt with the solicitor handling the probate of her will. Minnie had started going through Verity's clothes, putting them in bags to take to Oxfam.

"If there's anything you want to keep—" Clare had said.

Minnie hummed and haa'ed for a bit but then admitted that of all things she would love the camel coat that Miss Ashland bought last year. "If thass all right with you," she said.

"Of course it's all right. She'd want you to have it."

"And that blue silk scarf with the butterflies. I'd dearly love that."

"Then take it. Take anything."

"Dear of 'er, she already give me more than enough," Minnie said. "To think I could buy my own house now, if I wanted—"

"She was very fond of you, Minnie. You know that. She couldn't have done without you."

Slowly, aimlessly, Clare walked through the rooms on the ground floor. So many possessions, she thought. Furniture, pictures, ornaments. What was she to do with them all? She felt overwhelmed by the weight of the decisions that had to be made.

In the dining room she paused to look up at the portrait of Verity's father, Joseph Ashland. There he stood, stiff and unsmiling in his frock-coat, a typical Victorian *paterfamilias*, complete with a glossy moustache and the aloof kind of expression that seemed to say that he was fully aware of his own importance. It was Joseph Ashland who had bought this desirable site and built Lemorrick. His wife, Louise, faced him soulfully down the length of the huge rosewood table. She was dressed for a ball in a low-cut gown of palest blue, bosom out-thrust, bustle curving gracefully behind. She had pale sausage curls artfully tumbling over her

27

milk-white brow, and her apparently guileless eyes were set wide apart in her pretty face. Verity said it gave little impression of her true character.

"She was as artful as a wagon-load of monkeys," she told Clare on one occasion with rueful but affectionate amusement. "The kind of woman who could truly be said to enjoy bad health. The entire household revolved around her whims and wishes."

"She looks a bit like Mummy," Clare had said.

"Does she? I never thought—" Verity had frowned as she looked at the picture more carefully. "I do see what you mean. There is a kind of likeness, I suppose. Something about the mouth."

Her mother, too, was artful, Clare thought now. Manipulative. Throughout her life, she had done little but make sure her own nest was nicely feathered, even if it meant abandoning her own daughter.

"She doesn't care a bit about me," she had said once to Verity, when she was no more than thirteen or fourteen. "She never has."

"That's not true, darling," Verity had assured her.

"She'd rather live with horrid old Gerald—"

"She was fearful of the future. She needed the security, and she knew you were all right with me."

"We'd have managed somehow. She wasn't penniless, after all. There are loads of single mothers who get by perfectly well on less."

"Not Beatrice." Verity had looked sad, as if she felt this as some lack in herself.

"She could have got a job, or even come home here, to you. Then we could all have been together."

"It wouldn't have worked, Clare."

"I don't see why not."

"Use your imagination! Can you see her living here?"

"She might have got to like it. It's her home, after all."

"I doubt if she sees it like that."

"Then she jolly well ought to! Why is she so—" For a moment or two Clare sought the right word. "So *feeble*?" she finished at last. "She just has to have someone telling her she's wonderful all the time, and buying her things!"

This had made Verity laugh. "I don't suppose many of us would object to that. Don't be too hard on your mother, Clare. She's what life has made her."

Clare thought this over. "But surely," she said, "it's up to people to go out and make life what they want it to be."

And at that Verity had laughed again and had hugged the girl beside her and said how wonderful it must be to be young in the '70s, in this brave new world where women were equal with men, mistresses of their own destiny.

Which is what I am, Clare told herself, thinking of this long-ago conversation as she left the dining room with a new spring in her step. I am mistress of my destiny. I am not dependent on Claremont City Trust.

She longed, suddenly, for fresh air and went upstairs to pull on the old fisherman's smock she had found in the cupboard in her room, then made her way down the steps cut from the cliffs that led from Lemorrick's garden to the beach below. What *had* her mother done to think that Verity had never forgiven her, she wondered again, thinking of Verity's letter. No doubt it was some sexual escapade. Maybe Verity had caught her *in flagrente delicto*, which would have seemed a heinous crime all those years ago. And then there were Verity's own misdeeds that she'd hinted at but never explained. Why on earth hadn't she questioned the old lady while she was alive? Now she would never know the truth, and the thought irritated her like a nagging tooth.

But down on the beach she perched on a flat-topped rock and looked at the lacy-edged waves as they came and went, absorbed in the one thought that took precedence over all others. What was she to do about Lemorrick? The thought of losing it created a physical pain in her stomach, yet it was surely ludicrous to think of keeping it. It was far too big for her and ridiculously expensive to run. Anyway, much as she might regret it, her life was in London . . .

But need it be? And would she miss it if she decided not to go back? How could she tell? The waves surged and retreated, surged and retreated, in their own hypnotic rhythm, giving her no answer.

She was alone on the beach, for it was late autumn and the holidaymakers that flocked to Porthallic in the season had long gone. After a while she began to feel cold despite the thick, high-necked sweater she wore under the smock, and getting up from her rock she wandered towards the far end of the cove. The tide was out and her footsteps bleached the sand as she skirted the waves, occasionally stooping to pick up a suitable stone and skim it into the water. The air was tangy with the scent of salt and seaweed. Oh, *how* I do not want to go back to London, she thought, hurling a stone with particular violence. And no, I wouldn't miss it. I'm sure of it.

She turned at last to retrace her footsteps but stopped short, for coming towards her was the figure of a man who could only have come down the Lemorrick steps.

It was Nick. She felt a rush of delight, an urge to run to him, and was glad that she was far enough away to have time to adjust her expression, by the time they met, to one of mild pleasure.

"Nick, how nice!" she said, once he was within hailing distance.

"How are you?" They came together and kissed, briefly, two friendly acquaintances. "I was so sorry when I heard about Verity," he said. "I know how fond you were of her. My mother mentioned you were down, so I thought I'd drop by to see you, just to give my condolences. I've been in the Scillies, which is why I didn't make the funeral."

"It's nice of you to come. Thanks."

"You'll miss her."

"Yes. Still, she had a good innings—" Clare heard herself uttering the meaningless phrase and was astonished. Surely the sudden appearance of Nick hadn't reduced her to this particular platitude? "It seems very strange without her," she said, to make up for it.

"It must do." He smiled at her sympathetically, his eyes warm and friendly. They tipped up at the corners and were green, flecked with gold. She had never seen eyes quite like them. "Hey, are you just going back to the house? When Minnie said you were on the beach, I thought great, a bit of a blow is just what I need. Are you in a hurry? Why don't we take another turn?"

"All right." Clare turned and together they walked the way she had just come. "This place doesn't change, does it?" she said. "The minute I set foot on this beach, I have an irresistible urge to collect shells and build castles, just like I did when I was seven."

"You don't look a lot older now."

Clare laughed at him, aware, belatedly, that her face was devoid of make-up and her shoulder-length hair pulled back in a ribbon. It wasn't the way she would have chosen for him to see her after so long, but she felt relaxed about it. Maybe it was a sign of growing up, she thought. Maybe all that striving, all that showing how bright and talented and sophisticated she was, had come to an end. Maybe she had arrived at the comfortable realisation that people could take her as they found her, or not take her at all.

"I – I heard about your marriage," she said, a little awkwardly. "I'm sorry it didn't work out."

He gave a grunt of laughter.

"News travels in this place, doesn't it? The divorce only came through a couple of weeks ago. Still, Lorraine and I have been apart for the last year, so I suppose there was bound to be talk."

"I'm sorry," she said again.

"Don't be. I'm over it. Long over. We both knew it was a mistake and it's just a relief to have it all tidied away."

"I also heard you were back at Howldrevel."

"That's right. I have an apartment where the servants' quarters used to be – just *pro tem*, you understand! My parents are in the Dower House, so we're not exactly on top of each other, but I'd still rather be totally independent."

"What happened to your lovely house on the Fal?" Stupid question. Lorraine had it, of course.

"It's been sold," he said. "Lorraine moved to the States with her fancy man—" he shot her a quick glance. "I shouldn't have said that! He's a perfectly respectable oil executive who happened to fall for a pretty face. I don't bear him any ill-will. In fact I'm rather grateful, if the truth were known." Was he protesting too much? Impossible to tell.

"I hear the Courtfield Corporation is going great guns," she said, thinking it best to steer the conversation towards less personal matters. "Fingers in all sorts of pies, I'm told. And a fishing village Theme Park, no less."

"All done in the best possible taste, I assure you. And extremely popular *And* educational! Schools take parties to it, to show how life was in the last century."

"Why so defensive?"

"I could see that look in your eye. You don't have to worry. Even Fran and Sophie approve."

Fran and Sophie were his sisters and had always been his most rigorous critics.

"Are they well?" Clare asked.

"Fine. Fran's having another baby. She and Simon are living in Bath now, and Sophie's in the throes of renovating a rather nice Victorian house in Somerset, up to her eyes in builders and architects. Which reminds me, what's going to happen to Lemorrick?"

Clare found herself disappointed. That's why he came, she thought. Not to see me at all, or to say how sorry he was about Verity. Just to find out if Lemorrick is available to be sucked into the Courtfield maw.

"Why?" she asked guardedly. "Do you want to buy it?"

"Is it on the market?"

"Not yet. I haven't decided what I'm going to do."

"Well, my advice is don't do anything in a hurry – not unless you're desperate for the money." He had taken the wind out of her sails. "I mean," he went on, having seen her quick, perplexed frown, "it's such a wonderful place. I can understand why you might feel you have to sell, but if you do, you could possibly regret it for the rest of your life. If it were mine, I'd want to keep it at all costs. I've always loved it."

"But you don't want to buy it?"

"Well, I might if it were available. As a matter of fact, I itch to get my hands on it, bring it up to standard again. I imagine it needs a good deal spent on it." He paused for a moment in order to turn and point towards the house. "Look, you can see the deterioration of the roof from here."

"I know!"

"Have you thought of turning it into three or four apartments and keeping one for yourself? It wouldn't be at all a bad proposition if you can beg, borrow or steal enough capital, and heaven knows, you're in the right business to do that. The site's wonderful and any place with a view like that would sell like hot cakes."

"I suppose they would."

"On the other hand—" He stopped altogether, turning to look at the house at greater length. "It seems a shame to chop it about. You might regret it, once it was too late."

"I know, I know! To be honest, Nick, I'm in a complete spin about it, but it seems to me it'll have to be sold eventually. It's a little on the large side for a single woman, you'll admit."

"You might not always be single." He grinned down at her.

"Can't imagine why you are, as a matter of fact. You were never short of the odd suitor or three."

Coolly, she raised her eyebrows. "Maybe none of them came up to scratch – and I have had other preoccupations, you know."

"I know. Prestigious City institutions tremble at the mention of your name."

"Don't be mean!"

"I'm not. But if an old friend can't tease you, who can?"

Clare grinned at him. "Well, I wish the old friend would give me some words of advice. Should I really pursue the apartment idea? Or sell it as an hotel or to some other institution? What am I to do, Nick?"

He pursed his lips, still staring up at Lemorrick standing proud on its cliff top. "Nothing," he said at last. "Nothing rash, anyway. Give yourself time to think. Then, if you really want to sell, give me first refusal." He glanced at his watch. "I must be getting back. There's a planning meeting in Truro I have to go to."

"I ought to go, too. I have to make a flying visit to London on Friday and I must make a few phone calls."

Together, they retraced their steps, the conversation taking a less personal turn, but at the bottom of the steps Nick put his hand on her shoulder, turning her to face him.

"What happened to us, Clare?" he said. He was smiling, treating the question lightly. "We were so bloody good together, and then – wham! It all blew apart. Damned if I can remember why."

Clare laughed. "We were children, Nick. We quarrelled, that's what happened."

"What about?"

"Do you honestly not remember?"

"No. Well—" he corrected himself, "I remember being pissed off with Verity for some reason. She made it so abundantly clear she didn't approve of me. I thought you let her run your life for you."

"She liked to know where I was and who I was with. You can hardly blame her. I was only sixteen."

"It wasn't only that, though. She took agin me for some reason."

"Well—" for a second Clare hesitated. "She had a kind of a thing about your family, I admit."

"She made me feel two inches high!"

"She did rather go into her *grande dame* mode whenever you were around, I admit. But she wasn't the embittered spinster you accused her of being. Naturally, I defended her."

Nick looked at her, eyebrows raised as if in astonishment. "And that was it? You're telling me we split because we couldn't agree about the extent of Verity's sexual experience?"

"Hardly!" Clare was laughing at him. "You picked a quarrel because you were mad as hell that I wouldn't go to bed with you."

He grinned, reminiscently. "I hadn't forgotten. Just out of interest, why wouldn't you?"

"Hard to explain." Especially, Clare reflected silently, when I was so madly in love. This, however, was a thought she kept to herself, as she abstractedly picked at a fern that was growing out of a crevice in the rocky wall of the steps. "I – was scared, I suppose. And idealistic. And really quite incredibly innocent even for then, never mind now. Girls seem to grow up so fast these days, don't they? And everyone falls in and out of bed at the drop of a hat, but then – well, I suppose I just didn't feel ready. Girls at school talked about it, of course, but I felt—" She paused, and looked at him, shaking her head. "I don't know what I felt, Nick. Maybe I was a touch retarded."

"There was something else," Nick said, pointing an accusatory finger at her. "You brought up all that old tittle-tattle about my father killing the little boy—"

"I shouldn't have done that. Verity would have been furious – she always was if I repeated gossip, which is what it was. I suppose I just wanted to hurt you."

Nick expelled his breath in a puff of disbelief. "You're actually telling me that you and I fell out because of rumours and hearsay and village gossip, plus a childish desire to hurt each other?"

"Nonsense!" Clare had begun climbing the steps, but turned again to grin at him over her shoulder. "I told you why – we fell out because I wouldn't let you have your wicked way with me. Everything else stemmed from that. And then," she went on, "we were so busy showing each other how little we cared that we never did sort it out."

She heard him laugh.

"There was a fair-haired chap, remember him? He wouldn't

leave you alone. He played rugger for Marlborough and had piggy little eyes."

"Anthony Something. I don't remember anything amiss with his eyes. He was rather gorgeous, actually. Anyway, you weren't any better! There were those glamorous twins who wore matching leopard-print bikinis. Lord, I was so jealous!"

"Really?"

"They seemed the very acme of sophistication – and I'm willing to bet they didn't have my inhibitions."

They had reached the top, and laughing, he caught her arm. "Let me take you out to dinner," he said. "Let's pretend we've only just met. Two adults. No baggage from the past."

Clare considered the proposition for a moment. "All right," she said. "I'm back at the weekend. Why don't you ring me?"

She was smiling as, having waved him off in his car, she went up the front steps into the house, pleased that, after all, he had come in friendship, without any ulterior motive. He'd raised her spirits, made her feel young and hopeful, as if the future was not something to be feared but was full of exciting opportunities just waiting to be explored. He was like that, she remembered. Always had been. She hoped he would phone, as promised.

But don't make anything of it, she told herself as she went inside to make her calls.

Neil Fuller, in his capacity as Chairman of Claremont City Trust, was sitting at the far end of the long, highly polished table, with the dozen other directors distributed evenly along its length on either side. He had been speaking for some time in a general way about the desirability of the bank branching out into insurance. It would later fall to Clare's lot to enthuse about Diamond Assurance in particular.

She knew all the arguments; had reminded herself of them before the meeting and felt no qualms about having to lay the perceived advantages of this take-over before the assembled board. None of the men round the table, seeing her neatly-suited exterior, smooth hair and immaculate make-up, or listening to her crisp summing-up of the situation, could possibly have guessed how little interest she felt in the outcome.

Afterwards when the meeting was over and the other directors

had drifted away, Neil congratulated her warmly, exuding satisfaction that the vote had gone his way.

"Well done, Clare. That was a most persuasive performance.
You swung it for us, no doubt about it. Come up to my office and
have a celebratory gin."

"Thank you. I rather think I could do with one."

"It ought to be Veuve Cliquot of the finest vintage. You left Jim
without a leg to stand on."

Clare smiled but said nothing, content to listen as Neil continued
to enthuse about the satisfactory outcome of the meeting. Once
in his office, high over the City of London but insulated from it
by toughened glass and pot plants and diaphanous curtains, he
waved her to a chair. She went instead to stand at the window,
looking out for a moment at this high-rise, high-powered world
that surrounded them.

After a moment, Neil joined her there, handing her one of the
glasses he was holding.

"Your health," he said, lifting his glass in a toast. "And your
continued success."

"Thank you." She took a sip, silent for a few moments. "Neil,
how do you manage to stay so enthusiastic?" she asked at last.
"Don't you ever feel the slightest touch of *ennui*?"

He gave her a look of total bemusement.

"*Ennui*?"

"Boredom," she translated, as if he hadn't quite understood.
"Fed-up-ness."

"No," he said, after an astonished moment. "I love it. And so
do you."

"Do I? I don't know that I do. To be honest, it all seems to be
wearing a bit thin."

"You need that holiday."

"I'm aware of that. What I'm not sure about is if I shall want to
come back."

He looked at her with the air of an exasperated father contem-
plating the foolishness of a child.

"Of course you'll want to come back. Take your holiday. Go
somewhere exotic, lie in the sun, have a holiday romance. I'll bet
you a month's salary that you'll be raring to get down to work
again at the end of a couple of weeks." He gestured towards
the vista outside the window. "Take a look, girl. You belong

here, you know you do. You have a great job, a marvellous future. You've crashed through the glass ceiling that's supposed to thwart the ambitions of most women – not that I believe in that for one second, but undoubtedly there are plenty of women who'd envy you—"

"Like, think of the starving Somalis and eat up your greens?"

"No, not like that! You're a square peg in a square hole, and it would be criminal to give it up. If this Diamond Assurance thing goes the way I expect, the sky will the limit as far as you're concerned." He smiled at her, his best and most winning smile. "Look what a great job you did this morning. How on earth would I manage without you."

Clare laughed briefly. "You'd do very well," she said. "After all, there's always Mark – and no one's indispensable."

"Some are more indispensable than others. So let's have no more loose talk about not coming back, OK?"

"All right. You win," she said. But she sighed as she said it.

She had lunch with Duncan and mentioned her indecision over the house.

"Of course you love Cornwall," he said soothingly. "You always have, I know that. Why not turn the house into apartments and keep one for yourself?"

"You're not the first person to suggest that."

"Well, it makes sense. You could go down whenever the fancy takes you. Play your cards right and I might even come with you."

She didn't want him there. The realisation came to her suddenly and swiftly, inexplicable and possibly inexcusable, but valid just the same. She kept smiling, however, and said nothing.

Later Hannah, an old university friend whom she met for a drink, expressed astonishment that the idea of leaving London could ever enter Clare's head, staring at her as if she had taken leave of her sense.

"Darling, Cornwall's all very well, but you can't *live* there," Hannah assured her. "You'd go mad in a week. I know you love it for holidays, but you have to face it, here's where the heart is. How on earth would you sustain life so far from Harvey Nicks?"

She was laughing, of course, but there was a hard core of sincerity buried in the joke. Hannah, undoubtedly, would shrivel and die so far from London, and Clare thought: maybe she's right. It would be easy to get sentimental about a place like Lemorrick, but she'd always enjoyed London, enjoyed the challenge, loved the buzz.

She loved her flat, too, and disliked the thought of giving it up. Maybe Neil was right, she thought. She would probably want to come back after her holiday. But he wasn't right about going somewhere exotic. Lemorrick called her, and she had every intention of answering the call.

She collected her car from the garage where it had languished for the past week, picked up some cleaning, packed more clothes, made a few phone calls, so that it was lunch-time the following day before she left London and late evening by the time she arrived back at Lemorrick. She had intended to stop *en route* for something to eat and had told Minnie not to wait dinner for her, but as time went on and the weather deteriorated she decided that after all she would press on towards home without stopping to eat. Rain was now falling in a long-term, aggressive kind of way, gusts of wind hurling it with force against the windscreen, and she was unwilling to prolong the journey.

Minnie had finished her meal but insisted on cooking an omelette for her despite Clare's assurances that she was quite capable of doing it for herself.

"What's been going on here?" Clare asked, glad to be inside at last.

"I've been some busy," Minnie said. "Turning things out. Cleaning up. I've left some old stuff on the window seat for 'ee to look through – boxes and papers. On the shelf of that wardrobe in the blue bedroom, they were. Family stuff, for the most part. Photos and that. What they was doing there I don't know. Been there years, I reckon." She sprinkled the omelette with grated cheese. "And that Nick Courtfield phoned," she added, shaking the pan. "Said he'd got to go to America, sudden-like, but he'd be back by the end of the week." She darted a look at Clare. "You ent getting mixed up with him again, are ee?"

"He's an old friend, Minnie."

Minnie sniffed. "Thass as may be. Courtfields are folk to steer clear of, if you ask me." Deftly she folded the omelette and slid it into the plate that was warming on the rack above the stove.

"Isn't it time for everyone to forgive and forget?" Clare asked.

Minnie sniffed again. "Leopards don't change their spots," she said.

Clare took the plate she offered. "Thanks. That looks wonderful," she said, adding wryly, "I just hope I never get into your bad books."

Minnie gave her a warm smile. It transformed her face and would, Clare thought, render her almost unrecognisable to any passing Courtfield.

"You never will, my love," she said. "Not never."

After Clare had eaten they went into the sitting room together to watch the news. It was, as always, followed by the weather forecast which prophesied gales, particularly for the south-west. The warning was superfluous, for already the wind was howling around the house, and when Clare pulled the curtain aside she could see, even through the rain, the white tops of the huge waves that were pounding the shore.

Minnie went off to bed quite early.

"Early to bed, early to rise," she said, as she had done almost every night that Clare had known her. "I'll see you in the morning, my love. Oh," she added, coming back into the room, "they papers, they'm up on Miss Ashland's window seat. 'Tis dustbin day tomorrow, so maybe you could take a quick look and see if there's anything worth keeping. I'll throw them out, else."

"Family papers, did you say?"

"I think so, my love. Didn't look too close, but you'll want the photos, I expect. There were some school books, too. You'll have to see for yourself."

"I will," said Clare.

Her curiosity was whetted, for Verity had never spoken a great deal about the past, had never been one for poring over old photographs, and had reminisced only under pressure.

She went upstairs, pausing as she switched on the light, for this room still seemed to hold the essence of Verity. She looked around it with affection. One day, she supposed, someone else would sleep here, would impress their personality upon it. Not yet, though. Not for a long time yet.

She could see the boxes and the piles of papers that Minnie had put on the window seat, and crossed the room to examine them. There were pamphlets and catalogues, tied together with

string, and journals of the Lifeboat Institute and another bundle
of correspondence concerning a defective washing machine. A
small, square box held envelopes and a few unused Christmas
cards, together with a list of names running to several pages. It
was in a larger chocolate box that she found the photographs –
old, brown sepia pictures of people whose identities she could
only guess at. There, surely, was Verity as a child with her two
brothers, Harry and Stephen. My grandfather, Clare thought. No
more than eleven or twelve. So straight and bright and confident
and smiling.

In the next photograph he was older. This recorded a sumptuous
picnic complete, in the background, with uniformed maid and
a flunkey of some sort, and still further in the background, a
stately old car. Joseph was there, and Louise, hatted and gowned
in what undoubtedly was the latest fashion, and with gloves on, for
heaven's sake! She was sitting in a deck-chair holding a cup of tea.
Stephen was lounging elegantly on a rug, propped on one elbow,
wearing a striped blazer and straw boater. Harry was standing, a
plate of cakes in one hand as if caught in the act of passing them
round. Verity was scowling as if something had annoyed her. Or
perhaps the sun was in her eyes.

None of these must be thrown away. They were wonderful!
Perfect period pieces. Clare replaced the lid and put the box well
away from the papers, promising herself to look through them
more carefully at some later date.

She turned to the other box that lay beside it. This was bigger,
the size of a dress box. She lifted the lid and saw that it contained
the books Minnie had referred to. Schoolbooks, she had said.
Notebooks they certainly were, mostly of uniform colour and size
as if they had all been purchased from the same source. On top,
there was one that was quite different. Its covers were of stiffened
yellow silk, faded and a little worn in one corner, its gilt-edged
pages held together by a small, gold metal clasp. On the front of
it, in flowing gold letters, was written *My Diary*.

Clare's heart began to beat strongly with excitement, as if
she instinctively knew that she had found a treasure. With trembling fingers, she undid the clasp and opened it gently, for the
pages were dry and brittle and flaked away as she touched
them.

"10th January 1913," she read, the words written in a hand that was round and unformed, the ink faded to a sepia brown. "I, Verity Louise Ashland, have decided to keep a diary."

With reverential awe Clare turned the pages, then turned hastily to investigate the plainer notebooks. 1916, 1917, 1918, all were there. No 1919, she found, nor '20 – nothing, in fact, until 1923 when they began again and continued until 1944, a new notebook for every year, though not all contained an equal number of entries. Some years had clearly been more eventful than others.

Verity's youth – all here, all described. Details of the family she had never known, the great-grandparents, dead before she had been born. Her mother . . .

Did she want to know about her mother? Yes, of course she did, for good or ill. She had always wanted to know. But even now very little would be revealed for there was nothing beyond 1944 when her mother had been – what? Fourteen? Fifteen? No more. Just a child, really. But better than nothing; oh, so much better than nothing.

She repacked the box hastily, picking it up to carry it to her own room.

She was tempted to begin reading then and there but was overcome by a sudden overpowering weariness. It had been a long and trying journey. She would leave everything until the following day, she decided, which, judging by the sound of the strengthening wind and the rain which was hurling itself against the windows, would be fit for nothing but staying indoors.

Sure enough, she awoke to a grey and dismal world. The rain fell remorselessly and huge waves dashed themselves against the rocks at the far end of the cove, hurling a cloud of spray high into the air. There was no sea traffic this morning, no fishing boats, no yachts. And no reason on earth, Clare told herself, why she should leave the house. Consequently she went to the smaller sitting room, known always as the morning room, and stoked up the fire, explaining to Minnie that she had a great deal of reading to do.

"And no better day to do it, my love," Minnie said. "I shan't disturb you."

Clare barely heard her. Already, unable to control her eagerness, she had begun to read.

41

BOOK TWO

VERITY

Three

10th January 1913
I, Verity Louise Ashland, have decided to keep a diary. Most
people start such diaries on the first day of the year, but I am
starting on the 10th because it is my birthday (my thirteenth
because as Mother says "I was born with the Century") and
Harry has given me this beautiful diary to record my Doings.
I don't really know what I'm going to write in it, but it's so
lovely that I can't resist starting at once. Stephen says I won't
be able to keep it for more than a week, but I'm quite determined
to carry on, just to show him. If I am honest, though, I can see
why he thinks I might not, not because there won't be heaps of
Interesting Doings to record, but because I have a mind like a
grasshopper. Miss Pond is always telling me so. (She is always
telling me about my Argumentativeness, too, and of Not Thinking
Before I Speak!)
Miss Pond is the governess at Howldrevel (which is Cornish
for "Sunrise". I can't imagine why it was ever called that because
it is right in the middle of the woods and you don't get a lot of sun
at any time of the day.) It is the biggest house for miles around and
I go there every day to have lessons with Amelia and Catherine
Courtfield. I will save until later what I think about THAT, but it
isn't good. However, I will try to describe Howldrevel, because
it's worth a special effort.
It is very big and has a sort of Grecian front with pillars and
lots of steps going up to the front door which is absolutely huge,
and to the left and right of the steps is a terrace. On the right,
there are big windows that belong to the drawing room which
is very grand with lots of little tables with things on them which
are All Too Easy to knock over, and three huge Chesterfields,
one dark red velvet and the other two covered in gold and red
striped stuff. The curtains are of gold velvet. There are lots of

45

chairs, too, and a great big marble fireplace with a great big gold-framed mirror with cherubs over it. That's enough about the drawing room. Oh, there are lots of gold-framed pictures, too. (Not until I started to write about it did I realise how much gold there was!)

The terrace on the other side of the steps has long windows and leads to the ball-room which has three crystal chandeliers and lots of gilt chairs. Forget what else. Have only been in there once.

There are lots and lots of rooms but the only one that really concerns me is the schoolroom which is quite cosy but has Seen Better Days. We sit round a big square table and in one corner there is a blackboard and in another a dressmaker's dummy, and there are bookshelves with books but in my view not nearly enough.

There are three ways to get to Howldrevel. You can just drive down to the village, turn to the left, then to the left again where the signpost says Turner's Cross, and if you just keep on going you get to the place where there are just a few cottages and beyond them there are gates and a Gatehouse, and a long drive with woods on either side. An old lady called Mrs Ducky lives in the Gatehouse and comes out to open the gates. Honestly, that's her name.

Another way is to turn left before the village which leads to a much smaller lane and another drive that also goes through the woods. This is called the Lower Drive and it is hardly ever used because it isn't so convenient. I heard Lady Courtfield complaining the other day that it is going to Rack and Ruin.

The third way is to take the path beyond Lemorrick that goes up to the stile. When you get there, the left fork goes to the cliff path, the right to another stile into Howldrevel Woods and if you walk far enough, you get to the house. The Courtfields don't mind people going in, so long as they stop at the brook, but the Public are not supposed to go over the bridge into the second part of the wood because they say it's Invading their Privacy, though even at the brook you can't see anything of the house.

In the wood there is a house called the Dower House which belongs to the Courtfields but is empty at the moment since the Dowager Lady Courtfield died. And that is MORE than enough about Howldrevel! I'd so much rather go away to school, like

Olivia Rees who is my best friend and is a weekly boarder in Truro.

Mother and Father gave me a bicycle for my birthday which is wonderful because I have wanted one for ages and ages and now I will be able to go for rides with Livvy at weekends. She is Dr Rees's daughter and lives halfway down the hill between here and Porthallic. She's had a bike for over a year! Father would have bought me one last birthday but Mother suffers with her nerves and was against the idea because she said I might come to some harm, there is so much traffic about these days, and I'm likely to come whizzing down hills and round corners. This is ridiculous. I am not a child.

Stephen gave me five shillings, which was a great deal better than the pencil-case he gave me last year. I don't know yet what I shall buy with it, but am hoping to find Inspiration in Truro tomorrow.

I suppose I should start by writing all about myself. I live at: Lemorrick House, Porthallic, Cornwall, South West England, Europe, The Universe. The house is right on the edge of the cliff overlooking Lemorrick Cove and is about half a mile from Porthallic which is a fishing village. My mother's name is Louise Elizabeth, and before she married Father, she was a Fothergill, which makes her very proud. The Fothergills are an ancient family and if you go back a bit we are related to a Lord. Unfortunately my grandfather was only the youngest son of a cousin (female) and anyway the family has more or less died out so there won't be a title for Stephen. Father says he will have to earn one for himself, which knowing Stephen is quite possible as nothing is beyond him. Mother does not approve of this because she thinks that only inherited titles are any good, but Harry and I are Bolsheviks and we believe quite the opposite. Anyone can inherit a title, but only people of True Worth are awarded them. (I must find out if Bolsheviks really approve of titles at all, inherited or otherwise. They may not, which is a little worrying.)

My father's name is Joseph Bradley Ashland and he built this house in 1893, his father having made a great deal of money canning fish, which is something Mother never likes anyone to mention, but I have resolved always to be Completely Honest in everything I write. Anyway, I am fond of my Grandfather Ashland, even if he did have Lowly Origins and even if we don't see him very often. He is very kind and generous. (I forgot to say he sent me a five pound note for my birthday!) Mother says he has a Bristol accent, and that's true, but I don't mind it, in fact I find it sort of cosy, but Mother is against accents of any kind, especially Cornish, and Harry and I have only to repeat something we have heard in the village for her to have Fifty Fits. Father owns the fish warehouse on the quay and all the carts that unload the boats. The fish (mostly pilchards) are then packed into barrels and taken up to Bristol where we have a factory where fish comes from other places as well as Porthallic. It's canned and also made into fish paste. Father doesn't actually work there any more, but he goes there sometimes for Directors' Meetings and is there at the moment. I like the bloater sort of paste very much and Harry and I eat quite a lot of it, on toast.

I have two brothers, Harry who is sixteen and Stephen who is eighteen. They both go to Waltham College in Somerset, so I only see them in the holidays. Nicholas Courtfield goes to Eton and has another three days' holiday, but Harry and Stephen go back tomorrow—"

Verity stopped writing and sighed, her gaze wandering to the view beyond the window. It wasn't that she had already tired of keeping a diary. Actually, she found it rather entertaining, putting down everything in writing like this. It made her think more carefully about her brothers and her parents, and the Courtfields of Howldrevel, just as if they were characters in a book.

She'd always liked writing compositions. They were quite the best part of the lessons she took with the horrible Miss Pond, who had beady eyes and a moustache and a long, thin nose. Verity knew she should be sorry for her because, as Harry said, she must have been behind the door when looks were given out, and surely she would never in this world attract a husband. However, it was hard to feel anything but scorn as she was so humourless and dull and much given to the utterance of pious platitudes.

Her preferred method of teaching was to dictate notes or lists of dates from a book which she then required her pupils to learn by heart. Verity had understood early on that it was of little use to ask why things happened as they did. Questions such as how Henry VIII managed to get away with marrying six different women, or why was Queen Elizabeth so beastly to Mary Queen of Scots or what made Guy Fawkes want to burn down the Houses of Parliament remained largely unanswered. If it wasn't in the book, Miss Pond didn't know it, and worse, didn't appear interested in finding out.

The thought of returning to these uninspiring lessons was bad enough, but it was saying goodbye to Harry yet again that had sent her spirits plummeting and caused her to abandon the diary, at least temporarily. She supposed she ought to be used to doing without him, but she still felt miserable every time he and Stephen went back to school.

Harry was her friend, ally and confidant. She told him things she could never tell another living soul, even Livvy, and he told her things, too. He always understood her feelings when she complained to him about having to curtail her activities because of Mother's nerves, and sympathised completely with her desire to go to school. He'd even taken up the cudgels on her behalf about the uselessness of lessons at Howldrevel, attempting to persuade Father that she had a good brain and ought to have a decent education, but it was no good. She was doing very well with Miss Pond, Father had said confidently, and was clearly receiving, at comparatively modest cost, a highly suitable education which would more than adequately prepare her for her future as a wife and mother. No man, after all, wanted to marry a blue-stocking and the last thing he wanted was for a daughter of his to get all these silly, modern ideas in her head.

Which was all very well, Verity thought when this was reported to her, but suppose no one ever asked her to be a wife, let alone a mother? What was she supposed to do then? And if by 'modern ideas' father meant thinking women should have the vote, then such thoughts were already in her head and were unlikely to come out of it. She had a shrewd suspicion that it was the 'modest cost' part of Father's argument that was the most important.

Appealing to Mother was useless, both she and Harry were agreed on that. Not only was she adamant that she could never bear to let her only daughter leave home, but her offspring had long ago noted the pride with which she told new acquaintances that Verity went daily to Howldrevel to share lessons with Sir Geoffrey Courtfield's daughters. A baronet wasn't a lord, that was true, but it was a great deal better than nothing, particularly when he lived in a house as magnificent as Howldrevel.

At least Harry made her laugh about it all. He could do a wonderful imitation of Miss Pond to the point where Verity giggled so much she had to beg him to stop. He was a bit of a giggler himself, if the truth were known, and the pair of them were often rendered agonisingly helpless, usually at the most inopportune moments, like in church or when some friend of Mother's came to call and they were required to be on particularly good behaviour.

Stephen despised such conduct. Real men controlled themselves, he said. Real men didn't go into paroxysms of helpless mirth. He called Harry a Great Girl, and a sissy, but Harry didn't appear to care. He tried, he said. No one really wanted to collapse with uncontrollable laughter at awkward times, but it happened and there didn't seem a lot he could do about it.

"For heaven's sake, grow up," Stephen snapped at him on the last occasion this happened, which happily was when the three of them were alone in what was still called the nursery. It was at the end of the previous summer when he had stamped in, red in the face, to recount an incident in Porthallic when one of the village lads had called after him that his blazer would look better on a deck-chair. "I told him I wasn't standing for insults like that," he snarled, still smarting at the thought of such *lèse-majesté*. His handsome jaw was clenched with anger, his hands deep in his trouser pockets.

"Certainly not," Harry said, a little absently. He was, apparently, only half-listening, his attention mainly occupied by the particularly difficult jigsaw puzzle he and Verity were attempting together.

Stephen continued to fume.

"*Damned* if I'm going to stand for that kind of cheek."

"Of course not," Harry said, soothingly, adding after a moment in a faraway kind of voice, "But if he should feel like sitting down, I'd advise you to run a mile."

It wasn't much. Under any kind of analysis it might well appear rather a pathetic attempt at humour, but it was more than enough. Verity clapped her hand over her mouth, caught Harry's eye, and the damage was done. Furiously, blazing with anger, Stephen stood and watched them as they collapsed on to the table, jigsaw forgotten, their shoulders heaving, helpless with laughter; and unable to stay in the same room any longer, he delivered his verdict on their infantile behaviour and stalked out of the room, slamming the door behind him.

"Oh, Harry, I ache!" Verity hiccupped, minutes later, wiping her eyes and attempting to restore herself to order. "He was so on his dignity."

"He can't really help being a pompous ass, you know," Harry told her. "It comes from being such a Figg at school."

"Figg", Verity knew, was Waltham College slang for someone who excelled, particularly in sports. Harry was vague about its origin, but thought that years ago there was a famous fighter called Figg who beat all-comers, and his name had lived on in Waltham history. Waltham had all kinds of words peculiar unto itself. "Koppas" were lavatories, "larks" were playing fields, "giggers" dormitories, to name only a few. Verity prided herself on knowing them all. They were part of the enviable mystique of school.

That Stephen was a Figg there could be no doubt. To start with, he looked the part, he was so tall and handsome. Most of the Porthallic girls were in love with him, from the kitchen maids and the shopgirls in the village to the Courtfield sisters, Amelia and Catherine. You only had to see them gazing at him in church and witness their confusion whenever they were anywhere near him to know that. He was clever, too, and good at games. He'd been Captain of Cricket last summer and played Rugby for the Waltham College 1st VX. In the autumn, he was going up to Oxford.

"You'll find competition worthy of you there, my boy," Father had said at breakfast the other day. He was stroking his moustache at the time, always a sign of great satisfaction. Quite clearly it had never entered his head that his elder son could do other than to shine, in any company. Conversely, he had never made a secret of the fact that Harry's lack of prowess on the sports field was a great disappointment to him.

Verity admired Stephen, of course, and was proud of him, even if she did occasionally feel a sisterly urge to take him down a peg; she didn't miss him when he was away as badly as she missed Harry, though.

She sighed and picked up her pen again.

I am trying to view my bike as a consolation, as well as transport. Tomorrow I shall be going to Truro with Mother to see the boys

Barbara Whitnell

off at the station, so I shall have her all to myself after they have gone. I am hoping to take the opportunity to persuade her to let me ride to Howldrevel on fine days, though I am not hopeful, even though she intends to buy a new hat in Truro and should therefore be in a good mood. I daresay she will be overcome by horror at the thought of all the wild animals (i.e. lambs and the odd cow. Maybe even a squirrel!) that I might encounter between here and there!!! And there's always the postman's trap that might career into me – it must have been going at almost four miles an hour the other day!

One awful thing about tomorrow. We have to buy material for a new dress for me, and then go to Miss Penhaligan's to be measured up for it. There will probably be a battle for I refuse utterly to have another dress with smocking on it. No one of my age wears things like that, but Mother seems to want to keep me looking like an overgrown baby forever more. I shall fight tooth and nail.

Miss Penhaligan makes me laugh, though. She's so anxious to please that she agrees with everything Mother says, no matter what, sometimes even before she's said it. Poor old thing, it must be terrible to earn your living by sewing! I'd rather die in a ditch, for sewing is not, and never will be, one of my accomplishments. (What is????)

12th January 1913
Things I have to do:

1. Speak to Father about biking to school when he comes home from Bristol (from which it will be seen that Mother was not receptive to my pleas yesterday. Not that appealing to Father will do any good if Mother has put her foot down with a firm hand but it's worth a try!).

2. Make sure that he agrees I can go for rides with Livvy. He HAS to do that, or what was the point of buying me a bike at all?

3. Try to be better and to think before I speak. I said a rude and hateful thing to Mother because she kept going on and on at lunch in the Red Lion about how I should be nicer to Amelia and Catherine and go for walks when they ask, but honestly I see enough of them in lesson time and Amelia particularly is such a bore and a ninny. And not really very nice, if the truth is known.

52

She despises everyone and is not above making rude remarks about fish when she wants to get back at me for something, like getting good marks. She's older than me so hates it when I beat her, as I do most of the time. (I'm not being big-headed. Most people would beat her – even Tommy Penhale who's the village idiot and stands by the harbour wall banging his head all day.)

The dress business was all right, and I didn't have to fight about the smocking. It was really funny at Miss Penhaligan's. This is what happened.

Mother: I think a plain bodice with pearl buttons, don't you, Miss P?

Miss P: Oh yes, a plain bodice with pearl buttons will suit the material beautifully. You couldn't wish for anything nicer.

Mother (thoughtfully): On the other hand, a shaped yoke coming to a point in the front might be more becoming.

Miss P: Oh, I couldn't agree more, Madam! I can just see Miss Verity in a shaped yoke! A shaped yoke is always pretty, especially one coming to a point.

Mother: Unless, perhaps, you make it curved. Yes, I think that might be best. With three little bows at the front.

Miss P: Oh, you always have such excellent taste, Madam. I always love a curved yoke, especially when there are little bows at the front.

How I wished that Harry could have been there to hear it, but alas and woe is me, no Harry for three whole months!

Monday 3rd February 1913
I discovered a Truly Amazing Fact today. I was reading the Child's Guide to Knowledge. *(I'd finished my arithmetic exercise ages before Amelia and even longer before Catherine, so Miss Pond told me to sit quietly and find something to read.) All very well, I thought. I'd rather read than do arithmetic any day, but I've read everything in the schoolroom a million times over. Still, I hadn't noticed this bit in the C.G. to K. before. It said that when turtles lay their eggs, they always go back to the beach where they were born themselves. Isn't that clever? How do they remember?*

I asked Miss Pond, but naturally *she didn't know. She always glares at me when I ask her questions she can't answer, as if I'm trying to show her up in front of Amelia and Catherine instead of really wanting to know, but this time she put on her pursed-mouth, prissy face and said, "Verity, God's Word tells us there are more things in heaven and earth than we dream of."*

Well, I happened to know that this quotation (or something like it) is from Hamlet, *not God's Word at all, because Harry was swotting it up last holiday and I read it with him. So I told her. I thought she'd want to know, but she didn't and glared at me even harder.*

I am fascinated by the turtles, though. It's as if I were to be plonked down somewhere in Siberia, and was told to find my way back to Lemorrick without any signposts or maps or anything. I'd hate to live anywhere that was far from the sea, particularly my own special bit of it. So I would certainly want to get back home but I don't suppose I'd be clever enough to do so, so how do turtles manage? God does move in mysterious ways, there's no doubt about it.

While we were having our mid-morning milk, I mentioned this to Amelia out of interest, but all she did was glare at me.

"What a horrid little know-all you are, Verity Ashland." Amelia's eyes were black, like coal, and too close together. Her nose was thin, the combination giving her – so Verity had always thought – a look faintly reminiscent of a weasel, a resemblance made even closer by the fact that she now wore her hair scraped up which gave her a sort of skinny, inhuman appearance.

She and Catherine were sitting on one side of a small wicker table in the conservatory, with Verity on the other, a jug of milk and a plate of biscuits between them. "You always like to make sure everyone knows how clever you are, don't you?"

Verity looked at her in genuine astonishment.

"You mean about the turtles? But it's interesting!"

"I was talking about *Hamlet*."

"We haven't done *Hamlet*," Catherine put in accusingly, as if, this being the case, Verity had no right to know anything about it.

"Harry had to read it last summer." Verity's tone was defiant. "It's got an awful lot of quotations in it."

Amelia was unbending.

"There was no need to rub poor Miss Pond's nose in your superior knowledge."

Verity bit her lip. She supposed, now she thought about it, that it had been, well, tactless. However, she had no intention of meekly accepting reproof from anyone, least of all Amelia Courtfield for whose intelligence she had little respect.

"I didn't mean to hurt her feelings," she said, still on the defensive. "She shouldn't be so thin-skinned. Anyway," she went on, "since when have you thought of her as *poor* Miss Pond? You're far worse to her than I am."

This was undoubtedly true. All the Courtfields were in no doubt of their elevated place in society, and a mere governess was, to both Catherine and Amelia, little better than a servant and as such hardly deserved recognition, never mind consideration of any kind.

"I was just making the point," Amelia said loftily. "Nobody likes a know-all."

Verity continued to look defiant. Pride would allow of nothing else, but she knew in her heart that Amelia had a point and later, when they happened to be alone together, she apologised to Miss Pond who sought to excuse her gaffe by passing it off as a momentary lapse of memory.

"Which can happen to anyone," she said, still on her high horse. "As one day you will surely learn, Verity."

Verity pretended to believe her and later, thinking the whole thing over, found it in her heart to feel sorry for Miss Pond, in a lofty kind of way. It must be awful, she conceded, to be quite so dim and unattractive, and therefore unlikely to find herself a husband which was, as everyone knew, the only worthwhile thing a woman could do with her life.

What happened to the Miss Ponds of this world, she was moved to wonder, when they grew too old to teach? What did they have to live on? And where did they live? Some families provided a small pension, perhaps, but the Courtfields had never been noted for their generosity. Of course there was the Old Age Pension these days. Her father didn't approve of it. He said it encouraged fecklessness and people should be encouraged to save for their old age, not live off the taxes of those more industrious, but Harry believed it to be a good thing and she did, too. Still, she had a vague idea that it didn't amount to much. Thoughtfully, she considered the question.

Saturday 8th February 1913

Livvy came to tea today and I told her about my plan for founding a Home for Old Governesses when I grow up and we spent ages planning it. There would have to be single rooms for each, with pretty curtains and wallpaper and things and a bathroom on every floor, not just wash-stands in rooms. They would perhaps appreciate a library, too, and organised trips to Places of Interest. Livvy said Sewing Bees would be a good idea, and the Home would have to be near a church because governesses tend to be pious.

"Like Miss Pond," I said, pulling a Pondy kind of face. We looked at each other for a minute and then burst out laughing, thinking of how awful it would be to be surrounded ALL THE TIME with lots and lots of Miss Ponds, and I could feel all my good intentions leaking away through my toe-nails. Livvy said couldn't we make it a home for unwanted horses which would be much more fun and wouldn't demand so much in the way of wallpaper etc., horses not being noted for their appreciation of interior decoration. I couldn't help agreeing with her. I still feel sorry for Miss Pond, though. (But sorrier for me.) I'm ashamed to say that we got sillier and sillier in our suggestions for our governesses' entertainment, until we were laughing so much we had to stop.

It is very cold and wet and Februaryish at the moment, so no bike ride this weekend. Mother has relented a bit and I am allowed to ride along Lovers Lane and up the Lower Drive because there's never any traffic there except the odd farm cart, but she still won't let me ride into the village, or to Howldrevel the Turner's Cross way, though I haven't suffered a single scratch yet. I think Father is sympathetic to me, but he won't say so because of upsetting Mother.

Livvy and I played halma after tea until we got tired of it. Then she told me about a craze at school where you have to make a list of your favourite things in answer to questions, so we did that. These were mine:

Colour: Blue. Girl's name: Cordelia. Boy's Name: Jeremy. Famous Person (Male): Gerald du Maurier (I know as a Bolshevik I ought to put Lenin, but we swore to be absolutely honest and I do adore G. du M. though I've never actually seen him on the stage, just photographs). Famous Person (Female): (a) Mrs Pankhurst

(b) Miss Carne. Food: Coconut Ice. Song: I Hear You Calling Me. (It always makes me cry.) Animal: Horse (see above). Book: Treasure Island.

Don't think I've mentioned Miss Carne before, but she is the very musical daughter of the Vicar and she does her best to teach me the pianoforte. I really do love and admire her. Her name is Isobel, which is my second-favourite, after Cordelia. She is the Soul of Patience, and I wish like anything that I could be a better pupil! I'll never learn to play like Catherine, though I daresay I could be a bit better if I practised more. Is it too late to make a New Year Resolution?

Since we seemed to be in the mood for lists, we decided to make lists of all the virtues we would look for in the man we would like to marry. I put kindness to children and animals, a sense of humour, a liking for books and a nice mouth.

Livvy thought that was funny, and said, "Why stop at a nice mouth? I want nice everything!" But somehow it's mouths that seem to matter most to me, though eyes are important, too. And height, of course. I don't think I could ever fall in love with a really, really short man. Livvy said the very most important thing is that the man should be wildly in love with one, and I suppose that's true but so unlikely I can't imagine it. Love has got to come into it, though, because how else would you put up with it? Livvy (being a doctor's daughter) knows all about babies and things and she told me ages ago what you have to do. I think it sounds unbelievable and very shocking. She said she is quite sure she hasn't made a mistake, though. I wish I had the nerve to ask Miss Pond how babies come, just to see what she would say and watch her neck go red, like it does when something has embarrassed her, though come to think of it this would be breaking my vow to be nicer to her in future.

When Harry was at school Verity's week narrowed down to lessons at Howldrevel, calls made with her mother to other big houses in the neighbourhood, dancing classes, and piano lessons. Entries in the diary were often brief: "Same", she wrote on many occasions; or "Nothing worth recording", or "Dull, dull, DULL!!!"

Weekends were different, though, for then she was allowed to play with Livvy and together they roamed the cliffs and the woods, giving rein to their imaginations and their adventurous spirits, and went on bike rides together, far further than Louise Ashland would have allowed had she known about them.

Saturday 8th March 1913
Rode all the way to St Frayne today. Mother would have had a fit! It was lovely, though, especially sailing down the hill into the village. It was just like flying. The sky was a beautiful pale blue with hardly any clouds at all, no one would have believed how it had rained all week. There were primroses along the banks in all the lanes, and a sort of lovely fresh smell. We stopped by a field just for a rest and when Livvy went to explore we found two little baby goats there, one black and one white, and when you stroked them you could feel little nobbly horns under their fur. We christened them Blanche and Nigel and shall go and see them again next week, they were so sweet. Not that I am a lover of goats when they are grown-up, they have such nasty looking eyes, but B. & N. are different.

Sunday 16th March 1913
Mother and Father went to a ball at Howldrevel and Livvy came to spend the night with me. We talked and talked and didn't go to sleep till after midnight. Edith kept coming in to tell us to be quiet but we didn't take any notice and she said she'd tell Mother.

Livvy said she thought Mother looked really beautiful in her ball dress, and I agreed that she was very stylish and ornate, but quite honestly I'm not sure about beautiful because she has the Fothergill nose. I have, too, which is maddening because the Ashland nose is smaller and neater. In my opinion, anyway.

Her dress was apricot and gold, with a low-cut neck and a kind of puffy-out overskirt that rather reminded me of a very expensive Christmas decoration, but I know it's the fashion because I've seen that kind of thing in Lady's Home Journal. *Livvy said it was "le dernier cri" and that when she was old enough she was going to have one just the same, but I pointed out that fashions change. "Tell that to Miss Penhaligan," she said.*

Father looked distinguished, as always. He is a very good-looking man, in my opinion, and Stephen takes after him.

I don't think Edith could have split on us because nothing was said the next day, not that there was much time before Church as Mother had breakfast in bed and only just came out to the car in time. The sermon lasted for forty minutes! I timed it on my watch. We sang "Rock of Ages" and afterwards, in the kitchen, Cook said if she'd sat there any longer she would have turned into one.

Went back with Livvy to her house after lunch and had a lovely walk with Dr Rees who knows all there is to know about birds, and is quite funny. Home for tea. Learnt spellings. Read The Railway Children *for the 100th time.*

ONLY THREE DAYS BEFORE THE BOYS COME HOME FOR EASTER!!!

The ball, Louise Ashland reported to her daughter, had been everything that one could expect or wish for; a truly glittering occasion, where Amelia Courtfield had, for the first time, been allowed to join the adults, despite the fact that her presentation at Court wouldn't be until the summer.

"What did she look like?" Verity asked curiously.

"Quite passable," Louise replied. She caught sight of herself in the heavy, gilt-framed mirror over the fireplace as she spoke, and she pulled a few tendrils of hair over her forehead, smiling a little, happy in the knowledge that no one would attempt to describe her in such a luke-warm way. "Mind you, I don't think white is really her colour. She looked rather sallow, I thought. But then, does it matter when one is a Courtfield? She'll catch a husband before she's too much older, I feel quite sure." She turned from the mirror to come and sit beside Verity on the overstuffed sofa, taking her hand and smiling at her in a confidential manner. "You know, darling, I do wish you would put yourself out to be a little more friendly to the Courtfield girls."

Verity looked sullen. "Why? They're not very friendly to me."

"Oh, nonsense! I exchanged a few words with Amelia on Saturday and she asked after you in a most kindly way, and said how well you were doing in your lessons. You must realise," she went on, seeing no change in Verity's expression, "how great an asset it could be to you in the future, to be one of their intimates."

"*Mother*—!"

"No, listen to me, Verity. The Courtfields are the most influential family for miles around. They know everybody, and when it's your turn to come out in society you'll be glad to have the *entrée* to Howldrevel. I mean, you must face it, the Ashland side of the family will be quite useless in that respect.

"But I don't want—"

"Listen to me, Verity!" Suddenly Louise dropped her sweet, confidential manner and her voice hardened. "Please allow me to know best. In a little more than three years it will matter very much whom you know and to what places you are invited." She stood up and took a few restless paces across the room. "Believe me, I know what I'm talking about."

"Yes, but—"

"My family was poor, so there were no dances or parties for me. My father's cousin who inherited the title never married, never entertained. My social life was non-existent."

"But you met father—"

"People have told me I'm a beauty, you know," Louise said, ignoring this interruption. Verity looked at her, but said nothing. There was, after all, the matter of the Fothergill nose, and the fact that her mother was quite old. Nearly forty! "I take it you don't agree," Louise said acidly.

"Of course I agree," Verity said hastily. "You looked lovely on Saturday."

"And not too repulsive, even today, I trust."

"No. No, of course not. But what's that got to do with—"

"Who knows what my destiny might have been, had I moved in more elevated circles?"

"But you met—"

"Yes, yes, I know. Eventually, I met your father." Louise turned back to the mirror and stared sombrely at her reflection, drawing in a long breath. Verity watched her, frowning.

"So everything was all right in the end," she said.

Her mother continued to gaze in the mirror, saying nothing. Then she sighed. "Well, yes," she said, with a marked lack of enthusiasm. She whipped round to look at Verity again, shaking her finger. "But I was lucky, Verity. It might not have been all right. Your father was just about the first man I ever met. I want you to have a choice. I want you to meet someone – someone aristocratic. Someone worthy of you. Worthy of a Fothergill."

Verity thought this over. Then she, too, gave a sigh. "I can't make myself like Amelia and Catherine," she said. "And I can't make them like me."

Louise looked her severely. "You could make an effort," she said.

Four

11th January 1914
A whole year since I started writing a diary, and today I read it through right from the beginning. I am struck by how unexciting my life sounds, and how much the same it is, day after day. Sometimes I think it will never change and that I'll go on having lessons with Miss Pond for ever and ever until we all die of boredom! I'm afraid there are a lot of blank days. Blank months, sometimes. That's because of the sameness. Miss Pond is worse than ever and Amelia and Catherine just as infuriating, though I have really tried to be more friendly towards them, as Mother has instructed. There are days when I feel I could BURST, I am so longing to get on with life.

Thank goodness for Harry! How I wish he didn't have to go away so soon. He is my Best Friend and always will be. He dropped a bombshell yesterday. He told me he is having second thoughts about being a Bolshevik! He says he is seriously thinking of joining the Parliamentary Labour Party, but swore me to secrecy as Father would have Fifty Fits. As if I would say anything! I know Father thinks no more of Keir Hardy than he does of Lenin, and anyway he spends quite a lot of time in Bristol these days so that I hardly ever say ANYTHING to him.

Have bought this notebook so that I can keep on with the diary. Must try to write more. If I don't have many Doings to report, I can always record my thoughts on Life.

All through spring and summer Verity wrote about her problems with Amelia and Catherine, about birthday parties and excursions to the beach with Livvy.

5th June 1914
Family outing to Newquay and picnic on beach. Father has

brought a Mr Richard Rastrick from Bristol to stay. I am sorry Harry isn't here because I know we would find much to laugh at (perhaps, on second thoughts, it is just as well he is not as without him I am able to be on my Best Behaviour). Mother has warned me that Mr R. is a Very Important Gentleman. He certainly has a Very Important Moustache, but he can't say his R's which must be a grave disadvantage with a name like Richard Rastrick. I think he has taken a fancy to Mother. She has been a lot more Sprightly these last few days.

14th June 1914
Church this morning. Another hour-long sermon. I added up all the hymn numbers lots of times and every time the answer was different. I am quite useless at arithmetic. Went for walk with Livvy this afternoon. Mr R. has gone back to Bristol for which I am rather glad.

23rd July 1914
I'm not being any better this year than I was last in recording my Doings, mainly because nothing much happens. Now the boys are home and life is much more exciting. There was a charity cricket match at Howldrevel on Saturday. I had been praying all week that Stephen would bowl out Nicholas Courtfield and my prayer was more than answered as he bowled N. out for a duck! I was thrilled as N. is in sore need of being taken down a peg. One's prayers are not always answered so satisfactorily. N. thinks he's Everybody! I suppose he isn't bad looking, but in my opinion he has a Most Unpleasant Expression and he swaggers around as if he owns the earth and everyone ought to bow down and worship. He's a bad sport, too, and would hardly speak to Stephen for the rest of the day, but he's come round now because he needs S. to crew for him in the sailing regatta.

But by regatta week, there were more serious things to occupy them than sailing trophies. The declaration of war on the 4th August came to Verity, if not her elders, as a complete surprise. She greeted it with patriotic fervour and great excitement, rather in the same spirit as a Test Match against Australia.

We'll show them. The Germans won't stand a chance against our boys. Everyone says it will be over by Christmas.

Both Nicholas Courtfield and Stephen joined up at once, while Harry, under-age, waited in a barely contained fury of impatience until he should have finished his schooling.

By 1915 the war had begun in earnest, but at home there was little idea of the horror of it. As before, it was the more parochial matters that occupied Verity; the fund-raising fêtes, the musical evenings, the impact made by Stephen when he came on leave in uniform looking more handsome and dashing than ever. Amelia was married that summer, to a naval commander – a friend of her father, considerably older than herself, who almost immediately went to sea.

A cousin of the Courtfields was killed at Ypres, but Verity had never met him and though Amelia and Catherine were both very sad, this event had little impact on her. Agonising over whether or not she would be allowed to sleep over at Livvy's house after a long bike ride and picnic with several Rees friends and relations was far closer to her heart.

By October, Harry had joined the army, an occasion of great pride, particularly when he, too, came home in his uniform. She insisted on his wearing it to church and wrote afterwards that he looked every inch a hero and that no girl present could keep their eyes off him. But by July of the following year events had sobered her considerably.

Wednesday 19th July 1916
It's nine whole months since Harry joined the army, seven months since we have seen him and three weeks since we have had a word from him. The papers today were full of the terrible fighting on the Somme and they published a horrendously long casualty list. I feel sure he is in the thick of it and I am so worried about him. We all are. At least now Stephen is learning to fly we know that he is at home in England, though I can't imagine that's any safer really than being on the Western Front. I simply don't understand what keeps aeroplanes from plummetting out of the sky, which is horribly ignorant and old-fashioned of me, I know.

Isobel Carne has gone to Exeter to join the VADs. I do like her so awfully and will miss her a lot, but every cloud has a silver lining and I am thankful not to have any more pianoforte lessons. I will never be any good at it, if I have lessons until my dying day! Nicholas Courtfield is home on leave at the moment, still hobbling, but everyone says he will be all right though it's not certain he will be able to play cricket again, or indeed any sport at all which is a pity as he loved all games. It makes me feel ashamed of all the things I said about him the time Stephen bowled him out (and lots of other times, too). Catherine says he acted heroically during the naval battle and will probably get a medal, Admiral Jellicoe says so. To me, every time I see him now walking round the garden at Howldrevel leaning on his stick he seems a symbol of all the boys who have given up so much for their country. I can't help wishing, though, that it was Harry who was safe at home, stick or no stick!

Oh Harry, where are you? I am about to look out of my window at the moon which shines over you, too, and and I shall pray very hard that you are safe and that we'll hear from you soon.

Friday 21st July 1916
We had a letter from him today! He's all right! He says in another few days he'll be sent back behind the lines for a bit of a rest and that we're not to worry, trust an Ashland to know how to look after himself!

Mother cried when she read the letter, but I could see that they weren't sad tears and knew at once it was good news and was dancing around the breakfast table in my excitement. I wanted to rush out and turn cartwheels, but knew that Pascoe would be watering the flowers and thought I'd better not. After all, I am sixteen and a half. Amelia Courtfield was married when she was only six months older than I am now – just imagine! I find it impossible to think of her as Mrs Walter Urquhart (which Harry says sounds more like a hiccup than a name), even though she talks about "my husband" on every possible occasion. Her baby is due in six weeks' time and she has come home to have it because Walter is in Egypt. One can't help feeling sorry for her. She is so huge now that she won't allow herself to be seen in the village, or anywhere outside Howldrevel grounds, and spends most of her time lying on a chaise longue on the terrace, or in the conservatory if it's raining.

Even without the news about Harry, this would be one of the happiest days of my life because, believe it or not, we heard yesterday that Miss Pond, who went away at the beginning of summer to see her mother in London, won't be coming back because she has joined the WAACs! Catherine and I simply can't believe it! She was muttering a bit towards the end of term about us not really needing her as much as she is needed elsewhere, but we thought she was referring to her ailing mother who has cropped up in conversation over the years. But not a bit of it! The ailing mother, it seems, has taken a turn for the better, gone to live with her sister in Colchester and is helping to run a Guest House. For some reason this has inspired Miss Pond to throw her cap over the windmill, and do her bit for King and Country. To say Catherine and I were astonished is putting it mildly. C. says she must be hoping to meet a soldier and get married, but I think she's probably just looking for a change. I know we always thought of her as old as the hills, but now I come to think about it she can't be a lot more than thirty-two or three which is old enough, heaven knows, but not exactly in one's dotage.

So now my schooling is over. What am I to do with my life? Catherine is going to some kind of finishing place in Leamington Spa and Father says I could go too, but I don't want to. I'd still like to go to a proper school, but it's all too late. I know it would mean total mortification because I am so far behind. This Leamington Spa place just teaches useless stuff like flower arranging and folding napkins into waterlilies and managing servants and rubbish like that which I know would bore me to death, and anyway I don't really want to go anywhere with Catherine. She's a lot nicer when Amelia isn't around but even so isn't exactly a bosom friend, not like Livvy. Oh, how I wish Harry was here so that we could have a good talk about it. Failing Harry, I would like to talk it over with Isobel Carne. We used to talk about all kinds of things when she was struggling to teach me the piano. Just in between times, I mean, because she was very conscientious. She has promised to write to me, but I expect she will be far too busy.

Mother is really glad I don't want to go away and seems to think I will find plenty to occupy me here, like helping in the garden and the house now that we have so few servants and only old Pascoe and a half-wit boy outside. I don't mind doing that sometimes, but there surely must be something more! I am obsessed by the thought that I simply must Do My Bit.

Monday 24th July 1916
I have found my "something more"! I saw darling Dr Rees in the village this morning, coming out of Mrs Penrose's cottage down by the harbour. Her baby is expected very soon, but poor Mrs P. heard that Joe was lost at sea just a month ago and she is very down. Anyway, Dr R. waited until I caught him up, and we had a chat about Harry and Livvy (now working terribly hard for her exams. She wants to go to university and train to be a doctor, too. Lucky Livvy! I envy her so much. Not that I want to be a doctor, but I want to be SOMETHING.)

When I told Dr Rees I wasn't having lessons any more and was desperate to Do My Bit, he suggested I went over to Cranbrooke House, now a hospital for wounded sailors, to make myself useful by doing things like writing letters and reading to the men who have lost their sight. He says there is a great need for someone to do these jobs, and though I can't do much, I feel sure I would be able to do THAT! Mother doesn't want me to go because she says that I would find it too harrowing, and anyway no one could be spared to drive me over.

I'LL GO ON MY BIKE, I said, with all the determination I could muster! These days she doesn't make as much fuss as she used to, but I felt pretty sure she would raise objections on this occasion because I have to ride down that rather horrid bit of the Truro road. She didn't say anything, however. I think she could see from my expression that there was no point in arguing with me.

Dr Rees said he would talk to the Matron the next time he's over there (tomorrow) and would let me know the outcome.

Despite her determination, Verity was conscious of the fluttering of butterflies in her stomach as she pedalled the six miles between Lemorrick and Cranbrooke House.

She had dressed for the occasion with great care, putting on one of her favourite outfits, a light summer suit in cream shantung which had come from Harrods. Her mother, much to her relief, had recently decided that she was now too old to make do with any more of Miss Penhaligan's creations. She was, Louise told her frequently, almost a young lady now. In this suit and the little straw hat that went with it Verity felt quite sure she looked every bit of seventeen. Maybe more. And surely it was her patriotic duty to look as chic as possible, to cheer up the poor wounded soldiers?

It was a warm day and as she freewheeled down the sloping drive of Cranbrooke House, she marvelled at the change that had taken place since she had last visited there. Old Lady Polwhele, now deceased, had lived here before the war, and on one occasion Verity had reluctantly accompanied her mother when she had gone to one of the old lady's At Homes. The grounds then had been beautifully maintained by a regiment of gardeners; now they were showing unmistakeable signs of neglect, and the lawns were dotted with groups of men, some in wheel chairs, some leaning on sticks, or on the arms of crisply clad nurses.

A group of three men, one with a bandage obscuring one eye and another with a folded and pinned empty sleeve where his arm should be, were sitting on three garden chairs close to the drive. They whistled as she rode by, and called out to her.

"Don't be in such a hurry, darlin' – come and cheer the troops – be a sport!"

She laughed and waved and rode on. They didn't look so bad, she thought. Not nearly as harrowing as Mother had predicted. In fact in their bright blue uniforms, white shirts and red ties, they looked almost festive, and even the man with the empty sleeve had smiled and whistled.

Matron, once located, proved to be a far more sobering sight. She took Verity to her office, seated herself behind a desk, and spent what seemed like several lifetimes subjecting her to a long scrutiny which, by her expression, appeared to give no satisfaction.

She went on to list a comprehensive survey of what Verity was to do, and not do, say and not say. There was to be no personal involvement with the patients, no errands performed that were not approved by the nursing staff, no ill-considered remarks concerning the patients' condition, nothing said that could in any way lead to gloom and despondency regarding the current situation in France. Since Verity had clearly seen that some of the soldiers in the hospital were reading newspapers this seemed to infer that they were all congenital idiots, but she said nothing.

However, she was moved to murmur disagreement when Matron remarked that her current attire was more suitable for a garden party than work in a hospital.

"I *beg* your pardon?" Matron shot back, her face a mask of disapproval.

"I – I said 'not really'," Verity whispered. She gave a nervous laugh. "I mean, one wouldn't really wear this to a garden party, would one? It's very plain, I thought. M—more of a walking dress."

"See that tomorrow it's even plainer," Matron ordered, after a brief moment of eyebrow-raised displeasure at this effrontery. "A dark skirt and plain shirtwaister blouse will be suitable."

"Very well."

"You will say 'Yes, Ma'am' when I give you an order."

"Yes, Ma'am," Verity said woodenly, every bit as shocked as Matron had been. She had never called anyone 'Ma'am' in her entire life.

It was just one of the many things she became accustomed to during her time at Cranbrooke Hall. Her status remained undefined, but her time was fully occupied with odd jobs, mainly on behalf of the patients. Matron's embargo on running errands was soon disregarded; Verity's bicycle basket, more often than not, carried all manner of goods from the village shop, from cigarettes to birthday cards and packets of humbugs. She wrote letters that caused her secret amusement, others that made her want to cry. She read adventure stories to shells of men who were scarcely more than schoolboys, and love stories that made her blush with embarrassment. She played dominoes and bezique, and was instructed in the intricacies of nap and poker.

Some of the nurses were kind and companionable and made her laugh. A few were scornful of her privileged position and did their best to humiliate her. Whatever they were like, she had not been working at Cranbrooke more than a few months before she began to feel that she wanted to emulate them. She wanted, she felt quite sure, to be a real nurse. Yes, she *knew* that only last year, for a few short weeks, she had wanted to be a missionary, but this was different.

She was under no illusions about what it entailed. She had seen the hard work, the long hours, the emotional wear and tear for herself; that was unimportant, she told herself. Nurses were doing some good in the world, leaving it a better place than they found it, which was what she dreamed of doing. Not just now, during the war, though that gave her ambition an added urgency, but afterwards, in those unimaginable days when life returned to normal.

She knew that for the moment she was too young to undergo training, and knew, further, that even when she reached the required age her parents would do everything possible to dissuade her. It wasn't the sort of thing that ladies did.

Still, she was determined, and secretly she wrote away to discover how to go about fulfilling her ambition. 1916 turned into 1917, and in early spring Harry came home on seven days' leave. He was thinner, clearly more mature, but otherwise not much changed and their rapport was as great as ever.

"Are you really sure about this nursing thing?" he asked her, as, on a newly-minted day of duck-egg blue sky and scudding clouds they paused in their walk over the cliffs and sat together on a five-barred gate. Below them the sea glinted and sparkled, and all around the grass was starred with primroses. "You have to do some pretty beastly things, you know."

"Of course I know! How could I *not* know? I've been working at Cranbrooke for months."

"Yes, but—" Harry paused and sighed.

"But what?" Verity asked him.

"I dunno. Now is now, and beastly things have to be done; but whenever I think of the future, I picture soft colours and girls in silk dresses and sunshine and flowers and music and happiness. Will you want to do such things then?"

"People will still get ill."

"Well, of course, but you won't want to be looking after them. You'll meet a nice man and get married and have babies of your own to look after – though of course, there's always the question of who'd have you—"

"Watch yourself, now! One bad word and you'll be off the gate and into that mud. Oh, Harry, I want to get married one day, of course I do, and I'd absolutely love to have babies, but I don't want to be like Amelia, married straight out of the schoolroom and saddled with a baby before I'm twenty. I don't know who I am yet. Nursing will help me find out."

"You'll have a battle with the parents."

"Don't I know it! I'm getting tough in my old age, though. Anyway, I have a feeling that Father might be sympathetic, at least while the war's on. He's very patriotic."

Harry looked cynically amused. "You really think so?"

"Of course! He's proud as Punch of you and Steve."

"Oh, that—" Harry dismissed this aspect. "I was thinking of the business. I imagine he's doing pretty well out of the war, with all these army contracts."

Verity looked at him, frowning. "Soldiers have to be fed."

Harry shrugged his shoulders. "Yes, I suppose you're right. The troops must eat, and Ashland's pilchards are the best in the business."

"Not to mention the bloater paste! By the way," Verity said, "Dad seems awfully keen for you boys to go into the business after the war."

"I know."

"Do you think you will?"

"I can't speak for Stephen."

"But what about you?"

For a long moment Harry said nothing. He jumped down off the gate and held up a hand towards Verity. "It doesn't appeal much, I have to admit," he said at last.

Verity joined him on the ground. "You must have some idea of what you want to do," she said.

Harry smiled and looked away, saying nothing. Verity felt suddenly cold. He just wants to live, she thought, with the kind of panic that had been in abeyance during the days he had spent at home. Just to live. Oh God, please . . .

He went back to the front and life returned to what had come to pass as normal. There was work at Cranbrooke, social events with friends, balls in Truro where she danced with men on leave or men awaiting posting. Louise Ashland had been delighted, early in the war, to be invited by Lady Courtfield to serve on a committee devoted to raising money for naval charities which meant that there was always some fund-raising bazaar or concert in the offing for which Verity was pressed into service.

News of a new German Spring Offensive made terrifying headlines. Once again, a long period elapsed without a letter from either of the Ashland boys. Casualty lists were long, and grew longer. Feverishly, Verity prayed that they would be kept safe, without any great assurance that her prayers would be answered. Hadn't Mrs Truelove, who kept the inn in the village called the Lugger and was one of the most devoted church-goers in the village, similarly prayed that her Billy would return safely? And hadn't he fallen on the Somme, never to see his home and his sweetheart again?

Keep busy, Verity told herself. Work hard and play hard and don't think too much about the future.

There were, however, decisions to think over and letters to write. From time to time Verity told herself that she would, very soon, have to tell her parents about her long-term intentions. They would surely understand her feelings, would realise that anyone, of any age, could sell programmes at village concerts or man a stall at a bazaar, and they would see that it wasn't enough. Not nearly enough. Still she put off the moment, though, dreading the arguments that she knew in her heart would inevitably arise.

Since her father was so often in Bristol and her mother had never been an early riser, she was nearly always able to extract any letters addressed to herself without anyone of importance seeing them first. Then one day, having arrived home in the small hours after a dance at Howldrevel, she slept until mid-morning and came down to find her mother looking curiously at a long white envelope.

"Who on earth would be writing to you from the Devon and Exeter Hospital?" she asked.

"Oh—" Verity felt a flutter of panic, and lied accordingly. "Just one of the nurses I worked with."

Her mother looked at her narrowly, suspecting instead some unsuitable liaison with a patient who had passed through Cranbrooke. For all Matron's warnings, such things happened.

"Is that the truth, Verity?"

Verity took a breath, hesitated a moment more, then sighed heavily. "No," she admitted. "I lied. I'm sorry, Mother, but I've rather been dreading telling you. I've decided to stop playing at being a nurse and to train properly, and I think this may be a letter calling me for an interview with the Matron."

Still holding the envelope up by the corner, her mother was, momentarily, lost for words, her face a mask of disbelief, grown pale with shock.

"Have you taken leave of your senses?" she asked faintly, at last. "Your father will never allow it. That kind of work is not for ladies, as you know perfectly well." She looked up, her attention diverted. "Yes, what is it, Elsie?"

The Ashlands' pre-war indoor staff of butler, cook/house-keeper, parlourmaid, housemaid, 'tweenie and boot-boy having been reduced to an elderly cook/housemaid, a part-time charlady and a timid fourteen-year-old school-leaver, it was this latter who had appeared on the threshold of the morning room, seemingly unwilling to venture further.

"If you please, ma'am—" she began. She got no further. Verity's future career and her mother's annoyance were alike forgotten, for the attention of both was riveted to the telegram the girl held in her hand.

All three players in this drama seemed for a moment frozen in time, and it was a tableau that Verity was to remember for as long as she lived. The girl seemed transfixed by dread, unable to move and finally, as if in a dream, Verity found herself crossing the room, taking the telegram and opening it.

"Regret to inform you," she read tonelessly, "that Lieutenant Harry Ashland was killed in action on May 28, 1917. Lord Kitchener sends his sympathy."

She was aware of a rustle and a thump somewhere behind her and with difficulty, for somehow it seemed difficult to move, she turned her head. Her mother, she saw, had fainted dead away.

Five

4th June 1917
I don't even know why I'm trying to write anything. I seem to be in a state of suspended animation. Father has come home from Bristol and Mother has taken to her bed.

6th June 1917
I can't imagine why I feel so frightened, now that the worst has happened. I do, though. There's a horrible feeling of dread in my stomach that won't go away. We heard from Stephen yesterday. He is well, and is coming home next week for forty-eight hours' leave. It seems he met someone who knew someone else who knew Harry, so heard the news quite by chance, just before he flew over enemy lines, which must have been awful. Casualties among the RFC are very heavy. I do hope he takes care because if anything happened to him, I think it would be the end of Mother.
That is a stupid thing to say. Grief does not kill. I only wish it did.
We had a letter from a Captain Ward, who said that Harry was a brave soldier, much liked and respected, and that he died instantly. I hope he is telling the truth, but have a horrible suspicion that he tells all the families that. Poor man.

Saturday 9th June 1917
I went to the village for the first time yesterday and everyone was so kind about Harry and said wonderful things about him. I managed not to cry until I got home.
I am determined on Monday I will make an effort and go to Cranbrooke again. Dr Rees called to see Mother today and assured me I needn't and that everyone understands, but if all bereaved families behaved like me, where would the country be?
He brought Livvy with him, home from school for the weekend.

It was good of her to come and I was glad to see her, yet couldn't think of anything to say. It didn't really matter as she was just the same as always, but she did say I must write to the Matron to cancel next week's appointment and ask for another, so today I did. I can't imagine, though, that I will have the energy to do anything about it even if I am granted a second chance. On the other hand, it seems more important than ever that I should do something really useful. Livvy was very insistent on it and I know Harry wouldn't have wanted me to go to pieces like this. It's a cliché, but life has to go on. I just seem to be weighted down with this awful grief and inertia and fear. Why fear?

Mother is still very poorly and cannot face anything yet. Dr Rees can do very little, but at least he gave her something to make her sleep. Strangely, for my part, all I want to DO is sleep. It's waking up that's so awful – the moment one comes to oneself and realises afresh what has happened.

Father is still here, but seems anxious to get back to Bristol. I wish he wouldn't go away. Not yet, anyway. I think Mother needs him.

11th June 1917
Back at Cranbrooke. Rather a quiet day. Quite a number of the boys have moved out and the new lot not yet arrived.

Received a letter from Exeter offering me another appointment on the 20th. I wanted to tell Father about it at breakfast, but he retreated behind The Times *and was not in the mood for conversation. At dinner I tried again, but he talked a great deal about the business and how his presence in Bristol was really essential these days, and somehow the opportunity never presented itself. It seems that Ashland's Fish is making a lot of money because of government contracts, just as Harry said. I wish he hadn't mentioned that. I know the troops have to be fed, of course, but it seems all wrong to profit unduly by it – not that he would appreciate my saying so!*

I thought perhaps Mother might have mentioned my intentions to him, but apparently not. Maybe she's forgotten, after everything that has happened. Or thinks that I have.

13th June 1917
Finally managed to talk to Father about my interview, and of

course I should have known the outcome. He has absolutely forbidden me to go to Exeter. He has to go back to Bristol on Monday, he says, and it is quite unthinkable for Mother to be left alone, her nerves are so bad.

I knew that he would hardly welcome the idea of my becoming a nurse and was prepared to put up a fight on those grounds, but of course, it is an unarguable fact that Mother can't just be left to the servants. Foolishly, I thought that perhaps seeing her in such a bad way, Father would manage to find some way to stay at home for a few weeks yet, or at the very least cut down his time in Bristol to no more than two or three days a week. If the company is making as much money as he says, then one would think he could take on extra staff, but perhaps I am being unreasonable. His work is, after all, of national importance and good staff is not easy to find these days. Anyway, there is nothing to be done. I must try to put a good face on it.

Between me and this diary, however, I had managed to persuade myself that in hard work and new surroundings I might find some kind of relief for this awful nothingness inside of me, and I am severely disappointed to have to cancel my appointment yet again. I do hope it won't be too long before Mother feels herself capable of making an effort to face life once more.

It was spring again before she could bring herself to walk along the cliff path to the place where she had gone with Harry, that last time. She sat for a while on the gate, thinking of him; then walked on further, feeling him strangely close to her.

Below there were tiny coves, accessible only by sea, each with their own mysterious fascination and hidden secrets. In the past, they had visited them in the dinghy that bobbed all summer at Lemorrick's own private mooring.

Never again, Verity thought from time to time, looking down on them as she walked the cliff path. She couldn't bear to. They belonged to Harry.

She came at last to a place called Rocky Head that she and Harry had loved, perhaps, more than any other. It was a headland where a small, minor path narrowed as it wound downwards towards the rocky cliff that jutted out into the sea.

It led through encroaching gorse bushes, now covered with yellow flowers. For a moment she had hesitated at the top of the path, for the scent of the gorse, warmed by the sun, brought the pain back as sharp as ever, instantly transporting her to the carefree days when she and Harry had played here as children.

She took a breath and went on, however, and soon left the gorse behind, continuing over an area of tussocky grass and outcrops of granite boulders that had served as high mountains and castles and forts in the days of their childhood, and had provided seats and crannies, sheltered from the prevailing wind, in later years. It was here they had talked and planned, sharing their dreams.

This had to be done, she told herself. She couldn't go on avoiding these special, secret places for ever. And who could tell? It might even be some kind of comfort.

There was one large outcrop of rock almost at the end of the headland that had been the most special place of all. She and Harry had always called it the Cathedral because of its spire-like formation. It was possible to climb it on the landward side, then inch round to a ledge which gave an incomparable view of the entire bay.

Determinedly, knowing it to be the biggest mental hurdle of all, she began to climb, one hand pulling herself up on the rocks, the other lifting her skirt above her ankles. Even so, it became snagged. She looked down to free herself, then saw to her astonishment as she edged round to the ledge that she was not alone. A young man was already sitting there.

He was brown-haired, of medium height; superficially so like Harry that she drew in her breath with a great gasp and reached for a handhold to steady herself. Her heart, when it resumed beating, was racing and it was a struggle to compose herself.

"Good afternoon," said the young man, not moving. "I'm sorry if I startled you."

She relaxed a little. He was really nothing like Harry, she saw. Everything was different – mouth, nose, eyes, voice. It was only his colouring and shape and the unexpectedness of him that had made her think, just for a moment, that she was seeing a ghost. She shut her mouth, and swallowed.

"I – I just wasn't expecting anyone," she said. "For a second it seemed—" She broke off, feeling foolish, and looked at him more closely. "Don't I know you?" she asked curiously. "It's Laurie, isn't it? Laurie Grenfell?"

Mr Grenfell, Laurie's father, had been the postmaster in

Porthallic for several years when the children were small, but the family had moved away before the war, to where Verity couldn't remember. Laurie had been around Harry's age and they had become friends in a casual kind of way, swimming together or splashing about the harbour in a dinghy along with the other boys – much to her mother's annoyance, Verity remembered, for she disliked any of her children to mix with those of the village in case they picked up a Cornish accent or nasty, lower-class germs, or an infestation of some kind. Fine-tooth combs were instantly produced the moment such fraternisations came to light.

Laurie, therefore, had never been invited to the house or officially recognised in any way. The beach, however, was open to all, as were the surrounding woods and fields, and no parental edict could prevent a limited amount of association between the boys.

"That's right," Laurie said now. "But I'm afraid I don't recognise—"

"Verity Ashland." She took the last few steps up to achieve the ledge and settle herself at the other end of it. Strangely, though her immediate reaction had been one almost of outrage that someone else should be there – someone other than Harry – she felt now some measure of relief. Harry had liked Laurie, she remembered, and had told his mother so in no uncertain terms when she trotted out all her usual objections to the association.

"Miss Ashland!" Laurie Grenfell half rose a little awkwardly, then, as if realising that such niceties had no place on a narrow ledge at the far end of a Cornish headland, he sat down again. He smiled at her, rather charmingly, she was now in a fit state to notice. "Of course! I can see it see now. But you'll admit you've changed a bit."

"I should hope so! You've been gone for ages."

"I had to come past your house just now, and I thought of Harry. What's he doing with himself?"

"He was killed at Arras," Verity said quickly, getting it over. "Nearly a year ago now."

"Oh, God, I'm sorry. This bloody war!" Laurie shot her a glance, suddenly embarrassed. "I'm sorry," he said again, with a slightly different inflexion.

"You mean for swearing? Well, what else can one do?" She sighed, lifting her shoulders and letting them fall again in a gesture of resignation. "Sometimes – and only in private, I promise – my language would make a navvy blush."

He laughed at that. He really was extremely good-looking, she thought, conscious of a twinge of excitement. She had always liked that kind of thin, sensitive face. And such eyes! They were dark and thick-lashed. Any girl would have coveted them.

"What about your other brother?" he asked. "I've forgotten his name. Never knew him as well as Harry."

"Stephen. He's all right, so far. He's a pilot in the Flying Corps."

"He would be," Laurie said, obscurely. Verity glanced at him with a gleam of amusement in her eyes, but made no comment.

"Is it ever going to end, Laurie?" she asked instead.

Sombrely, he shook his head. "God knows. Sometimes it doesn't seem like it."

"It's gone on for ever. You're in it, I suppose?"

"Yes. Well—" He broke off and shrugged his shoulders. "I have been," he said obscurely.

"On leave?"

"That's right."

She glanced at him to see that he was looking out to sea, his brows drawn together, his lips clamped shut. Quite clearly, he had no wish to talk about the war. Well, she could understand that.

"Where did you go when you left here? I've forgotten."

"Falmouth." His expression lightened. "It was a good move. We were happy there."

"Weren't you happy here?"

He thought about it for a moment. "Well, not as happy as in Falmouth. Porthallic's a funny sort of place. You're either gentry or beyond the pale. My mother's an educated woman, she was a teacher before she married, and she felt she didn't belong anywhere. Falmouth was different. Bigger. People find their own level."

Slowly, Verity nodded, seeing how this could be so. "What brings you back here?" she asked.

He made a sweeping gesture towards the sea and the cliffs. "All of this," he said, smiling a little at last. "I thought of nothing else in the trenches. I wanted to come here again. I made bargains with God. One more look, I said. Just one more. I won't ask for anything more."

Verity looked at him, suddenly needing to swallow hard. "Well, He must have heard you," she said at last.

"Yes." He shifted a little on his ledge and she heard him sigh. "Tell you the truth," he went on after a moment, his voice a little gruffer now as if he spoke with difficulty. "I've been invalided out. No use to the army any more. I suppose I ought to be pleased. Daft thing is, I'm not. I'm bloody ashamed."

"Oh, Laurie!" Impulsively she turned to him and reached to touch his arm. "As if there's any need for that! Were you wounded?"

"I was blown up on the Somme. Lost a finger. Makes me a bit – clumsy, you could say. No use to the army any more."

"Oh, Laurie," she said again.

"Could be worse. It was my left hand."

"Well, then!" Verity was using the voice she so often employed at Cranbrooke; sympathetic but cheerfully encouraging. "You're right. It could be worse. Here, let me look." She inched a little nearer to him and calmly reached across him and took hold of the hand in question. He tried to pull it away, but she hung on, studying it closely. His middle finger was missing just short of the knuckle while the rest of his hand was heavily scarred. It was undoubtedly a mess, but her face showed no emotion.

"Yes, a lot worse," she said, looking up at him with a smile. "Which doesn't make it any easier for you, I know. Not just now, anyway. I expect you feel that the eyes of the world are focussed on it, but they're not, you know. I'd never have noticed it if you hadn't said. You'll get used to it."

He was scowling as he snatched his hand away and thrust it into the pocket of his jacket. "What do you know about it?" he said. "It's revolting. I can't ever imagine holding hands with a girl again."

"Oh, come *on*! You just have. Anyway, that kind of rawness will fade, I promise you. And after all, it is your left hand. I imagine you could do an awful lot of holding with your right one."

"Yes, but—" He turned and studied her, still frowning. "Are you a nurse, or something?"

Verity sighed. "Or something, I suppose you could say. I only wish I were! I help over at Cranbrooke House, you know, the mansion at Five Lanes. It belongs to the Polwhele family, but old

Lady Polwhele died and the family's dispersed so none of them are living there and it's been turned into a hospital. I'm a kind of volunteer assistant there three days a week, and believe me, I've seen far worse things than your poor hand." She touched his arm once more. "You must have suffered, though, Laurie. I do know something of what you must have gone through. Don't think I'm callous, or unsympathetic."

He attempted a laugh. "Oh, I'm not in need of anyone's sympathy. In fact you probably feel I ought to be congratulated for copping a Blighty. Many would be glad to."

"No! I don't think that. How could I?"

For a while he said nothing. Verity glanced at him, biting her lip, worried that she had said the wrong thing. She thought she could detect an attitude she had met before. They don't tell us what goes on out there, she thought, yet they resent it if we don't understand. She felt she had sounded callous, put things clumsily, didn't care a jot for his pain. Oh, when am I going to learn tact? she asked herself.

Suddenly, he gave a long sigh and she felt him relax beside her.

"I'm sorry," he said gruffly. "I know I'm too sensitive. I'm not always like that, and I really am everlastingly grateful that it's not my right hand. I know I'll learn to cope. It's just the *look* of the thing! It repels me, never mind anyone else."

"Any girl, you mean?"

He gave a mirthless grunt of laughter.

"I suppose I do."

"But it's of no importance! No girl worth her salt is going to take the slightest notice of it."

"Oh, no?" His tone was caustic. He knows differently, she thought. Maybe someone's already hurt him badly.

She took a breath and changed the subject. "Tell me, what are your plans, now you're a free man? You really ought to think of the future."

"Well—" he hesitated, sitting up a little straighter, as if making a determined effort to shake off the last vestiges of self-pity. "I want to get some proper qualifications. My mother wants me to go to university – and I could," he added a little belligerently, as if she had produced arguments against it. "I won a scholarship to Falmouth County School and did pretty well. It really depends on whether I can get a grant from the County because my parents can't afford to send me to college without a lot of help – and anyway, I'm not really sure that university is the best course for me to take."

"What do you want to do?"

"Horticulture." He looked at her as if daring her to say something flippant. "I've written to Kew for advice and I'm waiting to hear from them. If I could get taken on as a trainee, that might be better than any university, but they might say a degree in botany would be an advantage. I'll just have to see."

"Horticulture?" Verity looked bewildered. "That's just gardening, isn't it?"

He grinned at her. "And any fool can do that, of course!"

"No – I didn't mean—"

"It's a science, Miss Ashland, and the most important one I know. I want to grow things. Better things. Find new species. I think I've always known it, but these last few years . . ." His voice trailed away and he bit his lip as if afraid of sounding over-emotional. Or, perhaps, a little pretentious.

Verity looked at him, wide-eyed. "Of course," she breathed. "Of *course*! I understand absolutely. I think that's wonderful."

For a moment his eyes held hers, then he swallowed and looked away, out to the horizon.

"They do say that after the war there'll be all sorts of schemes for sending ex-officers to university, but no one has time for that now. First we have to win. After that I'll see what can be done."

He was an *officer*, Verity thought, surprised; then felt ashamed of herself. It was just the sort of amazed reaction that her mother would have felt. Why shouldn't he be an officer? He might be the son of a postmaster and still retain his Cornish accent, but he was clearly educated and a thoroughly decent person with the kind of idealism that she found inspiring. "I'm sure you'll do well," she said.

He gave an embarrassed laugh. "I'll certainly try. But meantime I must get a job of some kind so that I can save some money. That's why I'm over in this direction. I've been to Howldrevel to see Sir Geoffrey. He needs a head gardener."

"So he does," Verity said. "Old Carrivick died a couple of weeks back, and Nicholas Courtfield was saying the other day that none of the others is suitable to take over. Two are barely out of school, and the other is unreliable."

"It'll suit me down to the ground. I'm still clumsy at the moment, but I'll get better and I do know a fair bit about gardening. We've got a good garden in Falmouth, and an allotment. My Dad grows all sorts, and I've been helping him ever since I was small."

"Capability Grenfell," Verity said, teasing him, glad to see him looking so much more cheerful.

He laughed. "Maybe one day."

"Well, I wish you luck. All the luck in the world. And I'm glad to have met you like this." She got to her feet, holding on to the rock to steady herself. "I have to go now, or I'll be late for tea. My mother hasn't been too well since Harry died, and it fusses her if I don't present myself in her sitting room on the dot of four."

Laurie stood up beside her. "It's time I went, too. If I go across that field it brings me to the main Truro road, doesn't it? I may be able to catch a bus at the bottom of the hill. By the way," he continued when they were walking in single file through the gorse, "you mentioned Nicholas Courtfield. Is he around these days?"

"He's in the navy. He was wounded at the Battle of Jutland and has got some kind of a desk job in Plymouth so he gets home quite often." She looked at him over her shoulder. "You don't sound as if you care for him much."

Laurie hesitated. "I hardly knew him, and he certainly didn't know me. Harry—" He hesitated for the fraction of a second. They had come to a place where the path was wider, and he came to walk beside her. "Harry didn't think much of him, I remember. Said he carried on as if he owned the place. Used to call him a 'pishter', whatever that was."

"It was a Waltham College word, and not at all polite," Verity said, and though she laughed she was aware of pain. Would she ever be able to think of such things without it? "As for owning the place, he almost does, doesn't he? And I have to tell you, he's still a bit of a pishter, in spite of getting a medal. But you won't want to be rude about him when you're working at Howldrevel."

"Don't worry! I'll touch my forelock as often as he wants, so long as his dad gives me a job."

They parted at the fork, and Verity hurried towards home,

conscious that she would be very lucky indeed if she arrived there by the appointed hour.

Her mother led a strange and confined kind of existence. She had always been – as she was only too ready to say to anyone who would listen – highly strung. She had suffered from her nerves all her life, she said. And headaches. She had never been strong, had somehow *felt* things more than other people. All of which meant that her husband and children had always been required to tip-toe round her, sheltering her from any of life's unpleasantnesses, major or minor. Harry's death had apparently tipped her into a neuroticism that prevented more than a half-hearted attempt to live a normal life, and more and more she was adopting the role of semi-invalid, though Dr Rees assured her husband and daughter that there appeared to be nothing physically wrong with her. Visits to specialists in London had produced the same opinion, though never quite so plainly expressed. It cost Joseph Ashland many hundreds of pounds for one Harley Street consultant to diagnose neurasthenia, and even more for another to settle for nervous exhaustion – verdicts that Dr Rees greeted with silence and an expression of deep scepticism.

"I wish it were possible to get her interested in something," he said to Verity once, in private. "Nervous exhaustion is a condition that simply doesn't exist."

Verity did her best to carry out his wishes, but nothing worked. Once her mother had enjoyed collecting porcelain, arranging flowers, seeing friends. Now nothing held her attention; nor would she agree to go away for a change of air. Only the presence of her husband at weekends seemed to create any spark of interest, a spark that was all too quickly extinguished when he was driven back to Bristol on Monday mornings.

Her main preoccupation as far as Verity was concerned was that of procuring a suitable husband for her only daughter.

"Anyone would think we lived in Jane Austen's time," Verity complained to Livvy. "I wish Mother would get it through her head that I may be unmarried, but I am not in want of a husband. Maybe I never will be."

She didn't really believe that, but certainly she had met no one so far she felt she could bear to share her life with. However, as far as her mother was concerned, hope continued to flower. From time to time she met eligible young officers, either at dances or at the houses of friends, and occasionally one or other of them presented himself at Lemorrick for tea. Some Verity liked, some she regarded with indifference, but whatever her feelings towards them her heart sank whenever they called, for she knew that once they had gone she would be subject to a barrage of questions from her mother. Who were their people? Did they have a profession? Were they in trade? Did they own property? The quizzing was endless, and all quite pointless.

"Mother, I'm not ready to settle down," she said. "I haven't lived yet!"

"Don't be silly, dear," her mother replied dismissively.

After Verity's chance meeting with Laurie, she arrived home fifteen minutes late and had time only to wash her hands and smooth her hair before presenting herself in her mother's sitting room. There Louise Ashland, arrayed in a coffee-coloured tea-gown, was already sitting at the lace-covered table which Eva was always required to set with daintily cut sandwiches, scones and cream, and various cakes, all complemented by the finest china and immaculate napery. There was little evidence of wartime shortages here, though Mrs Saunders, the cook/housekeeper, constantly complained of having to make do with inferior ingredients.

"I haven't waited," her mother said, her mouth tight with disapproval. "You'll forgive me, I'm sure. As you know, I always feel a little faint if I don't have my tea on the dot of four."

"I'm sorry I'm late, Mother."

"It was rather thoughtless, dear; but never mind, now that you're here. Where have you been?"

"Oh, it was such a lovely day that I went for a walk along the cliff to Rocky Head. It was so beautiful!"

Louise sighed. "How I wish I could have accompanied you! Mind you, I don't think, however good my health, that I could face Rocky Head. It was one of our dear Harry's favourite places, you know."

Verity said nothing, concentrating on pouring herself a cup of tea. Of *course* she knew – none better – that it was one of Harry's favourite places. Hadn't she shared it with him, times without number? It was one of the things that most annoyed her about her mother, that her loss had to be treated as so much worse than anyone else's.

84

"You'll never guess who I saw there," she said, after a moment, hoping to provide a little diversion. "Laurie Grenfell! Do you remember him? His father was the postmaster."

"No-o—" Louise's reply was vague and long-drawn-out. "No, I can't say I do. But then I wouldn't, would I?"

Verity laughed, genuinely amused. "No, Mother. I don't suppose you would. He's done well, though. He's just left the army because he was slightly wounded, but I gathered he was a commissioned officer."

Her mother raised perfectly arched eyebrows.

"Good gracious!" she said faintly. "Whatever next! The *postmaster's* son, you say? Of course, there have been so many casualties in the field, I suppose they're reduced to promoting all kinds of people. I hope you haven't arranged to meet him again."

"Well," Verity said, outwardly demure, "I rather liked him, you know, and though nothing's been arranged, it might be a bit difficult not to bump into him from time to time in the village. He's coming to work at Howldrevel."

"Really?"

"As head gardener."

"Good gracious," her mother said again, with even more astonishment, as if the ways of the modern world were too much for her to understand. Her voice strengthened. "Then however much you might have 'rather liked' him, Verity, I trust you certainly won't be seeing him again! An officer he might have been, but there are limits."

"He seemed, actually, quite congenial," Verity said, some demon making her determined to provoke. "Pleasant, and very intelligent. He hopes to go to university when he's saved up some money."

"*University*! My dear girl . . ." Louise's trilling little laugh had an edge to it. "Really, what are things coming to? I'm sure he'll find that university entrance isn't as easy as all that! He'll need more than a field commission, I can assure you." Verity reached for a scone and said nothing, while her mother regarded her suspiciously through narrowed eyes. She instinctively distrusted talk of congenial young men of the wrong class. "Well, I don't suppose your paths will cross again. You must realise, Verity, that these are important times for you. You must not get the reputation for being – well, *eccentric* in your choice of friends. It's so easy for a girl to lose her reputation. I mean, what would Nicholas Courtfield think if he saw you hob-nobbing with his father's gardener?"

"Nicholas?" Verity frowned. "Why should I care what Nicholas thinks?"

Louise Ashland sighed, looking at her daughter with some exasperation. "Verity, you must start being sensible. Let me be brutally honest. You are a dear girl and I mean no offence, but you are no beauty, your features are far too irregular for that. Thank heaven you've inherited my skin, and you have a certain youthful charm at the moment which almost passes for prettiness, a liveliness which is quite attractive. I have seen men looking at you. I have seen Nicholas Courtfield looking at you."

Verity threw down her tea napkin. "Mother, I can't *stand*—"

"Attractiveness such as yours does not last, my dear," her mother went on, holding up her hand to silence her daughter. "I've seen it so often. The only thing for us to do is to take advantage of it while we may. It's not, after all, as I've said before many times, as if being a member of the Ashland family is of any great social advantage—"

"We're hardly poor, Mother!"

"I know that, of course. We live very comfortably, but it is nothing compared to the landed families – the Courtfields, and so on – and there is, after all, the stigma of Trade. One can't ignore it. It's something I have learned to live with, but it hasn't always been easy and one can't expect others to do the same."

Verity's voice rose angrily. "Mother, you're living in the past. After the war, everything will be different, you'll see."

"I want to see you settled," her mother said tremulously. "And settled quickly. And please don't raise your voice to me." She groped for a handkerchief and dabbed at her eyes. "My nerves simply won't stand it."

15th May 1918
It is an undoubted fact that Nicholas Courtfield has been paying me some attention lately. Can't imagine why, as every Courtfield I have ever known usually acts as if the entire Ashland family is barely worthy of their attention (with the possible exception of Catherine, to be fair. Being in Trade must give out its own particular smell. I suppose ours is distinctly fishy!) They really are

the most arrogant beings I have ever encountered, and Nicholas has always been the worst in this respect. No – Lady Courtfield is the worst, with Amelia and Nicholas vying for second place.

What Mother doesn't realise is that when N. looks at me (and I don't give him the chance if I can help it), I feel as if slugs are walking all over me. I don't know what it is about him. I know he is a war hero and I vowed to be kinder to him because of it, but there is something about him that repels me. I know that many people think him handsome, but I have never liked his mouth which is somehow thin and mean, or the way his nostrils curve as if he has a perpetual sneer on his face. He can be cruel, too. I have seen him beating his dog mercilessly for not coming when called. Anyway, for whatever reason, I wouldn't marry him if he were the last man on earth, no matter what Mother says. The very thought of kissing him, let alone anything more intimate, makes me shudder!

To be honest, when I stopped being cross I was a bit cast down when I remembered all that Mother said about my lack of looks, but now I've had time to think I am a little more philosophical. After all, I am only eighteen and have a few years (surely?) of youth in front of me. Anyway, it's not as if I am absolutely repulsive. So far I have had more trouble fighting suitors off than encouraging them. Mother doesn't know the half of it. I have liked one or two quite well (e.g. Capt. Chivers and Lt Masters) but I have only to feel myself on the brink of love to think: how would I feel if they didn't come back? and then I feel too frightened to let my emotions become really engaged. I don't know how I would cope with a second bereavement. I suppose, though, that if I really fell in love I wouldn't be able to choose whether my emotions were engaged or not.

It was nice to see Laurie Grenfell. I thought his views about the future most inspiring. It is wonderful to meet a man who has been through the hell of the trenches and can think only of the need to beautify the world.

I hope I didn't say the wrong thing about his hand. I fear that I did. It's so very hard to sound positive and encouraging without seeming heartless.

17th May 1918
Letter from Laurie Grenfell this morning, apologising for being so thin-skinned about his hand and going on to "burden me with

his dreams"! He said that after leaving me he walked across the field feeling full of hope and determination as if suddenly his life had taken a turn for the better, and he knew it was all because of me! He begins work at Howldrevel right away. Don't care what anyone says, I hope I see him again. I'm going to write back.

24th May 1918
Don't know where the time goes. A bit short-staffed at Cranbrooke, so I've been every day which doesn't please Mother very much. She keeps telling me that Charity Begins at Home, but she spends so much time either in bed or lying on the chaise longue in the conservatory that it seems such a waste of time for me to be there when there is so much to be done at the hospital. Besides, I am so tired of bezique!

They let me do all sorts of jobs at work now, not just the frivolous things I used to do, although I'm not excused those either. Had to write a terrible letter today for a man who'd lost his sight and his right arm, in answer to one from his fiancée breaking off their engagement. How could anyone do that? I could have wept for him, he was so upset, and after all he had been through, too! Maybe I should tell Laurie about him for surely his problem would fade in comparison. It makes me so cross when I hear people moaning about food shortages! They're not as bad as all that, just inconvenient, and no one shows any sign of starving yet.

Oh, I do wish it would all end, though. Things seem to have reached a kind of impasse at the moment.

Saturday 25th May 1918
A beautiful day. Very conscious that a year ago today Harry was alive but three days later his life was snuffed out. There are times when the grief simply swamps me and I can't do anything.

Father home, so I was free. Dear Livvy (I am sure she realises how I feel just now) asked me to go for a walk somewhere nice, but she sent a note round in the morning to say she had a horrid cold and sore throat and would I mind if she cried off. So I went alone to Rocky Head because it was Harry's favourite place, and – just as if it were Fate – Laurie was there! I could hardly believe it, and nor could he! He said he had been sitting there, willing me to come, and then, suddenly, there I was! He said that actually he has been several times since we met before because it's his favourite place on earth (just like Harry!) and there's a short cut across from Howldrevel via Turner's Cross which makes it a convenient place for him.

We talked for ages, all about everything. I was sure I must have bored him stiff, going on and on about Harry and all the things we used to do together, but he said no, not at all. He just listened for ages and said what a wonderful person Harry had been, everybody thought so, and how lucky I was to have such happy memories and such wonderful times to look back on. He got very angry about the war and the waste of life, and in the end I found that I was comforting him instead of the other way round. I don't think there is a single living soul with whom it would be easier to share my grief. He understands everything.

He likes his job at Howldrevel. The gardens there are wonderful – some ancient, departed Courtfield travelled all over the world to bring back exotic plants in the 1860s, but lately the place has become overgrown and Laurie sees it as his Mission to restore it to its former glory. He says he doesn't see any of the Courtfields much. Roy Parker, the estate manager, gives him his orders and leaves him to get on with it, but Lady Courtfield is very particular about the flowers that are sent up to the house and gets very annoyed if the things she wants aren't available. He said he thought he was going to get the sack the other day because all the Cornish lilies are over (and have been for some time) and Cornish lilies were the things she wanted above all else. Next time he's going to tell her to go and complain to God!

I told him all about my schooldays there and in spite of everything we found quite a lot to laugh at. He has a very shapely mouth and fascinating, slumbrous grey eyes. We are going to meet again tomorrow afternoon at the stile and if I am to be honest, I must say that I am looking forward to that very much. I told him today to stop calling me Miss Ashland and he blushed!

26th May 1918
I feel ashamed because when I think of Laurie, I can't help being happy in spite of losing Harry. Couldn't sleep all night for guilt and today, in church, I knew he was there with the other Howldrevel servants but I hurried past when I saw him outside the porch after the service, mostly because I felt suddenly overwhelmed and thought I was going to cry.

It's not at all that I forget Harry when I am with Laurie, just that other things seem important, and then suddenly it all swamps me again and it seems so unfair that everything is finished for him and just beginning for me. It feels like treachery even to contemplate being happy, though I know this doesn't make sense because Harry would be the last person on earth not to wish me a happy life. It's all such a muddle.

Mother and Father talked all through luncheon about plans for putting a small bronze plaque in the church in Harry's memory. I suppose it's a good idea but it seems a bit irrelevant. Those who loved him won't need any plaques to remember him by.

Decided not to meet Laurie this afternoon after all and went to my room, but then, five minutes after I was supposed to be at the stile, I decided I wasn't helping anyone by staying away. How would it benefit Harry's memory to let down a friend who had, like him, been through the hell of war? So I rushed out and got to the stile twenty-five minutes late – lucky for me there was no sign of Mother or Father to question my actions! Laurie was still waiting.

We were so pleased to see each other that we sort of rushed together and I thought for a moment that he was going to kiss me! Then he seemed to collect himself and drew away, which I suppose he would think (and Mother definitely would think!!!) was the only honourable thing to do. And of course they would be right for we have met only twice (three times if you count church!). We seem to know each other so well, though. I just hope I wasn't too eager in the way I ran towards him for I would hate him to think badly of me and it is always impressed upon one that men don't like girls who are too bold. Really, it was relief, because I thought he might not wait that long.

I was a little bit afraid of seeing someone I knew when we were together, not because I am in the least bit ashamed of going for a walk with Laurie, but because if word got back home I would be in so much trouble and it would spoil everything. However we didn't see a soul except some small boys we didn't know, climbing trees.

We sat on a log for a while and he told me a lot about life in the trenches. He didn't really want to, but I got it out of him. It's amazing how little we at home know of what the boys really go through, and I am astonished that any of them can stay sane. I really wanted to know about it because of Harry, but it brought back the pain all over again, however I'm glad I met Laurie after all because I think it did him good to talk. I am not the only one with a burden of grief.

In spite of that – or perhaps because of it – it was a lovely afternoon during which I feel Laurie and I became closer and more at ease with each other. The worst moment was when I said I couldn't meet him the following week because I was going to a dance in Bodmin at the Officers' Mess. I am to stay overnight with the Kempthornes at Kelynack Manor. I don't much want to go, but feel I have to. No sooner had I mentioned it than I could have cut my tongue out because I knew at once that Laurie felt I was putting a distance between us, emphasising the difference between my position and his. I assured him I would much rather be spending my time with him, and eventually he came round and said he was sorry, he just couldn't bear the thought of not being able to dance with me himself. He is very sweet-natured but far too conscious of class distinctions. What do they matter?

In my opinion he is far more handsome and intelligent and attractive than anyone I have met for a long time, or am likely to meet in Bodmin. In fact, strictly between me and the pages of this diary, I think I am falling in love, and I wish he had kissed me when we met. There! It's down in blue-black and off-white!

I must be even more careful to keep this diary under lock and key.

Six

6th July 1918
Cycled over to Howldrevel and met Laurie in the copse where we left my bicycle and walked to Kilva Cove to swim. It was totally deserted, and the weather was perfect, not a cloud in the sky.

We lay on a kind of grassy ledge half way up the cliff, and kissed and kissed and kissed. I shall never love anyone as much as I love him. He knows that, but he is very honourable and we never go too far although it's difficult for us sometimes (and strictly between me and these pages, there are times when I wish he wasn't so damned honourable!). Rather to my surprise, I find his nature can be changeable and sometimes he is very down in the dumps. Today was not one of those times, thank goodness.

He is very conscious that "he has nothing to offer"!! I put this in quotation marks, because it's something he often says when he is in one of his low moods, even though I assure him every time that I see it quite differently. I think he has everything to offer, not in the practical, monetary sense, perhaps, but every other way. He is good and kind and sensitive and decent and intelligent and hardworking and ambitious and wonderful company most of the time. One day we shall be together for ever and ever and then I shall make him so happy that I know he'll be quite different and never suffer from bad moods again. I shall be so proud to be his wife because he is quite the most handsome man I have ever seen, and far better read than many public schoolboys I have known. He really is very funny and can make me laugh and laugh and I love the way he gets fired up over flowers and all growing things.

There is nothing about him I would change. Except the moodiness, of course. At those times he can say very hurtful things, but I know now that he doesn't really mean them and he is always dreadfully sorry afterwards.

He hates it when I can't meet him, especially when this is because of a social engagement elsewhere, but I think mostly he is depressed because of the war. He says he still has nightmares, which I can perfectly well understand. Being with me makes him feel that all is well with the world in spite of everything, he says when in good spirits, which I think is lovely. (Even if things aren't at all well!)

Our love is, of course, still a secret and must stay one for the moment. I wish it were otherwise. Nicholas has started to pay me far more attention than is comfortable and of course Mother is highly delighted by this and encourages him as much as she can. She can think of no higher honour than that her only daughter should marry into the Courtfield family and, eventually, become Lady Courtfield!!! To me it would be the worst horror imaginable, and I shudder at the thought.

Catherine has been staying in London with her aunt and uncle and apparently, according to Lady C., enjoying a social whirl. She is home now and seems friendlily disposed towards me (probably because she is lonely without Amelia!).

Whether she will remain friendly after the events of last Wednesday, however, I very much doubt. What happened on that fateful day was this: she invited me to go for a sail and a picnic with her and Nicholas and her cousin, Bernard Crossland (a naval commander, temporarily stationed in Falmouth, and a most FORBIDDING man whom I can just imagine flogging ratings at the mast, or wherever such things take place!). I didn't a bit want to go, but it wasn't one of my days for Cranbrooke and I couldn't think of any excuse quickly enough so found myself saying weakly, "How very nice! Of course I'd love to come!", and other similar lies.

We sailed up the Fal to a beautiful creek where wooded hills came down to the river, but despite the beauty, all was doom and disaster! Nicholas insisted on taking me for a walk into the woods, away from the others, to look for wild orchids, he said. I didn't want to go, but Catherine gave me the kind of look which said she wanted to be alone with Cmdr Crossland. Quite unaccountably, she has fallen in love with him! So very reluctantly I went with Nicholas. I might have known it was asking for trouble.

Hardly had we got out of sight of them when N. tried to kiss me! And more! His hands were everywhere. He was really insistent, but I wouldn't give in. He just kept on thrusting himself at me and laughing in a horrid spittle-y kind of way. He said very sneeringly, "Come off it, old girl, I know you want it," which made me more angry than I have been for a very long time. I summoned all my strength to give him a great big shove and told him in no uncertain terms that he was completely wrong (nor was I particularly charmed by being called "old girl"!), in fact I was tempted to say that far from wanting it, I'd rather kiss Ned Pike who is the dirtiest old down-and-out I know! However, I managed to be slightly more restrained without leaving him in any doubt about my feelings. He wasn't laughing any more by the time I finished with him, in fact I was rather afraid I might have given him a black eye. Fortunately this proved not to be the case, but he was spitting nails about the whole thing, obviously thinking that I should be greatly flattered by his attentions, and he refused to address a word to me for the rest of the afternoon.

And now it's his twenty-fifth birthday party on the nineteenth and there is to be a ball at Howldrevel to which Mother and I were invited long before Wednesday's incident. Of course, I haven't said a word to her about what happened, and she is so delighted that we've been asked, though she goes on and on about wishing her husband and sons were able to escort us until I feel like screaming. I don't suppose N. wants me there now, but it can't be helped.

Of course it won't be as lavish as the Courtfields' pre-war dances, but apparently Lady C. is determined to celebrate this grand occasion in an appropriate manner, according to Catherine, and has arranged to get the regimental band over from Bodmin. She is also said to be extorting, with menaces, every last morsel of game and fish and any other comestible that friends and relations and grovelling tenants might be concealing in storecupboards the length and breadth of the county, so that all can be dazzled by the magnificence of her hospitality. (I must curb this discreditable tendency to make fun of the Courtfields on every possible occasion!)

At least I am getting a new dress out of it, pale blue chiffon with a deep V-neck, a tight waist and a very pretty skirt. I shall keep well out of N.'s way. Maddening to think that Laurie will be so near, yet I will not be able to see him.

Friday 12th July 1918
An awful, calamitous evening. Mother was angry with me for
"choosing my own company above hers" – i.e. wanting to go out
for a walk after dinner. The weather continues warm and cloudless
and the evenings are so beautiful that Laurie and I have taken to
meeting in Howldrevel Woods several times a week. I always take
my sketch book to give myself a kind of alibi, but tonight Mother
demanded to see it and has decreed that I am wasting my time!
When I consider that most of my drawings have been dashed off
in a couple of minutes just before leaving for home, I think I ought
to be hailed as a genius and hung in the National Gallery!!! (By
the neck, some would say.)

I am making a joke out of it, but I did not feel like joking then,
and even now feel more like crying than laughing, I had so looked
forward all day to seeing Laurie. When it became clear that I could
not possibly leave Mother in the kind of state she was in, I confess
I felt physically ill with disappointment. It was such a wonderful
summer's evening, just the kind a woman should spend with the
man she loves . . .

The sun was still warm on the stones of the small rear terrace overlooking the sea where Verity and her mother, calmer now that she had
achieved her purpose, had come to take their coffee after dinner.

"Come along, dear," Louise said coaxingly, addressing her
daughter's back. "The coffee's poured and I asked Eva to put
out the last of the sugared almonds, as a little treat. I feel we owe
ourselves a change from wartime austerity, don't you?"

Verity, standing with both hands gripping the wall, did not
move, but continued to look longingly across the bay where she
could see the winding path that led up the field towards the cliff
and woods, where the summer foliage was thick and green and
all-concealing. Laurie would be there at this moment. How was it
possible to bear such disappointment? She felt hollow with misery,
as if without the support of the wall she would collapse entirely.

"What a beautiful evening," her mother said, her voice determinedly bright. "I thought this afternoon that we might have some
rain, but I was quite mistaken. Pascoe was complaining of this dry
weather, but I must say I love the sun, don't you, dear?"

Verity heard the voice and knew that she must answer.

"Yes," she whispered at last. "Yes, it's beautiful."

The beauty was so intense that it hurt; a limpid, golden seascape with a paling sky and the gentlest of waves, the sea an artist's palette of blues and greens of every shade, glinting lazily in the evening sun.

She had longed all day for this hour to come, joyful because she knew that it would find her in Laurie's arms with his lips on hers. Knowing this, counting the hours, she had flown about the wards at Cranbrooke as if she had wings on her heels. The men had remarked on it, had teased her, demanding to know who was the lucky chap who'd put that smile on her face.

But she was selfish, her mother had said. Selfish and uncaring, paying no heed to *her* loneliness, she who had lost one son and whose other son was in constant danger and whose husband was absent on essential war work. She had been out all day, her mother complained—

"Working hard," Verity put in.

She had been *out*, her mother reiterated. Meeting people, following her own desires, and now she wanted to go out again.

"Just for a walk," Verity had pleaded, mendaciously. "I need the fresh air, Mother." She was painfully aware that if she missed seeing Laurie that night, she would have to wait days before seeing him again. It happened to be his mother's birthday that weekend, and he had special leave from his duties to spend Saturday and Sunday in Falmouth. The time seemed to stretch in front of her interminably, barren as an Arctic winter. And he was expecting her! What would he think? What would he do?

"We shall sit on the terrace for as long as the sun lasts. There's fresh air in plenty here. My eyes are a little tired, I thought you could read to me. There appears to be rather an amusing serial beginning in the *Ladies' Home Journal*."

The magazine was on the table beside Louise, and having poured the coffee, she picked it up and leafed through it.

"Do come, dear," she said after a moment, glancing up at Verity's rigid back. She frowned, growing a little impatient. "Really, Verity, you're far too old to sulk the moment you can't have your own way. Come at once before your coffee is cold."

Verity drew a long breath. "Yes, mother." Slowly, unwillingly, she turned and came to sit down, refusing the proffered sugared almonds with a shake of her head.

"There's no need to look so down in the mouth." Her mother

replaced the silver dish with an air of annoyance, as if it was she who had been rebuffed, not a few sweetmeats on a lacy doily. "It surely isn't unreasonable of me to expect a little cheering conversation from my daughter. I haven't felt at all the thing today. My poor head! How I hope it is better by next Friday when we go to Howldrevel."

"I wish we needn't go at all."

"What can you mean?" Her mother's voice was sharp. "Of course we must go!" She mellowed into roguishness, tapping Verity on the arm with a corner of the magazine. "A little bird tells me Nicholas would be very, very disappointed if we did not!"

Verity clenched her teeth and said nothing. She had conceded defeat, had given up all hope of going out, but she was *damned* if she was going to spend any part of the evening talking about Nicholas Courtfield! The very thought of the way he had attempted to force himself on her last Wednesday, and the look of vicious fury in his eyes when she had had the temerity to reject him, still had the power to make her shudder. She had always thought him arrogant and unpleasant but had never expected quite such incontrovertible proof of it.

She glanced towards her mother and saw the martyred look on her face. It was impossible not to feel irritated, remembering how often she was forced to subdue her own inclinations. Yet still she stood accused of being selfish and uncaring!

Was it true? She didn't mean to be and tried her best to be the kind of daughter her mother longed for. She worked at Cranbrooke only three days a week, unless the need was particularly great, and was therefore able to spend a great many hours in her mother's company. Hour after hour after hour, it sometimes seemed, playing interminable games of bezique, or listening to long reminiscences, or reading aloud. It was only the thought of her times with Laurie that made life supportable, and so made the disappointment of that evening so catastrophic.

He'd been in a funny kind of mood the last time they had met, troubled by memories. He'd rambled on about some friend in the army who had been killed but might have been saved if only he had given a different order at a different moment. By the time they had parted she had managed to calm him, but still she worried about him. Was he in a better frame of mind by this time? And if she didn't see him tonight, how would she know when to meet him again?

The weekend passed slowly. Then, to her joy, she received a letter from him on the following Monday morning which he had posted just before leaving to go to Falmouth the previous Saturday. He had waited for two hours that Friday night, he told her, and hadn't slept a wink. What had happened? Did she still love him, or had his behaviour the last time they met turned her against him? He was tormented with the thought that this must be so but he would be lost without her, she must know that. He adored her utterly and would do so until the day he died. The following week he would go every night to the stile in the hope that she would come.

Hiding the note swiftly – thank heaven it had arrived before she left for Cranbrooke on the Monday morning, and before her mother had put in an appearance – Verity's spirits soared again. Everything would be all right. They loved each other – that was the most important thing – and she would make sure that nothing prevented her walk that night.

Of course, he hated the thought of the Howldrevel ball even more than she did, but it was too much to hope that her mother's health would prevent their attendance, even though it was a long time now since Louise had put in an appearance at Lady Courtfield's fund-raising committee meetings. Other ladies of her social standing ran soup kitchens or crèches in support of the women of the village who were trying to cope with their families on the meagre pay of a soldier or sailor, but her war effort had dwindled to little more than writing letters to her husband and son, or making a pathetic effort to knit socks which never progressed beyond the first inch.

She had, however, made it clear that though the ball might tax her resources to the limit, she considered it something she and her daughter could not miss. Verity's future happiness could well depend on it.

"You'll dance with that – that *rotter*," Laurie said when they met on the Monday evening. "I can't bear to think of his arms round you."

"If you mean Nicholas Courtfield, neither can I," said Verity. "But I have every hope he won't ask me. Actually, I can't bear the thought of dancing with anyone but you. Oh, Laurie, I wish you were going to be there!"

"I can imagine what the Courtfields would think of that! I'd pollute the atmosphere. Bring muck in on my boots."

"But you're no ordinary gardener, they must know that. You were an officer."

"A ranker," Laurie said, a touch of bitterness in his voice. "A field-officer. The kind that doesn't count. They haven't even invited Mr Parker, and he's the estate manager and far higher up the social ladder than I am."

"Well—" Verity, her arm through his as they sauntered through the woods, gave him a comforting squeeze. "I don't suppose you'll miss much. But oh, I wish you could see me in my new dress!"

"I shall," Laurie said. "They're bound to have the long windows open, with the weather as it is. I'll lurk in the bushes, and if you come out on to the terrace I'll be able to see you in all your glory."

"Will you? Can you do that?" The thought amused her, but then she sobered again. "Oh, Laurie! I'm going to hate it, knowing that you're there but not being able to be with you. Listen, you're not to be jealous! Promise? I can't help dancing, if people ask me, but I won't want to, honestly. I shall be thinking of you all the time."

This was no empty promise. She did think of Laurie, especially when she saw the magnificent floral decorations that must have come from the Howldrevel gardens, but on the other hand it was impossible not to be diverted, just a little, by such a glittering occasion the like of which she had not seen during the past four years. Perhaps because the news from the Western Front was beginning to improve, spirits were high. The second Battle of the Marne had begun, and it seemed that at last the Germans were beginning to retreat, which was, in itself, good reason to cast gloom aside.

The blue dress was a great success and since she knew a large proportion of the other guests, her little programme with its tasselled pencil was soon almost full. As Laurie had foretold, it was a perfect summer's night and all the long windows that ran along the side of the ballroom were wide open to the terrace, the strains of the orchestra floating out across the lawn and through the shrubs, making the garden appear like some magical stage set. Couples wandered outside to sip their champagne or fruit cup and breathe the sweet-scented air between dances, and Verity, from time to time, enticed her partners to do the same so that she could stand by the balustrade, ostensibly for relief from the heat of the ballroom but in reality peering into the depths of the garden in the hope of catching a glimpse of Laurie. She couldn't see him, though, however much she looked, which was hardly surprising since as the moon climbed higher the shadows round the clumps of trees and shrubs grew more dense and impenetrable.

She went into supper on the arm of Clifford Minter, the son of friends of her parents whom she had known all her life. Clifford had metamorphosed from a shy boy into a rather dashing captain in the Duke of Cornwall's Light Infantry. They were joined by Catherine and Cmdr Crossland, as silent and grim-faced as he had been on the ill-fated sailing trip. What Catherine could see in him, Verity couldn't imagine. Well, she thought, at least Nicholas must have kept quiet about what had happened that Wednesday, which was a good thing. But still her heart sank a little when she remembered that she was due to dance with Bernard Crossland once supper was over. Why he had asked her she had no idea, for he gave every impression of despising her every utterance. And Catherine's too, come to that, though she seemed not to notice, or to mind if she did. She looked pretty that night, Verity thought generously. The pink dress was one she had bought in London, and it was most becoming.

The buffet supper, though perhaps not as sumptuous as it would have been in pre-war days, was nevertheless something of a treat. Where on earth had Lady Courtfield acquired the sugar necessary for all those meringues, people murmured? Not to mention the fat for the sponges. Perhaps it didn't do to speculate.

"I was so sorry to hear about Harry," Clifford said to her quietly as they sat together. "I know how close you were."

"Yes." Verity looked down, avoiding his eyes. "Thank you. It's still awfully hard to talk about it."

"How is your mother? I heard she had a nervous breakdown. It must have been perfectly frightful for her."

"For all of us." There was a trace of sharpness in Verity's voice. No one had been as close to Harry as she had been. Then she bit her lip, unable to ignore the familiar feeling of guilt that thoughts of her mother inevitably caused her. She *must* try to exercise more forbearance, she told herself. Perhaps it was worse for mothers, how could she tell?

She looked up at Clifford and forced a smile. "You've reminded me," she said. "I really ought to go and see how she's getting on. I promised I would." She made her excuses to Catherine and Cmdr Crossland as well as to Clifford, and the men rose politely as she left them to make her way across the room towards a large alcove flanked by potted palms where a few of the older guests had spent the evening.

She need not have worried about her mother's welfare, for she found her looking more sprightly than for some time past, about to go in to supper on the arm of a silver-haired, distinguished-looking gentleman, who was bending over her hand in a protective manner. His name was Sir Walter Spinks of Tavistock, a great benefactor and patron of the arts, her mother said proudly as she introduced him. And equally proudly, she presented Verity in her turn.

"Dear Verity," she added, smiling graciously. "Always so mindful of my comforts! Go back to your friends and enjoy yourself, my dear, and pray don't give your poor mother a thought, for Sir Walter is looking after me quite splendidly."

Verity watched them go, smiling a little cynically, willing to wager any money that there would be no talk of nerves or headaches for the moment; no reaching for the sal volatile on this occasion.

She would have gone back to the supper room there and then had it not been for two elderly ladies who were returning to the alcove as her mother was leaving. They, too, turned to watch the departing couple, blocking her way and causing her to step back a little to wait until they had settled themselves. There was something about their imperious noses that made her feel sure they were Courtfields. They were both old, both dressed in rusty black, both unknown to her, but undoubtedly there was a family resemblance. One walked with the aid of a silver-topped cane; the other held a pair of lorgnettes, raised now to watch Louise's progress across the room on the arm of her distinguished escort. They seemed in no hurry to sit down on the chairs that awaited them. Verity hovered uncomfortably behind them.

"Sir Walter seems to be enjoying himself," remarked the one with the lorgnettes, her expression implying that this was greatly to be deplored.

The other, turning, was fussing with shawl and cane before sitting down.

"I didn't quite catch the name of the lady with him," she said.

"Oh, you must know her! That's Mrs Ashland," said the other.

"Who, dear?" asked her companion, putting aside her other concerns for a moment to straighten up a little and tilt her head towards her companion. "Do speak up! You know I'm a little hard—"

"ASHLAND," said the other, more loudly and with more than a touch of impatience. "You know, Ashland's Fish." Verity took a step towards them and half-raised her hand as if to make her presence known, but neither of them noticed her, and with their next words she froze in her tracks, discretion forgotten.

"Someone told me," said the old lady in a voice pitched to reach her deaf sister, "that young Nicholas is paying court to the daughter. Can you imagine it? Ashland's Fish!"

"*Well!*" The owner of the lorgnettes looked suitably shocked. "I don't know the young woman, of course, but really . . . ! There's money, of course."

"Of course. They've done very well out of the war, I'm told, so the Ashland gel's a good prospect. One understands that Nicholas can't afford to be too choosy, the way things stand, but it's a great pity. One would prefer a lady."

"Excuse me." Verity had been transfixed by this passage but managed to find her voice at last. It sounded shrill in her ears, high and thin. "I am Verity Ashland, and I can assure you that I would rather die than marry Nicholas Courtfield!"

The lorgnettes rose, the better to survey her. "My dear gel—" their owner said faintly.

"And if ladies can speak as you have just done, then I'm glad I'm not one. So there," she finished, her voice trembling on the final words. And with that she pushed past them, knocking the walking stick flying.

She didn't wait to pick it up but swept away with her head in the air, tears of anger in her eyes, regretting only the final "so there", which seemed to hang on the air, childish and futile.

As if – as *if* she would ever marry Nicholas! He was so creepy, so arrogant, so repulsive, so – oh, so absolutely impossible! And implying that she had nothing to attract a man except her father's money! It was humiliating and horrible. She had never been so angry!

She found herself on the terrace without any clear idea of how she arrived there, all thought of the dance she had promised to

Cmdr Crossland gone from her mind. Most people were still at supper. A large and noisy group, braying with laughter, were occupying the wide steps that led down to the garden, and a couple, lost to the outside world, were gazing into each other's eyes at the far side of the terrace.

No one was taking the slightest notice of her as, still trembling with rage and barely able to breathe, she stood in the shadow of a giant urn, grasping the stone edge of the balustrade and fighting for control.

The moon was high now, the garden more beautiful than ever. Slowly, slowly the anger seeped away, leaving unhappiness in its place. What was to become of her? Her parents would never accept Laurie as a son-in-law. If ever she were to marry him, it would mean a total break with them. Oh, what a crazy world it was, when she was considered not good enough for someone like Nicholas, yet too good for a man as thoroughly worthy as Laurie. Yet I ask for nothing more, she thought. Not a title, not a great house like this. Not money. I just want to be with the man I love.

A low whistle from somewhere close at hand made her stiffen. It was Laurie's whistle; she recognised it instantly, yet she could still see no sign of him. Hastily she looked over her shoulder once more. The couple had gone inside, and the group on the steps were still shrieking with laughter.

She looked over the wall at the side of the terrace. Nearby there was a mallow which had grown almost to the size of a tree and suddenly, as she looked, its shadow seemed to lengthen and change shape.

"Laurie?" she said cautiously, peering into its depths. Once more she looked around, but she still appeared to be unobserved.

She could see him now, and he seemed so near, so reachable. If only she could go to him, everything would be all right again.

To use the steps at the front of the terrace was clearly impossible with all those people sitting on them. What other possibilities were there? Not through the conservatory. That, she knew, was crowded, too.

Of course, there was that other side door to the garden, in the other wing of the house. She had been through it several times in her schooldays, in Catherine's and Amelia's company, and clearly remembered that it opened on to a path, edged with a thick yew hedge, which in turn led to a garden within a garden. This, too, was enclosed by a tall hedge with a lawn and sundial at its centre, and was always known as the White Garden, for on the orders of some former Lady Courtfield it had been planted solely with white flowers.

Casually she leant her elbows on the wall as if she were simply admiring the garden by moonlight.

"Laurie?" she whispered again, a little louder this time. "Can you hear me? Go to the White Garden. I'll join you there. The White Garden," she repeated, just in case she hadn't made it clear.

With that, she turned, and went back into the ballroom. The music had not yet started again after supper and people were moving around, joining friends, chatting in groups. She smiled and nodded, acknowledging this one and that as she made her way around the edge of the room and out the other side, into a corridor where there were further groups of people. Smilingly, she ploughed on with a purposeful air, as if intent on making her way to the bedroom which had been designated the ladies' cloakroom; however she went straight past this, slipping into a further passage which led eventually, if one turned right, to the kitchens.

She did not turn right but went straight on, down a dimly lit passage, past the door that had once been Miss Pond's private domaine, past the entrance to a back staircase that went up to the old night nurseries, past a store room, until, at last, she reached the outside door. It was locked, of course, and bolted top and bottom, but the key was on a nail beside it and the bolts were swiftly dealt with.

It had been stuffy in the passage, which made the air from the garden all the sweeter as it rushed to meet her. Closing the door behind her, she hurried down the path and into the little garden where Laurie was waiting for her; and instantly everything else was forgotten in the joy of being with him, held in his arms again, giving and receiving kisses as if it were years since they had met instead of less than twenty-four hours.

"Oh, it's a horrid ball," Verity whispered, when at last she could speak, forgetting her excitement of earlier in the evening and remembering only the conversation of the two old ladies. "All the time, I've wanted to be with you. Isn't this the most beautiful little garden? Just smell those tobacco plants! We used to come here for elevenses, sometimes, because it's so sheltered, but it looks even lovelier in the moonlight."

Laurie only had eyes for her. "Oh, my darling, it was torture, seeing you at a distance like that! You look so lovely. Lovelier than any of the others."

Verity laughed at that. "Such nonsense!"

"It's true. Honestly."

"Oh, I love you, Laurie. One day we'll dance together."

"Why not now? We can just hear the music."

"So we can."

The orchestra had struck up a Viennese waltz with a great deal of brio and panache, and the strains were borne to them on the faint breeze as he stepped back and bowed with great formality.

"May I have the honour?" he asked, laughter in his voice.

Verity curtseyed low. "The honour is mine, sir."

They circled, decorously at first, smiling into each other's eyes.

"My shoes are getting soaked with dew," Verity said after a moment, laughing, not caring.

"Take them off!"

She kicked them high into the air, and still laughing they circled on, faster now, then more and more wildly as if drunk on the magic of the night, keeping pace with the music; then, breathless, no laughter now, they fell into each other's arms in a long embrace.

This, Verity knew, was a moment she would never forget, as long as she lived – not the moonlight or the white flowers and their heady scent, or the music, or the feel of the dew-soaked lawn, cold on the soles of her stockinged feet, or Laurie's arms around her. All was sheer magic, an idyll so perfect that she couldn't ever have imagined it, not in her wildest fantasies.

Then, suddenly and brutally, the idyll was shattered and there was noise and shouting, and people roughly tearing them apart. She recognised Nicholas and Bernard Crossland, Clifford Minter whom she had thought her friend, and two other young men she did not know.

"Stop it, stop it," she screamed, seeing how Laurie was reeling under their blows. "Leave him alone. We weren't doing anything wrong."

Nicholas grabbed her shoulders and thrust his face into hers. It was white and set, and she could see his eyes glittering.

"He deserves all he gets," he spat, shaking her as he spoke. "Bloody ranker! Who the hell does he think he is? He's my gardener, for God's sake."

Laurie seemed to see an opportunity and hit out at Bernard Crossland who staggered backwards, then suddenly the others were upon him and he was down, curled into a ball to avoid their concerted attack.

"Stop it, stop it!" Verity beat her fists on their backs, until at last, seeing the fight had gone out of the man on the ground, they stepped back and she dropped down beside him, sobbing with rage. "You're beasts, beasts, nothing but animals. Look what you've done!"

Clifford Minter had the grace to appear ashamed of himself. "Maybe we went too far," he said. "We thought you were being attacked."

Verity looked up at him. "I was here," she said, distinctly. "Because I love him."

Nicholas laughed, loudly and wildly, and Verity realised that he was more than half drunk.

"You're demented," he said. "As demented as he is. Don't you know he's mad? He was discharged from the army because of it, and we took him on out of the goodness of our hearts."

"He lost a finger, that's why—"

"He was shell-shocked," Nicholas said contemptuously. "There's another word for it. He's a bloody coward. That's why he was discharged, and if he told you different, he was lying. And this is the man you lower yourself to meet in secret like any common kitchen maid. You should be ashamed."

Laurie stirred and groaned and Verity bent over him. "Are you all right? Laurie, Laurie, are you badly hurt?"

"The bastard'll live," said Nicholas harshly. "He got what was coming to him. He should have been shot for cowardice, months ago."

Clifford and his friends were already melting away, but Bernard Crossland stayed with his cousin, standing back with his arms folded, aloof, austere, uninvolved.

"We must get him back to his quarters," Verity said. "He'll need help."

"Leave him. He can get there on his own." Nicholas grabbed her, trying to pull her up, but she resisted, and at last, as if in disgust, he flung her away from him. "You little slut," he said, almost more contemptuous than he had been before. "You common little trollop. To think that I—" He didn't finish his sentence, but turned to his cousin. "Come on, Bernard. If she wants to stay here, let her stay."

He took a few steps away from Laurie and Verity, then, as if thinking better of it, came back again. "As for you," he said, bending over Laurie, loathing in his voice. "If I see your face around here again, you'll wish you'd never been born. You're to be off the premises by morning." He straightened up and turned to Verity. "See that he is," he said harshly.

He and Bernard left the garden; and as he did so, Verity heard a harsh, tearing sound and realised that it was coming from Laurie; that he was crying, one arm across his eyes. She knelt lower, putting her arms around him.

"Don't," she begged him softly. "Ah, my dearest, don't! Did they hurt you dreadfully? Can you sit up?"

Still he sobbed, taking in great, painful gasps of air while Verity stroked his hair and kissed his cheek.

"Oh, Laurie," she whispered, in tears herself, "please, my love, let's move from here, before someone else comes." There was blood on her hands, she realised, and on her dress.

Laurie took his arm away from his face and she could see the gleam of his eyes. They looked wild, his whole face distorted. He drew in one more ragged breath, then pushed her away.

"Go," he said. "Go away. Leave me alone."

"No, Laurie. Of course I won't"

"Just go. Leave me. You heard what they said. I'm a coward. The finger was nothing. I lied to you."

"It doesn't matter. I'm not going to leave you."

"You must!"

"I think," said a new voice beyond Verity's shoulder, "that you should do as he asks." She turned to find a man she recognised as Mr Parker, the estate manager, standing behind her, known from long ago when she was a child and a constant visitor here. A kindly man, she had always thought, though he looked severe enough now. "Go along now, Miss. I'll see to him."

She looked at Laurie, but stubbornly he kept his face away from her, and though she spoke to him he did not answer. Reluctantly she stood up, collected her shoes and turned to go, though where she was to go, how she could possibly go inside unnoticed, she couldn't imagine. Her dress was torn and stained, her hair hanging round her face, but what did that matter? She had the feeling that the dress was not the only thing to be ruined that night.

"What on earth is going on here?" asked an imperious voice from the direction of the archway which led to the garden. Verity recognised it at once and her heart sank. There was no mistaking Lady Courtfield's voice, and less than no chance now of escaping discovery. The voice boomed out again. "Is that you, Mr Parker? Nicholas tells me I'm needed here. What girl is this? What *is* going on? Come here at once, girl. Who are you? Answer me!"

For a moment Verity was incapable of movement; then, facing the inevitable, she moved forward.

"It's Verity," she said.

Seven

23rd June 1923

Very neglectful of diary for ages and ages, but am resolved to start again. Not that I have a lot of time. Too busy, too much fun, too many parties. Too much racketing about altogether, to use Mother's pet phrase. Absolutely lethal *gathering on Tommy Vaughan's yacht last night. David C. drove all the way to Helford Passage at breakneck speed through narrow lanes at midnight with five of us in the car, shrieking with maniacal laughter the entire way, and I thought my last hour had come and hoped everyone would be inconsolable when our lifeless bodies were found by a village bobby next day. However things did not come to this, though I've had such a frightful head all day that it might have been better for me had they done so.*

Rex, Tommy, David, Jemima and Carla swam, quite starkers, but I resisted, not through an excess of modesty but because I knew that the water would be icy. Also, I may not have a great deal of common sense but I do know that when one is a bit squiffy is not the right time to take the plunge (cf. Adèle Trafford, though reminding people of her fate doesn't exactly do a lot to enliven a party. I learned yesterday that when at last washed up, after three weeks, she could only be identified by dental records, owing to the depredations of various marine creatures. Not an end one would willingly embrace.)

Also, Tommy had conjured up a rather divine artist called Evan Hughes, and at the time everyone was casting clouts and diving off the deck, he and I were curled up in the saloon, White Ladies in hand, talking about Life, which I found a lot more appealing as well as considerably warmer. He lives in Newlyn in the utmost penury, apparently, but clearly has a soul above material considerations – or so he would like one to think. He certainly didn't appear to have a soul above helping himself to

Tommy's liquor! Tommy likes him, he tells me, because he is so amusing as well as being divinely handsome. Definitely an asset to the group! I hope we might meet again, though Mother would undoubtedly disapprove of him and say that I was Wasting My Time. Again!!!

Her mother, of course, continually accused her of wasting valuable time, never failing to remind her that life was passing her by.

"'What, still alive at twenty-three, A fine upstanding girl like me?'" Verity misquoted, laughing as if she hadn't a care in the world.

"You're getting very hard," Louise said, coldly.

"Me?" Verity opened her eyes wide. "You can't mean it!"

She did, though, and with some reason, Verity had to admit. She couldn't quite pinpoint the moment when she had swung from utter despondency to the kind of feverish gaiety that suddenly seemed to make some kind of sense of her days. Maybe it was the time Livvy had forced her to go to that party, the Christmas of 1922. That's where she'd met David Crowder, who had somehow managed to spark some kind of response from her through sheer persistence. It must have been the challenge she presented, she thought at the time. Or novelty value. Girls tended to drop at his feet, not act with the supreme indifference she had displayed – at first, anyway. Later she had acknowledged that he was intelligent and really rather attractive. Different, anyway, from the kind of young men she had always known, whom she now regarded as stuffy and priggish and wholly predictable.

David, well-connected though he was, had emerged from his war with a total disregard for convention and a contempt for all the values of his parents' generation, despite the fact that their wealth allowed him to indulge his minor aptitude for art, gathering about him an equally cynical group of friends. It wasn't long before Verity had been totally accepted among their number, their hedonistic way of life answering a need in her. She wasn't in the least in love with him, or he with her, but they had indulged in a brief, spiky kind of *affaire* that both enjoyed, though it had been over for the past year and had now mellowed into friendship.

Louise had seemed to welcome the change in her daughter, innocently unaware of the group's more questionable activities, thankful that at last Verity was enjoying some kind of social life. Anything, in her opinion, was an improvement on those awful months after the terrible debacle at Howldrevel when she had seemed to withdraw from life altogether, not eating, not speaking, fading away to a total wraith. When David Crowder had come to call, Louise had thought him charming. It was certainly true that, should he wish it, he could display excellent manners, as indeed, could most of the friends and hangers-on that soon became frequent visitors to Lemorrick. She was even acquainted with the families of some of them, and felt quite sure that now Verity had entered society again it would not be long before she found a suitable husband.

Marriage, however, did not appear to be the thing that was on any of their minds, and before long Louise was forced to revise her opinion of them. Having a good time seemed to be all any of them thought about, which appeared to mean drinking too much, dancing until dawn, racketing around the country in fast cars. What, she asked, was the *matter* with young people nowadays? Even her precious Stephen wasn't immune to this virus, joining Verity's crowd with apparent enthusiasm whenever he was at home.

"It's doing your reputation no good at all," she told Verity, plaintively. "What man will want to marry a girl who thinks of nothing but pleasure? And it all could have been so different! If it hadn't been for that wretched Grenfell man—"

She broke off, seeing Verity's angry scowl, but it was a theme she returned to on the day the news came that Nicholas Courtfield was to marry an unknown young woman called Frances Gardiner, the wealthy daughter of a deceased Northern industrialist. "You could have had Nicholas, Verity, you know you could! It was all that man Grenfell's fault. If he'd let you alone, you might have come round to the idea, and now it's too late!"

Verity could barely control her exasperation. "Marrying Nicholas was never a possibility, Mother. I do wish you'd realise that. I could never stand the sight of him. I just hope that this poor unfortunate woman knows what she's doing."

"I'm told," Louise said, "that Sir Geoffrey and Lady Courtfield are delighted."

Time was, of course, when she might have been vouchsafed this information at first hand by the Courtfields themselves, but communications between Howldrevel and Lemorrick had not been restored since that unfortunate ball.

Was it never to be forgotten? Verity could see the expression on her mother's face and knew exactly what she was thinking. And in spite of her irritation she felt a pang of pity, for the disgrace of it had been without precedent or equal, a body blow which had affected her mother perhaps even more than herself – even more, in a way, than Harry's death had done, for that at least had been an honourable loss. The humiliation of Verity's disgrace had forced Louise once more into invalidism just when she seemed to be coming out of it, and she had drooped and faded and lost her looks, withdrawing from life with as much determination as that shown by Verity herself.

It was only last year that she, too, had come back to life, thanks to the new pills that Dr Rees had prescribed for her. One a day, he'd said, and usually that's what she took; only sometimes, when her mother's gaiety seemed as febrile as her own, did Verity suspect that the stated dose had been exceeded. She said nothing, though, for what did it matter? Louise was venturing out again, making new friends. If only Verity could find herself a husband, Louise said to Joseph, she simply wouldn't *know* herself!

That still left Stephen, of course. She worried dreadfully about him. He had succumbed to his father's wishes and gone into the business once the war was over, but made no pretence of liking it. Or anything, come to that. He argued with his father – about money, about the way the business was run, about the way he was expected to learn it from the bottom up, about the poky little flat that had been bought for him in a dreadfully unfashionable area of Bristol near to the factory. He showed, his father thought and often said, a distressing lack of commitment. Where was the son who had shone at everything he attempted? The favourite son who had shown so much promise?

It was the war that was to blame, of course. Louise said so constantly and Verity was sympathetic, for anyone could see that exchanging life in the Flying Corps for dogsbodying at Ashland's Fish was hardly the most exciting thing in the world. It was she who encouraged him to join her and her group of friends whenever he came home, just to cheer him up, which it had done, a little. It wasn't an unqualified success, however, for he stuck out like a sore thumb. He was too critical, too pompous, unwilling and unable to laugh at himself.

"But frightfully handsome, darling," Jemima Trefusis drawled one day when she was sitting at Verity's dressing table painting her pretty little cupid's bow mouth. "Dull, of course, you have to admit, but definitely the sort of man one ought to marry. Not the kind of rotter you and I run around with."

"Maybe you're right," Verity replied. And maybe she was. Perhaps Stephen was the kind of man who would be redeemed by the love of a good woman. Which rather ruled Jemima out of court, though wickedly she seemed to exert herself to charm Stephen whenever they met.

"I hope he's not getting serious about Miss Trefusis," Louise said anxiously, for Jemima was not one of Verity's friends she had ever approved of. She was no lady, in her opinion. All that paint and powder! And red nails, if you please!

"I don't think you need worry," Verity assured her. "Stephen has his head screwed on the right way."

Had he? In spite of her confident words she was by no means sure of this, and confided as much to her diary; still, whatever her differences with her brother, they stuck together when it came to facing their parents and she would no more have thought of confessing her doubts to her mother than of flying to the moon.

Louise appeared comforted by Verity's assurances, but nevertheless was a disappointed woman. She had thought that with the end of the war and with Stephen now working in the business, Joseph would be free to live at home once again, but this was peremptorily dismissed by her husband as being out of the question. They were introducing a number of new lines, Joseph told her. It was a far bigger operation now than it had been at the beginning of the war, and Stephen was nowhere near ready to take the helm. And anyway, he'd acquired a taste, all over again, for the cut and thrust of business life, viewing with horror the thought of immuring himself in the depths of the country.

In vain did she argue that it had suited him well enough at one time when he had chosen Porthallic as a site for their house.

"And it will again, my love," he assured her. "When I am older and ready to retire, but I don't think that will be for a year or two yet. Fifty-five is nothing these days."

"Fifty-eight," his wife corrected him, a touch acidly.

It seemed, then, that there was nothing for it but to keep on taking those miraculous pills and continue her solitary life at Lemorrick – which, after all, was quite pleasant now that she had her newly acquired friends. There was Mrs Radley, who had bought Fairlawns, one of the more imposing houses just outside Porthallic. And Mrs Tresidder, a war-widow. Newcomers, both of them, but then since the Howldrevel ball she was more comfortable, she found, in the company of people who weren't *au fait* with all the circumstances of that disastrous occasion. Not that anyone spoke of it, of course, but it was always *there*. Mrs Rees visited her from time to time, too. Such a nice woman! Not *quite*, of course, not at all the same class as dear Dr Rees, but so cheerful and kind. There was no doubt, as she often remarked to Verity, that the war had been a great leveller.

Yes, in spite of everything she had much to be thankful for. But then had come the news about Stephen.

20th October 1923
A bombshell! Stephen came home last night and announced at dinner that he has been accepted for the Colonial Service and after a short course of training will be sent overseas, probably to India!

Father almost had a fit and Mother burst into tears over the coq au vin. A terrible row ensued, and both Father and S. said things they probably regret today. It struck me how alike they are. Too alike, I suppose, which perhaps is the cause of all the friction between them. They are both, it has to be admitted, quite sure they are right about everything and are unwilling to listen to anyone else's point of view. But at least I understand how S. feels, even if I think he could have broken the news a little more tactfully and should certainly not have brought up all that old business about Father being nothing but a war profiteer. I cannot believe it to be true. I know Ashland's made money out of the war, but Father worked hard and put up with a great deal of inconvenience (i.e. living in an hotel instead of staying comfortably at home, as indeed he does to this day). He had a good product that the army wanted to buy. I cannot really believe that he can have acted corruptly in any way. He is not an easy man to know or understand and has never been an accessible kind of father, like Dr Rees, but I have always believed him totally honest.

One would think today that there has been a death in the family, there is such an air of tragedy about the place. Stephen went off somewhere on his own immediately after breakfast. Mother was in tears most of the day, only marginally cheered when Mrs Radley called and, on being told the news, said how admirable she thought it was of Stephen to want to take English values to some dark, unenlightened part of the Empire! Such a noble young man, she said – at which Mother burst into tears all over again.

When S. at last came home I asked him if this was what had motivated him, and he put on his pompous face and said yes, of course.

"Not because you think it might be rather a lark?" I asked him. "Not to mention getting you out of a very nasty entanglement?"

He was not amused, and threatened me with dire consequences if I breathe a word about Jemima to the parents. Which, of course, I wouldn't. He melted a bit then and said I'd always been a Good Sort (the kind of compliment that strikes terror into a girl's heart! How David would laugh.)

He is, however, immovable. The Colonial Service it must be. I caught him looking into the mirror over the drawing room mantelpiece this evening, positively preening! I'm sure he was seeing himself in a white uniform with the kind of feathers in his hat that colonial governors wear.

"Sir Stephen Ashland, MC, CMG," I said, teasing him. "You can depend on it," he said, without so much as a smile. And I daresay I can. Didn't Harry and I always say so?

Hyde Park Hotel, 30th January 1924
What were my feelings as the ship slowly moved away from the dock this evening? Envy, I think. London on a day like today wasn't at all cheerful and the thought of sailing away to sunnier climes was appealing. There was an icy wind blowing and frequent flurries of freezing rain which anyone would be glad to escape.

Stephen certainly was, and not just for reasons regarding the climate, or his disenchantment with fish. Marriage to Jemima would have been disastrous for him, especially as I know for a fact that she doesn't really think the baby is his, whatever she told him, and she certainly doesn't love him. She confessed to me in her cups last week that it's probably Evan's child, and in any case she has decided to come to London for an abortion. Carla knows some shady doctor who will oblige, at a price.

I hope Stephen finds someone good and sweet who can really love him – the antithesis of Jemima, in fact. Someone with a sense of humour, who can tease him a bit and laugh at his pomposity would be nice. Hark at me! I sound just like Mother. But it is somewhat unnerving to see the way he is now – overbearing as ever, of course, but somehow disorientated and so angry about everything. I think, now, that he's doing the right thing in getting away, but feel a little sorry for the natives to whom he is about to become the Big White Chief. Then again, perhaps total belief in the absolute rightness of one's opinions is an essential in a job like that. At least he and Father parted reasonably amicably, and of course Mother has forgiven him long ago for wanting to leave these shores. To hear her talking about him, you would think that this was the ambition she had cherished for him from the day he was born!

Met Rex and Tommy tonight (strange to see them in their usual habitat instead of mine; they seemed quite different) plus a little chit of a thing called Winky, a friend of Rex's, who had kiss curls and no bust at all and wore a tubular shift dress in a particularly repellent shade of lime green. We went to a night club, and one look round the room was enough to assure me that my dress (bought at Pophams of Plymouth only three months ago, at vast expense) was about as fashionable as Calpurnia's toga. Shall have to pop across to Harrods and do something about it. But at least the new hair-cut passed muster and I must say it feels wonderfully light.

Would I like to live in London? It is undoubtedly exciting, but I don't know if I could stand so many people and all that noise and traffic, not to mention the dirt and poverty (seen, rather more than usual, when we drove to the docks). There are too many ex-servicemen selling matches etc. on the street. Bought a little clockwork dog from one in Oxford Street. Hadn't the slightest use for it, but the man was blue with cold and it broke my heart to see him. The dog disintegrated during its first trial! Of course, there is poverty in Porthallic too, but somehow not the same kind of misery. Not so evident, anyway. So although London is nice for a change, I'm glad we're going home tomorrow.

14th February 1924. Lemorrick
Valentine's Day – and not a card to my name! Doesn't matter.
No one I want one from, thank you very much. Was supposed to
go to a Fancy Dress dance at Carla's tonight and had hired a
costume (Marie Antoinette – such originality!) but at the last
moment I decided I couldn't face it and rang her up to cancel.
She didn't mind. Too many women anyway, I suspect.

I note that my last diary entry spoke of my pleasure that we were
going home, yet now that I am here I wish I were almost anywhere
else, which I am only too aware reflects either on my character or
my state of mind, or both. Mother accused me of being silent at
dinner. I suppose I was, though she talked enough for both of us,
mostly about Mrs Radley's refurbishment of Fairlawns and her
choice of curtains.

Found it hard to take any interest in the relative merits of velvet
v. figured satin. Would London be more stimulating? Yes, almost
certainly. There wasn't nearly enough time while we were there
to go to all the plays or art exhibitions I should like to have seen,
and not even the opportunity to see Livvy, who is working all the
hours there are at St George's Hospital. I have never wavered in
my love for Lemorrick yet, at this moment, it is impossible not to
think that Life is going on somewhere without me.

A blowy night. Wrapped myself up in my Persian lamb and went
out for a walk after dinner. Mother thought I was mad and I think
suspected me of an Assignation (with, naturally, someone not
suitable enough to be brought home! Pascoe's sinister-looking
son, perhaps?) but she couldn't have been more wrong. I just
felt I would go crazy if I didn't go out and breathe some clean,
cold air.

There was an intermittent moon and scudding clouds. I walked
down to the cove and up the path as far as the gate. I leaned
on it for a while, just looking at the wonderful view over the
bay. How I love this place! Harry seemed very close to me
tonight. The grief is still there, of course, and sometimes I
really ache just to see him again, but tonight consciousness
of his presence was almost comforting. The moon was shining
on the sea and the Lemorrick lights were reflected in the water,
and further round the bay were all the lights of Porthallic.
Utterly beautiful, utterly familiar; but though the sight of it went
some way towards lifting my mood, one question still seemed

to beat insistently in my brain: what the hell am I doing with my life?

Nothing, is the answer. Nothing constructive, anyway. I am twenty-four, uneducated, perhaps, but intelligent, reasonably well-read and fairly capable, and all I do is enjoy myself. Not even that, lately. It all seems so pointless. Would I have been happier if I'd done that nursing training? Probably. I don't know. All I know is that no power on earth would have made me leave Porthallic while I thought there was a chance of Laurie coming back to find me. I was quite convinced that he was simply waiting until he had, after all, something to offer me (and more important, to offer my parents). But he didn't come and he didn't come, and finally I had to accept that he was never going to, by which time I had quite lost the urge to nurse, or at least had come to realise that it is not in my nature to stand being bossed about by the likes of that wretched Matron at Cranbrooke.

But why didn't he come? Oh God, how many times have I asked myself that question? I know he loved me. Of course, he was unstable. I wouldn't allow myself to see it at the time but afterwards it seemed clear as day – all that moodiness and those strange silences. But then the war left many men like that, and I am quite sure I could have helped him to get better. Ultimately it was his pride that kept him away. Not the class thing, though from the beginning that had been a stumbling block (to him, not to me). Worse shame in his eyes was the fact that he had lied to me, or at least, concealed the truth, and still worse in his eyes that he was the kind of person who suffered from shell-shock in the first place. Oh, the pity of it! Didn't he know that it was his sensitivity that I loved? Do I still? I wish I knew. There have been others since, of course, but I know he will always be very important to me. But it was such a long time ago, and it makes no sense to go on grieving for the unattainable. I do long to know what happened to him, though.

And what am I left with? A life that needs filling, that's what. There must be something I can do. I always wanted to write a book and I have tried in a desultory kind of way, but any efforts I have made seem to run out of steam by about Chapter Three. I somehow just can't seem to get my characters from Point A to Point B, and my conversations sound like a child's reading exercise. Perhaps I should try non-fiction – but then I don't know enough about anything. Good Works are always an option, of course, but I am ashamed to say that I am woefully unenthused by the thought of Fallen Women or Distressed Seamen or the Aged Poor. Of course, there is the proposed Cottage Hospital, which is a good cause if anything is. I suppose I could throw myself into raising funds, but though I'm more interested in this than anything else, I don't see bazaars and jumble sales as my life's work.

Marriage and a family is – as dear Mother keeps telling me – the only answer. But marriage to whom? Not David. Marriage is not a word in his vocabulary, and I don't love him. I think I might go to Plymouth and stay with Isobel Carne (now Powell) for a bit. I know her John is at sea so she might be glad of my company, and I should certainly be glad of hers for she is the sanest person I know, and the kindest. She must be, to remain friends with me after the trial by piano I put her through!

Saturday 23rd February 1924. Plymouth
Invited myself for the weekend. Isobel, thank heaven, as welcoming as ever. Baby Timothy is adorable. Am trying not to be too jealous, or to get too broody, which would plainly be ridiculous in the circumstances.

Isobel is an angel, patience personified, one of the few people I can talk to – and have we talked! She thinks I ought to go away from Lemorrick. Certainly now that Mother is so much better there is not the same need for me to be there, though I know Father will contest this view and say it is my duty to stay to keep her company. There are times when I agree with him that it is a daughter's duty, and times when I burn with frustration! Mother has lost both her precious sons in one way or another, and only has her husband at weekends. I know that she would feel lost without me, even if half the time she complains about my behaviour, but on the other hand – WHY ME? Why should it always be the daughter who is expected to stay at home and dance attendance? Surely Father bears some responsibility, too?

I know what his answer would be to that. He would have no time for the argument that this is 1924 and women are more liberated than they have ever been. And, almost to my own fury, I see his point. Yes, I am the obvious one to stay with Mother; but haven't I a duty to myself as well?

Isobel talks of "Enlightened Self-Interest" and says that for my own sake I must find a more satisfying way of life. I know she is right. But what?

24th February. Plymouth
Musical gathering in house of friends of Isobel called Fortescue – a small, grey, bespectacled couple who would be almost indistinguishable from each other except that one wore trousers and one a skirt. Mrs F. accompanied Mr F. in some German lieder – very accomplished, but definitely dreary and it went on a bit too long. Isobel played Chopin, a Nocturne and two waltzes, which were lovely. Talked (all right, flirted!) with a dark and handsome Irishman called Michael Casey, who played the violin like a dream. He belongs to a chamber orchestra based in London, is only staying here with his sister for a few days, and was really the raison d'être for the whole evening. His sister, Kathleen, plays the 'cello very well, but has none of her brother's looks. She wears her hair in loopy coils over her ears, which gives her the appearance of a somewhat lugubrious bloodhound. They played some lovely duets, however, and I thoroughly enjoyed the entire evening. How thankful I am that one doesn't have to be able to play an instrument to appreciate music! Whatever talents I may possess are certainly not in that direction.

Home tomorrow, with nothing much solved. I think Isobel is right, however. I must get away from Lemorrick.

It was only a few days later that Mrs Rees came to tea. Had it been Mrs Radley or Mrs Tresidder, Verity would probably have taken the opportunity, knowing her mother was being entertained, to absent herself, but she had always been fond of both Dr Rees and his wife and thirsted for news of Livvy who was far too busy to write very often.

"She's well," Mrs Rees told her. "Overworked, of course, and a little worried because she's been asked to vacate her room at the hospital. An entire wing is having to be rebuilt – something to do with drains, I understand – so she's rushing around trying to find somewhere to lay her head. She can't be too far from the hospital, of course, and it's an expensive area, which makes things difficult." Her usually cheerful face creased with worry. "Money never troubles me as a rule, but I must confess that this is one of those times when a little more would be very handy.

How I'd love to be able to buy her one of those little houses behind Harrods."

Louise nodded and smiled, and returned almost immediately to Mrs Radley's choice of carpets, and it was to Mrs Rees's great credit, Verity thought, that she listened with every appearance of interest.

The words she had spoken, however, seemed to repeat themselves in Verity's mind. A little house behind Harrods seemed, suddenly, to be the most desirable thing on earth. And she could afford to rent one. She had money invested, left to her by her Bristol grandfather, with the interest just piling up. Her mother might be upset temporarily, but she had her own friends, she would adjust, just as she had done to Stephen's departure. And she and Livvy could live together and have such fun! They could go to things – concerts, plays, anything.

And she could get a job. People did, in art galleries and hat shops, things like that. She could even go to classes and learn to type and keep books—

Well, maybe not that. But there would be something.

"So can we rely on you, Verity?"

Mrs Rees's voice brought her back to earth and for a moment she blinked, uncomprehending. The others laughed.

"Really, what are you thinking of?" her mother asked. "You look as if you were miles away. We were talking about the Cottage Hospital fête."

"Oh!" Verity blinked again. "Well, yes. Of course. At least, I suppose so. Is it far ahead? I might not be here . . ."

20th September 1924
No diary for ten days. That's because life has been very topsy-turvy of late, what with settling into the house, buying things for it, finding a maid, etc. Have settled on a Mrs Prettiman (quite young but, disconcertingly, no teeth) who will come in from eight thirty to five, Monday to Friday, will do laundry and prepare evening meal if required but not for a penny less than 22/6 a week! She will, she says, come in for dinner parties and on Saturdays to "oblige", but we'll have to pay extra! London prices seem terrible to us after Cornwall, but I suppose they're something we'll have to accept.

Must be more tactful about such things, however. Livvy is a bit thin-skinned about not contributing more – as if it mattered when I have so much! She works incredibly hard at St George's for a mere pittance. I really don't know how she keeps going, particularly when most of the male doctors are so beastly to her, but she loves the work so of course that helps. How I wish I had a vocation like that, or even the slightest inclination towards any kind of career. I really am useless.

Might have found myself a job, though. Through Winky, of all people. Went to party at Rex's flat the other night and met her again. Apparently she works in a beauty parlour, a high-class place somewhere off Bond Street where all the gorgeous ones of Mayfair go for manicures, facials, massages, etc. It seems they need a receptionist to welcome these ladies and make them feel at home. Winky opines that I would be Just the Thing. I have the right kind of voice, she says, and promises to mention my name, which is kind even though the position hardly seems one that would exercise the grey matter, exactly.

Livvy is dead against it and says it wouldn't do at all. I must, she says, get something that satisfies me intellectually. Like what? I ask, but she has no ready reply!

25th September 1924
Such a blow to my self-esteem! I was turned down for the beauty parlour job, voice notwithstanding. I'm not young enough or glamorous enough, apparently – which I think (and hope) means not made-up enough. The highly enamelled product of the beautician's art who interviewed me clearly thought I fell short by several hundred miles (even though I wore my Chanel suit) but I can't say I am sorry since I could tell I would never fit into the general picture. I am all for judiciously applied make-up and employ it all the time, but would find this shrine to it stultifyingly boring.

Livvy knows a woman who knows a man who might want someone in his antiques shop in Knightsbridge. It would at least be handy.

29th September 1924
Interview with Knightsbridge man; wouldn't take job if starving in gutter! Couldn't get out of the shop fast enough. Realised, after being manoeuvred between a Queen Anne escritoire and a

gate-legged table, that he obviously expects services far beyond the simple selling of antique furniture. He kindly offered private tuition in spotting fakes, to take place in his flat over the shop in the evenings. I said I was already very good at spotting fakes and rotters and marched out, clutching my umbrella like an offensive weapon.

However, hope springs eternal. Went to dinner party this evening at residence of people called Moorcroft. Mr Bill Moorcroft is a business acquaintance of Father's whom I have been doing my best to avoid ever since arrival in London. I thought he was bound to be boring, but I was completely wrong. Both he and Joan, his wife, were charming, and so were their guests. At dinner was inspired, no doubt due to excess of champagne, to give a spirited account of my search for a job, including incident with Knightsbridge antique dealer, which seemed to cause general amusement. Afterwards, one of the guests referred to by all as Dickie pressed his business card upon me and told me to contact him as he might find something for me to do. Inspection of said card tells me that he is Richard Mortimore Wellard, Editor-in-Chief of the Morning Standard*!*

Came home longing to tell Livvy but found her asleep, dead to the world. That girl works too hard.

6th October 1924
What a day! Thought I was just going for an interview with R.M.W., but all we did was talk about books for a bit. (He wanted to know what I thought of P.G. Wodehouse, which was an easy one to answer. I was so relieved that it wasn't Stendhal or the like!) He then handed me over to a formidable woman with an Eton crop called Miss Singer who said, without a great deal of enthusiasm, that I was required to write an amusing piece about Modern Life of not more than two hundred words and would I please have it ready by Friday!

Am excited and appalled and terrified, all at the same time. How can I be amusing to order? Have already written several drafts and torn them up. The awful thing about humour is that you think it's funny when you first write it down, but by the time you've read it over a hundred times it seems as dull as ditchwater. Am trying to do something on the job-hunting theme, but feel that if the job depends on my making Miss Singer laugh, I might as well make my way to the dole queue here and now. She has a mouth like a small but particularly savage rat trap.

8th October 1924
Having worked day and night, have now finished piece. Gave it to Livvy to read and she laughed here and there, which was encouraging. Must now get it typed by someone so that it can be handed in by the 10th. Obviously, if anything comes of this I am going to have to learn to type. Shall eschew the book-keeping, however. Accounts never have been, nor never will be, my métier.

"It was the most unnerving five minutes of my life," Verity said on her return home. Livvy, enjoying a day off-duty, was putting varnish on her nails. It was important, she said, to wave the flag for feminism, not try to be a second-rate man.

"What happened?" she asked.

"The wretched woman sat and read it with a face like granite."

"And she didn't laugh once?"

"Laugh? Her lips gave not the merest twitch."

"But she accepted it?"

"Only, she made it clear, because I was a protégé of Mr Wellard."

"You'll just have to show her that you're worth your keep," Livvy said.

Verity laughed. "Which turns out to be 17/6d a week! Five shillings a week less than we pay Mrs Prettiman."

"Ha! We'd both be better off charring." Livvy's voice was uncharacteristically bitter and Verity sobered immediately.

"What's wrong, Liv?" she asked, sitting down so that she could scrutinise her friend more closely.

"Oh, nothing." Livvy sighed, then gave a brief and bitter laugh. "Nothing unusual, anyway. Just the men ganging up on me. I should be used to it by now. They hate me even venturing an opinion if it doesn't echo theirs, and of course, the patients are often as bad. I can make a diagnosis I know perfectly well is accurate, but they still want to see a 'proper doctor'."

"Surely, women would rather see another woman—"

"No! No, they wouldn't. Well, maybe some that have a

particularly embarrassing women's problem would rather see me than a huge, hairy man like Glaister, but even then I get the feeling that they think they're being short-changed. In so many eyes, a woman will never be as good as a man. Which is absolutely ludicrous."

"Suppose you specialised in women's things – what's it called? Gynaecology? Wouldn't that be easier for you?"

Livvy sighed again. "Maybe. But that's not what I want to do, Vee. I want to go back to Porthallic and help Daddy with the practice – be a good old GP! It's what we've always planned."

"Your father's wonderfully enlightened."

"Yes, I'm lucky, aren't I?"

"Doesn't your mother get on to you about getting married?"

"A bit. She's against marriage at any cost, though, and she knows how much my career means to me."

"You really are lucky." Verity, too, heaved a sigh. "My mother is beginning to scrape the bottom of the barrel and come up with all kinds of creatures to parade in front of me. Twice my age, sans teeth or eyes or hair, nothing matters just so long as he happens to be an unmarried gentleman. Did I tell you she asked Commander Burton to dinner on my behalf? Do you remember him? He's ancient, like a very old lizard."

"Well, you know what they say about being an old man's darling—"

"He told me over coffee that dancing the Charleston was not only decadent but could easily damage the spine."

"And I'm sure he's the kind that thinks women's suffrage will endanger the delicate female brain. Anyway, he's surely a confirmed bachelor. I get the impression he doesn't really like women at all."

"Yes." Quite suddenly, Verity's smile died. "You're probably right. What I know he does think, because he pulled no punches in telling me so, is that my duty lies with my mother—"

"Well, take no notice," Livvy said briskly, waving one hand in the air to dry. "Your mother does very well, and Mummy said she would keep an eye on her so you have absolutely no need to worry. I think it's absolutely marvellous that you've managed to find a job like this and I know you're going to make a big success of it. It's what you need."

"Then for pity's sake, think of something funny I can write

about for next week," Verity begged. "My mind's a total blank."

"I'll work on it," Livvy promised.

In the end, it was Verity herself who thought of her next theme, that of a country bumpkin in London, her trials recounted with a self-deprecating humour that even wrung a reluctant smirk from Miss Singer.

Women's fashions, disasters in the kitchen, entertaining at home, all were grist to her mill over the ensuing weeks and all were well received. She found she developed a kind of nose for the kind of occasion she could turn into an article for the paper. She learned to take a quite ordinary event and by dint of a little fabrication here and a lot of exaggeration there, make it into just the kind of thing that was required.

By Christmas, in addition to this weekly task, she was given another. Mrs Macomber, the elderly lady who wrote the "Aunt Abigail Advises" page every Wednesday, was taken ill and Verity was asked to step in "for a week or two". When it became obvious that Mrs Macomber was never likely to return to work, the job was offered to her on a permanent basis and she accepted gladly. She had learned to type by this time and had bought herself a typewriter, on which she tapped happily away in her room feeling more contented than she had done for years.

For Livvy, however, it was a case of hanging on grimly until her year at St George's was completed, and for the most part she was able to throw off her frustrations once she arrived at the little house in Vanbrugh Gardens. One day in March, however, she came home in a savage mood.

"I can't stand it any more," she said, throwing her bag down on one chair, her hat on another. Her hair was wild, her eyes flashing. She looked, Verity thought, like one of the Furies. "Heaven knows, I've put up with a lot but today was just the end."

"For goodness sake, sit down! Have a gin—"

Livvy took no notice but raged around the room.

"I'll kill Glaister before I get through. I will, I'll kill him! Do you know what he did? Today he spoke to me, in front of a patient, as if I were twelve years old and mentally retarded at that. Nobody but a fool, he said, could mistake this chap's chest pains for a heart condition when quite clearly they were nothing more serious than indigestion. Go home, he told him. The ladies, God bless 'em, they do like to fuss, don't they?"

"So what happened?" Verity asked. "Or need I ask?"

"The patient had a coronary. He got up, got dressed, packed his things and collapsed in the corridor, right outside the ward. We still don't know if he's going to pull through."

"That's terrible!"

"It's not the worst of it. When Glaister was asked how this came to pass, somehow it turned out that it was all my fault! Would you believe it? I hadn't briefed him sufficiently about the symptoms, he told McNab. Of *course*, if he'd had the full picture—"

"But aren't there notes, and things?"

"They weren't complete. I was just writing them up when he came on his rounds, but he took them from me and took over. God, what a fool I was not to snatch them back and finish what I was doing! But he just wiped the floor with me, Vee, and I felt so humiliated with both these men chortling over the poor little inefficient woman who'd made such a great mistake. I *told* him what the symptoms were but he was so blinded by his desire to make me look a fool that he didn't take them in."

"Can't you tell McNab all this?"

Livvy slumped down in a chair. "What's the point? If you start from the premise that women are all stupid, it's impossible to take anything they say seriously. McNab will believe Glaister before me, now and forever."

"So what will you do?"

"What can I do? Hang grimly on, I suppose. I must do this year, at least." She sighed and ran her hands through her hair. "If only Dad could find some way of getting the hospital built in Porthallic, I could maybe go down there at the end of it."

"Well, everyone's raising money like mad. What's the latest news on that front?"

"They're still a long way short of the target figure, and the bloody Courtfields are still holding out for some astronomical sum for the land."

"Isn't there any other available?"

"Not in the village. You know they own practically all of it. You'd think that for the greatest good of the greatest number they'd treat us generously."

"We are talking about the Courtfields, aren't we? When did they care about anyone other than themselves?"

"One lives in hope." Livvy sighed. "You know," she said, managing a smile at last, "that gin wouldn't be at all a bad idea."

"Coming up," said Verity.

Livvy was off-duty that weekend, the first for many weeks, and to cheer her up Verity insisted on taking her to a concert at the Queen's Hall given by the London Symphony Orchestra.

"My treat," she insisted. "No, honestly, I shall brook no argument about this. It's therapy. Mostly Brahms, with a touch of Puccini. Do us both the world of good."

They took their seats, three rows back from the podium. The orchestra filed in, settled themselves, and began tuning their instruments.

"That has to be one of the most exciting sounds on earth," Livvy whispered. She had put away her weekday troubles and her eyes were shining. "Thanks for insisting on this, Vee. It was a great idea of yours, and marvellous seats, too! The place is almost full. Was it hard to get tickets?"

Verity didn't reply to this, didn't, it seemed, even hear. "I say, do look," she murmured. "You see the violinist on the front row, three along? I know him! That's the chap I told you about, the musician I met in Plymouth. Michael Something. He's Irish and so's his name – Casey, that's it."

"You didn't tell me he was in the LSO."

"He wasn't, then."

Verity was looking directly at him as, violin tuned to his satisfaction, he sat back and surveyed the audience. His eyes passed over her, then swiftly returned. He smiled. He'd seen her, recognised her.

"You didn't tell me he was so handsome, either," said Livvy.

"Didn't I?" Verity's voice was casual. Livvy gave her an amused, sideways look, eyebrows raised, but said nothing. Amid applause, the leader was taking his place. The music was about to begin.

10th October 1925
Concert at Queen's Hall, with surprising sight of Michael Casey in the orchestra. Went round to see him afterwards (I thought

it would distract Livvy) and found him frightfully friendly and happy to join us at a nearby cocktail bar for a quick drink afterwards. He's a highly entertaining fellow and I was happy to see that Livvy was looking far more cheerful when we arrived home than I have seen her for a long while.

We have for some time been thinking of throwing a party (have, of course, had lots of minor ones but this is to be a BIG one) and have agreed to invite him.

Eight

1st January 1926
My New Year's Resolution (one of them!) is to keep up this
diary. I have been very neglectful this past year – and, I see, the
year before that, too – but surely can plead pressure of work.
And play, of course. I can hardly believe that the time has gone
so fast, which I suppose implies that I am enjoying life. And oh,
I am, I am!

This was largely thanks to Michael Casey, of course, though her
work was still of absorbing interest. Sometimes she looked back
to that evening when she and Livvy had gone to the Queen's
Hall, and she shivered in her shoes to think how easily they
could have opted for the theatre instead of a concert, in which
case she and Michael would probably never have encountered
each other, a fate she couldn't bear to imagine. How did she ever
live without him?

He had come to the party a little late; not late enough to be
impolite, but late enough to make her anxious, for in the time
that had elapsed since she had issued the invitation the thought
of him had somehow lodged itself in her mind, the urge to see
him growing stronger with every day that passed. The possibility
that he had forgotten, or found something better to do after all,
was enough to take all the excitement out of the occasion.

Then, just as she was forcing herself to converse brightly with a
poet friend of Rex's without looking round at the door every few
minutes, she had somehow felt a presence at her shoulder and had
looked up, with a bounding of the heart, to find him there.

Despite this, and the fact that he was never far from her side all
evening, she denied any particular interest in him when everyone
had gone and she and Livvy were raking over the coals of the
party, as was their custom.

130

"I admit he's a gorgeous creature," she said. "What would be the use of denying it? But he really isn't my type, Liv – all that blarney, and the dimples and the twinkling eyes. You know perfectly well I prefer the more cerebral kind of man. Looks don't mean a thing to me. Never have."

"No?" Livvy smiled, unconvinced.

Events proved Livvy's scepticism justified. Michael Casey, by the sheer force of his charm and persistence, seemed to insinuate himself into their household, and Verity seemed only too happy to welcome him there.

"He's a life-enhancer," she said to Livvy on one occasion. "Haven't you noticed how the whole room comes alive when he walks in?"

Livvy could only agree. Verity was right; at the very sight of him, people sat up, became more animated. He was good company, she couldn't deny, yet there was something about him, only perceived after the passage of time, that made her wary. Once she came into the sitting room, Verity having left him for a moment, to find him reading a letter from Louise Ashland that had been left on a side table. The look on his face as he quickly replaced it and turned away could only be described as shifty. She had said nothing. He could, perhaps, be forgiven for curiosity about the mother he had never met, but she couldn't forget that expression, or the times when, thinking himself unobserved, she caught him looking at Verity with an expression that did not seem to her the look of a lover.

Again, she said nothing, not feeling that it would be of any avail, for by this time Michael had been universally accepted as Verity's particular escort. People referred to him as her friend, but of course he was her lover. They were invited together to the houses of friends in the country, and went as a couple to private parties at Henley and Ascot. He toured with the orchestra quite frequently, but when in London seemed to spend most of his time in Vanbrugh Gardens. Verity, always generous, was lavish with her gifts. A cashmere sweater, a leather travelling case, a gold watch when his old one gave up the ghost – he thanked her prettily, of course, but all were accepted, it seemed to Livvy, as no more than his due, and it annoyed her to see it.

She asked about marriage, one evening when they were alone.

"Yes, of course!" Verity said. "We have every intention of

getting married, just as soon as Michael sorts out some problem with his father's will. He's due to inherit the family estate in Killarney, but his father married for a second time not long before he died, some chit of a girl who's an absolute bitch and determined to see that none of his children inherit a penny, and so she's contesting it. Of course I've told him I couldn't care less about his father's will – let the girl have what she wants – but he says no, he can't come to me with nothing."

"I see," Livvy said, clearly unconvinced.

"You sound as if you think it's all going to end in tears!"

"Do I?" She looked at Verity anxiously. "I don't mean to. I want you to be happy, Vee."

"I am happy," Verity assured her.

But another year went by and still Michael seemed no nearer sorting out his financial problems, and in the summer of 1927 something happened to spoil Verity's happiness.

Thursday 9th June 1927

Dinner with the Moorcrofts. No sign of M. (three days now) so I went alone though God knows I didn't feel like it. Joan twigged there was something wrong but there was no opportunity to confide in her, and I wouldn't have done so if there had been, good friend though she is.

I regret the row terribly, but what could I do but face him with what Miss Brophy told me? I'm sure I wasn't confrontational about it! I just wanted to know the truth, that was all, and Miss B. did seem quite certain of her facts. She saw Michael quite clearly waiting for me outside the office. She knew his name, said she'd known his wife since she was a girl and was at their wedding in Dublin. They have two little boys! His wife, says Miss B., hears from him regularly and confidently expects to join him at any moment.

He denied it absolutely and was furious with me for believing the word of a comparative stranger, who must, he says, be half-blind and daft as well. He maintains he has several cousins who look just like him and she must have taken him for one of them when she saw him outside the office. One is even called Michael Casey – and wasn't his mother blind with anger when her sister-in-law gave her new baby the very same name as her own child? Sure, not an original thought in her head had Auntie

Maureen! But if I chose to believe the word of a daftie like Miss Brophy instead of his, then there is no trust between us and we have nothing left to say to each other. At which he stamped off in a rage and I haven't seen him since. I wish I knew what to believe. If Miss B. is telling the truth, it explains why he has never allowed me to invite his sister here to stay, although I know she is still in Plymouth because Isobel mentioned seeing her only the other day.

Saturday 11th June 1927
M. came round very late, after the concert. Says he has been utterly miserable and can think of nothing but our stupid quarrel and that I must believe him, he is no more married than I am! So let's get married right away, I say. Yes, yes, just as soon as all this legal business is sorted out, he says. And it really won't be long now, for the solicitor says the whole matter should be cleared up in a matter of weeks. He seems so sincere I feel I must give him the benefit of the doubt.

What Mother and Father will say when they know about him I have no way of knowing for they are both so conventional. He will charm Mother, of course, but she may well deplore his general Irishness and Catholicism. I doubt Father will approve of him, since musicians are among the category of people he considered untrustworthy fly-by-nights, along with actors, artists and most authors, unless they happen to be dead or exceptionally famous and not noticeably left-wing. Shakespeare might, just possibly, pass muster, but not many others.

On the other hand, they may be so relieved to get me off the shelf at last, that all will be forgiven!

Verity was smiling a little as she sat back in her chair, cynically amused at this thought; then slowly the smile died and she sighed. One person who would definitely not be pleased about the reconciliation was Livvy.

Once they had lived in total harmony, but there was no doubt that recently the little house in Vanbrugh Gardens had become a less agreeable place. She would never have believed it possible that she could fall out with Livvy.

Not that it had quite come to that. They were both too fond of each other, had been friends for too long, but somehow a gulf had undoubtedly opened up between them. It was, she thought, such a pity that these two most important people in her life couldn't be friends.

"Don't rush into anything, will you?" Livvy said one day. "Even when Michael sorts out his legal wrangles. Take it slowly."

"Slowly?" Verity laughed in astonished disbelief. "My God, Livvy, when have we done anything else *but* take things slowly? I feel Michael and I have been together for years and years, but we seem no nearer getting married, much as we want to be."

Livvy said nothing, asked no questions, but Verity was well aware of the look on her face which said, louder than any words could have done, that events could not move slow enough to please her.

The all-important thing, however, was that she and Michael were happy again. Happier, if anything, more loving and closer than ever. She longed to be able to take him down to Lemorrick for the summer, but knew it to be impossible, for the orchestra was going to be on tour in Europe for several weeks, and in any case she wanted matters between them to be resolved before introducing him to her parents. So she went alone, and though she had looked forward to seeing all her beloved places she was, even so, taken by suprise at the extent of her joy at being home again. It was the peace, she decided. The lack of tension. The knowing that she wouldn't be seeing Michael for at least four weeks and could do nothing about it except relax and wait calmly for the day when they were together again.

A letter had come from Stephen only days before she arrived in Cornwall, announcing his engagement to the daughter of an army colonel, Daphne Winslow by name.

> She is nineteen, and very pretty (see enclosed photograph), and I know you will love her as I do. Her parents are delightful people and look forward to meeting you when they return to England. They have a place in Somerset and are related to the Wiltshire Winslows whose son I knew at Waltham and whom I believe you may have met at the Waltham/Marlborough cricket match, my last year as Captain. He was the fair-haired chap who bowled the hat-trick, remember?

I have to confess that it is rather frowned upon for a junior officer such as I to get married on his first tour, but the fact that I am older than most and have an independent income seems to sweep away many barriers. In fact, Mother, you may not believe it, but being the heir to Ashland's Fish has done me no harm at all. Quite the contrary! Colonel Winslow maintains that the troops all but lived on our tinned pilchards during the war, which, he says, would undoubtedly have been prolonged even further without such nutritious and tasty rations!

We plan to marry in about four months' time. Daphne is very keen to spend our honeymoon in Kashmir, on a houseboat. . .

Verity, studying the photograph, saw a slim girl with blonde hair and a wide, eager smile with, in her opinion, rather too many teeth.

"She looks – jolly," she said, after a second's hesitation.

"Well, Stephen loves her, that's the main thing," her mother said. "And I'm so thankful she comes from a suitable family. I mean, one never knows and there's always the fear that these men far from civilisation might go native. But oh, Verity, I'm quite devastated not to be at the wedding. He is my first-born, after all, and the only son I have left! You would think he might have waited."

"But if they're in love, Mother—"

"Oh, I know, I know. Young people these days have so little restraint."

"Stephen is over thirty. If he feels Daphne is the girl for him, then I'm glad he's taking the plunge. She could be the making of him."

"She's very young," Louise said doubtfully.

"You wanted to marry me off even younger, if I'm not mistaken."

Louise sighed at this. "And here you are – what? Twenty-seven? Oh, I can hardly believe it! You can never guess how I worry about you! Is there really nobody special in your life, dear? Your father was speaking of it just last weekend. You're out and about so much, meeting so many people, it hardly seems possible you haven't found Mr Right. Of course, I know the war was to blame for almost wiping out that generation of young men."

"Well—" Verity looked at her mother's anxious expression and could well imagine the despairing conversations she and her father engaged in. Should she take pity on her? "Actually there is someone I'm fond of," she continued after a moment. "But it's too early to say anything yet. Believe me, you'll be the first to know when there's anything definite to tell you."

"*Really?*" Her mother's face lit up as if she had been handed a present. "Oh, but you must tell me, darling! Who is he? Where did you meet him?"

"In Plymouth, actually. Years ago, that time I stayed with Isobel. And lo and behold, I met him again in London, quite by chance."

"Oh!" Louise beamed with pleasure and relief. "He's a naval man, then?"

Verity, knowing that instant plans were forming in her mother's mind involving full-dress uniforms and guards of honour with crossed swords, hastened to disabuse her.

"No, no. Not at all. He's a musician. A violinist, and very, very talented. He plays with one of the top London orchestras."

"Oh." Some of the light died out of Louise's face. "Oh, well—" She was, Verity could see, making a determined attempt to rally her spirits. "Some musicians are quite respectable, I suppose. Do we know his people? Where does he come from?"

Verity did her best to deal with these questions, but her replies, judging from her mother's dubious expression, seemed far from satisfactory. However, Louise took a deep breath and did her best to look on the bright side.

"Well, if Isobel introduced you, then I'm quite sure . . ." Her voice trailed away and she sighed. "I confess it's not quite what I hoped for when you were young, but the years are going so quickly. When are we going to meet this young man?"

"Not yet," Verity said quickly. "I shouldn't really have said anything and I'd be glad if you didn't mention it to anyone. Not even Father. Please, Mother, do promise."

"Why?" Louise looked puzzled and a little anxious. "There isn't anything not *quite* about him, is there?"

Verity laughed gaily. "Of course not! He's divinely handsome, and the most charming man ever. You'll probably fall in love with him yourself. It's just that he's abroad at the moment, on tour, and we want to announce it together. So, Mother, you'll keep this to yourself, won't you? I don't want the whole world knowing about it just yet."

"I understand, dear." Louise leant forward and patted her daughter's arm, looking more approving of her than she had done for some time. "Of course your secret's safe with me."

And if I believe that, Verity thought with a sudden pang of regret at her rashness, then I'll believe anything.

4th August 1927

I shouldn't have said anything to Mother, of course, because she's bound to tell her cronies and news of my imminent betrothal will be all round the village in no time. Really there's no guarantee that Michael will be ready to marry as soon as we think. It's not the first time our hopes have risen at the prospect of an early settlement, so I was a fool to open my mouth. I'm sure she'll tell Father, which won't make matters easier.

Why did I mention it? Partly, I suppose, because I just wanted to talk about M. (although I managed to stop myself saying much), and partly because I wanted to give Mother a little hope. Poor darling, she does feel horribly cheated that Stephen's wedding is going to take place so far away. I suggested that she might like to go out there for a trip, but the idea horrified her. She has never cared much for travelling.

Come to think of it, she might feel differently if I were to go too. I must say I find the thought of visiting India exciting, but hate the idea of leaving M. for such a long time. Anyway, it's just not possible if I want to keep my job. I was able to prepare for this holiday, but to be away for any longer would not be viewed in a favourable light.

I wonder where M. is tonight? He didn't exactly know what the itinerary was after Berlin and couldn't give me any addresses, so we agreed not to write. He's not much of a one for letters anyway. I hope he's thinking about me.

Being here without him feels odd, almost as if I have reverted to childhood. I swim, sunbathe, listen to music, go for walks, speak nicely to Mother's friends, all in a kind of comfortable limbo. All the old gang seems to have dispersed. Jemima is married and has emigrated to South Africa. David is living in Paris, I understand – surely the Left Bank must be his natural home? – and Carla is married to a frightfully respectable country squire. Rex is in London, of course, and the rest heaven knows where.

I did visit the Rees's yesterday and was as kindly welcomed as ever. Livvy has obviously said nothing about our disagreements, or her opinion of M. Dr Rees is very fired up about the Courtfields and the amount they want for the proposed Cottage Hospital site. I hope for Sir Geoffrey's sake that he doesn't need an emergency operation, when and if the place is finally built. In Dr Rees's present mood, I wouldn't like to answer for his actions if he were to be confronted, scalpel in hand, with Sir G.'s insensate form!

Nicholas and his wife, I am told, are currently swanning round the Med. on a luxury yacht, having left their small son at home with his nanny. (He is called Geoffrey Hugh, after his grandfather, but Mother says he is always known as Hugh to avoid confusion. I hope he grows up with a nicer nature than his father!)

That could have been you on the yacht, Mother tells me, as if expecting me to turn green with envy before her very eyes! I have of course seen Frances Courtfield from a distance, but have never actually spoken to her. What is she like? I ask Mother. Colourless, she says. Too much of a doormat for a Courtfield.

But, say I, you have to agree she is stylish.

Too short, says Mother, and no personality!

I am amused by this and feel she is guilty of the same partisan judgement as whoever it was who told Cleopatra that Anthony's wife was "dull of tongue and dwarfish"! Mrs Rees, however, tells me she is sweet and kind. Marriage to Nicholas must, I fear, take all the sweetness the poor woman can muster. I hope he really loves her and didn't just marry her for her money, of which I understand she has plenty. (Which makes their meanness over the Hospital land all the more detestable.)

Am currently reading Virginia Woolf's To the Lighthouse. *Clever lady. Oh, I wish, I wish . . .*

Truthfully, she wished for nothing and regretted nothing just at that moment, not even that her dream of writing a book had never been fulfilled. The weather was warm and sunny and all her fears about Michael's past and his future intentions were utterly allayed, as if the beauty and the peace had conspired to calm any misgivings that Livvy might have instilled. Everything was going to be all right, she felt quite certain of it. It's London that's to blame, she thought, as she lay idly on the terrace, soaking up the sun. It's such a jangly sort of place, so wearing on the nerves. Here, at Lemorrick, everything seemed so much more simple.

As the days passed, however, she was conscious of passing into another phase and was beginning now to count the days that must elapse before she would see Michael again. She looked in the mirror and was pleased with the reflection that looked back. Porthallic had been as good as a beauty treatment; she was lightly tanned and looked less strained. Younger. Prettier. What would he think of her on his return?

He had not known the exact date this would be but knew it to be some time during the last week of August, and though she had not planned to travel until the 26th, the last Friday in the month, the thought that he might already be in England tormented her past bearing. On the Wednesday evening of that last week she broke the news to her mother that she proposed to leave the following day.

"I've suddenly realised that if I'm to start work on Monday there are people I ought to see before the weekend," she said. "If I go tomorrow, I shall have the whole of Friday to sort things out. You haven't planned anything specific for me to do, have you?"

Louise admitted that the calendar was clear. "But darling, I shall be so sorry to see you go," she said plaintively. "Your father's not coming home this weekend, you know, which makes the week seem endless."

"I know. I'm sorry, but I'd have to go before the weekend, anyway, and twenty-four extra hours will make such a difference to me. You do understand, don't you?"

Louise sighed and reluctantly acquiesced. Verity knew she should feel guilty, and indeed suffered the odd pang of conscience, but excitement was uppermost. She was going back, going to see Michael. Their absence from each other now seemed to have been going on for half eternity and the thought of prolonging it further, even by a single day, was something she couldn't bear to think about. Lemorrick had done what she required of it; it had rested and restored her, smoothed out the wrinkles, calmed the nerves, but now she was ready to begin living again.

On her return to Vanbrugh Gardens the taxi driver carried her luggage to the door but left it on the top step, so that it was she who heaved it over the threshold to be greeted by the sight of a totally unknown young man, standing in the hall with a tray in his hands containing a teapot and two used cups. For a moment they stared at each other, startled. Then he smiled, the wide grin transforming his long and rather lugubrious face.

"Hallo. You must be Verity," he said.

"Right first time. And who might you be?"

"Robert Collins. A friend of Livvy's," he added, by way of explanation. He raised the tray an inch as if to bring it to her attention. "I'm just taking this down to the kitchen."

"Who are you talking to?" Livvy's curious face appeared round the bend in the basement stairs. "Oh, it's you, Vee! I didn't expect you until tomorrow."

Which must, Verity thought, account for the note of caution that somehow was implicit in this less than effusive welcome. What had Livvy got herself into during the past three weeks?

"Sorry," she said. "I should have let you know."

"Not necessarily." The whole of Livvy came up into the hall. "It's good to see you. I see you've met Robert." The young man sketched a parody of a bow, still hampered by the tray. "We've just been having tea," Livvy went on. "Would you like some? I can soon make a fresh pot."

"Where's Mrs Prettiman?"

"Gone to Southend for a week."

"She didn't say—"

"She gave me about five minutes' notice, wretched woman – but it didn't matter. I haven't been here much, to be honest. Sorry the place is a bit dusty, though. I was going to have a quick flip round before you came."

"Oh, Livvy! As if I would care."

"Well, what about that tea?"

"No, thanks. I had some on the train and really all I want is a wash and brush up."

"If you take this," Robert Collins said, handing the tray to Livvy, "I'll help Verity with her cases."

He seemed quite at home, Verity noted, grimly amused in view of Livvy's strictures about Michael. He also was a doctor, it transpired on the journey upstairs with her luggage, but not one of Livvy's colleagues at St George's. He was a GP – "a humble GP", as he phrased it – and he and Livvy had met at a symposium on communicable diseases three weeks before.

"She's – she's a wonderful girl," he said, shy and a little hesitant as for a moment they stood together on the landing outside Verity's bedroom door.

"I know," Verity said. "Well, thank you for bringing all this up. I'll see you shortly."

"I hope so, but not today. I'm about to leave. I've an evening surgery at six."

"Another day, then."

She watched him for a second as he retreated down the landing towards the stairs. He was tall, gangling, not at all handsome. But *nice*, she thought gratefully, smiling a little as she foresaw a future for him and for Livvy, running the practice in Porthallic in perfect harmony.

Heaven forfend that I'm turning into my mother, she thought wryly, as she opened the door into her bedroom. Maybe Livvy doesn't feel that way about him at all – though what else could account for the wariness in her welcome? There had been, undoubtedly, a subtle undercurrent of unease, as if Livvy had been disconcerted by her unexpected appearance, wanting, perhaps, to break the news of the new man in her life before actually confronting her friend with him. Could that be the explanation?

With the grime of the Great Western Railway washed away and in a pale dusty pink voile dress that displayed her suntan to perfection, she eventually went downstairs to find out the truth, to indulge in a little light-hearted teasing, maybe, but ultimately to assure Livvy of her approval of Dr Robert Collins. It would be wonderful, she thought, if Livvy could experience the kind of happiness that she had found with Michael.

She found Livvy in the sitting room, apparently looking for something in a drawer, the French windows open on to the small, paved garden at the back of the house.

"Another gorgeous evening," Verity said, making for the cocktail cabinet. "Let's whip up a drink and take it outside, and then you can regale me with every last thing that's been going on."

"No, Vee, wait." Livvy slammed the drawer and straightened up, not smiling. "There's something I have to tell you—"

Verity looked at her. Her voice and expression seemed to imply a serious matter.

"What is it?" she asked.

"Sit down. Please." Silently, Verity sank down on the settee and Livvy perched herself uneasily on the edge of the chair opposite. For a moment she hesitated. "There's – there's no easy way of saying this," she said.

"Just say it, Liv."

Livvy drew in a deep breath. "Michael was round earlier."

"He's back?" Verity's face lit up and she jumped to her feet. "Oh, why didn't you say? Is there a concert tonight, or is he free? I must go and phone him."

"No, no, wait, Vee. He came and collected some of his things—"

Verity looked bewildered. "You mean he's going away again?"

"I'm afraid so. Oh God, Vee, this is so hard! He's gone. He's not coming back. He told me to tell you – the lousy, spineless rotter! He didn't have the guts to tell you himself."

Dazedly, Verity stared at her. "No. No, Livvy! It can't be true!" Her expression hardened and her voice grew louder. "It *isn't* true! You never liked him. You're trying to come between us."

"Vee, believe me, this is the hardest thing I've ever had to do, to tell you such an awful thing. I hate to hurt you, you must know that."

For a moment, every muscle tensed, Verity looked at her; then her shoulders sagged. "No," she said. "Sorry, Liv. But there has to be some mistake—"

"Go and see for yourself. He cleared out that cupboard on the landing, where he left his winter things."

Verity whirled around and pounded upstairs. In less time than it took Livvy to pace agitatedly from one side of the room to the other, she was back. "Tell me everything," she said urgently. "Tell me exactly what he said."

Livvy took a breath. "He said – he said he was going away, to live in France, and that he wasn't coming back. That I was to tell you." Livvy went over to her, and putting her arms round her pressed her down once more to sit on the sofa. "Oh darling, I'm so sorry. I'll get you a drink, shall I?"

Verity shook her off. "I don't understand. If he wants to live

142

in France, then we can live in France. I wouldn't mind, he knows that! I don't mind where we live."

"Vee—" Livvy's expression was one of anguish. "I'm so sorry, but it seems there's someone else. Some wealthy French woman – titled, he said – who followed the orchestra around, all over Europe. He had the gall to tell me about her, can you believe it? I said the least he could do was to see you and tell you himself, but he said he had to leave at once and wouldn't be back. Oh, Vee, I know how much this is hurting you. But if only you could see what the rest of us have seen for ages! He's no good, he's rotten right through and you're well rid of him!"

"Yes," Verity said woodenly, all the light and vivacity draining away. For a moment she did not move, then suddenly she seemed to disintegrate, her face crumpling like paper. She flung her head back, her eyes closed and her mouth distorted, tears suddenly pouring down her cheeks. Blindly she got up and hurried to the door, striking out at Livvy's arm as she attempted to restrain her. "No, no, no," she shouted. "Leave me alone. I must be alone."

Did she mean it? Helplessly, Livvy followed her from the room and for a little while stood uncertainly at the bottom of the stairs, looking upward, full of anxiety and apprehension. She heard the slam of the bedroom door.

For a few moments longer she hesitated then, reluctantly, she went back to the sitting room with a heavy heart, knowing that she had to respect Verity's wishes. It seemed the worst of ironies that this should happen, just when she herself was so happy.

4th September 1927
Have spent the entire evening attempting to write an amusing article concerning summer holidays. Result hardly up to my usual standard.

I don't, honestly, know how I can go on. All right, that's ridiculous. People get over worse than this every day of the week. Even so, I feel—

Pause while I think how I feel. To be honest, I don't really know. I'm hurt. Desperately miserable. Humiliated. Bitterly, bitterly angry. Perhaps that most of all.

He should have had the guts to face me. He should have written, at the very least. To leave a message with Livvy and just go without a word seems unforgivable after all we have meant to each other, though I dare say I wouldn't have forgiven him even if he'd delivered the news in person, on bended knee.

I feel such a fool. My ego is shattered beyond repair. But more than that, I miss him so.

6th September 1927
Spent entire day on Aunt Abigail letters. My God, there's a lot of misery in the world! I needn't think that the fates have picked me out for particular attention. One twenty-year-old girl with three small children and another on the way writes to say that she married at sixteen to get away from a brutal step-father. Her husband had a steady job at Smithfield Market and at first they were happy but then he changed and now he gets drunk and comes home and beats her for all kinds of misdemeanours, real and imagined. She wants to leave him, but he would only pursue her and anyway, how would she keep the children?

What the hell shall I say to her? I know from bitter experience the police are useless in these kind of cases. She's untrained, uneducated, inarticulate, with the handwriting and spelling of a child of ten. How could she possibly earn enough to keep herself and four children? And I think I've got problems!

The worst thing is knowing that everyone else could see Michael was a rotter. His poor wife! I'm sure now that Miss Brophy was right and that he is married. He just had me, as they say, on a piece of string. No doubt I was a more than adequate meal ticket, but now he has a better one, for I have discovered via friends in the orchestra that the French lady in question is the widow of the Comte du Roufigniac de l'Abeille, smart as paint, rich as Croesus, and owner of a fabulous chateau somewhere in the Ile de France. A la lanterne, is all I can say. Where is Mme Defarge when one needs her?

Why couldn't I see what he was after? Love is a terrible emotion, blinding one to reality and common sense. You could say I was mad about him, and that's the only way to describe it. Mad.

11th September 1927
Poor darling Livvy! She is head over heels in love with Robert Collins and he with her, and yet she feels it necessary to hide her happiness from me. It does hurt a bit to see them together, I

144

have to admit, yet honestly I don't wish things otherwise. Robert is a good man, and just right for her. She's taking him down to Porthallic for a few days at the end of the month. Must warn her that I gave Mother a hint about M. when I was down; I expect the news of my impending marriage is all over the village by now. What a fool I am! As if I did not make a sufficient laughing stock of myself over Laurie, long, long ago.

Livvy suggested tonight that I take a trip to India, to see the country as well as attend Stephen's wedding. I haven't a lot of enthusiasm for it, but then I haven't a lot of enthusiasm for anything just now. I suppose it might be as good a way as anything else to pass the time, if I can summon the energy. Quite honestly, I don't think I can cope with Aunt Abigail much longer, and am finding my own column more and more difficult. Maybe a change wouldn't be a bad idea.

15th September 1927
Letter from Mother in reply to mine suggesting we go to India together. She doesn't want to go, not even with me to keep her company. She is too fearful of heat, insects, native servants, etc. etc., but urges me to go alone so that I can give her a first-hand account of the wedding. I said I would think about it. Would Stephen be glad to see me, I wonder? Or would it remind him too much of those awful, wild days after the war when we both did things we'd rather not remember now? How young I was, and how foolish. And how little I have changed!

The mood she was in post-Michael was not unlike that she had experienced post-Laurie. Though more sensible now in many ways, she felt a desperate need to get away from London. She wrote to Stephen and in return received a warm invitation to go out to the sub-continent for an extended holiday. He would show her around as much as he could, he wrote. And who knows, she might meet this Mr Right that Mother was always wittering on about. She wouldn't be the first girl to meet her fate in India!

Verity gave a hollow laugh at this conceit. Men had no place on her agenda at the moment; still, the prospect of such an exotic trip succeeded in raising her spirits and she accordingly booked her passage on the SS *Ormond*, sailing at the end of October. She immediately flung herself into the absorbing quest for suitable clothes for a long sea voyage.

It was one evening at the beginning of the month, when both girls were in the sitting room, that the telephone rang in the hall, interrupting Verity's modelling of a colourful pair of lounging pyjamas, bought that afternoon.

"You take it, Liv," she said, already making for the door with the intention of going upstairs to change back to something more suitable for a London autumn. "I expect it's Robert. You are quite sure I don't look ridiculous in this?"

"You look marvellous," Livvy said, as she followed her out to answer the phone. "Glamour incarnate." Smiling, she took the receiver off its hook and held it to her ear. "Sloane 369." The smile died, and she held the earpiece away from her, pulling a face as Verity passed her. "Lots of crackles," she hissed. "I think it's a trunk call."

Verity paused, halfway up the stairs. Trunk calls sometimes meant Porthallic, which might mean an emergency for one or other of them. It might, she thought with a leap of her heart, even be Michael phoning from France – and at once berated herself for a fool. Of course it wasn't Michael. He had moved on to better things. And even if it *were* Michael, she had nothing to say to him (except Come Back, Come Back, Come Back!).

"Hallo? Hallo?" Livvy was still wrestling with the phone. "Oh, Mrs Ashland, is that you? Yes, she's here. Hold on." She held out the receiver to Verity who came downstairs again and took it from her, frowning a little. Her mother distrusted the phone and did not often resort to it. Letters were more her style or, in emergencies, telegrams of quite inordinate length.

"Mother? Is something wrong?"

That something was, indeed, wrong became very obvious to Livvy who was about to leave the hall, but stayed when she saw the shock on Verity's face.

"How bad?" Verity asked. "Are you sure? Yes, of course I'll go. First thing tomorrow. I'll ring as soon as I know anything. Please try not to worry, Mother; he's in the best possible hands, I'm sure."

"What is it, Vee?" Livvy asked anxiously, when the call was at last over.

"Father," Verity said. "He's had a stroke, and he's in hospital in

146

Bristol. I'm going down tomorrow." She caught sight of herself in the mirror over the umbrella stand and thought how incongruous she looked in her bright, flower-printed cotton.

"Vee, it might not be so bad. Did you get any details?"

"Not really. She was pretty hysterical – you know what Mother's like."

"You could phone the hospital."

"Yes, I suppose I could. Or better still, you could, Livvy. You'd be able to understand what they were talking about. I wrote down the number."

Further enquiries were not encouraging. Mr Ashland, a starched voice from the other end of the phone told Livvy, was as comfortable as could be expected. Even when she produced her credentials, there was only marginally more information. Mr Ashland was in a coma, the nurse said, and yes, the outcome was in the balance. It would probably be a good idea for his family to come as soon as possible.

"It's not good, is it?" Verity, still in the pyjamas with the Harrods label hanging down her back, looked worried.

"They have to be cautious. But I do think it would be advisable if your mother—"

"She won't go," Verity said. "She made that abundantly clear. Her nerves aren't strong enough to stand the shock, she says." She gave a breath of bitter laughter. "In my next incarnation, I'm going to have nerves. You'd be surprised the bother it saves you."

"You'll cope," said Livvy.

But next morning, having risen early to catch the train, Verity was not at all certain she was right. She felt sick with apprehension as the train took her to Bristol, and could not afterwards have described any of her fellow-passengers or the scenery that unfolded outside the window. In her youth she had adored her father and basked in his approval, seeing him as handsome and all-powerful, without flaw. Later, she saw the flaws clearly enough. He was opinionated, self-centred and rather vain, and his neglect of his wife was thoughtless, but even so the thought of a world without him made her feel hollow with grief. On the other hand, the thought of him living on, paralysed, was almost worse.

Perhaps it wouldn't come to that. He had always been strong, with a fine physique. She could hardly remember one single time when he had been ill or confined to bed.

At the hospital she was shown into her father's room by a stern-looking woman in a uniform so starched that it glistened in the shafts of light that filtered through the Venetian blind. Her cap was a confection of frills and pleats and seemed to sit uneasily on her narrow head. She was, Verity judged, very senior indeed; Mr Joseph Ashland, of Ashland's Fish, would merit no less.

He was still unconscious, and was breathing stertorously, his mouth open and his face a strange dark grey in colour and somehow pulled to one side. Fighting for calm, Verity sat down beside him and took his hand.

"Talk to him," the nurse ordered.

"Can he hear me?"

"We don't know, but it can't do any harm."

Verity took a breath, licked dry lips.

"Father? It's Verity. I've come from London to see you—"

Hearing the rustle of starch, she glanced over her shoulder and saw that the nurse had gone and she was alone with him. She looked at his poor, distorted face that had once been so handsome, so ruddy with health, and she bit her lips hard. Tears would help no one, she told herself. But what was there to say at a time like this?

"I'm – I'm so sorry you're ill," she said at last. "So is Mother, of course, but she couldn't come. She's not up to it – the journey, and everything; you, of all people know how upset she gets. She phoned me last night and I came down on the early train."

Still the heavy breathing went on, but was it slower? Noisier? Surely they shouldn't leave him like this! There must be something that could be done.

"Livvy sends her love, too. She says that often stroke patients make a complete recovery, though it can take some time. I'll look after you, I promise."

Dimly she became aware of noise in the corridor outside; an altercation of some kind, a feminine voice raised. She looked round as it seemed to get nearer and the next moment there, framed in the doorway, was a fashionably dressed woman, a young nurse, flushed in the face, pulling at her arm.

The sight of Verity seemed to take the woman by surprise

and for a moment she froze, her mouth open. "Oh! I – I didn't know—" she said, discomfited.

"I told you his daughter was here," the young nurse said, pleadingly. "Please, Mrs Hadlow, you've no business—"

The woman turned on her. She was breathing hard and her colour was high. "No business, eh? I'll remind you I'm the one who brought him in last night. You didn't say that then!"

"Are you a friend?" Verity got to her feet, feeling a measure of relief at this interruption with its promise of support. "I don't mind, nurse. Please let this lady in."

"But Sister said—"

"Tell her I had no objection. Do come in – Mrs Hadlow, is it?"

"That's right. Martha Hadlow. How is he?"

She had a Bristol accent which to Verity, brought up to categorise people on the instant, meant that she was not what her mother would call *quite*. So not a lady, then, despite the expensive clothes and the enviable little hat. The wife of a senior employee, perhaps?

"He's not good, Mrs Hadlow," she said. "He's still unconscious, and no one seems to know how long he could stay like this."

Tentatively, Mrs Hadlow approached the bed, her face so drawn with grief that Verity's expression sharpened a little. Who was this woman? She was, she guessed, in her late forties, a little plump, but pretty still, with clear blue eyes and a good complexion, enhanced a little with discreetly applied make-up. She smelled pleasantly of *muguet de bois*.

"Do you know him well?" Verity asked.

"Joe? Oh, yes." Tears had welled up in her eyes.

Verity frowned. She had never, in all her years, heard her father referred to as Joe.

"I don't think he ever spoke of a Mrs Hadlow."

The woman looked up, as if suddenly remembering that this was the umarried daughter; the girl Joe had spoken of so often, with a mixture of fondness and exasperation. She bit her lip and coloured a little. The silence lengthened between them, but just as Mrs Hadlow opened her mouth as if to speak the attention of both of them was jerked back to the man on the bed. His breathing, suddenly, had changed. He seemed to give a long, shuddering sigh, followed by total silence.

Mrs Hadlow gave a small scream and seemed to fall across him, while Verity ran to the door and called loudly for the nurse. The young probationer was there instantly, Sister only a second behind. Even so, there was nothing now that they, or anyone else, could do for Joseph Ashland.

28th September 1927. Bristol
Father died without regaining consciousness at 1.15 p.m. today. Mother requires me to stay here to make arrangements about getting his body back to Porthallic. She is quite distraught. Clearly I shall have to go down to be with her for a while, which means postponing my trip to India.

Mrs Hadlow is a complication. She, also, is distraught – so bowed down with grief that she wept on my shoulder and told me a lot more than I imagine Father would have wanted. It seems they have been lovers for years. He bought her a little house in Stoke Bishop in 1917. Why am I so surprised? Why didn't I twig that he had a woman here?

Because I loved and admired and trusted him, I suppose. I felt angry, sometimes, that he left Mother alone so much, but even so it never occurred to me that all the time he was being unfaithful to her. Did she know? I don't think she could have done. Apart from the odd complaint about his absence and her regret that he was not of noble blood, she never uttered a word of criticism. She could have been hiding it from me, of course, but I don't think so. She is not the stiff upper lip type.

But surely we should have guessed? He was a full-blooded male, after all; one had only to look at him to know that. And I daresay poor Mother, with her ailments real and imagined, lost any interest in marital passion long ago. Even so, I find myself angry on her behalf and will do all I can to hide any knowledge of Mrs Hadlow from her.

Not that I don't feel sorry for the woman. I think she genuinely loved Father, and only hope that he has provided for her. If he hasn't, then I will have to. In any case, Mother must never know.

It rather proves, doesn't it, that one mustn't live as if one will go on for ever, disregarding the probable results of one's actions? I've always thought the instruction to live each day as if it were one's last a particularly chilling one, but now I know first-hand that not to do so creates problems for those who are left to pick up the pieces. Suppose Mother had been the one to discover the existence of Mrs H! It doesn't bear thinking of. At least she can mourn now without any bitterness.

And I? Yes, I do feel bitter, even though I recognise it as a useless and destructive emotion. So often it has been my duty to stay with Mother during Father's enforced absences – all undertaken, so we were led to believe, for the good of the business. Now I know it was only so that he could pursue his own selfish devices and desires.

3rd October 1927
Father was buried today at Porthallic. Rained all day. Quite a big turn-out in spite of it. Mother barely able to stand upright and had to be supported. Obviously it is out of the question for me to go to India this month, and have cancelled booking, also written to the Standard *bringing forward the date of my resignation. They won't like it, but it can't be helped. My duty is clearly here (living each day as if it were my last?).*

Father has left Mrs Hadlow the house in Stoke Bishop and a small annuity. Nasty moment when Mother surfaced sufficiently to ask, "Who is this Mrs Hadlow?" but I stepped in quickly and said she was the wife of a trusted employee who died while at work and she seemed to accept that without question, though it brought on fresh floods of tears at the thought of Father's generosity, kindness of nature, selflessness, etc. etc. She won't, I am sure, give it another thought. It's not as if her income is reduced at all – or mine, come to that, for he has left me a considerable acreage of commercial property in the centre of Bristol which he has acquired over the years. Thank God, the business seems in good hands, but of course there are decisions to make about that. Mother wants to get shot of the whole thing, but I don't know. I think it would be wrong to do anything in a hurry.

Shall have to go to London soon to pick up clothes and decide what to do about the house. Keep it for the moment, I suppose. I can't throw Livvy out.

6th October 1927
Went up to London by rail but drove back, with the car laden to the

gunnels. Felt sad when I said goodbye to Livvy and the house. She insists she can take the rent over now, says she can afford it, and if she can't, she'll find someone to share. Robert, I suggested? But she shamed me by looking quite shocked. He is far too honourable for that, it appears, and they are Waiting for Marriage. It occurs to me that my life might have worked out better had I adopted this virtuous and conventional attitude to it!

Had a simply wonderful idea while driving over Salisbury Plain. If I sell the Bristol property I can buy the land for the hospital! Then Livvy and Robert can get married and come to Porthallic and we'll all live happily ever after. Shan't make any announcement yet, for there's probate to be proved, etc. but the more I think about it, the better it seems.

Arrived home just before dinner and had it with Mother in her room. Apparently she has been very poorly while I was away and Dr Rees has been in twice and has given her sleeping pills. My heart fails me at the thought of going through all this again, it is such a dreary way to live. But what else can I do? At least when, with a renewed bout of weeping, Mother said tonight that when I marry she might just as well do away with herself, I could assure her that my plans have changed and marriage is not now an option.

Or, I think, ever will be. In three months' time I will be twenty-eight. Given that the male population of my age group was decimated in the war and the number of surplus women are numbered in millions, I feel my chances are not good. Anyway, I seem, suddenly, to have gone off men altogether. How can I trust any one of them?

That's right, she said jeeringly to herself, sitting back in her chair. Go on. Dramatise things. You fell in love with a rotter, your father kept a mistress for ten years, so suddenly all men are swine.

She went to the window and pulled the curtain aside to look out at the cove. It was a tranquil night, starry, with gentle waves. It reminded her of so many other nights in the past when she had stood in this same place, longing for calm, for serenity, for a certainty that better times would come, that somewhere over that horizon she would find happiness.

"So here I am again," she said aloud. "Back to where I started."

But not quite, surely? There might be countless games of bezique waiting for her in the future, but there was also the Cottage Hospital to think about. The Ashland Memorial Hospital, Dr Rees suggested it should be called. What better way of spending her father's money – gained for the most part during the war in ways she had learned to view quietly with a touch of suspicion? It was right it should be used for the good of the community. It would be some kind of atonement. Harry would approve.

She let the curtain fall, but stood without moving for a second or two, depression washing over her. Who was she trying to fool? Was this project, worthy though it might be, any substitute for Michael? For a husband, a family, babies of her own?

Of course it wasn't. Never could be.

"But you can put all that behind you, my girl," she said grimly, as she prepared for bed. "It's good works from now on."

Nine

13th January 1928

My twenty-eighth birthday. As I was opening my birthday cards, Mother asked me, with perfect timing, what was the matter with me these days and why have I let myself go! Stared at myself in the mirror afterwards and had to admit that she has a point. I agree absolutely that there is little to be gained and much to be lost by looking the way I am looking now – my own self-respect for one thing – and it is high time I pulled myself together. Not just where outward appearances are concerned, either. I must take a more positive attitude to life. It's no good going on like this, just drifting about, doing nothing very much. My New Year's/Birthday resolution is to make a new beginning. Oh God, I quail at the thought even before I have begun!

However, an idea is beginning to form inside my head, but I want to think about it properly before I present it to Mother. Suppose, it occurred to me in the night watches, that I took over the business? She, of course, can't wait to rid herself of the last whiff of fish and wants to invest her all in gilt-edged securities, which is what Stephen is urging her to do in a positive barrage of letters. I can see the sense of this in a way, but while I was in Bristol and in conversation with Mr Brownlow (temporarily in charge and an extremely nice man) I suddenly realised that business itself is quite exciting, no matter if the commodity is fish or textiles or clothes-pegs! Things in the fishy world are looking very healthy at the moment, Mr B. assured me, with new overseas accounts and also some additional sources of supply and I feel it would not only be a sin and a shame to let it pass out of the family, but that it would be a wonderful outlet for my energies. I could learn about it, I feel sure. Indeed, I am more energised by the prospect than I have been by anything for some time.

Meanwhile, the sale of my land in Bristol has gone through

154

and we will soon be able to complete the purchase of the site for the Cottage Hospital.

15th January 1928
Mother seemed in better spirits tonight, so I waited for what seemed a good moment, then told her about my idea about taking over the business. What a fool I am ever to think she would have given it any serious thought! It is, she maintains, out of the question to think that any woman could manage to do such a thing – and what kind of woman would want to?

A woman like me, I tell her. Can't she see that if I don't have something to occupy my mind I shall go stark, staring mad? She said that I was being hysterical, that my first duty was to keep her company and run the house, that in addition there were any number of good causes desirous of my services, that no man would ever look at me if I were up to my eyebrows in fish, and that in any case she had agreed only that day to the price offered by the Phillipson Foods Company. It is, she said, what Stephen would want.

I am so glad, I said, with heavy irony. It is so important to do what Stephen wants when he is thousands of miles away and totally unaffected by it. To which she replied, "Yes, dear, I knew you'd see it that way," just as if I were being serious.

She is the owner of the company now and the decision is hers. I argued, of course, but she is absolutely adamant, so that's another good idea gone west. I am astonished how long this myth of my eventual marriage takes a-dying, or how difficult it can be in the year of our Lord nineteen hundred and twenty-eight for a woman to plough her own furrow.

When, the following year, the Depression began to bite Louise Ashland was modestly triumphant. She'd got rid of the business just in time, she said; and though it was true that the return on her investments was down, she had speculated in nothing risky, thanks to good financial advisors, and undoubtedly the good times would return.

Verity said nothing, though in her opinion the same went for the fish business. It would survive.

Meantime, despite reduced dividends, their life style – always fairly modest – was little changed by the bad times endured by a large part of the country; indeed, they must have seemed very comfortably off to most of the other inhabitants of Porthallic who, along with the rest of the country, were forced to tighten their belts. The fisherman, as in the whole of Cornwall, were poor as church mice. Tin mines were failing, as they had been doing now for many years, so that vast numbers of miners were out of work. But then neither tinners nor fishermen had ever lived off the fat of the land. At least the walls of the Ashland Memorial Hospital were rising, and every penny possible was being raised to equip it.

Livvy and Robert were married at Easter, and according to plan came down to join Dr Rees in his old-established practice. Their arrival provided a great boost to Verity's spirits. That summer the three of them took off in her car to drive through France as the fancy took them and ever afterwards she regarded this holiday as a kind of turning point, coming back to Porthallic refreshed and invigorated. Life, she felt, maybe had good things to offer after all. She really ought to make the effort to travel more. Maybe in a year or two her mother would be well enough for her even to take that trip to India, for Stephen still mentioned it from time to time. In 1929 he mentioned something else, too.

8th September 1929
Letter from Stephen this morning announcing that Daphne is expecting a baby in February. Must be something about the time of year – Livvy is expecting in March. Mother is absolutely delighted at the thought of being a grandmother and has started knitting bootees already.

Livvy wants me to stand as godmother, and of course I shall adore to do so. Am more or less reconciled now to the thought that I shall never have a child of my own, though I think it's an awful waste! I love children and feel sure I would make a pretty good mother. Have refused to take on the Girl Guides, though. There are limits, and that's mine.

Frances Courtfield had become one of her more intimate friends. It was the Hospital Committee that had brought them together, but each had soon recognised the other as a kindred spirit.

3rd October 1929

I don't think I have ever met such a truly good *person as Frances. That makes her sound rather pi, but she's not. She is clever and humorous in a quiet sort of way, but never in the slightest bit waspish (not at all like me!). If I say I think her marriage to Nicholas is less than happy, it isn't because she has ever said so; just instinct. He is often away, shooting in Scotland, fishing in Wales, attending shareholders' meetings in London, etc. etc. but Frances doesn't seem to mind at all. He appears to toil not, neither does he spin, which is quite different from his father who, though far from my favourite person for many reasons, did at least show a great deal of commitment to the County and its problems.*

Another clue: I have seen with my own eyes that even when Nicholas is at home he largely ignores Frances, or treats her as if nothing she says is of any worth, which to my mind is far worse. I can't imagine how any woman could *be happy with him! (There I go again, showing my waspish side!)*

I think her serene acceptance of her lot in life is simply because she married him in the clear knowledge that it was a marriage of convenience and knew from the beginning, therefore, that it would be unrealistic for her to expect much in the way of romance or companionship. Her parents died when she was young and she was brought up by an aunt who sounds perfectly horrible. Almost any husband was bound to seem an improvement – and anyway, like so many of us, she felt there was nothing else she could do. The wretched aunt seems to have undermined any self-confidence she might have had. She even convinced her she was unattractive, which is ridiculous as she has a distinctive kind of style and beauty that is quite her own. So poor Frances saw capturing the heir to a baronetcy as something she couldn't possibly reject. Or only on pain of death!

A pity, as I have learned this past year that she has an incisive sort of mind that gets to the heart of a problem in no time and I am quite sure she would have been a success in business. What we'd do without her on the Hospital Committee I can't imagine. She is also highly knowledgeable about gardens and all growing things and has proved herself a great asset at Howldrevel, however dismissive Nicholas may be.

I drove over to Howldrevel with the minutes of the last Hospital Committee meeting yesterday and happened to meet Nicholas just as he was leaving. As is my wont, I wished him a polite "good morning", only to receive a glare in return. Was moved to ask him if it wouldn't be possible for us to at least maintain a semblance of good manners towards each other if only for Frances's sake, to which he replied that if he had his way, his doors would be closed to me! How can any man be so small-minded? I realised for the first time that this is not, as he pretends, in response to my terrible sin of dancing with the gardener (over ten years ago!) but rather that I humiliated him by spurning his advances on that picnic with Catherine and Bernard Crossland. She, by the way, is in Simonstown and has just given birth to twin boys. All well.

For my part, I shall continue to be outwardly polite to N., but admit I find it impossible to look at him without thinking: this is the man who ruined my life. I don't think this is exaggeration. If my love affair with Laurie had been allowed to run its course, I feel certain I would eventually have defied my parents and married him. Or am I deluding myself? Perhaps.

Nicholas told Frances about Laurie, of course, and of my totally despicable behaviour, but she thought the whole thing typical of masculine over-reaction and all her sympathies were with me.

Hugh, now four years old, is a strange little boy, very quiet and reserved. Jittery is the word that comes to mind. Frances worries about him. She says Nicholas demands too much of him. I can imagine it. He demands too much of everybody, except himself.

It was in the spring of 1932 that Stephen, Daphne and their daughter Beatrice, now two, came home on leave from India. To say that Lemorrick was in an uproar for months beforehand was to underestimate the situation considerably. Louise impatiently brushed aside any need for economy and insisted on redecorating the drawing room which involved long and – to Verity – tedious discussions with Mrs Radley and Mrs Tresidder.

The purchase of a new bed for the guest room was, Verity allowed, possibly essential, but was it really necessary to break through the wall of the small bedroom next door in order to install a bathroom for their visitors?

"I'd have thought they'd want to put Beatrice in that little bedroom," Verity said, when Louise expounded her plans. "It would be very handy for them."

"But my dear, there's the old nursery, ready and waiting! All it needs is a lick of paint."

"It's miles away!"

"What does that matter? We'll take on a nanny, of course. You must write to this Norland place. And get a girl in from the village to help."

"If that's what you want—"

"It's what *they* want that counts. After all, Daphne is hardly accustomed to managing without servants, is she?"

"I wasn't advocating that. Not entirely, anyway. I simply didn't realise that this would involve more of them actually living-in."

Verity sighed at the thought. The servant situation had changed since the war. Kitchen maids and general workers were still plentiful in Porthallic owing to the current labour situation, but while one might think the same would apply to trained and experienced staff, this had not been Verity's experience. Cooks, she found, were particularly difficult to find, and once found were hard to keep. She had lost count of the number who, after a few months, had left the house in tears or high dudgeon or both, either due to her mother's unreasonable demands or a general distaste for country life or an inability to get on with the other staff. Instinct told her that the acquisition of a suitable nanny might prove equally difficult, providing yet one more member of staff for their present cook to fall out with.

However, she took herself to London at her mother's bidding in order to interview prospective candidates for the position, and having spoken to several and examined their credentials, opted for a bright-faced woman, younger than many applicants, with a ready smile. It was arranged that she would arrive in Porthallic two days before Stephen and his entourage, to make sure that everything in the nursery was just as she required it to be. To assist her, Verity engaged the gardener's grand-daughter, Molly Pascoe, at his urgent request. She was a good girl, he said, and needed a job, adding, a little darkly, that he'd see she worked hard and minded her manners.

By the time the day dawned for the family to arrive, excitement was high, but there were also last-minute doubts.

"Do you think Daphne will like the bedroom?" Louise fretted at breakfast. "Really, I'm not at all sure about those curtains! Blue might have been more restful. And perhaps we should have left the hiring of the nanny to her after all. I can't help thinking that you should have chosen someone older."

"She's a very nice girl," Verity assured her, not for the first time. "Older than she looks, and very experienced. Her references were impeccable. Really, mother, everything is taken care of. As for the room, it looks simply lovely. And after all, they're not royalty!"

"They are to me," Louise asserted piously.

10th April 1932
Well, they arrived, three days ago. I thought at first Stephen had changed. He looks leaner and certainly seems happier, but is, unfortunately, as pleased with himself as ever. It is as well that Daphne is also pleased with him, and he with her. I had expected that she would, perhaps, need putting at ease in this new environment, but not a bit of it; I have never known anyone more at ease! Not a trace upon her face of diffidence or shyness, as dear G & S would say. This is not meant to be a criticism, in fact I am rather envious of her assurance. She is a good-looking girl – handsome, perhaps, rather than pretty, with corn-coloured hair, china-blue eyes and an athletic figure. It seems she excels at all sports and so far as I can detect has little interest in anything else. I don't think she noticed the curtains!

She hasn't at all taken to Molly Pascoe. Says she looks sly. I say all the Pascoes look like that, it doesn't mean a thing, but I can tell she is not satisfied. Thank heaven, she has said nothing derogatory about Nanny, though on reflection she hasn't said anything nice, either.

Beatrice is a pretty little thing, but not surprisingly seems unsettled and fretful. No doubt she will settle after a while.

15th April 1932
Long discussion tonight about forthcoming party for all the neighbourhood to meet Stephen and Daphne, my plea for a series of dinner parties being dismissed out of hand. This plan at least has the merit of getting it all over in one go, but I can see that it's going to involve a lot of work. Date fixed for 30th. I am impressed by the way Daphne knows exactly what she wants in the way of food, flowers, etc. Can see that she will make an excellent Governor's First Lady when the time comes, so perhaps

must be regarded as the perfect wife for S. even though my desire for him to meet someone who will tease him out of his pomposity has not been fulfilled. D. has, I find, no sense of humour at all. And she simply KNOWS *that she and Stephen are right in all things! Comforting for them, but a little trying for us lesser mortals.*

Daphne says the nursery isn't cleaned properly and that Molly clearly has no idea of how to treat children, and will have to go. I beg for a few more days' grace and promise to speak to Pascoe who will speak to Molly. In addition, assure her that M. has looked after children all her life being the oldest of six, but D. remains unimpressed.

Unfortunately, Nanny has come in for disapproval, too. Daphne believes in strict discipline and no drinks after five p.m., not even water, to guard against bed-wetting. Nanny assures me that not only is this inhumane, but it doesn't work. Oh dear! I tried to keep the peace by pointing out to Daphne that Beatrice would grow out of it, as we all have done – adding, lightly, that there aren't many twenty-one-year-old bed-wetters around, after all. At which D. gave me an astonished stare and said, "I should hope NOT!*" Meantime, there is the problem of Molly. Apparently there is little improvement, according to D., though I can't see much amiss. I mentioned that Pascoe would be upset were she to be given her marching orders, at which D. announced her readiness to Deal with him! I implored her to leave him to me as he has always needed handling with care and the last thing I want is to be without a gardener at this juncture. A second chance has been agreed (reluctantly!).*

20th April 1932

Nanny has left in tears due to stand-up row with Daphne. Molly still here, but under notice. Cook presents herself to me and says she doesn't know how to carry on, it's all too upsetting, however is placated by offer, by me, of a further ten shillings a week, on top of additional wage already negotiated for duration of S. & D.'s visit. What else can I possibly do, in view of impending party? My life is, at the moment, dominated by it.

1st May 1932

Well, it was All Right on the Night! But only just. A major upset occurred when, the Courtfields having been invited and

Frances having accepted in Nicholas's absence, N. came back from London where he has been disporting himself for the past few weeks and apparently decreed differently. He sent round a curt note to say that he regretted they would, after all, not be able to attend. No reason was given, but Stephen had no hesitation in informing me it was entirely my fault owing to my incredibly bad behaviour at the Howldrevel ball! I pointed out that this event took place twelve years ago, since when I have been the very model of probity, but this cut little ice, neither did he agree that the past of almost any one of us, and even the present of many – especially Nicholas – would reveal skeletons of one sort or another. (His brief affaire with Jemima and her consequent abortion is apparently forgotten, and I could hardly be cad enough to mention it in front of Daphne!)

Both he and D. were extremely cool towards me for a while, which irritated me somewhat seeing that I am racing round like a mad woman getting things organised for Saturday. Daphne is very good at visualising the Grand Scheme, but demands many willing foot soldiers to carry out the actual work!

Fortunately most of the others that were invited were able to come and it turned out to be a delightful occasion, with many old friends present whom we haven't seen for ages. Daphne looked most attractive in a sky-blue silk dress that exactly matched her eyes and Stephen positively glowed with pride in her.

Beatrice, thank heaven, slept peaceably through it all. She has been very difficult since Nanny left. A Mrs Tremaine from the village is sleeping in at the moment and seems kind enough, but B. doesn't seem to have taken to her and cries a lot. Now that the party is over I intend to take on the job myself, if Daphne agrees. I'll have to approach the subject tactfully, but it seems to make sense to me. B. is a dear little soul, rather solemn but very affectionate.

10th May 1932
Dreadful weather all week. Dreadful week altogether. Mrs Tremaine discovered the worse for gin and summarily thrown out. Molly also gone. Pascoe in state of umbrage. Took Daphne and Beatrice to tea with Livvy in order that B. could play with Alex who is much of an age, but the outcome not entirely happy since D. talked of little but the awfulness of Cornish servants as

opposed to the excellence of their eastern counterparts, almost every sentence beginning "Now, in India . . ." Afterwards she was highly critical of Livvy's methods of bringing up Alex. She is, D. opines, far too lax. Children need discipline.

He has discipline, I say. And love. And the stimulating companionship of his mother who talks and plays with him constantly and doesn't believe in leaving him entirely to the mercy of untrained girls. When will I learn to think before speaking? Not unnaturally, D. takes this as criticism and is mortally offended, which I fear may influence her when I make my suggestion about taking over Beatrice's welfare.

12th May 1932
Stephen all for the idea, and D. has accepted it faute de mieux, *in the absence of any other candidates for the position and her own total absorption in all things sporty. Molly has been given One Last Chance, and reinstated. What happens when they go to the Winslow parents in Salisbury is up to them. I do not wish to be involved.*

20th May 1932
S. & D. left for Salisbury this morning, so all is peace for a couple of weeks. The house seems to be vibrating quietly and ever more slowly, as if it's gradually winding down and becoming settled again.

Long talk with Stephen last night after D. went to bed – almost the first time we have had a chance to talk alone since they came. He asked if I still missed Harry! Imagine! How could he possibly think otherwise?

Only every day, I said. Hard to imagine, he said, what Harry would have done with his life.

I thought about this afterwards, and decided it was rather a foolish remark because we all do things no one would ever expect. After all, who would have thought Stephen would take himself off to an outpost of the Empire? And no one, least of all I, could have imagined I would still be living at home, aged thirty-two, dancing attendance on Mother.

Harry was so young. He joined the army straight from school. He never had a chance to be anything, except a wonderful brother and a brave soldier, but the potential was there for him to do almost anything. Couldn't, afterwards, sleep for hours, thinking about him.

Why only two weeks in Salisbury? You'd think Daphne would want to see her parents for longer than that.

Louise Ashland was very quiet after Stephen and Daphne had gone to Wiltshire. She had longed to see her son and his wife and hated to admit, even to herself, that the reality of having them in the house was proving such a strain. And who would have believed that one two-year-old child could upset a household so much?

"She does seem a most *contrary* child," she complained fretfully to Verity. "So prone to tears! Stephen was never like that."

"She's hardly more than a baby, Mother," Verity pointed out. "And her life has been turned upside down. You can't blame her for being a little upset."

"That's no excuse for crying all the time."

"She doesn't cry all the time. And if she did, one could hardly blame her."

Verity would not say so to her mother, but she blamed Daphne for much. After all, with everything else new and strange, it was surely up to the child's mother to provide stability. Yet Daphne's attentions were brief and when they occurred were often confined to administering discipline of one sort or another. It seemed obvious to Verity that even a child of two could see that her mother was anxious to get away from the nursery and out on the golf course or tennis courts at the earliest possible moment.

She bit her tongue, however, and made no overt criticism, either then or later after the family had returned from Salisbury, merely devoting herself to the little girl and finding a great deal of pleasure in doing so. Beatrice seemed pleased to be back at Lemorrick and became more contented, sleeping well and crying less.

"You're sure you don't mind?" Daphne would ask as she and Stephen prepared to go out to this engagement or that. "Oh, you're an angel! Bless you! What would we do without you?"

And what will I do without Beatrice? Verity asked herself from time to time as the weeks and months went by. It was with mixed feelings that she viewed the approach of October when the family were due to return to India. Living in the same house with Stephen and Daphne was undoubtedly a strain and a return to normality seemed greatly to be desired, but on the other hand she had become very attached to her small niece. She loved looking after her – the bedtime ritual of bath and storytime and cuddles had become precious to her, the walks and the games and the sandcastles on the beach as much a joy to her as they apparently were to the little girl. (Within moderation, she provided drinks after five p.m. if required, cheerfully ignoring Daphne's strictures even when this involved bare-faced lying.)

"I hope Beatrice won't miss all this too much," she remarked once to Daphne. She had indicated the sea and the cove as she spoke, though her real fear was that Beatrice would once again suffer from being wrenched from the one who had become her constant companion. Daphne, however, had pealed with hearty laughter at her fears.

"Miss this?" she asked. "Good Lord, no! Children have a wonderful time in India and Beatrice's ayah is frightfully good at her job. Not like some who let them get away with murder."

"She'll be six when I see her again. It's hard to imagine."

"Yes." Daphne's brow clouded. "I wonder what we shall do with her then. I suppose there are boarding schools that take overseas children at six—"

"You wouldn't—?"

"We'll have to, Verity. We have no alternative."

"Are – are there to be any more?" Verity asked hesitantly. "Children, I mean."

Daphne pulled a face. "Not if I have my way. I'm not the most maternal of women, you know, and really children do interfere with one's life quite dreadfully." She glanced at Verity as she spoke, and seeing her expression had the grace to look slightly conscience-stricken. "Sorry, Vee. I suppose I shouldn't have said that to someone in your position. But it's true, you know. People without children can't imagine what it entails. You're simply never free." At this she consulted her watch. "Oh, Lord," she went on. "Look at the time! I must dash down to the Yacht Club. I'm supposed to be meeting Stephen there for lunch."

15th September 1932
Two and a bit weeks of this visitation to run. I had a letter from

Isobel this morning, inviting me to stay in Malta with them when all is over. John doesn't expect to be stationed there after the end of this year, so I ought to take the opportunity. Isobel has kindly invited Mother, too, but I know she won't want to go, and won't want me to, either, but I have to admit there is a great deal of attraction in the thought of a holiday. Stephen says that perhaps I could now think once more about going to India, since Mother seems in better spirits. Perhaps I could, I say, hoping that a bubble had not appeared over my head, as in children's comics, saying "Thinks: Not On Your Life!" Not even for a trip to the East could I put up with a month or more of dear Daphne.

It's not that I can't see her good qualities, and I readily admit that she has made Stephen happy, for which I am truly grateful, but the fact remains that we are chalk and cheese. In addition, she has no conception of the need for diplomacy among people who have no choice but to live together, and seems to regard it not only as her right, but indeed a positive virtue to Speak Out regarding the deficiences of others. Telling the truth, she calls it. Consequently, today she berated Livvy for saying she felt that the time had come for her to get back to work. A woman's place is with her child, Daphne said piously. Since I have already documented her own manner with Beatrice, I will say no more except that I was open-mouthed with astonishment and speechless with fury on Livvy's behalf!

Or am I wholly honest about this? Is it the way she patronises me, personally, that I find unforgivable? I know she looks down on me as a fuddy-duddy, frustrated spinster, the archetypical maiden aunt without sufficient looks to attract a husband. She constantly delivers herself of advice about everything, from fashion to the care of children, of which, of course, I can know nothing, not having entered the blessed state of matrimony. With as much calm as I could muster, I pointed out that I have spent considerably more time with Beatrice this week than either of her parents, at which she trilled with laughter and said what a funny old thing I am! I really must learn not to be jealous and really I mustn't envy her for having such a wonderful life, because the kind of social round she and Stephen enjoy in India really wouldn't suit me at all, I'm such a dyed-in-the-wool country-woman. Her voice suggested that this could better be expressed as "village idiot", if common politeness didn't prevent it!

I opened my mouth to refer her to the years I spent working as a journalist in London (surely evidence of a modicum of sophistication?) but shut it again without saying anything. I suppose she's right. I turned my back on that years ago. There is no doubt I am a countrywoman at heart and have no wish, now, to live anywhere but here. But envious? I should love a little girl like Beatrice, I readily admit to that, but otherwise I envy Daphne not at all.

It was a relief, as always, to talk to Isobel. As expected, Louise had not smiled with approval on the proposed visit to Malta, but urged by Frances and by Livvy, both of whom promised to call at Lemorrick as often as they could manage, Verity finally decided to go and felt much restored by the experience.

"Would the sun make nicer people of us all?" she asked Isobel, lying back in a deck-chair in the little courtyard garden, looking up at the sky through a tracery of pink bougainvillea.

Isobel, beside her, gave a lazy chuckle. "From what you tell me, the Indian sun has done little to sweeten Daphne's nature."

Verity sighed. "I shouldn't have said so much about her. She's not all bad – and Stephen adores her, which is the main thing." Then she, too, laughed. "I suppose it's hardly surprising that I'm finding it much easier to appreciate her virtues now that we're thousands of miles apart."

"It must have been a strain, having her under the same roof for so long."

"Yes, it was." Verity laughed again, reminiscently. "But you know me! The worst thing was keeping quiet. I had to keep everything sweet – well, as sweet as possible – for the baby's sake. And for mine. I didn't want Daphne to turn against me, because of Beatrice."

"As if she could!"

"Oh, she could, believe me! And I think would have done, very easily."

"Didn't Stephen have anything to say?"

"Stephen can see no fault in her. Which, I suppose, is as it should be. It must be wonderful," she went on dreamily, "not to be seen any fault in."

"I can't believe you won't find someone," Isobel said after a moment. "Tomorrow. Next week. Some time when you're

167

least expecting it. Maybe tonight, who knows? I did tell you I've invited some people for dinner on Friday, didn't I? Two rather nice couples, the Deardens and the Taylors. You'll like them. John's No.1 is coming, too. He's called Frank Gillam. He's Cornish, by the way, comes from Penzance. John thinks the world of him. Not," she added after a moment, "that I hold out any hope that you'll find he's the man of your dreams. Honestly, I'm not really matchmaking . . ."

Frank Gillam was, Verity could see, quite probably worthy of being thought the world of. She assessed him at intervals throughout dinner. He was stocky, with a broad, dependable kind of face. Brown eyes, dark crinkly hair. Smoked a pipe. In his thirties, she judged, and a little shy. Rather stiff in manner. A man's man.

The talk was largely general, and he seemed to have little to say, but later he waxed more loquacious about various places he had visited in the course of his duties. He thought highly of South Africa, had suffered from the heat in Hong Kong. Verity found, unsurprisingly since he came from Cornwall, that they had acquaintances in common. When, at the end of the evening he stayed on for a last drink after the other guests had gone, it seemed quite natural that he should agree to come on a beach picnic that Isobel had planned for the following day.

"I hope you didn't mind," she said to Verity when he, too, had gone. "He often comes out with us and I could see you were getting on reasonably well."

"As long as you don't throw me at his head—"

"Oh, I wouldn't do that!" Hotly Isobel denied any such intention. "It's just that it seemed a good idea. The boys always get on well with him, and clearly he was delighted to be asked. After all, he's on his own. No family."

"Of course I don't mind, Isobel. He seemed very pleasant. And he knows the Frobishers. Did you ever meet them? Polly and Edward, an awfully nice couple. Live near Manaccan."

"I thought you might have friends in common," Isosbel said, looking pleased.

Frank seemed more relaxed during the day at the beach. He played cricket with the children, nine-year-old Tim and six-year-old Tony, and afterwards masterminded the building of an ambitious sandcastle.

"Great kids," he said to Isobel as he returned to sit down under the shade of the umbrellas.

The remark did much to endear him to Verity, as did the obvious admiration in his eyes when he looked at her. It made her feel young again, and hopeful, as if, after all, life might still hold a few surprises for her.

"He does seem nice," she admitted to Isobel afterwards. "Why isn't he married?"

"I gather there was someone once. She married Another. It's not always easy for sailors, you know. One has to be somewhat dedicated to make a successful naval wife."

On Sunday they met at church, and all went on to a sherry party in honour of a visiting rear admiral. It seemed inevitable that in the mêlée Frank should gravitate towards Verity. No one could call him handsome, she thought as he came towards her, but he had a lovely smile. Good teeth.

Before the party was over he had invited her to go sailing with him the following afternoon. She temporised, saying that Isobel might have made plans, but when she reported the invitation Isobel urged her to accept it.

"Do go," she said. "I've got this wretched dentist's appointment, so you won't be spoiling my plans, and you'll see the island in a totally different way."

She did, and she enjoyed it, the fact that there were long silences between them not mattering in the least. In fact she thought it sensitive of him, to let her enjoy the beauty in peace.

She said as much to Isobel afterwards. "The only thing is," she said after a long pause, "I don't want him to get the wrong idea. I like him well enough, but I'm not really attracted to him."

"No. Still, he's a good man, Vee,"

"I know. It's just—" She shrugged her shoulders, not finishing the sentence. The fact was simply that Frank Gillam, nice though he might be, rang no bells for her. He was too stolid, too practical, too unconcerned with anything he couldn't see or touch or taste.

On the other hand, who was she to think she rang any bells for him? Maybe he was just being kind, doing his best to see that his friends' friend was having a good time. So she went sailing with him again, and later in the week went with Isobel and John to a dance at the Club where, of course, Frank joined them. They danced together, first a foxtrot, then a slow blues number during which Frank held her closer. Gradually – the potency of cheap music, she wondered? – she became aware of his hand on her back, his breath on her cheek, and almost in spite of herself she felt her nerves tighten and her own breath quicken. She looked into his face and smiled tentatively, aware that he, too, could feel the tension.

It had been such a long time. And she was still young, after all, the blood pulsing in her veins as urgently as ever. Was it possible? Was Frank, after all, going to prove that he was the one? Instinct told her he was hers for the taking if she chose to encourage him. She'd be safe with him. He was dependable. He liked children. He was a man!

For a second or two after the music stopped, he held her without moving, as if reluctant to loose his hold on her; then they both laughed as the spell was broken and she led the way back to the table.

Another couple were now sitting with Isobel and John, engaging John in laughing banter regarding some past naval manoeuvres that had not worked out to plan, so that it was only Isobel whose more sensitive antennae picked up the fact that subtly things had changed between them; that each was more aware of the other. Verity, catching her eye, saw the quick frown, the small, worried smile.

He took her out to dinner the following evening, to a small fish restaurant overlooking the sea, and ridiculously Verity found herself changing her mind half a dozen times about what she should wear. What could she be thinking of? It was, she felt, almost unseemly in a woman of her age.

The restaurant, he told her as they drove out of Valetta, wasn't at all a grand place. It was very simple, really, but with good, local cooking and not a bad selection of wines.

"It sounds wonderful," she said, but smiled a little with secret amusement. She could have guessed that he would choose somewhere simple; it seemed all of a piece with his uncomplicated, down-to-earth nature.

It was necessary to park the car on the road above and walk down a tortuous path lit by lanterns. There were fireflies and crickets chirping, and the sky was full of stars. Below them, they could see the creamy tops of gentle waves lapping against the shore. Frank drew her hand through his arm, smiled down at her.

"I've been looking forward to this," he said.

Cherished was the word, she thought. That's what she felt and that, she felt certain, was how it would always be with Frank. How wonderful it could be, to have someone to lean on, someone to take responsibility; someone who, like Daphne with Stephen, could see no faults, even when faults were there.

They were given a table in the window overlooking the sea, the candle flames barely flickering in the offshore wind. Verity sat back and smiled at him.

"This is lovely," she said. "What a hard life you poor sailors lead!"

"It's not always like this."

"You'll be sorry to leave Malta."

"Yes – except that I've been told I'm to have my own command."

"Really? That's wonderful! Congratulations."

He coloured a little and gave an embarrassed smile, saying no more but dealing instead with ordering the wine and food.

Once the waiter had gone, he folded his hands on the table's edge and looked at her, apparently content to do so interminably. A pause ensued.

"Do tell me more about this promotion," Verity said at last, aware of awkwardness. "What kind of vessel might you be commanding?"

"A frigate," he said, his eyes losing their look of dreamy contemplation and lighting up as at the thought of a lover.

"Is that the same as a corvette? I'm terribly ignorant, I'm afraid," she added hastily, seeing the look on his face.

He explained the difference. Both were escort vessels, he said, but a corvette was smaller than a frigate.

"I see," Verity said.

"And there are other differences, of course," he went on, proceeding to explain these in great detail, pausing only for sufficient time to allow their food to be served.

There was one thing to be said, Verity thought, some time later. When it came to talking about ships and the navy, there were no long, awkward pauses where Frank was concerned, and beyond the odd "Really?" or "How interesting!" no need, either, for her to contribute to the conversation. Of course it was entirely laudable that he should be so enthusiastic about his life's calling, but – oh dear, she hoped her eyes weren't becoming too glazed over. He really was going on at inordinate length.

His, she saw, were warm as they rested on her, the waiter having removed their empty plates.

"I must say," he said, his voice low and earnest, "that it's a delightful change to meet a woman who is so sympathetic to the way I feel. I hope I haven't bored you."

"No, no. Of course not." Hastily, mendaciously, she denied it, but thankfully took the opportunity to turn the conversation to other things. Did he enjoy reading novels about the sea? Joseph Conrad, perhaps, or Herman Melville?

He never read novels, he said.

Did he enjoy the cinema? She'd seen a marvellous film with Marlene Dietrich—

He didn't much like films. Or the theatre. The dramatisation of fictitious events seemed, to him, pointless when there was so much drama and excitement in the real world. At sea, decisions had to be made, actions taken, that affected the lives of everyone on board. That, to him, was drama.

Well, Verity asked after a pause, what did he think about the new air service that had been running from London to Cape Town since April? Did he think that aeroplanes would ever replace ships as a method of transport?

He gave a short, dismissive laugh. "I doubt it," he said. "Speed isn't everything, after all. Safety is more important, and I fail to see how the man in the street is ever going to feel safe a thousand feet in the air. No, no," he said, taking the menu from a hovering waiter. "Make no mistake. There'll never be any real alternative to sea travel."

Heavens above, Verity thought, suddenly pierced by a perceptive shaft of light. What am I thinking of? I'd be bored by him in a week.

She remembered Isobel's words: it takes dedication to be a naval wife; and that, presumably, was if one genuinely loved the man involved. She wasn't within miles of loving Frank! The little flutter of desire she had experienced at the dance was no more than the demands of a hungry body, long deprived of sexual fulfilment. She simply couldn't begin to imagine, however good and kind and devoted he might turn out to be, what it would be like to be tied to him for life, packing up and following the fleet at the drop of a hat.

Well, she thought, amused at herself. It was a nice fantasy while it lasted. She could kiss goodbye to all those children her fevered imagination had conjured from the empty air. But on the other hand, she was free. Free as a bird. Relief washed over her and she gave him a wide smile.

"I think," she said, handing the menu back to the waiter, "I'll have the crème caramel."

Ten

There was no side about Frances Courtfield, no airs and graces. Everyone from Jack Jago who had, with his family, taken Mrs Ducky's place in the Gatehouse to Jim Truelove at the Lugger and the Reverend Mr Blunden, vicar of the parish, were unanimous on the subject. Mrs Pawley at the village shop went so far as to say she was as different from the last Lady Courtfield as chalk from cheese – the poor soul, she nevertheless added, for the dowager Lady Courtfield was now crippled with arthritis and was not often seen in the village. She had removed herself to the Dower House from where, daily and imperiously, she phoned her daughter-in-law demanding this service or that.

"She must hate the fact that you and I see each other so much," Verity commented to Frances one day in the spring of 1933 as, enticed by the bright, warm weather, they walked through Howldrevel Woods, now starry with primroses. "I was never exactly her favourite person. In fact I've been totally *persona non grata* since 1918."

Frances admitted the truth of this. "She does make the odd acid comment, but I take no notice. Actually, she's quite careful not to upset me because I think she's afraid I might leave Nicholas and she wouldn't like that at all."

"I should think not! What other daughter-in-law would run around after her the way you do? But might you?" Verity added after a pause. "Leave Nicholas, I mean?"

Frances sighed. "I've thought of it, I admit," she said at last. "But he'd make quite sure I'd never see Hugh again if I did, so I feel I must hang on for the time being, at least till Hugh is old enough to make his own decisions. And really I've learned to live with it. Oh, yes, I know he's unfaithful to me. I've known for ages. He almost always has someone on the go in London, and there's a woman in Paris—"

"And you're truly able to live with that?"

"Yes." Frances shot a quick look at Verity, sensing her astonishment. "Well, it's not as if I'm desperately in love with him, is it? Or that I ever thought he was in love with me. It would be different, then."

"But you must feel—" Verity paused. How on earth would a wife feel under those circumstances? And who was she even to hazard a guess?

"Insulted? Slighted? Well, yes, there is that." For a few moments they walked in silence, neither of them speaking. "But as I said, it's something I've learned to accept. Even feel responsible for. I should never have agreed to marry him."

"That's easily said!"

"I know. What did I know of life, or men? I really was exceptionally young and foolish. And gullible! He promised me the earth, of course." They walked for a moment without speaking. "I think," she said at last, "that the moment I understood how little it meant to me, personally, was when it dawned on me that the very worst aspect of the whole affair wasn't that I felt jealous of his women, merely humiliated when I realised that other people must know about it."

"It's so sad," Verity said, halting for a moment before resuming their slow walk. "You deserve love."

Frances laughed ruefully at that. "Doesn't everyone?" she asked. "Oh, I don't deny that sometimes I long for a knight in white armour to come and sweep me off my feet, but it's not going to happen so I might as well settle for what I have got – my son, a beautiful home, this garden, incredible scenery on the doorstep, good friends, no money worries. Well," she amended, "no serious money worries, anyway."

Verity made no comment on this. Money was not something that was ever mentioned between them, but it had occurred to her that the tin industry had been in a parlous state for many years and that the Courtfield mining and shipping interests must surely have been hit by the recession along with everything else. Was it, she wondered now, Frances's money that was keeping them afloat? If so, it seemed more than short-sighted of Nicholas not to treat her with more consideration.

"Look!" As if dismissing all her troubles and disappointments, Frances had crouched down and was peering with delight at a patch of blue among the yellow of the primroses. "Forget-me-nots! They grow quite wild here. The sun must have brought them out. Oh, and look over here – there are some Lords and Ladies. I'm going to lift some of these for planting in the White Garden, in that corner by the willow."

Mention of the White Garden would only, ever, mean one thing to Verity, but she was able now to think of that childish escapade with a kind of affectionate sadness, as if it had all happened to someone else. Frances, in fact, had effected quite a number of changes there. Gardening was a passion with her, particularly the cultivation of camellias which seemed to grow very readily at Howldrevel. She had somehow induced a sweet-scented white variety to grow, espaliered, against one wall of the garden, looking so spectacular when in flower that enthusiasts travelled from far to see it. Verity could only marvel at the depth of her knowledge. For her part, while appreciating the beauty of flowers, she had always been content to leave the growing of them to Pascoe's somewhat curmudgeonly devices.

The garden at Lemorrick was, in any case, not large by country house standards, but standing on the cliff as it did, with an incomparable view of the sea and coastline, it seemed as if its grounds were almost limitless.

A great deal of shipping on the horizon today, Verity wrote in her diary during the early summer of 1934. as she sat on the window seat in her bedroom. *I wonder where it's all going to and coming from. It occurs to me how little I have strayed from the place of my birth (if I were a turtle, I wouldn't have far to return to lay my eggs!). Apart from the holiday in Malta the year before last, and the tour through France with Livvy and Robert, I have been nowhere outside this country. And not too many places inside it, come to think of it. Should like to go to Italy before I die, however. But alone? It's not a very appealing proposition.*

She and her mother went, instead, to Torquay, at Louise's earnest request – made, Verity felt sure, merely because Mrs Radley had expressed astonishment that neither had ever been to such a fashionable watering place. It proved, in Verity's eyes, a pointless exercise. Torquay was pleasant enough, but to have nothing much to do except sit on the hotel terrace amid the palms or take gentle strolls along the sea-front bored her to extinction. If it were sea that was required, she preferred the untamed variety to be found at Porthallic; still, for her mother's sake, she bore it all as cheerfully as she could.

It was a relief to get home again and immerse herself once more in all the activities that had now become her life; little, parochial things, perhaps, but important to the people she loved. There was an urgent need for equipment for the new maternity ward at the hospital, and Robert had set his heart on an X-ray machine. A fund-raising fête was being organised, to take place at Howldrevel, for which a million things still had to be arranged. There was to be a village concert, too, for which Verity had assumed responsibility, but which was still woefully short of willing "turns".

She went, at the earliest possible moment, to Howldrevel in order to consult with Frances, and was shown into the sitting room that had always been the domaine of the lady of the house. It was small, cluttered, cosy. An oversize desk in the window spilled over with seed catalogues, account books, unanswered letters and fashion magazines. Frances had replaced the heavy pictures that had been her predecessors' taste with numerous flower prints and had taken down the dark red curtains to put pale green ones patterned with leaves in their place, but in essence the room was much the same as it had always been. Two Queen Anne chairs faced each other across the fireplace, a more modern Chesterfield upholstered in pale green was at right angles to them, in front of it a long, low rosewood coffee table.

"Please, Miss, Lady Courtfield is on the telephone and says she'll be with you in a moment," the maid said.

Verity sat down to wait, and because she would choose to read the telephone directory or the back of a sauce bottle if nothing else presented itself, she reached for a magazine that lay on the coffee table even though it was clearly a serious publication devoted to gardening.

There was an article on mulch, another on making your own compost, another on the Defence of the Conifer. (Were they under attack? If so, by whom?)

Idly she turned the pages, and as she did so, a name seemed to jump out at her. Startled, she brought the page closer to study it more carefully.

Dr Lawrence Grenfell, BSc, PhD. There it was, in black and white. She hadn't imagined it, then.

With a mouth that was suddenly dry, she read on. Dr Grenfell was the author of an article entitled "Camellias: Their Care and Propagation". Inset in the centre column was a small panel. Dr Grenfell, it informed readers, was an assistant director of Kew Gardens, an authority on camellias and the author of *Gardens in the South West, The Camellia Quest* and *From the Old World to the New: A History of Camellias*. He had, it further stated, travelled widely in Asia in search of new species.

Surely, it had to be Laurie! She was still staring at the name when, moments later, Frances entered the room, full of apologies. Blankly, Verity looked up at her.

"Vee, what is it?" Frances stopped in mid-sentence and stared at her, concerned by her expression. "What on earth's the matter?"

Wordlessly, Verity handed her the magazine, and Frances looked at it, her brows drawn together. Puzzled, she looked up after a few seconds. "I don't get it—"

Verity found her voice at last. "You see who wrote it? Dr Lawrence Grenfell, it says."

"Yes. He's quite well known. I've got one of his books—"

"It's Laurie, Fran. It must be! It's the sort of thing he always wanted to do."

"Laurie?" Frances was still uncomprehending, then light dawned. "You mean *your* Laurie? The Laurie who worked here?"

"I think it must be."

"Oh!" For a second, Frances seemed unable to grasp the full import of this. Then her expression melted in sympathy. "Oh, Vee!"

"Ironic, isn't it?" Verity gave a tight, humourless smile. "He wasn't good enough for me when we were young. Now he's a well-known botanist and author, respected in high places. My mother would have the red carpet out for him in no time at all."

"Oh, Vee," Frances said again.

"Well, there we are," Verity said, briskly dismissing the subject. "We were both young and foolish. Now come on, show me your plans for the fête. Where do you propose to stage the dance display?"

Frances took no notice of this. "You've never really forgotten him, have you?" she said.

For a moment Verity said nothing, then briefly she closed her eyes and shook her head. "No," she said. "My first love. I know

I made a fool of myself over Michael, but that was—different. Looking back, I think it was sex, pure and simple. Well, simple, anyway! Laurie was—" she broke off, shaking her head again. "Oh, I'm probably deluding myself, Fran. We were young, after all, and he was very mixed up about a lot of things. And moody."

"But you loved him."

"Oh, I did. I did."

"Well—" For a moment Frances looked at her, a small, cynical smile twisting her lips. "Maybe you should regard it as an enriching experience. I've never loved anyone like that. I don't know what it's like."

Verity laughed, briefly. "It's heaven when it goes well, hell when it doesn't. A mixed blessing, you could say."

"At least it's living," Frances said.

For a moment they looked at each other, each occupied with their own thoughts, then Frances took a breath and reached for a folder. "This is what I thought about the dance display," she said. "At the bottom of the lawn in front of those rhododendrons there's a kind of natural amphitheatre—"

With an effort, Verity concentrated on the fête and nothing more was said about Laurie; Frances even managed to avoid mentioning the clump of camellia bushes which she intended to form a backdrop to the garden stall.

They drank coffee, chatted of Torquay and of Frances's forthcoming holiday in the villa of a friend of Nicholas's in Tuscany. It was only as Verity was leaving that the subject of Laurie was introduced once more.

"He might not be married," Frances said. "Why don't you write to him, Vee? You could write care of the magazine. Just say you read the article and are glad he's achieved his ambition. It couldn't hurt."

Slowly Verity shook her head as if reluctant to dismiss the notion.

"I don't think so, Fran. After all, I may have only just discovered what he's doing, but he's always known where to find me. No, I'll just write it off as a half-happy ending. I am truly pleased he's doing what he wanted to do."

"Maybe you're right," Frances conceded.

But she looked sad, Verity thought as she drove away, as if she would have loved there to be a romantic end to this story.

The year moved on. The fête was pronounced a great success, and soon after, Frances, Nicholas and Hugh went to Tuscany. The family who were to be their hosts were very grand, Frances told Verity before they left, and Villa Prezzolini was of palatial proportions, far more luxurious than Howldrevel. There was a swimming pool made of Carrara marble and any number of horses to ride; even so, Frances declared that she was not looking forward to it.

"I'm uncomfortable there," she said. "And so is poor Hugh. The Prezzolinis are incredibly cold and formal, not a bit as one imagines Italians to be. I've always thought they loved children, but that's one trait that seems to have been left out of their make-up. The old *nonna* is quite sweet, but all the others scare me to death. Nicholas just adores it there, of course. He and Giovanni are thick as thieves, always off on some huntin', shootin' and fishin' expedition, while I'm incarcerated with the Prezzolini women, so we have to stay there for three whole weeks."

In view of this, Verity was surprised when, less than a couple of weeks later, she received a telephone call from Frances, made from the Courtfields' town house in Lowndes Square.

"Frances! What are you doing in London?" she asked her. "Shouldn't you be in Italy?"

"I made an excuse and came back with Hugh," Frances said. "I said the heat was too much for him – and so it was! Too much for me, anyway. In fact, everything was too much for me. Listen, Vee, I've had a marvellous idea. Couldn't you come up here for a few days? We could shop and go to a few shows together. It would be fun. Do say you will!"

It took a little arranging to leave at short notice, and as always Louise Ashland was not best pleased. Sudden decisions and changes of plan invariably brought on headaches, attacks of nerves, and (as Verity reported to Livvy) dry rot in the wooden leg; but Livvy advised turning a deaf ear to the complaints, assuring Verity that there was nothing wrong, as far as she could see.

"And I'm only at the end of a telephone," she said. "I can be at Lemorrick within minutes if necessary – which it won't be, I'll bet my bottom dollar. Go on, a break will do you good."

It was with a feeling of pleasurable anticipation, therefore, that Verity caught the Cornish Riviera Express to Paddington. It was some time since she had been in London, even longer since she had seen a good play, and she was looking forward to the change that this short excursion promised.

Frances and Hugh were at the station to meet and greet her, Frances effusively, but Hugh with his usual reserve. He was a tall child for his age, and the Italian sun had given him more than the usual amount of colour in his cheeks, but he still managed to appear nervous and rather fragile. He had taken, lately, to wearing spectacles to correct a minor eye problem. Frances, Verity knew, worried about the fact that he was to go to prep school when the term started in September. He seemed unready for it, she said. Too shy and too unable to stand up for himself.

Verity, knowing it to be inevitable, was bracing. "Maybe it will be the making of him," she said.

"That's what Nicholas says."

"He could be right."

"He says I molly-coddle him. But Vee, have you ever known a child of eight suffer from insomnia? Hugh does! He's awake far into the night, I've tip-toed up and seen him! He won't admit it but I think he's terrified about going away to school. He lies there worrying about it. It breaks my heart."

Verity sympathised, but she knew, just as Frances did, that Hugh's fate was sealed as far as his schooling was concerned. He would go to prep school and then to Eton, just as his father had done before him. In Nicholas's opinion there was nothing else to be said.

She felt sorry for the child, and it was a matter of regret to her that her usual ease in the company of children seemed to desert her with Hugh. Amicable overtures were greeted with the barest twitch of a smile and a flicker of the eye. Any conversations she might initiate died still-born. Maybe she tried too hard, she told herself.

Mrs Probert, the housekeeper who looked after the house in Lowndes Square, had considerably more success with him, probably because Hugh had known her from the time he was a baby. She was a plump, motherly soul who talked without ceasing, which, said Frances, was probably the secret of her success. Hugh felt under no pressure to respond.

That morning, prior to meeting the train, mother and son had spent several hours together at the Natural History Museum.

"He must have enjoyed that, surely," Verity said.

Frances looked worried. "Yes, I think so. It's so difficult to tell with him."

"Does he open up a little more with Nicholas?" Verity asked.

"Nicholas? Heavens, no! He feels far too much on trial," Frances said. "Something happened in Italy that was so typical. Nicholas insisted on his riding a particularly fearsome-looking horse. I shall never forget the expression on that poor little boy's face until my dying day. He was, quite literally, petrified. He simply couldn't move, which of course meant that his father shouted at him and called him a miserable coward, humiliating him in front of several assorted Prezzolinis. The poor child hardly wanted to come out of his room after that." She sighed. "Nicholas says I spoil him, of course. I don't think I do. I just try to restore the balance a bit. The funny thing is," she added, "the one thing on earth that Hugh wants to do is to please his father. He longs to make him proud, longs to ride and shoot like he does. It sometimes seems to me like the making of a tragedy, with nothing I can do to make things better."

"I'm sure that's not true, Fran," Verity said comfortingly. "Just knowing you're on his side must make a difference. And under the circumstances, school might not be so bad. It can rub the corners off, after all."

Frances looked far from convinced but she did not pursue the matter, for it was time for them to go and change before joining some of Nicholas's Courtfield relations for cocktails in Cadogan Square.

"I'm sorry about this," Frances said when later they met downstairs. "I simply couldn't avoid it. At least we have tickets for the theatre so have an excuse to leave before too long."

"I don't mind a bit," Verity said. "That dress is gorgeous, Fran. Is it new?"

"I bought it yesterday. Do you really like it?"

It was a pale gold satin shift, artfully cut on the cross, with a long-sleeved bolero in the same material. Frances twisted a little to catch a glimpse of her backview in the gilt-framed mirror over the fireplace.

"It's really lovely," Verity assured her. "You simply must help me with some concentrated clothes shopping before I go home. I need your advice."

"Love to," Frances said. "It'll be fun."

The heat had gone out of the day and they enjoyed the short stroll to Cadogan Square. They had tickets for Ibsen's *A Doll's House*, and in view of the cocktail invitation had decided to eat after the theatre.

The Courtfield cousins were pleasant and had invited some entertaining guests. It was all a million miles away from Lemorrick, Verity thought, as she stood, glass in hand, beside an open window overlooking the square, exchanging frothy conversation with a man from an advertising agency. It was superficial chat, totally without any hint of profundity, but he made her laugh and for a few moments she felt young and carefree again. The light curtains were blowing gently in the welcome breeze, the faint hum that was London a background to it all. It all seemed highly civilised, reminiscent of other, more exciting days.

Eventually a taxi was called and they left to go to the theatre. They were both in good spirits as they took their seats, and the excellence of the acting absorbed them both from the beginning. It was a little before the end of the first act that Verity became aware of her companion's almost unnatural stillness. Was Frances seeing a parallel between her own marriage and that of Nora and Torvald, she wondered? It seemed possible. Nora was an intelligent woman, forced to act like an irresponsible ninny to feed the ego of her husband. On the face of it, it did not appear too far removed from the relationship between Frances and Nicholas.

Frances was leaning forward slightly, her eyes fixed on the figures on the stage, her breathing barely perceptible. At the interval she seemed subdued, but assented quickly when Verity asked her if she were enjoying it.

"Oh, I am." She peered at her programme. "Who is that girl who's playing Nora? She's marvellous, isn't she? D'you know, I had no idea of the story. I even thought it was a comedy. How dreadfully ignorant I am! I expect everyone else in the entire world knows it back to front."

"I wouldn't say that."

"I'm sure you did."

"Well, yes, but. . ." Verity's voice trailed away. Frances wasn't listening. It was as if she were still hearing the actors' voices, as if they were communicating something to her that only she could hear.

Alerted to her reaction during the first act, Verity glanced towards her as the play reached its climax. On the stage, across a bare table, Nora was facing the husband who had become a stranger, hating his lack of morals, coldly tearing him to shreds before walking out and slamming the door behind her. Frances, she saw, appeared mesmerised, her lip caught between her teeth, breath apparently suspended.

She was, perhaps, quieter than usual on the way home. Mrs Probert greeted them with her customary cheerfulness, and assured them that Hugh went happily to bed after beating her at halma. She'd left a cold collation in the drawing room, she told them, with a bottle of champagne on ice.

"Then please don't wait up for us," Frances said. "We can take care of ourselves."

"What an excellent woman," Verity said appreciatively as she poured a glass for each of them and handed one to Frances. "And my goodness, Fran, this food looks wonderful – lobster and prawns and a scrumptious-looking salad. She can prepare a cold collation for me any time she likes."

Frances barely looked at the meal. "Actually, I'm not the least bit hungry," she said. "But yes, Mrs Probert is a gem, I suppose. At any rate, she's always been good with Hugh." She took a few sips of her champagne and gave a shrill little laugh, quickly cut off. "She doesn't approve of me, of course."

Verity looked at her, frowning. "Why on earth not?"

"Well, Nicholas uses this house far more often than I do, and when I do come here, I always have the feeling that she regards me with a kind of – I don't know. A kind of contemptuous pity, I suppose. I'm sure she knows exactly what Nicholas gets up to and thinks I ought to put a stop to it. Be more forceful. Not just stay down in Cornwall and let him get on with it."

"It's your life, Fran. You must do what suits you."

Fran gave another brief, despairing laugh. "I wouldn't go so far as to say it suits me. I'm weak, Vee. Like Nora, in the play."

"You're not in the least like Nora."

"There are ways and ways of being weak. Nicholas doesn't cosset me or call me his little squirrel, but he knows I'll put up with anything he cares to throw at me. I've proved it, over and over."

"Nora wasn't weak in the end, was she? You don't have to go on putting up with things."

Fran sighed, moving about the room in an agitated kind of way.

"I think I do," she said, after a pause. Then she gave a brittle little laugh. "Oh, take no notice of me, Vee! You see what a little taste of the high life does? It brings out all my latent restlessness. Why can't I be more like you?"

Verity looked astonished. "Like me? What on earth can you mean?"

"You're so – oh, I don't know. Sane. Balanced. You've had some lousy luck in your time, but you just get on with your life, never moping or complaining."

"Don't you believe it!" Verity looked at Frances with a worried frown. She had never seen her in this kind of mood before. "When it comes to moping, believe me, I take the cake. Of course," she said, attempting to lighten the atmosphere a little, "I'll never be quite up to my mother's standard when it comes to complaining, especially when she gets on to the subject of my single state."

"Take it from me," Frances said bitterly, "you're better off single."

"She had high hopes of snaring Nicholas at one time. Did I ever tell you?"

"You had a lucky escape. She ought to be thankful."

"Oh, Fran!" Verity's tone changed again and she looked at her friend with affectionate compassion. "What is it? Has something happened?"

Abruptly Frances turned and poured more champagne into her glass.

"Nothing very unusual," she said. "Just Nicholas, losing control of himself. It's why I came back from Italy."

"How do you mean?"

For a moment Frances said nothing, then she put her glass down and very deliberately took off the bolero. Along the length of both arms there was massive bruising, black and purple and livid yellow.

Verity stared at her. "Fran! Are you saying Nicholas did that?"

"Yes."

"Does he often—?" For some reason she could not bring herself to utter the words.

"Quite often."

"Oh, Fran!" After a horrified moment Verity went to her, holding her rigid, unyielding body in her arms. "You've got to report it. Tell the police."

Gently, Frances disengaged herself. "I know I should," she said. "But I can't. There'd be a scandal and it would be bound to hurt Hugh. I shouldn't have told you. It must be all the emotion of this evening. The play—"

"But you're not in a play, Fran. This is life, and I don't see how you can go on living it like this."

"I suppose in a way it's my fault."

"How can it be? Nothing excuses a thing like that."

"Well, you see—" Fran sighed and replaced her concealing jacket. She picked up her glass, wandered over to a chair and sat down. "There are times," she went on in a tight, hard voice, looking down into her drink, "when I am—" She paused, then with a touch of defiance looked up at Verity. "When not to put too fine a point on it, I'm less than happy for him to exercise his marital rights. Times when he comes home and I know damned well he's been getting all he wants from women up here. And even if it weren't for them—" Her voice quavered suddenly, and she paused again, biting her lip.

"Fran," Verity said gently. "Talk if you want, but don't think you have to."

"I want to," she said. "Now I've started. The thing is that – oh, I know I'm inexperienced about men! I married out of the schoolroom and I've only, ever, been with Nicholas. But surely, surely, there has to be some tenderness, even if there's no love? There can be kindness, can't there? With him, everything is so sudden, so brutal, so lacking in any kind of consideration or humanity. Oh, Vee, I'm sorry! We were so happy tonight and now I've spoilt everything."

"Don't be silly! You should have told me long ago – told someone, anyway."

"I didn't think anyone would believe me. He's always careful not to mark me anywhere where it shows."

"That time you had a black eye, the time you said you'd walked into a door—"

"Well, yes. That was an exception, I admit. But usually there's nothing to show at all, and on the surface he seems quite – well, ordinary. And he's a Baronet, don't forget. Men like that don't knock their wives about. That's the prerogative of the lower classes after closing time on a Saturday night."

Verity thought this over. "I've always known he had the capacity for violence," she said slowly. "But I never guessed – Fran, you can't go on like this! There are years ahead of you."

"And a child to think about. I can't leave him."

"If you divorced Nicholas for cruelty, you would have custody of Hugh."

"Hugh loves his father. Oh, he's afraid of him, as I told you, but he still looks on him as some kind of hero. And of course he was, in the war. And he's frightfully good at shooting defenceless birds and riding and hitting a ball about – all the things that Hugh would love to be able to do and doesn't seem to have any natural talent for. I don't know if he'd forgive me if I took him away from his father. And then there's Howldrevel. I'm not sure he'd forgive me if I took him away from that, either. Anyway, Nicholas would fight it, tooth and nail, and I have no doubt he'd win. As I said, he's Sir Nicholas Courtfield, with heaven knows how many friends in high places from school days and the navy. I don't think I'd have a chance."

"Don't you hold the purse-strings? That must give you some say in things."

"That's not how it is. Oh, I did have money – lots of it – when he asked me to marry him, and I was allowed to keep some, but not very much. I was such a little fool that I allowed Nicholas – and my aunt, who was so keen to get rid of me – to talk me into signing over an enormous sum as a dowry. It seems quite senseless now. I can't imagine what made me do it, except that money didn't seem important to me then. And of course, I was persuaded that it made no difference, that after we were married we would be as one, with a common purpose and common desires. How totally fatuous that turned out to be! So, as people say under these circumstances, I've made my bed and I must lie on it. And usually I manage to. It was just that damned play that somehow churned up my emotions. So come on—" She made an effort and attempted a smile, holding out her glass towards Verity. "More champagne, please. Let's eat, drink and be merry. Maybe things will look better in the morning."

2nd September 1934

Such revelations! I responded to Fran in a quite inadequate way, but I am so truly appalled that it was hard to know what to say. Appalled, but not entirely surprised, for I have first-hand experience of Nicholas's violence; not just that attack on me,

187

but the way he laid into Laurie that terrible evening. I've never forgotten it. The look on his face was terrifying. My heart aches for Fran who is such a gentle soul. Too gentle. There must be something she can do.

Astonishingly, the next morning found Frances paler than usual, but calm, and apparently looking forward with pleasure to taking Hugh to the Science Museum as she had promised, and to shopping with Verity later in the day.

And as they tried on the new dresses and fingered materials, it was a marvel to Verity to see how normal she appeared, how funny and carefree, laughing as together they egged each other on to spend far more than either had intended.

Verity was pleased with her purchases, particularly a slim-fitting linen dress with a matching flared jacket. "Though when I'll wear it, heaven knows," she said.

"It's the sort of thing you can wear anywhere."

"You sound just like that poisonous saleswoman."

"Modom can dress it up, with a pearl choker, and a brooch placed *so*," Frances said, in strangulated accents.

"Poor soul! Imagine being dependent at that age on the whims of other women for your livelihood."

"Well, at least we didn't go away empty-handed. We bought things. Maybe too many."

"I'm beyond caring."

In the evening, they went to see the play which had been Verity's particular choice, *Richard of Bordeaux*. It was as good as anything she had ever seen, but in spite of that she found her mind wandering during the second act.

What a lottery it all was, she thought. And how much worse was an unhappy marriage than no marriage at all. She wished, very much, that her mother could come to this conclusion and stop fretting about her inability to find a husband; even more, she wished that there could be a happy outcome to Frances's predicament.

But when two days later she caught the train back home, she was fully aware that whatever her wishes, nothing very much was likely to change.

Eleven

10th June 1935
Cloudless sky and azure-blue sea. Livvy had a day off, so
we walked over the cliffs as far as Portrec for a swim. There
were larks singing, and dragonflies skimming over the gorse
and countless butterflies. The talk, mainly, was of old times, and
we laughed a lot. Had lunch at the Old Ship Inn. Fresh-caught
mackerel and fried potatoes. Wonderful! We both agreed that we
didn't remember the water being quite so cold in our younger
days, which is a rather distressing sign of the passage of years.
Still it was, as we kept assuring each other, lovely once you're
in, and all in all it was a lovely day. Good to be able to talk,
too. Normally, on the occasions Livvy isn't working, she has Alex
with her, but today his grandmother collected him from school to
give L. an uninterrupted break. He is a very nice little boy and
I am devoted to him, but it was very good to have a child-free
conversation for once.
It seems L. is expecting another baby in seven months' time,
but not a word to anyone as she wants to go on working for as
long as possible and people tend to look askance. I do not look
askance, but am very happy for her even if I have to admit to a
touch of envy. More than a touch.
Returned to find that a letter from Daphne had arrived . . .

"And she's already talking about their leave next year," Louise
told her, before she could read the letter for herself. "And would
you believe it, it seems they might be leaving India! After all this
time! Stephen's been offered promotion, but it means moving to
Singapore. Didn't I always say he would do well? I knew it was
only a matter of time! I remember saying so to your dear father
. . . Of course, it involves a lot of disruption. They think it would
be best if little Beatrice comes home to school."

189

Verity stared at her. "Surely not! She's not six yet—"

"Daphne has been in correspondence with several schools that take very young children. It seems it's not unusual."

"And what about the holidays? She's to come here, I suppose."

"Well, of course, dear." Louise looked at her daughter with mild astonishment. "I must say I expected you to be pleased. And so did Daphne. Look, read her letter for yourself. Here it is, on the second page. 'I know one person who'll be delighted at the news. Auntie Verity will be able to have our little Bea all to herself.' There!"

"You can write back and tell her that Auntie Verity is disgusted that she should contemplate sending a child of five away from home."

"She'll be almost six by then."

"She's still a baby, Mother. Look at little Alex. Can you imagine Livvy packing him off to boarding school? I won't connive at it, or make it easy for them. Daphne can make all the excuses she wants about disruption, but she's been wanting to get shot of Beatrice ever since she was born."

Louise remonstrated a little. "That seems rather hard, dear."

"Don't you remember what she was like when they were home last time?"

Louise put on the glasses that hung on a gold chain around her neck and skimmed through the letter again. "Well, I don't think anything we say will make any difference," she said at last. "It does sound as if she's made up her mind."

"Then she'll have to unmake it," Verity asserted stubbornly. "Unless—" she added in another kind of voice, a few seconds later.

"Unless what?"

"Unless," she amended thoughtfully, "she allows Beatrice to be educated at home. At a day school, I mean. She could make her home here, couldn't she, and go to school in Truro? That would be rather a different cup of tea. I wouldn't mind taking her every day."

"Have her here? All the time?" Louise looked dismayed. "Oh, I don't know if I would want that, Verity. Holidays are one thing, but to have a child here all the time—" Lost for words, she shook her head dolefully. "Why, think of all the crying,

190

and the paddies she used to get into! My nerves would be in tatters."

"She was tiny and her world had been turned upside down. She wasn't like that by the time they left and she won't be like that now."

Louise still looked doubtful, but having talked the matter over with Mrs Radley, a most enthusiastic grandmother, she came to the conclusion that perhaps the arrangement might, after all, have something to be said for it.

"Young life about the place," Mrs Radley gushed. "My dear Mrs Ashland, there's really nothing like it. Mark my words, you'll be all the happier for it. And think what a difference it will make to poor Verity's life."

Louise remained unconvinced that Lemorrick would be in any way enriched by the presence of a child, but saw the point about Verity – poor Verity, whose chance of having a baby of her own had surely gone for ever.

"Well, dear, I've thought it over," she said, a few days later, "and if you're determined to have little Beatrice here, I won't raise any objection even though there's no doubt it will be very hard on me. I shall just have to bite on the bullet and think of the greatest good of the greatest number. Perhaps it would be best if you were to write to Daphne. It'll come better from you, though of course I shall be writing myself to dear Stephen before too long to congratulate him on his advancement. I must say," she added with an air of dutiful, if painful, self-denial, "that it seems an excellent idea for them to rent a house nearer London for at least part of their leave. When you write, tell Daphne that if it's more convenient for Stephen's visits to Whitehall, then I am quite prepared to sacrifice the pleasure of having them here."

Verity looked at her with some amusement, but there was no trace of irony in her mother's expression. Louise's capacity for deluding herself seemed endless, she sometimes thought.

She wrote her letter; in fact, she wrote several letters before she achieved what she considered the right tone. It was no use overtly opposing Daphne's decision, nor did she wish her now overwhelming desire to keep Beatrice at Lemorrick to appear too much like the obsession of a crack-pot maiden aunt. It was not easy to hit the right note of caring breeziness, but she felt, on the fourth attempt, that she had done as well as

191

possible and went to post the letter before she could change her mind.

"I wouldn't put it past Daphne to insist on boarding school just to put me in my place," she said gloomily to Frances.

Frances looked at her quizzically. "You're terribly keen on the idea, aren't you? Better not build your hopes up."

"I'm trying not to." Verity cocked an eyebrow at her and smiled ruefully. "Pathetic, isn't it? Poor, childless old maid—"

"You're no such thing!"

"What am I, then? I'm unmarried and I have no children."

"Well, you're not poor, in any sense of the word. Or pathetic."

"Perhaps not." Verity drew in her breath determinedly. "No, I'm not! I refuse to be. I've got a pretty full life, one way and another. Did I tell you I'm putting up for the Council? Mr Pawley suggested it to me. It seems the regulars at the Lugger agreed I would be the right person, and I confess it rather tickled my fancy. But oh, Fran, I do want Bea to come here! I want her to grow up free and fearless and secure, and I want her to have the kind of education I never had."

"You'll have her for the holidays, wherever she goes to school."

"She's too little for boarding school. Much, much too little."

It worried her, thinking of how little she was; how lost she would surely be if she were to be plunged into some large institution, no matter how accustomed it was to accepting small girls from the colonies.

The letter she finally received from Daphne was non-committal. It was sweet of Verity to offer to have little Bea, she wrote, and they were thinking the matter over carefully. Once in England, they would inspect the recommended schools and see how they felt then.

It was a bleak day in the February of 1936 – a day when the sea and the cove were alike painted in shades of grey and even the seagulls looked cold – that Stephen and his family arrived from London. They had been in England three weeks by that time and had settled into the rented house they had found in Twickenham. All were laid low with colds.

"This frightful climate!" Daphne said. "How on earth do any of you manage to live in it? We've been miserable as sin ever since we got here, haven't we, darling? What with the weather and the servant situation and the impossibility of getting the house warm, we're all just about on our last legs. Beatrice, stop sniffing like that and blow your nose, for heaven's sake."

It was a miserable beginning to a miserable two weeks' stay. The cold seemed to paralyse Daphne and she seldom stirred from beside the fire in the morning room, snapping Stephen's head off if he so much as suggested a walk, let alone a round of golf. She even lost her enthusiasm for driving around the countryside inspecting schools.

However, the family returned to Twickenham with no final decision made about Beatrice's future. Letters flew between them. Beatrice had a bad attack of measles.

"Such a bore," Daphne wrote. "The nurse we engaged was quite unsuitable so I had to care for her myself."

"Oh, the poor soul," murmured Verity sarcastically on reading this.

"Of course, if little Bea comes here there will be all those childish ailments to cope with," Louise reminded her. "There are bound to be bad times as well as good." But Verity smiled and said nothing.

1st March 1936
Daphne has arranged to see a school in Surrey, and seems hopeful that it will be suitable, but still no positive decision about Beatrice.

Wish I could think clearly and dispassionately about the whole question. Is my desire to have B. here entirely motivated by love for her, or am I affected by (a) my desperation to have a child of my own and (b) the far less worthy desire to prove how far my own mothering skills are superior to Daphne's! I do not like her, I have to admit. Not that I would make any attempt to alienate B.'s affections. I have faced that danger and warned myself off. On the other hand I admit to pleasure when B. turns to me rather than her mother, which seems a highly unedifying emotion.

It is one thing for me to think in my heart that Daphne shouldn't be allowed within a mile of any child, but quite another to say that Beatrice would be better off without her. Mothers remain important, no matter what their failings – and really, children seem to survive any amount of neglect and still grow up in a perfectly satisfactory way.

Arranged today to go up to Twickenham next week to thrash out whole affair.

9th March 1936. Twickenham
Terrible day, cold, wet and windy. Leafy suburb. House, owned by ex-India hand, full of Benares brass, with a particularly obscene amputated elephant's foot umbrella stand in the hall.

Stephen has grown very like Father in his manner and tends to stand on the hearthrug in front of the fire, thumbs in armholes of waistcoat, rocking heel to toe just like Father did before delivering himself of some weighty pronouncement concerning the government. No weighty pronouncement from S., though. Just a non-stop monologue concerning his various triumphs among the natives. Daphne smiles through it all, reminding him of various successes he has unwittingly forgotten.

Spent the entire evening exercising tact on many diverse fronts, which – not at all to my credit – I found extremely trying.

10th March 1936
Stephen, once more in position on hearthrug, informs me that they have decided to leave Beatrice with me for the next three years, though would like her to go to boarding school at the age of nine.

Cannot begin to describe how pleased I am. Later, when alone with Daphne, I attempt to assure her that I will never attempt to take her place in B.'s affections, at which she gives her hard little laugh and says that in any case, that would be impossible. Beatrice adores her.

I get the impression that Stephen has, for once, over-ridden her wishes in this matter, probably for financial reasons.

Reasons didn't matter. Verity was simply overjoyed that she was, after all, to give a home to Beatrice. She travelled back to Porthallic with her mind full of plans, seeing little of the countryside that sped past the window. There were all kinds of arrangements to be made, a school to be found being perhaps the most important. She'd heard good things about Fairlawns, in Truro, and would immediately set about investigating it.

It was Stephen who brought Beatrice down to Porthallic at Easter, Daphne having decided to stay with her parents over the holiday. They still had two months of their leave to run, but it seemed sensible, he said, to get Beatrice enrolled in her new school so that she could start the term after the Easter holidays. Besides, they had decided to spend much of their remaining time on the Continent.

Beatrice waved him goodbye quite happily when the time came for him to go.

"Now can we go and buy my school clothes?" she asked eagerly, the moment his car had gone out of the drive.

"Tomorrow, I promise," Verity said. "Let's go down on the beach while the sun's shining, shall we?"

"*Yes*! Come on, Auntie Vee—"

The beach was sheltered from the wind and it felt warmer down there, the sun glinting on the shallow pools left by the receding tide. Beatrice jumped from rocks and splashed through pools until, tiring of this, she set about collecting shells in her little tin bucket embellished with the picture of Mickey Mouse, while Verity sat on a sun-warmed rock and relished the moment, a little awed, now it came to the point, by the responsibility she had taken on. She would do her very best, with God's help, she thought humbly. What more could anyone do?

The warmth went out of the spring afternoon, and they went home to toast crumpets in front of the fire. Verity, watching Beatrice's small, flushed face as she held the toasting fork to the blaze, was suddenly conscious of an all-consuming happiness in which her previous diffidence had no place at all.

"I'm glad you're here," she said to Beatrice.

"Me, too. Can we go tomorrow *morning* to get my new clothes?"

Fairlawns School was run by two elderly sisters, the Misses Heycroft, in a large house at the top of Lemon Street, the elder Miss Heycroft being known as Miss Violet, the younger as Miss May. It was Miss May who became Beatrice's teacher. She was a sweet, gentle soul, and Beatrice seemed to settle down well under her tutelage.

"Such a dear little girl," Miss May said to Verity when she inquired about Beatrice's progress. "So anxious to please, and quiet as a little mouse. I wish they were all like that, I can tell you."

"Is that natural, do you think?" It was a point that worried Verity. Sometimes it seemed to her that Beatrice was too quiet, too neat, too anxious to please, in spite of which she seemed to have few friends and when asked, never wanted to invite any of her schoolmates home to tea. Miss May, however, brushed aside any doubts.

"The other children have all been here since the age of four," she said. "Settling in is bound to take time. And as for being anxious to please – well, she's just a little girl who thrives on praise. Don't we all, Miss Ashland?"

With which Verity had to agree; still, it did seem strange to her that Beatrice should be quite so amenable. She never seemed to rebel against any rules that might be laid down; never begged for an extra half-hour at bedtime, or flew into the kind of paddy she had indulged in when she was a toddler.

Her bedroom was always neat, with her toys arranged in careful rows. The small desk which Verity had bought for her was never cluttered, nor were the books and crayons she kept inside it ever in any kind of disorder. Thinking back to her own chaotic nursery days, Verity was astonished by such inborn tidiness. It didn't seem right, somehow. She would positively have welcomed some minor naughtiness.

"Just think yourself lucky," Frances said one day when, during the summer holidays, Verity took Beatrice to tea at Howldrevel. It was a glorious day and the two women were sitting on the terrace, watching the children in the garden below as Hugh kicked a ball and Beatrice, uncomplainingly, ran to find it. "Hugh has changed so much since he went to school. He seems to regard as a point of honour the necessity to argue about every single thing he's asked to do."

"At least he's playing very nicely with Beatrice."

Frances laughed. "Making sure she takes a female, subservient role, you notice."

"She seems happy," Verity said.

But as they drove home through the lanes, Beatrice seemed, even for her, unnaturally quiet and unresponsive to her aunt's conversational gambits. Later, when Verity went upstairs to tuck

196

her up and say goodnight, she found her sitting up in bed, her face strangely pinched.

She sat on the bed and took her hands. "Is there something wrong, darling? Are you unhappy?"

Beatrice shook her head vigorously, avoiding Verity's eye by lying back on her pillows.

"You're sure? Everyone's unhappy sometimes."

More headshaking was the only response.

"Well—" At something of a loss, Verity bent and kissed her. "You know I'm here if you want me. And you know I love you."

The curtains were drawn and the room was dim as Verity went to the door, but she was conscious that Beatrice's eyes were on her and was not altogether surprised when, just before she closed the door with herself on the other side of it, Beatrice spoke.

"Auntie Vee," she said, in a small voice.

Verity went back inside and sat on the bed again. "What is it, darling?"

"Does Mummy really hate me?"

"What?" Verity laughed, opening her eyes wide in horrified surprise. "Whoever put such an idea in your head? Of course she doesn't! Your Mummy and Daddy love you very much."

"Then why did they send me away?"

"You know why. Because there weren't any schools for you."

"There are some schools. For little girls."

"Ah, but you're thinking of India, aren't you? They had to go to Singapore, and they didn't know what it was going to be like there. Anyway, it's much healthier for you here. They love you so much they wanted you to live in the very best place possible." She leant forward and put her arms round the thin, rigid shoulders. "And I love having you," she said. "So let's have no more talk of anyone hating anybody."

Beatrice returned the hug but sighed as she settled back again. "It's just that Hugh said—" she broke off, biting her lip.

"Oh, it's Hugh who's been putting those silly ideas into your head, is it?" Verity held her by her shoulders and looked into her face. "Well, take no notice of him."

"He says his Mummy and Daddy hate him and that's why they've sent him away."

"He thinks that? Surely not! He knows that all boys of his age go away to school. He's a very naughty little boy to say such things."

"He's not little. He's big," Beatrice corrected her.

"Well, yes. Certainly big enough to know better. But he's absolutely wrong. Now give me another hug and settle down to sleep."

Beatrice did both and Verity sat beside her until her steady breathing made it obvious that she was asleep. Only then did she tip-toe from the room.

Should she say anything to Frances about Hugh's remark? She felt like doing so. He shouldn't be allowed to upset a small girl whose parents were so far away; on the other hand—

She paused on the landing for a moment, frowning. Could he really think that of his parents or was he simply pretending, in order to upset Beatrice? Even if Nicholas made it abundantly clear that Hugh failed to come up to the standard of physical prowess that he looked for in a son, certainly Frances had never stinted her unconditional love. Her first thought was always of Hugh and she had agonised at the prospect of sending him away. What a strange, unknowable child he was.

Maybe, Verity thought, it was Hugh who needed sympathy every bit as much as Beatrice.

Everyone said how remarkable it was that Beatrice had settled down so well and showed so little sign of missing her parents or the life she had known before.

"Which of course is entirely due to you, my dear," Mrs Radley said to Verity, seeing the way she devoted herself to her small niece. "Oh, how cruel fate can be sometimes! What a wonderful mother you would have made!"

By the Christmas of 1937, Verity herself was beginning to have doubts on that subject. Her love for Beatrice and her determination to give her a happy home and a glorious future was undimmed, but she could see that even with the best of intentions, the path of parenthood was strewn with difficulties, not the least of which, in this particular case, was Beatrice's desire to monopolise her every moment. She appeared to accept that attending school was obligatory, but objected to taking part in any other activity if it meant she would be separated from her aunt.

Verity sought advice from Livvy, now the mother of seven-year-old Alex and baby Rose.

"I simply don't understand it," she said. "You and I never wanted grown-ups around, did we? Not often, anyway. All we wanted was to push off on our own somewhere and talk secrets, or play our own silly games yet I practically have to dragoon Beatrice into having friends to tea, and even when she does, she always wants me to be there as well. And look at what happened when I tried to enrol her in the Brownies! She sat in a corner all evening without joining in a solitary game and utterly refused to go again. Dancing classes were the same. It can't be good for her to cling like this."

"You must give her time, Vee."

"Surely, I have given her time! Heaven forbid that I should ever make her feel I don't want her around, that's not my intention at all and simply wouldn't be true, but it does seem important to me that she should at least begin to show some sign of independence. Oh, I know that I represent security in her eyes, but surely she should realise by now that even if she goes to someone else's house I'm there when she gets back? Don't forget it's only a couple of years until she goes to boarding school, at Daphne's insistence. I simply have to make her a bit more self-reliant before then."

"Two years is a long while in the life of a child. She'll be over this kind of behaviour by then, I feel sure."

Robert seemed less sanguine. "Boarding school doesn't suit every child," he said. "Maybe you should be prepared to make other arrangements."

"But Robert, I'm under orders," Verity reminded him. "It's hardly my decision, is it?"

She resolved to be even more patient, but her efforts were not rewarded by any visible result. So long as Beatrice was alone with her and the recipient of her full attention, then she remained the sweet, biddable child she had seemed at first. Adult visitors commented openly on the excellence of her behaviour and her charming manners. It was only when other children came to the house that a devil seemed to enter into her.

On a summer's day in 1938, Livvy telephoned with an urgent SOS. Her nursemaid had been rushed to Truro with appendicitis, her parents were away on holiday in Wales, they were short-staffed at the hospital. Would it be possible for her to leave the children at Lemorrick just for the afternoon? Verity, naturally, agreed at once.

"That'll be fun, won't it?" she said to Beatrice, as she put the telephone down.

"We were going on the beach."

"Well, this won't stop us. We can all go. Alex and Rosie love the beach, too."

"Rosie's too little."

"No, she's not. We'll take her for a paddle, you and I."

Beatrice looked mutinous, but said nothing more. All afternoon she played on her own, refusing any friendly overtures from Alex and openly hostile to Rosie, pushing her away angrily when the toddler blundered into her sandcastle, causing much drama and many tears.

Back at Lemorrick, she refused tea even though it included the kind of chocolate biscuits she particularly liked, and went upstairs to her room, slamming the door behind her. Grimly, Verity ignored her, knowing, however, that the time of reckoning had surely come. This kind of behaviour simply wasn't acceptable.

"Have they been good?" Livvy asked when she came to collect the children.

"Yours have been marvellous," Verity assured her. "I wish I could say the same for Beatrice."

"Where is she?"

"In her room."

But when Verity went to look for her, the room was empty. Mild surprise developed into anxiety as time went by without a sign of her. She was nowhere in the house or garden, nor, it seemed, on the beach where, after a while, Verity went down to look for her. She approached a few families who had spent the afternoon there and asked them if they had seen a little girl in a pink flowered dress, the little girl who had been with her earlier. Nobody had.

By half-past six she was definitely worried. The cliffs were so high, the drop from them so great. Could Beatrice have taken herself off, along the cliff path, where she had slipped and fallen? Had – heaven forbid – someone abducted her? Some maniac, perhaps? There were plenty of strangers about now the holiday season was upon them.

Verity rounded up help: Mrs Harmer, the cook, Gladys, the kitchen maid, and Tilly, a young school-leaver who helped in a general kind of way. One of them ran for Pascoe, and together they searched the beach again, going further this time, where there were no families, and where granite rocks took over from the sand, rocks after rocks after rocks, leading right around the coast as far as the next village.

"You'll have to tell the police, Miss," Pascoe said at last. "Or the coastguard. The little maid's missing—"

"I know that," Verity snapped. Instantly, she apologised. "I'm sorry, Pascoe. It's just that I'm so worried. You're right, of course. I'll go back to the house and telephone right away. Would you keep on looking just a little longer? I suppose she could have gone inland, towards the woods?"

"Mrs Harmer and the girls can take the cove road. I'll take the path to the woods."

"Thanks. Thanks to all of you. I'm really grateful."

She turned and made her way back along the beach where the tide was coming in fast. At the far end were the stone steps that led from the beach to Lemorrick, and she took them as fast as she could, anxious now to get official help; and as she turned the last corner, she saw Beatrice sitting calmly on the top step in the evening sun, smiling as she stroked Ginger, the kitchen cat.

"Oh, Beatrice!" Weak with relief, Verity sagged against the rocky wall. "Where on earth have you been?"

Beatrice giggled. "Wouldn't you like to know? I saw you all, looking for me—"

Her smile died as Verity sprang up the few steps that remained between them, and grasping her arm, jerked her to her feet. The cat, deprived of a lap to sit on, skittered off into the bushes.

"You did *what*? You naughty girl! How dare you worry everyone like that? I was out of my mind!"

At the sight of her anger, Beatrice shrank away and began to cry. "It was only a joke," she sobbed. "I'm sorry—"

"Don't ever do such a wicked thing again. I thought you'd gone for ever."

Beatrice continued to sob, but glanced up through her fingers with a discernible gleam of satisfaction. This, Verity realised belatedly, was just the reaction she had intended. Slowly her fury abated, replaced by a kind of helpless, angry pity. The child was still so insecure. What on earth was she to do about it, when all the devotion she could muster seemed to have no effect whatsoever?

"Go to your room," she said sternly. "And go straight to bed. On second thoughts, you're all sandy, so you'd better have a bath and then go to bed. I shall come up in twenty minutes, so get moving—"

Beatrice turned and ran. For a moment Verity watched her until she was in the house and out of sight, then wearily she set about getting word to the search party that the wanderer had returned, reflecting as she went that dinner would be late that night, undoubtedly having the effect of upsetting both Mrs Harmer and her mother. Pascoe, probably halfway to Howldrevel Woods by this time, wouldn't be best pleased, either. Where had Beatrice hidden herself? Somewhere quite close at hand, if she'd been watching them all on the beach. The answer occurred to her almost immediately. If you ducked under the fence and edged along the cliff from the top of the steps, it was possible to get to a declivity where bracken grew thickly. She'd hidden there herself as a child when she and Harry had played hide-and-seek. She should, she supposed, have thought of it earlier, but then it hadn't entered her head that Beatrice could be deliberately hiding from them. She sighed dispiritedly, horribly afraid, after all, that she had bitten off more than she could chew.

"I know exactly what sparked it," she said later to Livvy and Robert. "Beatrice had been forced to share me with Alex and Rosie instead of having my undivided attention."

"You shouldn't be such a whizz at sandcastles," Robert suggested dryly.

"It goes deeper than that."

"I know. What I don't know is how you can do more than you're already doing."

"Patience is the only answer. I'm convinced of that," Livvy said.

"That's never been my strong suit."

"I think you're doing marvels. We both do. She'll improve, given time."

"What a complicated business it is," Verity said. "She seems such a mixture of emotions."

"Which," said Robert, "is a fairly comprehensive description of the human condition."

This Verity acknowledged to be true, but it could be said that as the summer of 1938 drew towards its end, the emotions of the nation became concentrated on a dread of the war that seemed to be brewing in Europe.

7th September 1938
Gas masks delivered today. Don't know who made the most fuss, Mother or Bea. If Mother doesn't want to have anything to do with such things, then she's big enough and old enough to make her own decisions, but I had a terrible time with B., trying to talk her into putting the wretched thing on just for a few seconds. Of course they are claustrophic and I understand how she feels, but still she must get used to it somehow.

11th September 1938
I am terribly afraid that war seems inevitable. Mother thinks I should make arrangements immediately for Bea to go to her parents, and I must say I am tempted to do so, for having the responsibility of keeping her here seems almost too heavy to be borne. If there is to be a war, everyone seems to accept that the civilian population will have a far greater involvement than they did the last time, and I would never forgive myself if anything happened to Bea simply because I didn't send her away while there was still time. Have written to Stephen and await his reply.

It seems so monstrous, so utterly unbelievable that the horror is to start a second time and that Harry, and all the millions of others, died in vain, after all. Twenty years has gone in the twinkling of an eye, all those years of false security dissolved into nothingness as if they'd never been. I confess to this diary, if nowhere else, that I am scared stiff.

On the other hand, there are terrible stories coming out of Germany where Adolf Hitler seems to have become some kind of god who can do no wrong. Livvy and Robert were there early this year and witnessed a rally which they said chilled the blood. I can quite see that we can't just sit around waiting for the wretched man to walk all over other small countries that can't defend themselves, but I do dread the thought of war.

1st October 1938
Crisis over, thank God. Chamberlain back from Munich with assurances of peace with honour – which is fine, and nobody more relieved than I, but will this stop Hitler in his tracks or merely encourage him to annex some other part of the globe just as soon as things have died down a bit? Churchill doesn't seem to think so.

Your father never trusted Churchill, Mother says, which is true, I remember it well. However there is a still small voice within me that seems to say he could be right this time, though God knows I hope he's not. However, one can't close one's eyes to the reports coming out of Germany: i.e. that every Jew in Vienna is to lose his job, and that Pastor Niemöller has been taken to a concentration camp to be "re-educated", whatever that means. Also we have the evidence of all the Jewish refugees that have come to Britain. Clearly it is an evil regime and I can't help wondering whether, though we may have peace, there is any honour in it.

No word from Stephen yet. I haven't said anything to B. about the possibility of her leaving England and have sworn Mother to secrecy. I have no idea how she would feel about it, but there seems little point in unsettling her unnecessarily. Deep down, and despite all my assurances, I still think she believes she was sent away because her parents couldn't be bothered with her and have a suspicion she would feel that I was sending her back for the same reason. As it is, she has begun campaigning against going to Luscombe Abbey next year, as decreed. I can't help thinking it seems a nonsensical decision. She could go to the High School as a weekly boarder, but Daphne won't hear of it . . .

The awaited letter from Stephen arrived at last. He and Daphne had talked the matter over, he wrote, and felt that in view of the fact that the possibility of war seemed to have receded, they thought it best to leave things as they were, at least until they came home on leave in 1940 when they could review the situation again in the light of the current climate. Singapore did not provide an environment that was at all suitable for children and she would understand that his position demanded a great deal of entertaining which kept Daphne more than fully occupied.

Meantime, they were both so grateful for everything she was doing for Beatrice . . .

"School sounds horrible," Beatrice said. "I shan't stay there. I shall run away."

"No, you won't." Verity's voice was bracing. "You'll go there and work hard and make us all proud of you, and then you'll come back here for the holidays and have a wonderful time. You know, when I was young the one thing I wanted on this earth was to go away to school."

Which was, she thought as soon as the words were out of her mouth, as foolish a thing to say as could be imagined. Why should her own childish frustration with Miss Pond affect the way Beatrice felt? They were two utterly different people and she could only hope and pray that by the autumn of 1939 both the international situation and Beatrice's attitude would have undergone a major improvement.

Verity found, as 1938 turned into 1939, that few seemed to share Stephen's optimism that war was no longer likely. Certainly there was no such comfort to be had by the earnest student of *The Times*, which is what, more than ever before, she had become. In March, German troops goose-stepped into Prague. In April, conscription was introduced. There were helpful articles on constructing an air-raid shelter and rendering a room gas-proof. Inexorably tension rose; but through it all, Verity did as instructed by Daphne and prepared Beatrice for her entry to boarding school in September. She comforted herself by the thought that, set in the middle of Exmoor as it was, Luscombe Abbey was probably as safe as anywhere in the entire country.

It was towards the end of Beatrice's last term at Fairlawns, in June 1939, that Verity, having driven her to school, went into the garden to cut roses for the house. It was a heavenly morning, warm but with a light breeze, and she took her time as she enjoyed the sunshine, pondering idly, without a great deal of originality, on the tranquillity of the surrounding scene as opposed to the gathering threat from across the stretch of blue water that she could see to left and right of her. She jumped a little as Tilly approached her unawares across the grass and announced the presence of a visitor.

"'Tis a gentleman, Miss. I put 'un in the sitting room."

"Thank you. Did he give his name?" Verity put the question

without a great deal of curiosity and continued to snip a last rose or two. She now had a seat on the Council and was frequently lobbied on this matter or that, the provision of air raid shelters being a current preoccupation. No doubt this unknown gentleman had something to do with the subject.

"It's a Dr Grenfell, Miss," Belle said.

For a moment Verity froze, the last rose held suspended over the basket on her arm. Then, taking control of herself, she laid it with the others, took a breath and smiled at the girl.

"Is − is my mother there?" she asked.

"No, Miss. She's still upstairs, in her room."

"Well, tell Dr Grenfell I'll be with him in a few moments."

Once alone, her composure left her and she stood, incapable of movement. Laurie! Here! She was surely dreaming.

Pulling herself together, she went into the house, leaving the basket of flowers in the scullery.

"Could someone put these in water for me, please?" she said, putting her head around the door that led to the kitchen where Mrs Harmer was chopping parsley. "I'll come and arrange them later."

"Shall Tilly bring coffee for you and the gentleman, Miss?" Mrs Harmer asked.

It might help, Verity thought. Give her something to do with her hands. Break the ice. It was always helpful, having to dispense things.

"Yes, thank you. Good idea," she said.

"See to it, girl," Mrs Harmer said, continuing to chop. Just as if this was an ordinary day, an ordinary visitor, Verity thought, bemused. What do I look like? Is my hair all right?

She rinsed her hands at the deep, scullery sink and squinted at herself in the inadequate mirror that hung over it. She'd have to do, she thought. And what did it matter, anyway?

Oh, it mattered, it mattered! She went swiftly along to the sitting room, pausing only momentarily outside the door to steady herself. He was there, by the window, looking at the view, but turned as he heard her come in.

"Laurie," she said. "Can it really be you?" She went across, smiling, her hand outstretched, giving no sign of the turmoil behind the calm exterior. Her first impression was that he had changed; his face was different, not so thin as when he was

206

younger. But then he smiled and she saw that he hadn't really changed at all.

"It's me, all right. Dare I hope I'm welcome?" His voice was definitely different; one would need to listen hard for the West Country undertones now.

"Why, of course!" Her voice was brightly social, the one she used for jollying along recalcitrant committees. "It's lovely to see you! But what a surprise! Do come and sit down. Coffee will be coming in a moment. I'm dying to hear everything that's happened to you. Of course, I know you've done frightfully well – I saw one of your articles. You're a world authority on camellias, I hear." He made a modest disclaimer, but she ignored it and rattled on. "Are you still at Kew? I couldn't be more delighted that you achieved all your ambitions. But tell me, what on earth are you doing in this neck of the woods?"

For a second he looked at her in silence, an unreadable, rather baffled expression on his face as if this cascade of words was the last thing he had expected.

"Just – seeing you," he said at last. "I'm actually on my way back to London and was tempted by the Porthallic signpost. I don't get down to Falmouth as often as I'd like, but my mother's on her own now and not in very good health, so I made a quick dash—"

"I'm so sorry," Verity said. "About your mother, I mean. I hope she's – ah, here's the coffee. Thank you, Tilly."

There was a pause in conversation as Tilly set down the tray and left the room.

"Black or white?" Verity asked politely, coffee pot poised.

"White. Thank you."

"Sugar?"

"Just milk, thank you."

She handed him the cup and sat back in her chair, surveying him with a bright, if mocking, smile. "So the signpost tempted you," she said reflectively. "But never before this?"

"Well, yes. I've seen it many times, of course, but – but there were reasons—" He broke off uncomfortably, his expression reminding Verity, for the first time, of the insecure young man he had been. "I – I heard you never married," he said. "My mother often sees your name in the local paper. You seem to keep very busy."

Verity gave a light laugh. "Good works," she said. "The refuge of the unmarried gentlewoman." Suddenly she seemed to drop the brittle cheerfulness. "Why now, Laurie?"

For a moment he was silent, very deliberately turning to set his cup down on the little table beside him before looking up to face her again.

"I just wanted to see you, that's all. Explain what happened. The way I treated you—" He broke off, his face set and strained.

"It wasn't fair," Verity said, conscious herself of the change in her voice. She wondered if he noticed it, heard the tremor. "But Laurie, it all happened twenty years ago. Twenty-one, to be exact. There's not a lot of point in resurrecting it, is there?"

"I know. I shouldn't have come."

"Yes, you should." She gave her bright, social smile again. "It's good to see you. Tell me everything that's happened. Are you married?"

"Yes. My wife – Marjory – is another botanist. We met at Kew."

"How lovely. Your garden must be a show place."

"Pretty good, yes, but more thanks to Marjory than to me, I'm afraid. At home I'm the hedge-trimmer and mower of grass."

"You live in Kew?"

"In Richmond, actually."

"Ah! A charming town. I was there a year or two ago when my brother and his wife – Stephen; you knew Stephen, of course? – rented a house in Twickenham when they were home from India. Daphne and I went shopping in Richmond one morning, and I thought it quite delightful. And of course, it must be very convenient for Kew. Do you have children?"

"Two. A boy and a girl. Robin's nine and Celia's just—"

"Oh Verity, you have a visitor. Forgive me, I didn't know—"

As one, both Verity and Laurie turned towards the door where Louise Ashland had made an entrance. She was dressed in pale blue shantung, her ample bosom hung about with her suspended reading glasses and several additional gold chains. She held a folded copy of *The Times* under one arm and a knitting bag was looped over the other. It was clear she intended a prolonged stay and seeing her, Verity's heart sank.

"Mother – do come and join us," she said, putting a good face on it. "I'll ring for another cup, shall I?"

"No, don't bother, I won't have any coffee, thank you, as I've only just had breakfast, but of course I'd love to join you. Darling, aren't you going to introduce me?" Laurie had risen to his feet at the sight of her and she was smiling at him as she spoke, the kind of smile which Verity could interpret all too well. Her mother had no idea who this stranger was, but was delighted that such a personable man had seen fit to call on her daughter.

There was no help for it, Verity could see. He would have to be introduced, but with any luck the name would mean nothing to Louise after all this time. She took a deep breath.

"Mother, may I introduce Dr Grenfell? He's an eminent botanist from Kew, an expert on camellias."

"Really? How interesting!" Louise allowed him to take her hand for a moment, then with a great deal of fuss and flurry she settled herself in a small armchair. She put her spectacles on her nose, the better to survey him. "Camellias grow very well in the south-west, Dr Grenfell, as I am sure you know."

"Yes, indeed—"

"We have one along the front drive, but of course it's not flowering now. You must come back in the early spring to see that." Graciously she smiled at him again, pleased with him, pleased with herself. Briefly she turned her attention to Verity. "Even so, you should show it to Dr Grenfell, darling. It might possibly be of interest to him. Pass me the footstool, there's a good girl. Of course," she went on, pulling the footstool into position and crossing her still-shapely ankles upon it, "if Dr Grenfell is interested in camellias, Verity, you should take him to Howldrevel—"

As if the name had sparked something in her memory she fell silent and her expression changed from sociability via suspicion to dawning hostility. Her mouth opened and shut, then opened again as, very slowly, she turned to Verity. "Grenfell!" she said. "Not – not—"

"I'm Lawrence Grenfell, Mrs Ashland," Laurie said, cutting in quickly. "An old friend—"

Any trace of affability had gone from Louise's face, and she stared at him, outraged. "Friend, you say? Friend?" she said.

"Well, of course it's up to Verity whom she invites here, but I can only say, young man, that you caused a great deal of trouble and unhappiness to this family. I can't imagine why she let you over the threshold. *Doctor* Grenfell, indeed," she added, as if suspecting him of being an imposter.

"Mother, please—" begged Verity.

Laurie, having sat down, stood up again. "I'd better leave," he said. "I am truly sorry, Mrs Ashland, that I was the cause of any unhappiness to any of you, most of all to Verity. She meant more to me than I can possibly say, and the last thing I wanted was to hurt her. There were extenuating circumstances, but I won't go into that now. I've felt guilty for years, and simply wanted to apologise." He gave an awkward little nod of the head in the direction of each of them before making for the door.

"Wait, Laurie," Verity said, getting up from her chair and running after him, totally ignoring her mother's indignant instructions to let the wretched man go, and a very good riddance. "Please don't leave like that."

But I suppose I should have let him, she wrote in her diary later. *It might have been better in the long run. Instead, I ran outside and grabbed his arm and when he swung round to face me I could see how terribly upset he was. I was upset too, and for a moment we just stared at each other and then, without any thought or warning we were in each other's arms, both closer to tears than either of us could have wanted.*

He asked if we could go somewhere private, and as the tide was out I suggested the beach. We walked a bit, but then found a shady corner under the rocks and we sat and talked and talked.

What happened after that awful night was that he had a complete breakdown and was in Bodmin asylum for months. Fortunately he had enlightened doctors looking after him and eventually he made a full recovery, to the point where he was able to go to university and get his BSc. degree, after which he went to Kew in some quite lowly capacity from which he has worked his way up to where he is now, an assistant director of the gardens. I am so glad for him, but oh, why didn't he contact me years ago? If only he had!

He said he was quite certain at the time that I was not only better off without him but that, as I suspected, he was terribly ashamed because he had lied about the reason he was invalided out of the army. The loss of his finger, he said, was really the least of it. When Nicholas Courtfield said that he was a coward, then he was only speaking the truth. Many men had been shot for less.

Of course, that's nonsense, and I told him so. He was shell-shocked. He'd had a terrible time in the trenches and it wasn't his fault he was so badly affected by it. I would have understood, and stood by him. He said he tried to write, lots of times, but couldn't seem to get the words right, and the longer he left it the more difficult it became. I suppose I can understand that, in a way. I think he genuinely did think that I'd meet someone "of my own class" and be far happier without him, he was so class-obsessed in those days. Thank heaven, he seems to have got over that.

Well, too late now. Twenty-one years too late. One wife and two children too late. We didn't touch again – at least, only when I took his hand to say goodbye. I lifted up his left hand and had a good look at it, and of course it was just as I told him all those years ago. The scars have faded and no one meeting him casually would notice; and I don't think he would care if they did. He said he scarcely notices it himself now and has become adept at doing without one finger.

I don't suppose I'll ever see him again. I know I fancied myself in love with Michael, but I can say this now with absolute certainty. Laurie was, and is, the love of my life.

Twelve

All through the summer the possibility of war grew closer, but while Verity agonised over the impending calamity, nearer home she had to deal with the problem of equipping a rebellious child for boarding school. It involved the purchase of a vast amount of clothing, most of which could only be bought from the school outfitters in Exeter, all to be marked with Cash's woven name tapes.

Throughout the whole process Beatrice sulked to the point where even Verity lost patience.

"Look, sweetheart, please don't make up your mind that you're not going to be happy," she said.

"Well, I won't be, so there!"

Really, the only gleam of light on the horizon was the navy-blue cloak lined with green silk that constituted part of the winter uniform. Beatrice would have died rather than admit it, but she was entranced by it and even on the warmest summer day liked to try it on and posture in front of the long mirror in her bedroom.

"I'm being Maid Marion," she said once, when Verity caught her in the act.

"More like a fourth Musketeer," Verity suggested. "Something frightfully swashbuckling, anyway. It really does look nice, Bea, and so does the rest of the uniform."

"It's not bad, I suppose," Beatrice admitted. And Verity allowed herself a vestige of hope that the poor child would, after all, settle happily. Not that anything was certain, not even the date of the beginning of term, for as the international situation grew ever more threatening, schools were forced to make new arrangements. A letter arrived from Luscombe Abbey saying that in the event of war, St Hilda's Girls School, Ealing – a school of equal standing catering for girls of refinement, Luscombe Abbey parents were assured – would be evacuated to Exmoor and would share the

Abbey premises. Luscombe Abbey had ample space at its disposal and, with the addition of two nearby houses, would be able to cope. This did mean, however, that the term would start one week later than planned, i.e. on Tuesday, 19th September. The letter ended with the pious hope that, in this time of national emergency, all the parents and girls involved would see the need to pull together and understand that some small compromises would necessarily have to be made.

"So you have a reprieve," Verity said to Beatrice, handing the letter over to her to read.

"Perhaps the whole place will be bombed before we get there," Beatrice said hopefully.

However, not surprisingly in this case, no such event took place. Nor did the heavens fall in any other region when, finally, the worst happened and war was declared.

3rd September 1939
It's started, and I have to say that it's almost a relief to know where we stand. Chamberlain made an announcement on the wireless at eleven o'clock today. It was relayed in the church, after which prayers were said and the service broke up early.

Fruitless to wonder what the coming years will bring, or how long it will last. Nearly throttled Ted Chambers after church when I heard him say it would all be over by Christmas! I so well remember people saying that the last time, and look what happened. Four ghastly years. This time, we all know that Germany has a head start on us when it comes to re-arming.

Everyone expects London to be bombed immediately, and apparently it said on the wireless this evening that they did have an air-raid warning just after the declaration of war but it was only a false alarm, thank heaven, and we heard nothing here.

Several train-loads of evacuees arrived from London over the weekend. Frances is the Queen Bee of the WVS so is much occupied in finding homes for the poor little things. I feel SIMPLY TERRIBLE about not volunteering to have any, because (a) we have the room and (b) I should genuinely love to give a few children a home, but I just can't imagine how Bea would react if I were to take in some strange children just at the time when I am sending her away from home. Am I just pampering her? On the whole, I don't think so. This boarding school business is really terribly traumatic for her.

Fortunately Frances understands. She says she will not call on me unless all else fails, and I must say that as far as I can tell most people are proving themselves hospitable and generous towards these poor children. One can only imagine how totally bereft and at sea they must feel, suddenly being torn from their mothers' arms, as it were.

Frances tells me that Nicholas is going to the Admiralty tomorrow to see if he can sign up again (for some desk job, presumably). Council work keeps me busy – an Emergency Committee is being formed, of which I am a part, its energies much engaged at the moment by the question of shall we/shan't we invest in new fire-fighting equipment. Given the times we live in, I am in favour as the current equipment is totally inadequate as well as being archaic, and I have therefore been deputed to find out just what is required, and cost of same. Much annoyance caused by note saying that those at County Hall see no need to allocate a motor ambulance specifically for this district. Must agree it seems most unsatisfactory. Shall pursue the matter.

Meantime, there are still quantities of blackout curtains to make, necessitating a further trip to Truro since the Pawleys' shop sold out of black lining material long ago. I remarked to Mrs P., thinking of her profits, that it just shows that every cloud has a silver lining, and she said no, dear, they have to be black, the Government says so. Very strange, looking out of windows here towards the village and seeing nothing but unrelieved darkness. Ron, Pascoe's ne'er-do-well son, is now an Air-Raid Warden and goes around shouting threateningly at those who unwittingly show a glimmer. Impossible not to think that he has at last found his métier. Threatening shouts have long been his speciality.

The belated start of term arrived, and a silent Beatrice, her small face pale and set, was duly delivered at Luscombe Abbey. Though it broke Verity's heart to see her, still more to leave her there, she was a little cheered by the humanity of the staff she met and the general homely atmosphere that seemed to prevail. Beatrice clung to her on parting, but was almost instantly whisked away by a charming sixth-former who seemed to have been assigned the task of taking the newcomer under her wing. Very close to tears herself, Verity was nevertheless thankful that the moment was less emotionally charged than she had imagined might be the case and she left swiftly, only stopping on her way home to have a large, restorative brandy at one of the inns she passed by the roadside.

There were, after all, no immediate air-raids. The fishing boats continued to go in and out of Porthallic harbour, though without many of the younger fishermen who had joined the Royal or Merchant Navy. There were shortages of certain goods in the shops, but on the whole there seemed plenty of food to go round. It was, Pascoe opined, a funny kind of war, and in his view, that Hitler didn't knaw which way to steer nor turn and neither did they clowns in London. If you asked him, 'twould all be called off before the end of the year.

Verity was not so sanguine and was glad that the Council took matters more seriously, conscientiously preparing for the bad times that might lie ahead. The fire-fighting equipment was approved and purchased, and air-raid shelters constructed; meanwhile controversy over the ambulance rumbled on. Much to her relief, the evacuees seemed satisfactorily housed, though many tales were told of children who had never seen a sheep or a cow, or who had no idea how to use a knife and fork. Mrs Pawley sold more fine-tooth combs than ever before and there was a certain amount of language difficulty on both sides, but on the whole the newcomers seemed, with a few notable exceptions, to be assimilated into the village without a great deal of trouble; in fact, as Christmas approached, they engendered a considerable amount of community spirit as various groups joined together to give the evacuees a party they were never likely to forget.

Beatrice, turned ten during the previous term, came home from school and seemed to have settled down better than Verity had dared hope. She chattered of hockey and riding lessons and how Miss Potter was really foul and unfair and much too strict, und gave lines just because people talked when they shouldn't, but Miss Sanderson made them laugh and gave them sweets and came to the dormitory to tell them stories sometimes. And everyone was scared to death of Miss Longman, the headmistress, but really she was nice, and Jennifer Laver-Rice, the sixth-former who Verity had met that first day, was *awfully* nice and often spoke to

Beatrice to ask her if she was all right, which, apparently, was not something that sixth-formers did, as a rule, but then Jennifer Laver-Rice wasn't like anyone else. She was Games Captain and terribly good at hockey *and* netball, and everyone thought she was marvellous.

"So, on the whole, you're happy there?" Verity asked.

Beatrice's expression changed at once. "I didn't say that!" Her voice was full of indignation. "I hate it, just like I said I would. I wish I didn't have to go back."

Verity made no comment, distracting her thoughts by sending her to find the Christmas tree ornaments that were always kept in the attic.

Christmas dinner was eaten with Livvy and Robert, and on Boxing Day Verity took Beatrice to the pantomime in Truro. The entire journey was enlivened by a detailing, on Beatrice's part, of her many grievances regarding Luscombe Abbey. The food, the lack of comfort, the incredibly hard work, the meanness of Miss Potts – all, it seemed, were unendurable, but seeing her laughing, animated face as she joined the other children in the theatre in shouting urgent "Look Behind Yous" to Buttons. it seemed to Verity that no lasting damage was being done to her niece's psyche; in fact, when the time came to go back to school, she thought she detected a certain amount of eagerness in her manner. By the time they drove down the avenue and came to a halt in front of the school's impressive steps, she was peering excitedly to left and right.

"Look, Auntie Vee," she said, spotting the object of her search. "There's Jennifer Laver-Rice. No, *there*! The pretty one. *And* she's got a new hockey stick! I bet she'll shoot thousands of goals with it, she's absolutely marvellous at hockey—"

And inwardly Verity smiled, and gave thanks for the admirable Jennifer. If she had succeeded in deflecting to her own person just a little of Beatrice's dependence on her aunt, that, in Verity's view, could only be a matter for rejoicing.

13th January 1940
My fortieth birthday. A milestone in anyone's calendar, I suppose, but I can't say I feel any different. Is this a woman's tragedy, that externally she ages, while internally she feels eighteen, so that the merest glance in a mirror can produce a ghastly trauma? Looked

*long and hard at my visage this afternoon, and decided that for a
woman of forty, I don't look so bad.*

*Letter from Miss Longman to say how well Beatrice seems to
have settled in this term. Have to admit (reluctantly) that Daphne
seems to have been right. Left to myself I would have kept her at
home but boarding school does, after all, seem to have effected
a great improvement in her. Such a relief! On the other hand,
Jennifer L.-R. can surely have no more than another year at
school, if that. How will B. feel when she finally leaves?*

Sunday 21st January 1940
*Seems strange that only in my last entry I wrote of feeling,
perpetually, no more than eighteen. Such prescience! Who could
have predicted what ensued after the momentous phone call that
came right out of the blue?*

When she answered the phone that Friday afternoon, she had no
idea that by doing so, her life would never be the same again.

"Verity?"

The voice at the other end of the wire was unmistakable and for
a few seconds she could say nothing, unable to catch her breath.

"It's Laurie," he said, when still she was silent. "I'm in Truro.
My mother's in hospital. She had a stroke earlier in the week, and
it's touch and go—"

"Oh Laurie, I'm so sorry."

"At least she's in good hands and she seems glad to see me even
if she can't speak very coherently. But Verity, the reason I rang—"
he hesitated a moment, then came straight to the point. "Can I see
you? I want to, so much. I – I can't very well come over to you,
can I? Not the way your mother feels. But if you could come here,
we could have dinner. Do say you will!"

"Are you alone? Isn't your wife with you?" Not that it made
any difference, Verity thought, even as she asked the question.
She and Laurie were old friends, nothing more. Surely no sensible
wife would object to such a meeting.

"No, she's not. She and the children have evacuated themselves
to Hereford, to Marjory's parents. They have a farm there, and
they were anxious—" He pulled himself up short, apparently
deciding that all this was irrelevant. "Do come, Verity. Please,"
he added, when she said nothing.

"I can't tonight," she said at last. Another pause ensued. "But I'm free tomorrow," she added quickly, as if the words emerged of their own volition.

"Good. The Red Lion, then? Seven-thirty?"

"Very well." She felt strange. Fluttery. Eighteen, she thought suddenly.

Her mother had grown so accustomed to her being out and about on Council business that she had, much to Verity's relief, stopped cross-questioning her about the hours she spent away from home, or who she spent them with. Getting ready for the evening with particular care, she chose a dress in a soft, dark red wool which she had owned for some years and knew was flattering to her skin and hair. She felt reckless, heady with nervous excitement; conscious, confronting herself in the mirror, that this meeting was significant, that at the end of it something would have changed in one way or another. Recognition of this fact brought a flush to her cheeks and brightness to her eyes.

"I feel I'm in a dream," she said to Laurie, once they were facing each other across a table in the Red Lion. "Nothing seems quite real. It's unbelievable, that we're sitting here."

He seemed on edge, she could see. He fidgeted with the cutlery until he saw she was watching the tremor of his hands, at which he clasped them together, holding them out of her sight.

"Unbelievable, perhaps," he agreed. "But at the same time—" He looked at her, his eyes moving over her face. She saw him swallow convulsively. "Inevitable, don't you think? That last time – I told myself I'd never see you again, but I can't do it, Verity. I can't! I've thought of nothing and no one but you." She looked at him, but said nothing. "I'm being presumptuous," he said. "I'm sorry."

"No! It's not that. It's just that – well, we can't turn back the clock, can we?"

"We can make the best of the time we have left."

She looked at him, at the face she had once known so well and which was the same, but not the same. There were lines around his eyes, furrows running from nose to mouth, an almost imperceptible thinning of the lips. An older face, of course, but one she found even more attractive than before. She looked away quickly, the anguish of mourning for all the lost years almost too much to bear.

From the first, she wrote afterwards, *there seemed no barrier between us, no pretence that this meeting wasn't a highly-charged affair. No matter how we, and external events, have changed, we still love each other. It hardly needed to be said. I suppose if one saw it in a film one would deride it as impossibly sentimental and say life isn't like that. One could also say that common morality decreed that we should renounce our feelings and spend the evening discussing the finer points of the Russo-Finnish war or James Joyce's impact on contemporary literature. We did neither of those things. We simply held hands and looked into each other's eyes, just overjoyed that, for this short time at least, we were together. I don't know what we ate or drank (except that, in the case of the latter, it was probably too much), or who else was in the dining room, just that everything seemed as it was before.*

I asked him about his marriage. To his credit, he said little, but I gather it's been under strain for some time and that he was relieved when Marjory took herself off to Hereford, and so was she. He adores his children and misses them terribly. Of course he's glad that they are in a safe place, but the possible danger from bombs was, in M.'s case, just an excuse for leaving him, at least for a while. Any rift is his fault entirely, he says, because he's always been a difficult bastard. I can imagine this to be true. I can imagine being angry with him, losing all patience, throwing things, all of that, but even so I know it would make no difference. I shall always love him.

He said he knew, long before the wedding, that he was doing Marjory a grave injustice in marrying her, but events got out of hand and he was swept along with them.

You must have loved her once. I said. Well, maybe, he admitted. In a kind of way. But not enough. It was never, he said, remotely like the way he loved me – and still does. I was unable to speak for a while after this, totally unmanned by the thought of the wicked, wicked waste of both our lives. If only he had stayed in contact this would never have happened, and thinking of this I was suddenly overwhelmingly angry with him – or maybe just with life. It lasted no more than a moment, though, for when I looked at him I saw that he was suffering too, not only because of the waste but because he knew that he was the one who caused it.

He is staying in a holiday cottage in St Hennah, lent to him by a colleague, as it's very convenient for Truro and the hospital. We went back there and at last we were together as we should have been all those years ago. I know I should feel guilty, but I don't. Marjory can spare me this much. I got home around four-thirty.

He had to go back to work today but we are determined that we shall meet again. He has in the past gone walking and camping in the Quantock Hills on his own and says he knows of a remote inn where we can stay. He went on to say that on one occasion he took his son, Robin, camping with him in the area and that they had a wonderful time together, walking and fishing. I was so struck by the way his voice and face change when he speaks of Robin! He is so proud of him.

I'm going to do it. Because I want to do it. And if that sounds wicked, then I'm sorry, but really I do seem to have spent an awful lot of my life doing what other people want me to do and I think it's my turn now. However, life is so uncertain these days that making any kind of plans seemed to be tempting providence. Is that why I feel no guilt, because we all may be blown to smithereens before too long, so what the hell does it matter? Or is that sheer sophistry? Probably. I just want him, that's all.

The war seemed to come a little nearer with heavy shipping losses in the Atlantic, including the loss of a Porthallic man who had been one of the first to join up. Bacon and butter were rationed, and further rationing promised for the near future, but still there was no air activity over Britain, and many of the evacuees began drifting back to London. It seemed premature, in Verity's opinion. The war was only five months old.

Later that month Mrs Grenfell had another stroke and died in hospital, and though Laurie came down to Cornwall for the funeral Verity knew nothing of it until after he had gone back to London, for he stayed only a matter of hours due to pressure of work.

In March, only two weeks before Beatrice's arrival home for the Easter holidays (by train, this time, since petrol was in short supply), Verity announced her intention of going away for a few days. Council business, she said vaguely, and went on to talk about the need to brush up on her first aid skills. Louise had never taken a great deal of interest in her activities as a councillor and though she complained at being deserted for an entire weekend, she accepted the need for it without question.

The arrangement was that Verity should travel to Taunton by

train where she would meet Laurie, and that they would go to the Swan Inn, Cawbiscombe, where they would stay together as man and wife. In preparation, feeling vaguely ashamed, she raided a little-used jewel case of her mother's to find an ornate ring that had been her grandmother's wedding band.

All the way to Taunton, she felt strangely detached from her surroundings, as if it were not she but some other woman who was on her way to meet her lover. She sat in the corner of the carriage staring blindly at the scenery, discouraging, albeit politely, the conversational gambits of the naval officer who sat opposite her. Some giant, invisible hand seemed to be squeezing her internal organs causing a strangely hollow feeling inside. This, she thought dryly, must be a manifestation of what her mother referred to as Nerves. If so, she felt thankful that normally she was immune.

At Taunton station she crossed to the other platform to wait for Laurie, only to find that his train from London was delayed. She found it impossible to sit in the ladies' waiting room despite the cheerful fire that blazed there, but instead paced up and down the platform, the tension mounting with every step she took until she almost yearned for the peaceful, unthreatening, uncontroversial life that was her usual lot. I'm too old for this, she thought, worriedly. It's not in my nature any more. And I hate wearing this ring! It's a shabby, cheap thing to do. How appalled her grandmother would be to know what use her ring was being put to! And who could blame her? Who wouldn't condemn a love affair with a married man?

When the Cornwall-bound train from Birmingham and points north drew to a halt beside her, her panic had escalated to such an extent that she almost climbed aboard to go straight home again; but seeing it leave without her, she was conscious of a strange feeling of relieved helplessness, as of a die being cast, an irrevocable step taken. And when, moments later, Laurie's train steamed in, crammed to the gills with sailors bound for Plymouth, she greeted him with a feeling of calm as well as joy. This was the man she loved, would always love. How could this possibly be wrong when it felt so right?

11th March 1940
Home again, after a magical weekend. Lovely, if sodden country-
side. Gorgeous little pub, by a river. It rained most of the time,

but it didn't matter. The Swan was warm and cosy. We had a log fire in the bedroom at night and excellent food provided by the landlady, who appeared to accept us without question as a perfectly respectable married couple.

We wrapped up and walked when we could, and we talked endlessly. Laurie's sad about his mother but realises that she would have been badly paralysed had she lived, which makes it easier to bear. He's been to all manner of places in the Far East in search of camellias. I feel such a country bumpkin by comparison. Told him how I longed to see Venice and never had, and he said neither had he and we would go together, after the war. But I wouldn't let him talk about "after the war". I feel, in some strange way, that we can only justify our behaviour because the war has somehow suspended normality.

I feel irradiated with love. Cannot believe that Mother sees no difference in me now I am home, but apparently she does not and does not even seem curious about my activities while away, concentrating instead, for most of the evening, on the impossible behaviour of Miss Dawkins at the library who has been showing a marked tendency to give books reserved by Mother to other, far less deserving, subscribers.

Beatrice will be home in a week as Easter is early this year, but once she has gone back to school L. and I have arranged to meet again.

It was during the Easter holidays that Germany invaded Norway and Denmark which, despite a brave defence, were eventually conquered. In May, it was the turn of the Low Countries, where there was little resistance. Verity was once again with Laurie as, sitting together in the parlour of the Swan on a Sunday evening in May, they listened to Winston Churchill offering the country nothing but blood, toil, tears and sweat.

For a long moment after the speech was over, they sat in silence.

"Our concerns seem so small," Verity said, finally. "Oh, Laurie – what's going to happen?"

"Britain will rise to it."

Verity said nothing. Of course Britain would rise to it, that went without saying, but despite her former strictures on planning for the future, she had, just then, been thinking more personally. What would happen to them?

222

She did not press the matter, however. She knew it would be foolish to do so, acknowledging to herself that there were no certainties any more except those offered by Churchill. Everyone spoke now of a long war and there were few who doubted that the worst was yet to come. Silently she contemplated the bleak prospect, and a kind of despair seemed to invade her whole body and chill her to the bone, despite the warmth of the weather.

"What's the matter, darling?" Laurie asked her, putting his arm around her. "You're shivering."

"No I'm not. It's just a goose walking over my grave."

He leant towards her and kissed her lightly. "Not allowed," he said. "Not while you're with me."

And she smiled and pretended that it had been just a passing aberration, not the ominous shadow that, try as she might to rid herself of it, refused to be dismissed.

The times they could spend together remained few in number and never lost that aura of other-worldliness. Her daily life, by contrast, revolved around her duties as a councillor and a member of the Emergency Committee, which meant negotiations with the St John's Ambulance Brigade to initiate first aid demonstrations in Porthallic, the organisation of social events to entertain the various members of the forces who found themselves stationed in the district, the collection of tin-foil, and the continued raising of money for the Ashland Hospital – duties that she felt to be parochial and probably without significance of any kind, but were still totally time-consuming. Twice a week, she wrote to Beatrice; less regularly, to Stephen. There was also the house to run.

"There aren't enough hours in the day," she said to Louise, who complained on a regular basis that Verity never seemed to spend any time with her these days.

In June, there was the drama of Dunkirk, and only days later Paris fell.

"There's not a lot to rejoice about," Verity remarked to Frances one summer's day. "But say what you will, it's an ill wind that blows nobody any good. Stephen and Daphne were due home this year, but of course they've had to postpone their leave indefinitely. Call me heartless, but I don't feel I could cope with them at the moment."

"Does Beatrice mind?"

"She doesn't seem to. I think they've grown rather unreal to her, after all this time."

"How horrible! You can hardly blame them for stopping at one child, can you? It's a rotten kind of life, to have children and then be forced to let them go."

"It seems to suit them. And me, of course."

Sunlight filtered through a tracery of beech leaves as they walked away from Howldrevel, across the gardens and into the woods. The scent of summer seemed all about them; honeysuckle and bramble and ground ivy and the rich mixture that made up the undergrowth. Wood pigeons called, sweet and plaintive. For a moment Frances stopped and sniffed the air.

"So peaceful," she said. Then she sighed. "Oh, God, Vee, the thought of Paris in German hands seems impossible. I've thought of little else all week."

"I know." Verity paused too, reaching out to rub her fingers over the knotted wood of an ancient oak with a slow, sensuous touch as if to remind herself that despite man's follies, some things remained constant. "We're next in line, of course. Things are going to hot up from now on, I fear. The general view seems to be that invasion will come, but not before Germany softens us up. I was talking to the chap who runs the district first aid post yesterday and he seems to think that air-raids are inevitable."

Frances nodded. "It's the thought of all those children that worries me," she said. "All those who were evacuated but then went back to the big cities because it seemed that nothing was going to happen. What'll become of them? Children are so vulnerable, aren't they? So helpless. So utterly dependent on the whims of their parents – and heaven knows, being a parent doesn't grant one infallibility."

"Far from it!"

"I think I must be an awful mother, Vee."

"What utter nonsense!"

"No, it's not. Hugh was always a funny little boy, I know that, but when he was small we were always close. Now we're not. He doesn't talk to me, doesn't take any notice of what I say—"

"They call it growing up. You'll get close again."

"I hope you're right. I can't help wondering, are we doing the right thing by keeping our children at school? Or did all those parents who took their kids back home have the right of it? Maybe families should stick together, come hell or high water. If there's an invasion—" Frances seemed suddenly to realise the enormity of her words and she stopped, appalled. "God help us, Vee. We must pray it won't come to that."

Verity gave a mirthless breath of laughter. "I don't think I ever stop," she said.

They turned down a ride which led through towering rhododendrons to the main drive leading to the house and for a while neither of them spoke, both lost in their own thoughts.

"Do you mind very much if I drop in on Mrs Jago at the Gatehouse?" Frances asked after a while. "It won't take a minute, but I feel I ought to."

"Isn't she well?"

"She's fine, as far as I know. It's just that—" Frances broke off and sighed. "Nicholas came home at the weekend and managed to upset her," she went on. "You know how he can be. Apparently there was some domestic crisis; their little girl had fallen over and cut her head open, and Mrs J. was busy staunching the blood and didn't hear him hooting so didn't come out to open the gate as smartly as he thought she should have done. Such drama! Meantime," she added after a short pause, in a faraway kind of voice, "jackboots goose-step down the Champs Elysées. I told him he should get his priorities right."

Verity laughed without a great deal of humour. "I don't suppose he'll ever change."

"Unfortunately, I agree. I've told him, time and time again, he's going to lose Jack if he goes on treating the Jagos like serfs on some medieval estate. And that would be a disaster because now we've lost the two younger gardeners I don't know what we'd do without him. He does all kinds of odd jobs about the place as well as being the mainstay of the vegetable garden."

"So it's your job to keep things sweet?"

"I do my best," Frances said. Again, they walked in silence for a moment or two.

"Does Nicholas still knock you about?" Verity asked at last, her voice tentative.

"Well—" Frances seemed to hesitate. "Not really. Not now. I've threatened to leave him, you see, and he doesn't really want the kind of scandal that would involve. I know I would end up the loser as far as Hugh is concerned. I've always known that . . ." She sighed, and hesitated, as if she feared that Hugh was already a lost cause. "Even so," she went on, "he doesn't entirely trust me not to go to court. Even though he'd be bound to win in the end, there'd be an awful lot of dirty linen that could be washed in public if it should come to that, so at the moment he's treating me with kid gloves."

"I'm glad to hear it. I wish you were happier, though."

Frances laughed at that. "I could say the same about you," she said. "I suppose we all want our friends to have ideal lives, but not many people do."

Verity opened her mouth, longing to confide, longing just to say his name. Remember Laurie, she would say? Remember Dr Grenfell? The camellia man? We're lovers.

But the gates were ahead and Frances was talking about the Jagos once more and their daughter Minnie who seemed quite a bright little girl, so the moment passed. In a way she was glad that she had resisted the temptation, not at all sure that this was the ideal life that Frances had in mind for her. With her concern for children in general, she might well bring up the matter of Laurie's son and daughter, Robin and Celia, which was a subject that Verity did her best not to think about.

June turned into July, while the country held its breath, still fearful of invasion. The much heralded bombing raids became a reality as Germany sought superiority in the sky, concentrating on the ports and air-fields. Laurie wrote of fire-watching duties in Kew Gardens, much of which was now turned over to growing vegetables. But despite all, he and Verity arranged to meet at the Swan towards the end of July, just before Beatrice was due to come home for the long summer holidays.

Verity arrived there before him, having travelled independently. Laurie had warned her he could well be late. He had been co-opted on to a government committee concerned with the growing of food and there was to be a meeting that afternoon in central London. He had no idea how long it was likely to last, and in any case, the trains were unpredictable these days and often subject to delays.

"Your usual room's been took," Mrs Harrison, the landlady, informed her. "Sorry about that, Mrs Grenfell, but there's this old couple from Southampton wanted it permanent-like, on account of the bombs. I've had to put you in the back."

"I'm sure we shall be perfectly comfortable," Verity said.

It was a shame, though. They had loved that front bedroom, with its white walls and sloping roof and blue curtains, the high, white brass bedstead and the blue and white candlesticks on the mantelpiece. It had become familiar and meaningful, had been the scene of much happiness, many gradations of emotion. You could hear the burbling of the stream outside as you lay in bed, and sometimes there were nightingales singing in the wood.

The back room to which she was now banished was quite different, with nowhere near the same degree of comfort. It was small and dark and almost entirely filled by a cheap, modern bed covered by a slippery gold eiderdown. The paper on the walls was a tobacco colour, badly discoloured by damp in one corner, and the windows were curtained in dull brown, the outlook consisting of a blank wall, once white, but now green and black with mildew.

It didn't matter, Verity told herself as she unpacked her few possessions, arranging brush and comb on the dressing table, hanging up the dress she would wear that evening. Laurie would find it amusing. They'd laugh about it and draw the curtains so that whatever it was like, it would be their own enclosed little world.

It was a relief to leave it behind, however, and take a walk beside the river in an effort to fill the time before he arrived. She climbed the hill at the end of the lane that they had climbed so many times before. There was a wonderful view of the surrounding countryside from there; undulating fields and woods, the spire of a church, clusters of cottages, all spuriously peaceful. She leaned on a five-barred gate and gazed at it appreciatively. She felt calm and contented, sure in the knowledge that she would soon be with Laurie, soon feel his arms around her. And she smiled as she thought of him, still feeling that this unexpected rebirth of love was a miracle she could never have imagined.

It was almost eight before he arrived and she was beginning to get a little anxious. It was impossible not to, these days, for life was so uncertain. However, he walked into the room just before dinner, just as she was changing her dress for the evening. He looked tired, she thought, but perfectly safe and sound.

"You're here!" she said joyfully, turning in relief and holding out her arms to him.

He dropped his small overnight case and kissed her and held her, as she had known he would.

"I'm sorry I'm late, sweetheart."

"It doesn't matter, not now."

He looked around the room over the top of her head. "Is this the best they could do for us?"

"Ghastly, isn't it? The other one's let to someone else, permanently! Isn't that awful? We'll never be able to have it again. Still, it's not really important, is it?"

Laurie made no further comment on their surroundings but held her away from him at a little distance, surveying her near-nakedness.

"Mrs Harrison said we ought to go straight in to dinner as soon as you arrived," Verity told him.

"Did she, now?" They were both smiling, for both knew that they would do no such thing. Yet, after the passion was over, there seemed none of the sweet intimacy that she valued beyond any other element of their love.

"What is it, darling?" she asked, stroking his face. "Is something worrying you?"

"No, no." He seemed to make an effort to shake off his sombre mood.

"Have you had a bad day?"

"Pretty awful," he said. But he forced a smile, exclaiming in horror as he looked at his watch and saw the time. "That bloody meeting went on and on – but come on, we must get moving! I'm willing to bet Mrs Harrison is going to know exactly what we've been up to—"

"Let her! Who cares?"

"She'll probably let our dinner burn, just to pay us out for being late. Come on, last one dressed is a cissy!"

It was, she thought, a good effort; but she wasn't in the least convinced. Something was worrying him. Or maybe it was just tiredness. He spoke very little about his work but she knew that it now involved a very great deal more than growing camellias; the meeting had probably been exasperating as well as long-drawn-out. Committee meetings could be, she knew that from experience.

All through dinner – rabbit pie, home-grown vegetables, strawberries and cream, which in Mrs Harrison's hands seemed as fine a meal as could be found anywhere in England – it seemed to her that he was working hard to appear normal. Afterwards, with bats swooping low and a nightingale singing somewhere in the woods beyond the river, they strolled together up the lane towards the hills so that Laurie could, as he said, get the taste of London out of his mouth. He had fallen silent now, and she, too, was quiet. And though she told herself that in these surroundings silence was natural and something to be appreciated, she was conscious of a heaviness in the atmosphere. Suddenly she was apprehensive – without reason, she tried to assure herself. He was tired, that was all. Tired and strained. Something was worrying him. She sensed it in his silences, in the sentences that seemed to tail off and go nowhere, in the tenseness she detected in his face.

"Tell me what's the matter, Laurie," she said at last, very softly.

He said nothing, but she heard him sigh.

"Oh, my darling, it's all such a mess," he said at last.

"What is?" She spoke softly but even so the question was forceful, for there was something in his voice that seemed to say his worries were more serious than she had thought. "*Tell* me," she added with more impatience when still he said nothing.

Still he remained silent, then she heard him take a deep breath. "Marjory came home a couple of nights ago," he said flatly. "She's come back to me. Wants to make a fresh start, try to make our marriage work."

It was like a hammer-blow and Verity stood with her head bent, absorbing the shock. "And what do you want?" she whispered.

He seized her roughly. "You know what I want! It's you I love, but—" he broke off and very slowly, as if it hurt her to do so, Verity lifted her head to look at him.

"But—?"

"It's the children," he said, sounding defeated. "What can I do, Verity? I can't lose them; can't be responsible for breaking up the family."

The pain spread through her, slow but inexorable, and she squeezed her eyes shut. Children get over things, she wanted to say. They're tougher than you think. Marjory wouldn't stop you seeing them. She opened her mouth to speak the words, but closed it again and bit her lip, her eyes suddenly full of scalding tears. There was no guarantee of any of these things, she realised, and no other ending possible. No other ending had ever been possible. She should have known it; should have been prepared for it from the very first time they were together.

"That dinner, in Truro, at the Red Lion," she said bitterly, when she could speak. "You had a family then. You should have remembered."

He reached for her and although initially she resisted, she could not do so for long and turned to bury her face in his shoulder, feeling his lips against her hair.

"I know I should," he said. "Everything that's happened is my fault. I'm so sorry, so very, very sorry. You must believe I love you. I always will." He continued to hold her. "Let's go back," he said at last.

She pulled away from him and looked up into his face. "And make love? Is that what you want?"

"Darling, we both know how we feel—"

"You may." She began to walk away from him. "But I don't know, Laurie, I don't know at all." The tears were pouring down her cheeks and she walked on, waiting after a while for him to catch up with her. When he did so, she said: "I do know. I love you, but I can't go back there." She felt strangely breathless. "I can't spend another night with you, pretending everything is just the same. I just can't, Laurie. I'm going to get a car to take me to Taunton. I'm not staying here."

"What?" He caught hold of her. "Darling, don't talk nonsense, you have to stay. It's too late. You can't get any transport now." He reached again to hold her close. "Oh, sweetheart, let's be together one last time."

She stood, stiff and unyielding in the circle of his arms, and after a moment she pushed him gently away and without speaking turned for home.

22nd July 1940

I am, so Mother tells me, looking "peaky". Mrs Harmer calls it "wisht". I'm not surprised, I feel wisht. In fact it is a total mystery to me that I'm able to move and breathe and function in any way. But with Bea home in two days' time I must somehow pull myself together.

That terrible time in Somerset now seems totally unreal, the stuff of nightmares. That poor farmer whom I dragooned into taking me to Bridgewater with him must have thought I had escaped from the nearest lunatic asylum, but I felt then, and feel now, that fate must have led him to have dropped into the Swan that evening on his way home. However, I wish I could have left with a little more of my dignity intact!

I was angry with Laurie, so very, very angry. Not fair, I know. I am big enough and old enough to know that I was just as much to blame for the whole débâcle. I knew he was married (which makes me morally no better than him, or my father, or – come to that – Nicholas Courtfield!). I knew, also, that he adores his children. But why, why, did he have to come and see me? Why ask me to dinner and start everything up again when the years had healed the pain long ago?

Because his wife had left him and he was lonely, that's why. Because he thought it might be amusing, a little diversion, seeing I was still a poor, unwed woman, to look me up once more.

Do I really think that? Sometimes yes, sometimes no. I don't, honestly, know what to think. I just know that at this moment, I really don't care if I live or die.

Thirteen

While many of the beaches of Britain were sealed off by barbed wire and concrete for reasons of national security, Lemorrick Cove remained accessible to those members of the public who cared to walk to it.

"I suppose the powers-that-be think we're too insignificant even for an invading army," Verity remarked, her eyes on Beatrice, Alex and Rosie as they chased each other towards the sea.

Livvy, sitting beside her, was regarding her closely and made no direct reply. "You," she said, "are not looking at all well. Are you feeling all right?"

Verity groaned. "Not you!" she said. "I just wish people would stop telling me how ghastly I look. It's quite extraordinarily demoralising."

"You should see a doctor."

"Well, maybe I would if I knew of a decent one."

"Very funny! Seriously, Vee—"

"I'm all right, Livvy. Don't go on about it. Actually, you'd be better employed going to rescue Rosie – it looks as if Beatrice and Alex between them are set on drowning her."

Livvy straightened up for a moment and looked at the children now playing in the sea, shielding her eyes with her hand.

"They're all right," she said. "Rosie can stand up for herself, and she swims like a fish. You must be so pleased that Bea is better with other children these days." Comfortably, she settled back again and lifted her face to the sun. "Mm, this is the life," she said. "I feel a bit guilty, though. Poor Robert has more work than he can cope with at the moment, with my father so poorly. I ought to be doing my share."

"You work too hard as it is. It's only right you should have an afternoon off, once in a while. How is your father, anyway?"

"Progressing, but still very weak. This particular bug is a real nuisance; it seems to be cutting quite a swathe through the village and really there doesn't seem much one can do about it. Rest is the only thing, but try telling Dad! He can prescribe for other people, but won't take advice himself."

"I thought doctors were all like that." Verity was still watching the children, but relaxed a little when she saw they were all frisking quite amicably in the shallows. "This bug," she went on after a moment, "does it involve nausea and sickness?"

Livvy turned to look at her once more, this time even more closely. "Mm. Can do. Why? Is that what you're suffering from?"

"Sort of. Sometimes. It kind of comes and goes."

"Vee, do come up to the surgery and have a proper check-up, there's a dear. I'm serious. It's ages since you've been."

"It's ages since I've needed to. Actually—" she paused and shot a glance at Livvy. She sighed. "Actually, Liv, I do feel rather wretched, but I don't think it's anything physical. I've – I've had a bit of a bad time lately." Though she had thought herself over the worst, embarrassingly, and to her complete surprise, she found herself on the verge of tears. Even more disastrous, she couldn't seem to locate a handkerchief.

Livvy reached out to her. "For heaven's sake, Vee, what is it? What sort of bad time?"

Verity sniffed, struggling for control. "Sorry," she said indistinctly, relieved, at last, to have discovered a handkerchief in the pocket of her skirt. "This is neither the place nor the time—"

"Tell," Livvy ordered. "No one's listening."

"It's quite a long story. Remember Laurie?"

"Laurie—? You mean—? Yes, of course! He called, didn't he? Quite unexpectedly. I remember you saying."

For a moment, Verity hesitated, but the temptation to unburden herself at last was too great.

"I don't expect you to approve of this," she warned, "but he and I have been meeting at intervals for most of this year. We were lovers."

"Were?" Livvy's voice was gentle.

Stumblingly, Verity told her the story. "So you see," she finished at last, "I think that's why I'm under the weather. "I – I just can't seem to get over it."

"Oh, *darling*, I'm so sorry!" Livvy was biting her lip, almost in tears herself.

Shakily, Verity gave a small, sobbing laugh. "You don't think of me as a scarlet woman?"

"Don't be ridiculous! I'm just devastated you're so miserable. Look, come and see me at the surgery. I don't pretend to have the panacea for the kind of thing you're going through, but if we deal with the physical under-the-weatherness, maybe you'll be able to cope a bit better with the rest. It's just possible that I could prescribe something that would buck you up a bit."

"Thanks," Verity said. She managed a half-hearted smile. "Trust you to take the practical view." She was prevented from saying more as the three children came running towards them in a flurry of sand, demanding tea. "I will come, I promise, when time allows."

This proved to be in mid-September, after Beatrice had gone back to school, by which time the long-dreaded bombing of London had begun in earnest, with the East End bearing the brunt of it. Each day's news bulletin reported another night of horror, of Londoners spending hours in shelters and on tube stations, emerging to find streets in ruins and houses gone. How, Verity wondered, could people bear it? Yet bear it they did, somehow, and there was even something in her that longed to be bearing it with them. It seemed almost indecent to be so far away from the present danger.

Prompted more than anything else by the depressing image of herself that confronted her in her mirror, she eventually went to see Livvy. She looked like a ghost, she thought. Pale and gaunt and thoroughly miserable.

Livvy examined her carefully, asking questions that to Verity seemed quite irrelevant. When she had finished, she stood for a moment, looking down at her with an unreadable look on her face. "Get dressed," she said, going back to her desk.

Obediently, Verity got up from the examination couch and began to put her clothes on, eyeing her friend and doctor with some anxiety.

"What is it?" she asked as she buttoned her blouse. "You look horribly inscrutable. It's nothing serious, is it?"

"Sit down," Livvy indicated the chair in front of the desk. She took a breath. "Well," she said. "I have a shrewd suspicion you might think it serious, but I doubt if it will prove terminal. Had it crossed your mind that you could be pregnant?"

Verity stared at her and swallowed with difficulty. "No," she said faintly. "It really hadn't."

"Honestly, Vee!" Exasperated, Livvy looked at her in total disbelief. "I suppose it didn't occur to you to take any precautions, either? Or see that Laurie did?"

Wordlessly, Verity shook her head.

"But my dear *girl*—!" Livvy seemed, herself, beyond words. "What on earth could you have been thinking of? Didn't anyone ever tell you the facts of life?"

"But I'm too old for babies! I'm forty—"

"That's not too old!"

"But I haven't been what you might call regular for ages. Livvy, are you sure? You could be mistaken, couldn't you?"

"I could," Livvy admitted. "But I don't think I am. Anyway, we can confirm it within days."

Verity hunched her shoulders and wrapped her arms around herself, staring into space. "Pregnant," she whispered at last. There was a dazed look about her as she turned her eyes to Livvy. "I can't believe it. I *don't* believe it! It's a bad joke, isn't it? When you think how much I've always wanted children . . . Lord, Livvy, what am I going to do?"

"Have it," Livvy said. "You're healthy. I can't possibly recommend anything else."

Verity sat up straight, her eyes flashing. "I wouldn't even want to get rid of it, if that's what you mean! I'm just thinking of – practicalities. The disgrace will be the end of my mother. As if I haven't disappointed her enough—"

"Maybe she's tougher than you think. She can hardly send you out into the snow, can she? Or tell you not to darken her door again?"

"But think of all the tittle-tattle in the village! She'd be mortified, Liv. And so would I, come to that. I'm a respected Councillor, for heaven's sake. Miss Ashland of Lemorrick! Oh, what a juicy morsel for the village gossips."

"I suppose you could find some reason to go away in a few months' time. The baby could be adopted—"

Slowly, as if these words took time to sink in, Verity lifted her head and stared across the desk, her expression one of outrage.

"Adopted? Are you crazy? Livvy, this is *my child*, the only one I'm ever likely to have, and I'm not losing it, not by abortion or adoption or anything else. If there's adopting to be done, then I'm the one who'll do it." She spoke without thought, but then, as if once the words were released into the ether they made the utmost sense, she relaxed in the chair. "That's it, Livvy. That's what I'll do. I'll go away."

"Where?"

"I don't know. I'll think of somewhere. I could go away to do war work."

"Where?"

"I don't know. Anywhere." She paused as if in thought. "London, maybe. Yes, that's what I could do." She was warming to the idea, even growing excited. "I could go to London and offer my services somewhere. You can't tell me they don't need voluntary workers up there. I could renew my old contacts—" She came to a halt, biting her lip. "No, that wouldn't do at all, would it? Secrecy would have to be the watchword. Well, never mind, I'm sure I could find something useful to do, and a place to live. Then, in the fullness of time, I would come back home having adopted a poor little war orphan. People are used to me looking after other people's children. It's the perfect answer, you've got to admit."

"Maybe." Livvy was looking worried. "But London, Vee – is that a good idea just now? Why put yourself and your baby in danger?"

"Because that's where it makes sense to be. I'm hardly going to look for war work in rural Devon, am I?"

Livvy gave a rueful laugh.

"And knowing you, London, let's face it, is where everything's happening and where you want to be. But what about all your activities here? And your mother? I can't imagine she'll be too pleased to see you go."

"Yes – well . . ." Some of Verity's ebullience faded. "It's going to take some organising, I admit, but organise it I will. And Livvy, I've got to go quickly. I'm not having people look at me sideways, speculating, wondering why I've put on weight."

"And what about Beatrice? There are the Christmas holidays to think of."

"I'll meet that problem when it arises. Oh, heavens, Livvy,

anything could happen by then! Surely you can see this is the only answer?"

"Maybe. I don't know. I just hate to think of you on your own up there, without support just when you need it most. Aren't there any old friends you could trust?"

Verity thought this over, but ended up shaking her head. "Not really. Joan Moorcroft might have fitted the bill but she and Bill are living in Manchester now. I had a letter from her just the other day."

"But you'll need friends, Vee. You'll be so lonely, otherwise."

"I'll make new ones." Verity sat back with an expression that was suddenly bleak. "I know it won't be easy, Liv, and Ted Chambers is going to kill me for leaving the Council in the lurch. My name will be mud, I'm fully aware. Even so, it's the only course of action I can think of at the moment."

"Will you tell Laurie?"

Verity sighed and frowned, saying nothing for a moment. "I don't know. I hadn't thought."

"It's his baby as much as yours."

"I know, I know. But Livvy – I don't think I could go through it all again. Seeing him, leaving him. Anyway, he's made his decision and it's not one he's likely to change."

"Wouldn't this make a difference?"

Dumbly, Verity shook her head. "Why should it? No, I'm on my own with this. I'm going to have to do some very careful planning." She got to her feet. "I must go. You've got a waiting room full of patients out there. Meantime, you'll get on with the job of seeing if all this is really necessary?"

Livvy raised an eyebrow, and expressionlessly reached into a drawer to bring out a small glass beaker which she presented to Verity.

"It's something only you can do," she said.

She would have to confide in Frances, Verity decided. She had high-level contacts all over the place, including, probably, London. It seemed more than likely that one of them might know of something she could usefully do.

This child must have been conceived in mid-July on that last weekend – that last, hurried coupling when Laurie had already left her in his heart and Mrs Harrison was wondering why they were late for dinner. It meant that she had seven months left in which to come to some kind of conclusion. Seven months of exile! It seemed to stretch out before her like a prison sentence.

On the other hand, London again . . . the thought of it was undoubtedly exciting, stimulating. She'd be where history was being made.

London, 2nd October 1940
Thank heaven for Frances! Thanks to her I've been able to find not only some voluntary work but also somewhere to lay my head. Someone she knows slightly knows a man who has been taken prisoner in France, poor chap, but this very ill wind has blown me some good because the unfortunate man happens to have a small flat in Paget Court, Bloomsbury, and what is more, he has left the key with the said friend who thought it made sense for him to accumulate some rent instead of letting the flat stay empty. I am very grateful for it, for accommodation is like gold-dust. It's hardly palatial, just two tiny rooms and a sliver of a kitchen, plus what must be the smallest bathroom in London, but it's as much as I need or wish to cope with.

The bombing continues nightly and is unnerving, to say the least, with vast tracts of the East End all but flattened – which is why my services were welcome in a Rest Centre in Clerkenwell set up for the homeless.

I thought when I first saw the Centre that I would never be able to stand it. It looked like a scene from Dante's Inferno, *full of weird, unwashed people who appeared, at first sight, to be shouting at the top of their voices. The noise seemed to bounce off the bare walls of this cavernous warehouse where hundreds eke out an existence. I have been there two days now and still find it overwhelming, but have found it's not as bad as the first impression would have one believe. (Not quite!) I spend my time in the canteen dispensing tea and various items of food – soup, baked beans on toast, tomatoes on toast, sardines on toast, pilchards on toast (NOT Ashland's, I'm sorry to say, though of course the company is called West Country Products now). Also helped in picking through sackfuls of clothes for people who have lost everything. Human nature incredibly resilient. Much ribald joking, some of it, I think, a kind of hysterical reaction to still being alive in the midst of such chaos.*

Everything seems totally disorganised because these places have only just been set up and nobody knows quite who is responsible for what. We keep getting conflicting orders.

Am also called upon to dispense advice. Have been asked all kinds of questions from how to make a will to the best treatment for an ingrowing toenail, and am forced to adopt an entirely false appearance of omniscience. Would be entirely at sea except for woman called Josie – large and capable and full of confidence who seems to know what to do and say by instinct. I think she thinks I am a hopeless, gormless toff, but I am learning and she is kind.

The sound of the ack-ack guns are slightly muted in the Centre, but several bombs fell in the next street yesterday and we heard them without difficulty! Almost immediate influx of three distraught families who had survived by a miracle, though the son and grandmother of one lot were wounded and taken to hospital.

Back at the flat, NOTHING is muted! The first night here I was woken about midnight by the siren followed immediately by the ack-ack guns, so I dressed quickly, got my torch and went to the nearest shelter, only yards away up the road. Had miserable night. Sat on a bench until the all-clear in extreme discomfort, next to a woman who boasted non-stop about Near Misses She Has Known. Hoped fervently, in view of the bombs we could hear, that her luck would hold. It did, but it was hardly the most entertaining topic I could think of. Guns non-stop. Afterwards, we were told that the bombs we heard were incendiaries, mainly over the dock area. Was dead with tiredness and back-ache next day and decided not to bother with the shelter again. The flat is on the ground floor and has an exceptionally solid-looking oak dining table, so I put my mattress under it and slept there last night. Tried to, anyway. Was so tired I managed a few hours, despite the guns, the noise of which is truly horrendous and shakes the building. Still, one does feel (probably erroneously) more protected when one hears them. Josie assures me you get used to them and that she sleeps quite well now, which I find hard to believe.

Lay, in my many waking hours, wondering if I am mad to be here. Have I done the right thing? Are these the kind of surroundings for my unborn child? If not, where else can I go? Should I decamp to the country and just pretend *that I'm in London? I can't honestly imagine why I didn't think of this course of action sooner, except that I had this purely selfish urge to see what was going on up here. But there would be, of course, the problem of how to communicate with Mother. She would begin to smell a rat if my address was somewhere away from town. Also there is the fact that I think I am doing quite a useful job.*

Haven't been sick for three days!

Sunday, 13th October 1940
Still surviving. Am taking a day off today, the first for a couple of weeks. Stayed in bed (under the table!) for most of the morning. Everything quiet, was able to sleep for several hours and felt better for it.

Thought of taking a walk, but it's raining and miserable outside and the spirit has weakened. Feel quite good physically, however. No more sickness.

I think I would like the man who owns this flat. I like his pictures, anyway, and his books. Am currently (and slowly because there's not much time) reading his entire collection of Trollope, which I am enjoying much more than the first time round for some obscure reason. Shall start on Hardy next. I think he must be some kind of academic as there are all kinds of books on Spanish literature (in English) and poems (in Spanish). Some of the pictures look as if they are Spanish, too – lots of white buildings and intricate balconies and splashy-coloured flowers. They make me feel warm just to look at them. I wonder if he sits in his dreary prison camp and thinks about them. I hope he's all right. His name is Rupert Finn.

Keep changing my mind about whether or not I should contact Laurie to tell him of my condition. Swing between thinking he ought to know and feeling that it would only serve to upset me more if he attempts to have a hand in it (as it were). Yet I feel so utterly alone that there are times when I know I would jump at the chance to see him, let alone go back to him. What an utterly foolish, weak and irresolute woman I am!

I just wish I had someone to talk to! I know I'm with people all day every day but even if there were time to talk of personal matters, there is no one I would want to confide in. Josie is the kind of woman generally known as a Good Sort – good-natured, relentlessly cheerful and full of clichés. It occurred to me the other day that she never really listens to anyone despite her appearance of doing so. If I were ever stupid enough to tell her all, I know exactly what her reaction would be. She'd grin and slap me on the back and say well, poor old you. Never mind, love. Worse things happen at sea, and there is a war on, you know. Chin up and all that. So I tell her nothing.

It's odd, really. When planning these months away, I convinced myself that the thought of the baby would keep me company. What I didn't bargain for was not really believing in it. It simply doesn't seem real, that in roughly six months' time another soul will exist, for whom I will be entirely responsible.

12th November 1940
Haven't written up diary for ages due to pressure of work and a disinclination to do anything but slump when I get home, but feel I must record the events of last night. Left the Centre at eight-thirty at night, having been there since eight in the morning. Siren went just as I left, but I thought I'd plough on and get home as the Centre is only about a fifteen-minute walk away from the flat and I was dying for a hot bath. It was a lovely night, starry and clear. Guns going, of course, and the occasional warden yelled at me to take cover, but I just hurried on. Was concentrating on getting home as fast as I could when suddenly there were two distinct whistles, and two bombs suddenly seemed to drop from nowhere about a hundred yards in front of me, no more. There was a sheet of flame and then mud and stones and all manner of debris simply shot up in a kind of huge fountain. Instinctively I flung myself on the pavement behind a handily-placed horse trough, at the same time as another bomb went off somewhere not far away.

I just lay there for a while unable to move, until I realised that a warden was crouched over me asking me if I was all right. I said I thought so, and he helped me up, my knees trembling so much I couldn't stand at first. He wanted to take me to an Ambulance Post, but I said no, there was nothing really wrong and anyway I was almost home, so he very kindly escorted me there and we both had a rather large brandy that I was keeping for emergencies. I thought this probably was one.

After the warden had gone, she had sat on, sipping her drink slowly, to the accompaniment of ack-ack gunfire.

You are being a fool, she said to herself. You are being selfish. You are responsible for someone else now, a small, helpless being who is utterly dependent on you, and what do you do? You bring him into danger, to be bombed and shot at and starved of fresh air and decent nourishment. And why? To be away from prying eyes, yes, but also because something in you craved for change and excitement.

When had she last had a good, balanced meal? She couldn't remember. For the last few weeks, it seemed, she had eaten beans, and sausages stuffed with sawdust, and chips, and bread, bread, bread. Helpers at the Centre tended to eat whatever was left over, and once home, she found she was too tired to think of food. It was, she recognised, a foolish way to conduct a pregnancy.

But how could she quit now? The work she did was quite valuable in a mundane kind of way, particularly now that she knew the drill and understood the people more. She'd grown to like them – most of them, anyway. There was one evil, foul-mouthed old man she wished she would never have to see again, but then everyone felt like that about him, even his family. And there was Mrs Wisden. Dorrie. She had a thin, miserable kind of face, and three thin, miserable children, and all four of them whined and complained and demanded more attention than all the other inhabitants of the Centre put together.

But apart from these and a few like them, for the most part she had learned to respect the tough, irreverent Londoners with their defiant and subversive humour. Would everyone, put to such a test as these Cockneys had been, prove as resilient, as impossible to defeat? Perhaps. She only knew that if Hitler thought he could break their spirit, he was mightily mistaken.

She'd soldier on for a bit longer, she thought. But she would be careful. Not take the kind of risk she'd taken that night. Make sure she ate properly for the baby's sake. This nightmare couldn't, surely, go on for ever. At the last count there had been sixty-four nights running when sirens had sounded, bombs had dropped, casualties had mounted. There had to be a let-up soon.

Only two nights later it came, and she woke on the morning of the 14th November to realise, with astonishment, that she had slept soundly for seven hours, undisturbed by sirens or

242

guns. The Luftwaffe, she learned later, had switched its attention to Coventry, which was effectively flattened. Bristol, too, was raided.

Dressing to go to the Centre that day, she paused a moment to look at herself critically in the mirror, turning sideways to study her silhouette.

She could still get away with it, she thought; particularly now that winter had come and she could hide the fact that the waistband of her trousers no longer fastened by shrouding herself in thick sweaters and an overcoat. Time moved on inexorably, however, and it wouldn't be too long before her condition was obvious to all, overcoats notwithstanding. She ought, she knew, to see a doctor. Book in at a nursing home.

Contact Laurie?

No. It was a day for being strong, for holding on to her anger. She had coped on her own for so long, and would continue to do so.

She arrived back at Paget Court that evening and was about to put the kettle on to make a cup of tea, when the front door bell rang. This was a sufficiently unusual happening to startle her.

Outside the front door, standing in the corridor, she found an unknown, elderly woman; a bizarre figure, tall and thin, with wild, white hair beneath a wide-brimmed black felt hat which was set at a rakish angle. Against the chill November air she wore a black and white checked cloak thrown dramatically over one shoulder. Her features, too, were dramatic: heavy black eyebrows, and a prominent, beaky nose.

"Cynthia Finn," she said with a wolfish smile, thrusting out her hand in Verity's direction.

"Who – oh!" The flat-owner's wife? Surely not! She had imagined him to be a much younger man. His mother, maybe. Verity took the proffered hand.

"I'm Verity Ashland."

"I know. May I come in?" Mrs Finn's head was on one side, her large nose giving her the appearance of some strange, exotic bird.

"Yes, of course. Please forgive me."

The small hall would hardly permit two people to stand side by side and there was a moment's confusion as Verity ushered the visitor into the sitting room, suddenly uncomfortably conscious of the layer of dust which misted the furniture. Her crowded life did not seem to permit a great deal of dusting. Cynthia Finn, however, was looking around approvingly, smilingly pointing her nose in this direction and that.

"Not exactly a palace, is it? Still, not bad – not if one's forced to live in this monstrous wen."

Verity found her heart sinking, sure that this visit boded no good. Mrs Finn must want the flat herself; for what other reason could she have come?

"It's convenient," Verity said. "And I'm extremely grateful for it."

"I should introduce myself properly. I'm Rupert's mother. Had to come up to town today to see my solicitor, so thought I'd pop round to see if all's well." Her voice was hearty and full of self-confidence, aggressively upper-class.

"Everything's fine. I – I know it's a bit dusty," Verity hurried on, feeling rather like an incompetent housemaid, "but I haven't got around—"

"Dusty?" The nose went up and down and from side to side as its owner checked the surroundings. "Can't say I notice such things. Thought I ought to see if the place is still in one piece, though. Still got its windows, and all that."

"Oh, yes. The windows of the flats upstairs were shattered, but these survived, I'm glad to say. Tell me, how is your son?"

"Surviving, like the windows. Says he's well. These cards they send don't say much more, you know, but if I know Rupe he'll be making as much of a nuisance of himself as possible. He was always a rebel."

"I'm glad! Glad that he's well, I mean. Please sit down, won't you? Let me get you some tea."

"D'you know, I'd love a cup? Thank you, my dear. That would be very kind."

Verity went at once, and when she returned with a tray in her hands, she found Mrs Finn standing with her back to the room, surveying one of the pictures.

"What do you think of this?" she asked, looking at Verity over her shoulder. She had flung her cape over one of the chairs and was now revealed in a tweed skirt and a mustard-coloured jersey, darned in several places.

"I love it," Verity said, putting the tray down and going to stand beside her. "It warms up the entire room, don't you agree? Makes me feel that one day there'll be colour and sun and lovely things to enjoy."

"Excellent," said Mrs Finn beaming and slapping her tweedy thigh. "Glad you like it. I painted it in – oh, let's see 1922, I think. I was a bit of a bolter, I'm afraid. I got tired of living in England, so swept up young Rupe and Caro, my daughter, and pushed orf to Spain."

"You painted it? And the others?"

"I plead guilty."

"They're lovely! How very clever. You must have been a professional."

"I dabbled, that's all." She sighed, heavily. "To my shame. Should have concentrated on it, I suppose, but there were always so many other – ah!" She broke off suddenly, and swooped upon an ornament on the mantelpiece. "The little dog! What memories that brings back! It was given to Rupe, you know, by a Spanish nobleman. Juan Balthasar Gonzales-Grandes." She spoke the name lovingly, as if savouring every syllable. "It's quite valuable, he gave us to understand, made in the sixteenth century, just outside Seville."

"Then please, please take it home with you," Verity begged. "And anything else your son values."

Mrs Finn looked at the figure of the dog for a moment, then replaced it.

"Well, perhaps," she said. "And perhaps not. He's probably happier here. Rupert doesn't set much store by worldly goods, you see. He's like me in that respect."

She sat down and accepted the cup of tea that Verity offered, and all at once, as if a spotlight had been turned on her, Verity felt herself the object of Cynthia Finn's entire concentration.

"I suppose," she said, "you're busy with war work of some kind? Can you talk about it? Or is it hush-hush?"

Verity laughed, amused at the thought of events at the Centre being in any way secret. "Not at all," she said, and proceeded to give an account of her days.

Mrs Finn was an appreciative audience: admiring, amused, curious. "I take my hat orf to you," she said at last. She was speaking metaphorically, as the dashing hat remained on her head throughout. "The society of too many of my fellow men

245

has always made me run for cover. I'm a country woman, you see. Just come up from the depths of Hertfordshire. Mellon's Green. You won't have heard of it. It's not far from London as the crow flies, but a million miles away in spirit."

"I'm a country woman, too. From Cornwall," Verity said.

"Cornwall! How wonderful! I adore Cornwall. I lived with an artist in St Ives back in – oh, who cares when! It was a long time ago. Anyway, I utterly adored every moment, except when he got drunk, which was almost every night. It all wore a bit thin, you know, and we began to have rows and throw things at each other. He told me to bugger orf, so I did, with an engraver of immense talent and absolutely no sense of humour at all. *That* didn't last very long, I can tell you. Pity, but there you are. George Hoffman, his name was. He was quite famous in his time, but of course he's forgotten now. Probably in another hundred years . . . Tell me, what on earth persuaded you to leave the safety of Cornwall to come here? Patriotism? Love of good works?" Her head was cocked on one side, her beady brown eyes bright with curiosity.

"I – wanted to do my bit," Verity said. "Naturally."

"Of course, of course! At your age I would have felt the same. Now I feel I'm doing what I can for the common weal by keeping out of everyone's way." She consulted a watch that was pinned to her mustard-coloured bosom. "Good lord, look at the time! Thank you for the tea and the chat, my dear. I've enjoyed it, and Rupert will be glad to know I've met you and that the flat's still in one piece. I really must fly, however. There's a train in half an hour I can catch if I hurry. I might even find a taxi, with a bit of luck."

The cloak was swung round her shoulders, and she departed without ceremony, leaving Verity strangely cheered.

"Come again," she called after the old lady's retreating form as it proceeded down the corridor towards the door that led to the street. Mrs Finn did not turn, but merely waved her hand in the air. Whether this was denial or acceptance of the invitation, Verity had no idea, but she found she was smiling as she closed the door once again.

Christmas was rapidly approaching, bringing its own worries. Vaguely, Verity had thought she would write to Beatrice's headmistress asking if any of her friends could have her niece for the holiday since she was unable to get away, but as the time approached she began to think that perhaps it might be possible to conceal her pregnancy for a couple of days. At five months, her increased girth was still only noticeable to herself, just as long as she wore suitable clothes. If she attended the midnight service at church, she would wear her beaver coat which would hide all from the village; and if she bought a long, loose cardigan to wear at home, her mother might (and undoubtedly would) deplore her taste, but would have no suspicion of the real reason for it. Beatrice, she felt sure, would notice nothing amiss.

So she risked it, travelling down to Cornwall on Christmas Eve, and back to London on Boxing Day. The journey in both directions was long and uncomfortable, but she was glad she had made the effort, though once back in Paget Court and able to hide within the confines of her own four walls, she collapsed with relief. The whole experience had proved to her that she had done the right thing in getting away from home. Louise, while welcoming her with tears of joy, had nevertheless been relentless in her criticism. Verity, she said, looked tired and was far too pale. And surely she had put on weight? She was eating the wrong things, that was the cause of it. Too much starch. Not enough fruit and vegetables. She wasn't looking after herself properly.

It was, Verity admitted, a pretty fair assessment of the situation.

"But Mother, there is a war on, you know! And really I do a useful job."

"That's as maybe," Louise granted. "But why you have to cling to that dowdy cardigan, heaven only knows! You look like a retired missionary! Just because there's a war on, it doesn't mean you have to lose every last morsel of dress sense, surely?"

"I know it's not exactly the *dernier cri*," Verity admitted. "But it really is incredibly comfortable. And," she added, tongue in cheek, "it's so lovely to be home and able to wear just what I like in the sure knowledge that no one is going to criticise me."

She couldn't, she felt, have kept up the charade for long, but at least the purpose was fulfilled and she was able to make sure that Beatrice enjoyed a reasonably festive Christmas. She appeared well and cheerful and rather proud of her aunt's wartime exploits. In fact Verity had a shrewd suspicion that she habitually made much of them at school and suspected that her own extremely humble role in this war had been exaggerated out of all proportion, thus allowing her niece to bask in reflected glory. Livvy – as worried about Verity's pallor as Louise had been – promised to keep an eye on Beatrice once Verity returned to London, and took this opportunity of ordering her to take more care of herself.

"You *must* see a doctor when you get back," she said. "Promise me, now! You should be taking vitamins and orange juice and all kinds of things, as well as having your blood pressure monitored. At your age you can't be too careful."

Verity had pulled an indignant face at this, but had promised that she would ensure that she took care of herself in future.

It was the day after Verity was back in London that Cynthia Finn called again. She drank tea and sat and chatted as before, but astonished Verity by suddenly breaking off a spirited account of her activities in the Suffragette movement (dear Christabel, she *meant* well, of course, but she was always in her mother's shadow and it made her a little difficult, sometimes) to look at her sharply, her black brows drawn together. "You're pregnant, aren't you?" she asked.

Verity put down her cup carefully. "Does it show that much?"

"No," Mrs Finn admitted. "Not really. It's just that I can tell. Always can. Must say I wondered, the last time we met. Who's the father?"

Verity looked at her for a moment. "I don't think that's any of your business," she said, polite but cold.

"Very true. Still, I take it he can't marry you. I suppose he's away in the forces—"

"Not that I know of," Verity said.

The eyes that surveyed her were inquisitive, but kind. "I'm very difficult to shock," said Mrs Finn. "And clearly, you're troubled. Thought so, the last time. Might help to get it orf your chest, you know. Often does."

It did, Verity found, when after some initial hesitation she told her story. She knew, of course, that she was lonely, but the relief she found by confiding in Cynthia Finn took her by surprise.

"Reluctant as I always am to give advice," Mrs Finn said when she had finished, jabbing her nose forcefully in Verity's direction, "I think you should give up this job and get out of London.

Come to me. To my cottage. Mellon's Green is a delightful little place, quiet and peaceful. We get the odd air-raid warning, of course, but so far no enemy activity anywhere near. You can tell your family you're travelling up every day. People do, poor sods. Don't suppose your mother will know the difference. Can you type?"

Verity stared at her, surprised by this apparent *non sequitur*. "Yes," she said. "I used to be a journalist."

"Excellent! I'm writing me memoirs, you see. Could do with a bit of help, to tell the truth."

"I see," Verity said, faintly.

"How about it, then? No!" Mrs Finn held up a commanding hand. "Don't answer now. Give it some thought. I think we could rub along rather well."

Could they? Would Cynthia Finn be too suffocating? Bossy? Living in somebody else's house would be bound to need adjustments of one sort or another.

"I – I still can't make up my mind whether I should tell the baby's father—"

"That you're expecting?" Again, there was a jab of the nose towards her. "He doesn't know?" Verity shook her head without speaking. Cynthia Finn pursed her lips and narrowed her eyes. "What would he do if he did?" she demanded.

"I – don't really know." Verity spoke hesitantly.

"I do! He'd rush around like a blue-arsed fly, my dear, that's what he'd do. He'd parade his conscience, weep all over you, upset you thoroughly and in the end would bugger orf back to his wife. Take my word for it."

"You don't think he has a right to know?"

"Not at all! He gave up any rights the day he decided to play fast and loose with your affections. Sever all connections, my dear. You're better orf without him."

Verity was smiling. "You may be right."

"Of course I'm right! Now, say that you'll come and give me a hand with me memoirs. You'll enjoy them, I guarantee. Some of them will make your hair stand on end."

"I don't doubt it."

"So how about it? At least come out and see my place. You don't mind animals, do you? I have a couple of Jack Russells and a few cats, but I don't let them get out of hand. And then there are the goats, but they're outside, of course. With the ducks. Why don't you come for Sunday dinner?"

"I'd love to," said Verity, and was conscious, as she spoke, of a profound and all-embracing feeling of relief.

Fourteen

The sea was a calm, cold silver, and towards the east the sun was rising in spectacular fashion, staining the sky with pink and gold.

Verity, sitting in the window seat of her bedroom with the baby in her arms, saw the colours and was transported by their beauty and the tranquillity of the scene before her.

The peace was illusory, for by this time the war had come closer to home than ever before. Plymouth was now a total ruin, flattened by the bombs that had rained upon it earlier in the year. The evacuees were back once more, this time from Plymouth and Bristol as well as London, so that Frances and her cohorts were kept busy finding billets for them. No less than four school-age boys had been housed at Lemorrick for an entire month, until their mother found a house to rent nearer to Truro, more convenient to the school and to the work she had been able to find there.

"And if you take anyone else in, it will be over my dead body," Louise said with great force after they had gone, her chins quivering. "We have quite enough to cope with, thank you very much."

She meant Jeremy, of course, though heaven knew he caused her little enough trouble. At three months, Jem, as everyone called him, had lost his new-born crinkliness and had developed into a pretty baby, plump and good-natured and glowing with health. He slept well, ate well. She was lucky, Verity acknowledged. His arrival in the Ashland household had been controversial enough as it was; a more troublesome child would have been even less welcome.

"I really can't imagine what could have possessed you," Louise had said, when Verity had come home with the baby in her arms. She had, of course, been well primed to expect him, but predictably had failed to reconcile herself to his actual arrival.

251

"It's all very well to say there was no one left to look after him, but there are institutions for children like that. He would have been well cared for."

"But Mother, I told you. I knew his parents. I wanted to have him."

"He must have relatives somewhere. It's not up to you to take him on. It's a responsibility, you know, bringing up a child."

"I do know," Verity said, patiently. "But the deed is done, Mother. There was no one else and I *have* taken him on. It's all above-board and legal, so really there's no point in arguing about it. I thought, just possibly, you might think it a good idea. After all, what other babies am I likely to have? I love him as if he were my own, and when you get used to the idea, I'm sure you'll learn to love him, too."

Louise's mouth had set in a disapproving line, and although she had said no more just then, Verity knew from experience that there was still much that she would like to say. And would, given time.

It all washed over her head. From the moment she had given birth, her very bones had seemed to melt in adoration of this baby. She felt, these days, as if she had been presented with the keys of a kingdom she had never hoped to enter.

Beatrice's reaction, when she arrived home for the Easter of 1941, had been as hostile as her grandmother's, though she, too, had been equally well prepared.

"He's the dearest baby," Verity had written. "He'll be like a little brother to you, won't he? And how I shall depend on you to help me look after him! He's going to grow up loving you so much."

Beatrice had, however, pointedly withheld any interest in the new arrival. She didn't like babies, she told Verity. They were boring. It was, Verity found, her new word. Porthallic was boring, the beach was boring, Alex and Rosie were boring, writing to her parents was boring.

"You know what kids are like," Livvy said, reassuringly. "It's yet another phase. At least you can console yourself that she seems thoroughly settled at school these days. And in a way, a touch of jealousy is understandable."

"I've tried so hard not to let her feel that Jem has usurped her place here."

"I know. But she has had your undivided attention for a long time now, hasn't she? And you have to admit she's never been very good at sharing anything. She'll learn. And after all, it's not given to everyone to love babies. Jem might appeal to her more when he's a bit older and toddling around. Tell me," she went on, following another line of thought, "do you think your mother has the slightest suspicion—?"

"Not the slightest," Verity assured her quickly. "She never ceases telling me how foolish and quixotic I was to take on someone else's child. What about the village? Have you heard any whispers?"

"No. Not one. It's just as you said, folk are used to thinking of you as someone who takes on other people's children. Beatrice has given you the perfect alibi."

And Beatrice was now back at school, which was, Verity had to admit, something of a relief.

"And how are you, personally?" Livvy asked.

"I'm fine," she replied. "Really," she added a little more forcefully, looking up with a smile when Livvy's continued silence seemed to imply scepticism. "I mean it. Laurie Grenfell is firmly confined to the past and Jem is the only thing that matters. Meeting Cynthia Finn when I did just about saved my sanity."

"I wish I knew her."

"Oh, you'd adore her! She seems such a scatty, eccentric sort of person, but believe me, hearts don't come any bigger or kinder. I can't imagine what I would have done without her. She just swept me up and took charge, which is exactly what I needed at the time. She wasn't judgemental or disapproving—" Remembering Cynthia's memoirs, Verity laughed. "She couldn't afford to be! I tell you, the typewriter almost self-combusted at some of the things I was asked to record. My pathetic little sins positively paled into insignificance."

"Is she coming down here at all?"

"I've asked her, but I don't think she will. Being away from Mellon's Green for a single day is as much as she can stand because of all the animals. Anyway—" Verity broke off, and laughed again. "I somehow can't see Cynthia and my mother having a great deal to say to each other. Cynthia is quite as likely to launch into a blow-by-blow account of life in Paris as an opera-singer's mistress as she is to give advice on pruning roses. And if Mother raised any objection, Cynthia could well tell her to bugger orf! No, I'll go up and stay with her one day, but I'm pretty sure she won't come here."

"Are you going to tell Jem about his parentage?"

"Yes, of course. One day, when he's old enough to understand. But no one else, Livvy. Never anyone else. Not Laurie, not anyone. You and Frances and Cynthia are the only people who know, and none of you are likely to say anything, are you? This is one secret I intend to carry with me to the grave."

"Because of what people would say?"

"Because I've already brought enough disgrace to this family."

"You exaggerate, Vee."

"Maybe. But you know what they say about the sins of the fathers. I don't want Jem to suffer from the sins of the mother."

"Well, I swear a word will never pass my lips. And listen, don't worry too much about Beatrice. Mark my words, once he's walking and talking he'll win her over, I'm sure. He's a born charmer."

Verity hoped she was right. The Easter holiday had proved that there was ample room for improvement. Dispiritingly, she found that the summer holiday was no better.

The war dragged on, all their lives dominated by the moral necessity to hear the six o'clock news on the wireless. There was bitter fighting in Greece and in Russia, where the losses of men and equipment were said to be enormous. There were heavy losses at sea, too, with two more Porthallic homes left without their sons.

Then came Pearl Harbor and America's entry to the war, almost immediately followed by news of the Japanese bombing of the Philippines and of Hong Kong. At Christmas, Hong Kong fell.

"Thank God we didn't send Beatrice to Singapore," Verity said to her mother, who uttered a scream and put her hand to her mouth.

"Oh, surely, surely, they won't get to Singapore!" she moaned. "Oh, poor Stephen! Poor, dear Daphne! It's simply too much for me to bear."

"Don't say a *word* to Beatrice," Verity warned her. "Please, Mother. Promise me? There's no point in worrying her until we know if there's anything to worry about."

It was not long before they knew. On Sunday, 15th February 1942, came the news they had been dreading. Singapore had fallen. The following weekend, Verity left Jem to Mrs Harmer's mercies, and went up to the school to see Beatrice.

23rd February 1942
Hard to know what Beatrice is feeling. She said very little, but that isn't much indication. Of course I put as good a light on it as possible, saying that Stephen and Daphne might well have got away since they were civilians, but in my heart I am fearful for Stephen. He is, after all, next to the Governor in seniority, and as such was surely bound to stay until the last gasp. I can't imagine he would ever do less than his duty. However, Daphne might well have got out in time. I do hope and pray there is some definite news from them soon. I think Beatrice was appreciative of the fact that I came to see her, leaving Jem at home. I really don't know what to do about that situation, which doesn't seem to improve. I suppose time is the only answer.

A year later, however, things were no better. Beatrice was home for the Easter holidays once again and had, at Verity's request, taken Jem to the nursery while her aunt was called away to the phone. After no more than five minutes, the sounds of shouts and screams and tears caused Verity to finish her call hastily and run upstairs in panic, to find Beatrice rushing to meet her, her face scarlet with fury.

"That *wretched* boy! Just look what he's done! Look, he's knocked my jigsaw off the table and I'd almost finished it and it was *terribly* hard, it took me ages to do the sky—"

"I'm sure he didn't mean to—"

"He won't do it again. I hit him. *Hard!*"

"Beatrice, you shouldn't—"

"He deserved it! He mustn't touch my things."

Verity swept the bellowing Jeremy into her arms, and looked around at the scattered pieces and the low table where only a fragment of the puzzle remained.

"Beatrice, *really*! You don't mean to tell me you left it on that little table? Then you've got no one to blame but yourself. For heaven's sake, child, why didn't you put it somewhere higher? You could have done it on the big table—"

"Oh, it's always my fault, isn't it? You always blame me for everything. He's got to learn not to touch my things."

"Of course I don't always blame you! But Jem's still only a baby. He doesn't understand—"

"Well, he'd jolly well better learn!"

"He will. But I'm not having you hitting him, Bea, Do you hear me? I won't have it!" Verity spoke sternly. "You can let him know you're not pleased with him, he can tell by your voice. But you are not to smack him. Do you understand?" Seeing Beatrice's face, she took a breath and moderated her tone a little. "I'm sorry about the puzzle. I do understand how infuriating it must have been for you, but we do have to think a bit before—"

"Why should we?" Still beside herself with rage, Beatrice spat the words in Verity's direction. "He's nothing but a pest and I don't see why you had to bring him here. We were perfectly happy without him."

Verity looked at her, bereft of words. The child had troubles of her own, she reminded herself. No one had heard any news of either of her parents since the fall of Singapore the previous year.

"Beatrice—" she began.

"I'll hit him if I want to," Beatrice muttered, turning away and bending down to pick up the pieces.

"What did you say?" Verity's control was slipping again.

"I said I'd hit him if I wanted to. I'm fed up with having a baby to look after all the time."

"All the time?" Verity repeated the words. "All the time?" She gave an exasperated laugh, but warned herself to be careful. It wouldn't do to blow this out of all proportion. Adults often said terrible things in the heat of the moment; it was only to be expected that Beatrice, sorely tried as she had been, might do the same. "Come off it, Beatrice! I asked you to keep an eye on him for five minutes! Don't pretend I treat you like some kind of put-upon skivvy."

"Well, it's not fair," Beatrice said again, not meeting her eye. "Other girls don't have babies to look after. You should get a nanny for him."

Verity took a deep breath, looking at her in silence for a moment over Jem's head as she continued to soothe him. "Don't move," she said, quietly but in the kind of way that ensured she would be obeyed. "I'm going to put Jem down for his nap now, but when I come back, I think we ought to have a real talk, don't you?"

Beatrice said nothing to this, but she was still there when Verity returned, morosely picking up the last few pieces of her jigsaw.

"Look," Verity said, calm now, as she bent to help her. "I'm truly sorry about the puzzle. But darling, you must stop and think before lashing out. Jem is still hardly more than a baby, and it's quite wrong for you to hit him for behaving like one. It's natural for him to pull himself up by holding on to things, and scattering your jigsaw was just a game to him. He didn't know he was being naughty."

Beatrice said nothing in reply to this, and after a moment Verity realised that she was crying, making no sound, the tears slipping silently down her cheeks. She sat down close to her niece and put her arms around her,

"Oh, Bea darling, don't be unhappy. I know you must be worried about Mummy and Daddy. It's a terrible situation for you, for all of us—"

Beatrice put her head on Verity's shoulder and wept uncontrollably.

"Everything's horrible," she said, when at last she could speak. "I don't know what's happened to them, and you love Jem more than me, and I want everything to be the same as it was."

4th January 1943

I'm not surprised that the poor child is in a state. There seems to be no light anywhere. It is said that the Japanese navy is crippled, but Singapore is still occupied and there is no news whatsoever of Stephen and Daphne.

I tried to explain to her that because I love Jem, it doesn't mean that I have less love to give to her – love isn't rationed like meat or butter, I told her, with only a limited amount to be distributed. I don't think she was at all impressed! In a way it doesn't help that Jem is such an attractive child, for everyone makes much of him. Even Mother! Hardly believable, after the unpropitious start, but true. I can see B. looking daggers when she calls him her little angel, her little cherub, etc. etc. The other day she said he was just like Stephen as a child! I held my breath for a moment, but I don't think she saw the significance. I have a feeling that if he were a poor, unloved little misfit, B. would take him under her wing and smother him with love.

A good thing, perhaps, that she goes back to school on Thursday.

The much-admired Jennifer Laver-Rice had, of course, left school long since, but her early influence lingered on. Hockey was Beatrice's passion, and it soon became clear that she excelled in it, playing first in the under-fourteen team, the youngest girl ever to do so, then later taking part in inter-school matches.

Verity, seeing the increased self-confidence that this distinction conferred, was relieved and delighted. Beatrice visibly became more sure of herself, more assured of her worth. As predicted, her attitude towards Jem became more tolerant, too, though it was clear that she was not particularly maternal by nature. However, she seemed more understanding of Verity's need for the occasional helping hand. Nannies were simply not available, even if she had wanted one.

"Beatrice is becoming quite a pretty girl," Frances remarked during the summer of 1944 – the summer of the D-Day landings and the departure of the American troops that had been stationed in Cornwall for months beforehand. "She has a good little figure. How old is she? Fourteen?"

"And a half," Verity reminded her. "You mustn't forget the half. It's very important at that age."

"She looks older."

"I know."

"She'll be having boyfriends soon."

Verity sighed.

"I know," she said again. "In fact, to tell you the truth I'm relieved that all the Americans have gone. Last holidays, she suddenly seemed to become very aware of them. Natural, I know, some of them were pretty glamorous. I wasn't exactly unaware of them myself. But it was reported to me that she often got into conversation with them on the quay and I couldn't help being afraid that one thing would lead to another. I don't think they could possibly have known how young she is. As you said, she looks older."

"It's quiet without them, isn't it?" Frances said after a moment. "They did add a bit of colour to the place."

"Yes." Verity, engaged in giving Jem his lunch, spoke absently; then she seemed to realise the import of Frances's statement and looked up, a gleam of mischievous amusement in her eyes. "I do believe you're missing Colonel Wainwright."

For a moment Frances did not reply, apparently absorbed in folding a small, blue cardigan belonging to Jem that had fallen on the floor.

"Yes," she said, looking up with a touch of defiance. "Yes, I am, Vee."

The amusement died from Verity's expression. "You're serious," she said.

Frances gave a nervous breath of laughter. "I know. Isn't it crazy? I think I must be rather a late developer."

"You're in love with him?"

"Yes." Suddenly she was ablaze with happiness. "And he with me. Would you believe it? We had so much in common. He's a keen gardener, you see, and – oh, it's not only that! He's just the kindest, funniest, most gentle—" she broke off. "Are you shocked?" she asked.

Verity shook her head. "Me? After what I know about Nicholas? Of course not! I'm just – well, fearful, I suppose. Endings can be pretty shattering affairs."

"This is going to have a happy one. I'm going away with him, after the war. I'm going to get a divorce and go to America—"

"Oh, Fran! You're really sure?"

"Never more so. Oh, I know the love-'em-and-leave-'em reputation of the Americans, but Ross is different. His wife died six years ago, so he's free as a bird. He really does love me, Vee."

"Well! You're a dark horse, aren't you? All this time and never a word!"

"I wanted to tell you, but I had an awful lot of thinking to do. I held out against him for a long time. I've always taken my marriage vows seriously, whatever Nicholas got up to, but he was particularly beastly the last time he was home and suddenly the iron entered into my soul. I can't take any more of him. It's not as if Hugh is a child any more. If he's old enough to leave school and join the army, then he's old enough to understand that I've had enough of his father. More than enough."

Jem had been shovelling food into his mouth throughout this, apparently without any regard to the conversation going on over his head. Now, however, he laid down his spoon with an air of exasperation. "Well *I* haven't had enough," he said with great asperity, pushing his plate towards Verity.

"Little pitchers," murmured Verity. "Well, young man, what do you say?"

"Please may I have some more?" Jem grinned, wrinkling his nose, sure in the knowledge that she would grant all his wishes.

"Of course you may. But leave some room for chocolate pudding, won't you?"

Nodding earnestly, Jem attacked his second helping with enthusiasm.

"Greedy guts," Verity murmured dotingly.

Frances, too, was looking at him with affection. He was an endearing child, no doubt about it, and was growing so fast.

"It seems no time since Hugh was that age," she said. "And now look at him."

Verity made some indefinite murmur of sympathy. The truth was that she related to Hugh no better now that he was an officer cadet stationed somewhere on Salisbury Plain than when he was a schoolboy. His awkwardness when young had somehow translated itself now that he was older into a cockiness that she found deeply unattractive. No doubt it was a kind of defence, she told herself. Probably beneath the arrogant surface he was as insecure as ever.

Frances had said, long ago, that she feared he was bullied at school. Nowadays he probably endured the sarcasm of a disrespectful sergeant major who cared not a jot that he was a Courtfield of Howldrevel, heir to the baronetcy. Could anyone blame him for throwing his weight about when at home? It was, perhaps, only natural that now he had a uniform to give him some authority he took delight in swaggering through the streets of Porthallic or racing through the lanes in the little MG that Nicholas had given him for his eighteenth birthday. It was second-hand, of course, since even Sir Nicholas Courtfield was unable to buy a new car in these troubled times, but it was still the most dashing sports car in the neighbourhood and somehow he seemed to be able to get enough petrol to keep it on the road.

She had been in the village square only a few days ago,

choosing tomatoes from the display outside Mrs Penrose's green-grocer's shop when he had roared past and up the hill, causing those who witnessed him either to shake their heads and prophesy disaster or give a sigh of longing, according to age. Jim Truelove, landlord of the Lugger, happened to be beside her at the time.

"Who do 'e think 'e be?" he asked, more bitterness in his voice than seemed reasonable. "Too good for the rest of us, that's 'im. It takes more than the car to make the man, you know, and if you ask me, that Lord Muck there will never be a man no matter how many wheels he sits behind."

"He's eighteen, Mr Truelove," Verity reminded him, more tolerantly. "He's got time to improve."

"What I'd like to know," said Mrs Pentecost, poking through the cabbages, "is where do 'e get 'is petrol?" At which Jim Truelove had laughed and winked and said there were plenty in Porthallic wouldn't want *that* gone into too carefully! There was always petrol if you knew where to find it.

"And you'd better keep your trap shut, Jim Truelove." Old Wally Thomas joined in the conversation, taking his foul-smelling pipe out of his mouth and pointing it dramatically towards the landlord. "You'll have the police sniffing round. You don't want questions asked 'bout petrol, any more than the rest of us."

"Get away," said Jim Truelove, laughing as he sauntered off in the direction of the quay where the ancient old pub had offered sustenance to Porthallic's inhabitants for several centuries.

Villages, Verity thought as she paid for her tomatoes and plodded homeward up the steep hill that led from the village. Everyone knew everyone else's business. She had long suspected that there was a black market in operation among those in the know, and this seemed to bear out the theory. Well, they'd better watch their backs. Secrets didn't often stay that way in Porthallic.

It made her even more sure that she had done the right thing in going miles away to have Jem. And made her realise, too, how the years were flying, for it seemed only the other day that Jim Truelove was Hugh's age, and equally devoted to speed, equally the target of his elders' disapproval. He'd been very slim and handsome then, she remembered. Now he had several chins and a pendulous stomach and was the father of a growing family.

It was some weeks later that she switched on the wireless just in time to hear the news of the liberation of Paris. It was the most exciting, uplifting news that she had heard for a long time, and swiftly she went to tell Beatrice, longing to have good news to impart.

She had last seen her playing with Jem in the garden, which was a sight that gladdened her heart. Things were so much easier this holiday, and how right Livvy had been, saying that Beatrice would show more interest in Jem when he was a little boy rather than a baby, for now he was three she seemed to enjoy taking him for walks, or down on the beach. Hardly a day had passed that week without her taking him to the playground in the village for an hour or two. He liked the swings, she said; and Verity, off the Council now but still busy with many other activities, had welcomed it, both for the break it gave her and as a sign that relations had improved.

Beatrice, however, was nowhere to be seen on this occasion.

"She went up the woods," she was informed by old Pascoe, who still, arthritis permitting, put in a few hours' gardening a week. "She took the little 'un with her. Some 'andsome little tacker, en un?"

Verity smiled and agreed. Pascoe, despite his crusty nature, had from the beginning made much of Jem and had never minded having him beside him to "help" with the gardening, encouraging him indulgently to dig the beds with his little spade or pick up leaves to put in the wheelbarrow. She wasn't best pleased about Beatrice going off without a word, however. Much as she appreciated the improved relationship, she liked to know Jem's whereabouts.

Oh, don't be such an old fuss-pot, she reproved herself, going back inside the house. Just be thankful that Beatrice was proving such an excellent nursemaid. Jem had probably pestered her to take him to the woods; he adored playing there.

It was almost tea-time and she was beginning to hope that the children would be back soon when she heard the slam of a car door and came into the hall to see, through the open door, that it was Frances who had arrived and was running up the front steps. One look at her face made the blood freeze in her veins.

"What—?" She found she had no breath to say more.

"Vee, there's been an accident. You must come—"

"Jem?"

"I'm afraid so. He's at the hospital."

"How bad?"

"Very bad." Her lips were trembling. Verity swallowed convulsively.

"He's dead, isn't he?"

"No. No. They're trying to save him."

What happened? Where? Who? Questions seemed to hammer in Verity's brain but she could say nothing, do nothing. Frances took her arm and led her down to the car where she sat, white and tense, leaning forward a little as if by doing so, she could somehow hasten the journey to the hospital. The car took her down the hill into the village. People were there – a few shoppers, a small queue waiting for the bus to town. Strangely it seemed to her as if they had withdrawn from her, become unreal, turned away, leaving her alone in a soundless vacuum.

Through the village they drove, and up the hill that led out of it, as far as the gabled white building that had been so much part of her life from the moment of its planning. The words "Ashland Cottage Hospital" were set into the front fascia, picked out in green-painted stone.

She was out of the car almost before Frances had brought it to a halt, running up the steps and into the door, but was shocked into stillness by the sight of Livvy coming towards her. She was crying.

"Vee – oh, Vee," she said, holding out her arms. "We tried. We tried so hard."

Beatrice, it later transpired, had taken Jem to Howldrevel Woods, those same woods where Verity and Laurie had met and kissed and vowed undying love. She had been playing hide and seek, she said, just her and Jem. She didn't see anyone else. And then he ran off out of sight and while she was chasing after him she had heard a car accelerating away down the lower drive and had run there, only to find Jem, unconscious.

"Like a rag doll," she sobbed. "All limp, with his legs twisted and his head on one side." No, she said. She hadn't seen a car. She'd heard it, that was all. Heard it racing off down the drive. Or maybe up the drive, she couldn't really tell. It had all been such a terrible shock.

It was the following day that eleven-year-old Minnie Jago from the Gatehouse had come up with a different story. Beatrice hadn't been alone, she said. She'd seen her with Alan Truelove. She'd been in the woods looking for different kinds of ferns – her teacher had wanted them for a nature lesson – and she'd seen them. Kissing. She'd watched them for a bit and then crept away.

"No," she said. "There weren't no sign of the little boy."

"But honestly, Auntie Vee," Beatrice sobbed when confronted with this second version of events by the local policeman, "I *did* look after Jem, honestly I did! I didn't take my eyes off him for more than a second. I didn't say anything about Alan because I thought you'd be cross—"

Cross, Verity thought, sitting numb and silent. Cross! She has no conception of what I'm feeling.

Alan Truelove was the fifteen-year-old son of Jim Truelove of the Lugger. When he was questioned, he corroborated Beatrice's story. They had only heard the car on the lower drive and had seen nothing.

"And when you found the little boy, what did you do then?"

"Well—" The boy looked a little shifty at his less than glorious part in this tragedy. "Like Beatrice said, she ran all the way to Howldrevel to get help. She said I'd better go home, because she didn't want her auntie to know we'd been together. So I legged it."

Everyone said it must have been Hugh who drove the car. All of Porthallic seemed to have seen him the previous day when once again he had roared through the village, and all had prophesied disaster. Mrs Penwarne of the Post Office even claimed to have had a presentiment. It was, she was quoted as saying, like a big black cloud looming over her, all the day long.

Mrs Jago confirmed that she had seen Hugh drive out of Howldrevel, past the Gatehouse.

"At dinner time," she said. "We was just having our pasties, Jack and me and Minnie and he whooshed past the window."

She hadn't seen him come back, she said. But Hugh swore that he had done so. He'd just dashed out for cigarettes, he said, and had been back in fifteen minutes.

"You didn't come back on the bottom drive?" the policeman asked him. Vehemently he denied it.

"I haven't been that way for years. The surface is terrible. I came back along the top drive. I don't know why the Jagos didn't see me. Too busy feeding their faces, I suppose."

His arrogant manner did nothing to endear him to the police, but it had to be admitted that there appeared to be no bumps or scratches on his car; no trace of an untoward incident of any kind.

But on the other hand, no one could confirm his alibi. In an establishment that swarmed with servants – less densely than in the past, perhaps, but Howldrevel was still a well-populated place – it seemed strange that no one had seen him or could vouch that his car had been in its garage all afternoon. But no one could prove anything against him and he was allowed to go back to camp once his leave was over.

A few days later, Jem was buried in the Ashland plot beside Porthallic church. People said that Miss Ashland looked as if she'd aged twenty years, the poor soul, dear of her.

6th September 1944

A week today since we buried him. Many people and flowers, and everyone in tears at the sight of the tiny coffin. Many letters, too. It will, I think, be a little while before I can face answering them.

I cannot write about it. There is no point, for I shall never forget.

So very short, my experience of motherhood. Three years, five months. Every hour was a joy to me, and I shall mourn for the rest of my life.

Harry. Laurie. Jem. All gone, all my dearest loves. Laurie not dead, of course, but gone from me just the same.

Once I told Beatrice that she must not blame Jem for behaving like a baby. I, similarly, must not blame her for behaving like a fourteen-year-old girl and must struggle to overcome this bitterness towards her. She could not possibly have foreseen the outcome of her little adventure – but oh, how I wish she had! If she had gone alone to meet this boy, and left Jem playing in the garden—

And Hugh. Can I ever forgive him? Of course he may be as innocent as he professes and if this is the case then he has my apologies, but if it were not him, then who? No one uses that bottom drive any more. It is weedy and potholed and quite dangerous in places. Yet someone did. Apart from a lorry delivering coal and Hugh going out for cigarettes, no other traffic passed the Gatehouse that day and the only people in the wood were Beatrice and Alan who are still children, too young to drive. Both say they saw no one else. The police appear to have reached a dead end.

I am inconsolable. I pray for solace, but all I can think of is that incomprehensible text: From him that hath not shall be taken away even that which he hath.

BOOK THREE

CLARE

Fifteen

The gale had moderated, but at what stage during the weekend it had done so Clare was unable to say, so total had been her transportation to this world that, with all its joys and tragedies, was now far in the past. She had, at intervals, slept and eaten, showered and clothed herself, had spoken to Minnie, even answered the phone, but she had taken the minimum amount of time over such necessities, barely conscious of interruptions, hardly noticing the wind and the rain, anxious only to immerse herself once more in Verity's compelling story.

Now, having come to its sudden and tragic end, she felt numb with shock, as if it were she who had been bereaved, she who had suffered this appalling grief. She sat for a while, the book in her hands, not able to think or to move.

The fact that Jeremy had died in a tragic accident was a fact she had always known, Verity's sadness something that she felt she had understood and sympathised with. Now she knew without doubt that she had not truly appreciated the half of it.

"He was like my own," Verity had said to her more than once. How strange, how tragic it seemed that never in her life, not even in later years, had she claimed the little boy as truly her son. From the perspective of the 1990s it seemed unbelievable.

"I'm going out for a walk," Clare called to Minnie, putting her head round the kitchen door. She put on boots, zipped herself up in a windproof jacket, and powered her way down the drive, along the road past the cove, up the field to the stile, hands thrust deep in her pockets. She needed the air and the exercise; needed to get away from the house; needed to think and assimilate. The wind was still strong and the sky was leaden, but though the ground was wet underfoot the rain had stopped, at least for the time being.

Once at the top of the field where the path forked, she leaned against the gate beside the stile and looked back the way she had come. There it was, just as it had been all her life and all Verity's life, too. Lemorrick. The cove. The timeless, fathomless sea, the waves slate grey, breaking white on the rocks.

How could Verity have borne such grief? How, after suffering like that did she contrive to age into the serene, humorous, thoroughly human woman Clare had known, with prejudices and peccadilloes the same as all humankind, but with her faults far outweighed by her virtues many times over? There were those who, similarly stricken, would have withdrawn from life, turned in on themselves – and perhaps, at first, she had done so, too. But there had been no trace of bitterness in the character Clare had known. Her love, as she had said to Beatrice long ago, was not a commodity to be rationed but had extended in all directions; perhaps not as far as the Courtfield family, but that, too, was understandable.

And what of Beatrice? No wonder she had felt guilty. No matter how well Verity had hidden her instinct to lay the blame for Jem's death partly at her door, she must still, in her heart, have held herself accountable. What a burden to carry into her adult life! For the first time for many years Clare felt compassion for her – compassion and understanding for the young girl who, foolish though she might have been, surely had no intention of hurting the one person who had loved and comforted and stood by her.

And Hugh Courtfield? Did he, too, suffer from an unquiet conscience? Did he have nightmares? Or was he as innocent as he had professed himself to be? Minnie thought him guilty, that was obvious. And so had Verity, in her heart. It was hard not to think that they had a point.

She turned and, climbing the stile, took the left fork to walk the cliff path. The wind was stronger than ever here. It seemed like a living, breathing force, intent on hurling her back the way she had come, but still she battled on. The struggle seemed to answer a need in her, seemed in tune with her battered emotions and the turmoil in her mind.

She came at last to a five-barred gate, the same gate – well, maybe its successor – where Verity and Harry had sat and talked on his last leave, and here she stopped, grasping the top rail to anchor herself as she looked again at the mountainous waves. Out to sea a small boat made its dogged way towards harbour, borne up only to plunge down again almost out of sight, but on land there was no sign, anywhere, of another living soul on this inhospitable morning

– just like that other terrible day, she thought. No one had seen the car that killed Jeremy Ashland, yet it had existed. Someone must have driven along the lane from the village and turned into that little-used track that led to Howldrevel.

Who? Surely it had to be Hugh. No tradesman would have used that route. No chance visitor.

Then why would Hugh? Would he have considered it a short cut? A test of his driving skills? Such questions must have gone round and round in Verity's mind a million times.

Clare walked, in the end, as far as Rocky Point, the scene of the first fateful meeting of Verity and Laurie, but the wind was too strong to go out to the end and it carried a hint of rain now so that she turned for home, her thoughts still obsessed by the past.

It had been strange, reading of the youth of those she had known only as elderly. Frances Wainwright, Hugh's mother and Nick's grandmother, had come over from America one year soon after old Sir Nicholas had died in the 1970s. Clare had met her only briefly, but still remembered the joy with which she and Verity had greeted each other.

Clare had liked her, she remembered, and had been rather dazzled by her glamour and style, which seemed strange to the twelve-year-old to whom Frances seemed old as the hills. She had put it down to living in America but afterwards Verity had said no, Frances had always been like that. Clare had liked her American husband, too. He had made her laugh and had, secretly, given her a five pound note when he left, which made him, at least in her eyes, one of the more welcome guests to come to Lemorrick.

She had known Livvy and Robert, though both had been dead for twenty years at least. They had founded a medical dynasty – or, more accurately, Livvy's father had done so. Alex had taken over from his parents and now his son, Nigel, was part of an enlarged group of doctors who worked at the Health Centre.

And there were still Trueloves at the Lugger. Alan, the boy her mother had met in the woods, still pulled pints behind the bar even though it was his son, Greg, who was in charge now. Alan was a man who had been darkly handsome, just as Verity had described his father, but he had enjoyed too much of his own beer over the years and he, too, had become fat and florid, inclined to leer at girls, particularly those who came into the pub in summer in their brief shorts and halter tops.

The Lugger itself had changed. It had a juke box now, and a fruit machine in the public bar, though the last time she'd been there Greg Truelove had confided that he'd wanted to make further changes – refurbish the place, go up-market a bit. He'd get rid of the terrible flock wallpaper, he said, and put something more tasteful on the walls in place of the tat that had been there since the days of his grandfather.

Clare thought over the concept of continuity. Was it something to be admired, or did it imply stultifying boredom? She knew many who would think the latter.

For herself—

Oh, what did she want? Right now, looking down towards Lemorrick as with the wind at her back she was blown homeward, she longed above all things to make it truly hers, to fill it with life and love, just as Verity, all her days, had wanted it to be. The life she lived in London seemed suddenly sterile and empty, like a cup she had drained to the dregs. She was, it seemed, just as much in thrall to her career as Verity ever was to her mother and her good works; and, like Verity, she wanted children, before it was too late. She could picture it so easily, could almost hear them calling to each other.

"Coming down the beach?"

"I'm going for a sail."

"Hey, wait for me—"

Fool, she thought. She'd always had too much imagination, now here she was calling into life children who had never been born and probably never would be. But oh, what a sweet thought it was, and how easy to imagine a life here.

She went in through the scullery door, sitting down on the bench to take off her muddy boots.

"Hi, Minnie, I'm back," she called, hearing movement in the kitchen. "I hope there's some coffee on." She was conscious, over her left shoulder, of a figure appearing in the kitchen doorway and looked round with a smile. To her astonishment she saw not Minnie, but the less familiar and far more elegant figure of her mother who stood there with her arms stretched wide.

"Darling, you're back at last," she cried dramatically. "Come and give your mother a kiss."

"Good heavens," Clare said faintly, getting to her feet and going to greet her. "Mum! What a surprise! You got my messages, then—"

"I came as soon as I could. I've been away – in Paris – but the moment I got home and heard the news I turned right round and headed straight back to the airport. So here I am! Too late to see poor Vee, of course, but I thought I should come anyway. There must be so many decisions to be made about the house and so on—"

Clare looked at her guardedly. Surely Verity had told Beatrice that she was leaving Lemorrick not to her but to her daughter? That her own inheritance consisted of blocks of shares and some family jewellery? She said nothing, however. Time enough for that later.

"Tell me," Beatrice said, smiling brightly and standing back a little as if for inspection. "How do you think I look?"

"Wonderful!" Clare said, attempting to rise to the occasion. "Love that dress! Did you get it in Paris?"

Beatrice's smile died. "No, I didn't," she said testily. "A little woman in Palma ran it up for me and I've had it ages, as a matter of fact. I wasn't referring to the dress."

"Well, as I said, you look wonderful. Very well indeed."

"Six weeks ago," Beatrice said, speaking very precisely, every word separate and as brittle as ice, "I spent a considerable amount of money having my face lifted by one of the best cosmetic surgeons in Paris. I thought that just possibly you might have noticed the difference. I suppose I should have known—"

She turned her back on Clare without finishing the sentence and re-entered the kitchen. Clare stood in her stockinged feet and watched her go before shrugging helplessly and following her. Just two minutes in each other's company, she thought, and already I've disappointed her.

"Mum, be fair! It's almost three years since I've seen you," she said, in her own defence.

"And I told you then to call me Beatrice!"

"Sorry. Beatrice it shall be. Truly, you look terrific and you should take it as a compliment that I didn't notice you'd had anything done. You always look great to me. Minnie, dear, you have got coffee on, haven't you? I'm dying for a cup."

"I've told Minnie to bring it to the sitting room," Beatrice said, very much the lady of the house. Clare and Minnie exchanged a look, but said nothing. "Come along, dear," Beatrice went on. "We have so much to talk about. By the way," she said, pausing on the threshold to turn to Minnie once more, "I shall be sleeping in the master bedroom, so make up the bed there, will you? I don't see why I shouldn't have the benefit of the best view."

Minnie, coffee pot in her hand, stood as if suddenly turned to stone, her mouth open and Clare, too, remained transfixed for a moment.

"No, Beatrice," she said at last. "I don't think that's a good idea. There are still too many of Verity's things there."

"I don't mind that."

"It's not ready—"

"It's not ready?" Beatrice repeated the words, her voice swooping derisively. "Then Minnie must make it ready."

"Come along." Clare took her mother's arm. "Let's go and have some coffee. There are a few things you ought to know, Beatrice, before we go any further."

"The coffee's made, Clare," Minnie said, without expression. "You can take it with you."

"Right. Thanks." Clare picked up the tray. "Lead on, Mum. Beatrice, I mean."

"You allow Minnie to speak to you like that?" Beatrice asked in tones of horror, once they were out of earshot. "That's something that's going to have to change. She was always too familiar."

Clare said nothing, but entered the sitting room behind her and put the tray down on a low table.

"Beatrice," she said, her voice firm but friendly. "There's something I must make clear to you right away. Verity left Lemorrick to me. She must have told you! She didn't forget you," she added hastily. "I think the best thing is for us to go and see the solicitor so that he can explain everything."

Beatrice laughed, moving to the fireplace to look at her reflection in the mirror over the mantelpiece. She fluffed out her hair, apparently unfazed by this information.

"Of course I knew she was going to leave Lemorrick to you, silly child," she said. "On paper, anyway. She told me ages ago. It was all because I was living in Majorca and there were going to be endless complications about Spanish tax. She never intended me to be disinherited."

"You're not disinherited," Clare said. "She left you all her mother's jewellery, as well as all her gilt-edge stock. It'll give you an income for life. Actually, as I was always saying to Verity,

I was pretty sure this could be enhanced quite considerably if she'd only reinvest, but she didn't want to bother about making changes. Nothing to stop you doing so, though."

"And you intend to advise me?"

"Well, it is my job!"

"Exactly. And your job is in London where, I understand, you have a very nice flat. Not that I've seen it—"

"Well, you haven't been here to see it, have you?"

"The point is that you don't need Lemorrick. Pour the coffee, darling."

After a short, perplexed glance at her mother, Clare did so in silence. Beatrice took the cup from the tray and went to sit down.

"Forgive me," Clare said after a moment. "I really must put you straight on one point. Verity left Lemorrick to me because – and I have this in writing, in a personal letter she wrote to me before she died – she truly wanted me to have it. She said nothing about leaving it to me merely on paper, nothing about Spanish tax laws. She did say, however, that you had never wanted to live here, and I must say that the last thirty years seem to have demonstrated that quite forcibly."

Beatrice lifted her eyes to heaven. "Darling, how pompous you sound! I suppose it's this important new job of yours. I must say I rather feared it would make you lose your femininity and I seem to have been right. Now, look—" Beatrice put down her cup of coffee and leant forward in her chair as if to engender an atmosphere of confidence. "You don't need Lemorrick, do you? You have this wonderful flat overlooking the Thames that Vee told me about – quite the most chic part of London, I understand. There's no way you'll want to live here, except for holidays, and you can still do that. You'd be more than welcome to come as often as you like."

"Very kind of you," Clare said dryly. "One thing I don't understand. You've never liked living in England. Last time you were here, you constantly regaled us with accounts of your marvellous life in Majorca and never, for one moment, did you stop complaining about the weather. So why is it suddenly so attractive? And where, for heaven's sake, does Gerald fit into life in Cornwall? You know he'd hate it."

"Well—" Beatrice hesitated a moment. "I haven't had time to tell you. Gerald and I aren't living together any more."

"You haven't left him?"

"No, no, nothing like that. Well yes, in a sense I suppose I *have* left him, but not in the way you mean, not because I want to, you mustn't think that for a moment. He's ill, you see. Forgetful. Confused."

"He hasn't got Alzheimer's? Oh, poor Gerald."

"Yes, poor Gerald. And still poorer me. He's in the early stages, they say, so we decided it would be best if he went into a place in Barcelona that we'd heard of. A kind of clinic, run by nuns – quite terribly sweet, all of them." She saw Clare's expression and hurried on. "It's the best in the business. All kinds of wealthy people go there. He couldn't be better looked after, and really, it was quite impossible for me to cope in Deya. He could see that. So we've put the villa up for sale. I'm sure it will go in no time."

"And Gerald doesn't mind?"

"Well, he didn't *like* it, of course. He was always very fond of the villa and he adores me, so naturally he was a bit upset when I left him. He actually cried, bless him, but he knew it was for the best."

"Poor old chap." For the first time ever, Clare found herself in sympathy with Gerald Pryde. "But surely, you've been a bit – well, precipitous, haven't you? I mean, if he's only in the early stages, couldn't you have coped for a bit longer? You had help, after all, and could have got more."

"Oh, easy to *say*," Beatrice said, annoyed at the implied criticism. "But can you imagine what my life would have been like, stuck away on that hillside on my own? I wouldn't be welcomed at the Club any more, I know that quite well. My so-called friends would drop me. No one would ask me to dinner parties. I've seen it happen with women who've lost their husbands – people are sorry at first, but they get heartily sick of having an odd woman about the place, and there I would have been, neither fish, flesh nor good red herring, with none of the freedom of a widow but none of the kudos of being a wife, tied to a man who was becoming more and more vegetable-like every day. There's no cure, you know. People just deteriorate."

Clare assimilated this without comment. "What about Bonnie?" she asked at last. "She'd have stood by you, surely? You've been friends for years."

"Oh, Bonnie's the worst! You'd never have believed it was she who told me about this Barcelona clinic in the first place.

She showed not a shred of understanding when I told her I was arranging to have Gerald admitted, though I know for a fact she would have dropped me like a hot brick if I'd stayed."

"But why Lemorrick?" Clare asked after a moment. "You won't be short of money, will you? Why don't you buy an apartment in Barcelona when the villa's sold, so you can be near Gerald?"

"Because, my dear, it costs an arm and a leg to keep him there! It's simply frightfully expensive – these places are, you know – and I can see all our capital dribbling away until there's nothing left. Living here seems the obvious answer."

Clare took a breath. "But I'm thinking of selling it," she said. "It's too big for either of us, and needs thousands spent on it."

"You can't do that!"

"But, Beatrice, that's just where you're mistaken. Lemorrick is mine and I can do what I like with it. Of course, you're welcome to stay until you can make other arrangements, but you really can't count on any kind of permanency here. And another thing," she went on, putting down her cup very carefully. "I would rather you didn't sleep in Verity's room, if you don't mind. It's too soon. We still think of it as hers. We're still busy going through her things."

Beatrice glared at her daughter, lips pressed together. "I was right," she said. "You're hard and unfeminine. How I contrived to have a daughter like you, I can't imagine."

Clare managed a rather strained smile. "Well, face it, Beatrice," she said. "You didn't really have a lot to do with it, did you? Now, if you'll excuse me, I've got things to get on with, so I'll leave you to your unpacking. Would you prefer the blue room or the rose room? The rose room is probably nicer," she went on, when Beatrice continued to glare without speaking. "I'll take your case up there, shall I?"

I've been bounced, she thought when, a little later, she was grimly packing up the large-print books that Verity had borrowed and which she should have taken back to the library days before. Selling Lemorrick had been, a little earlier, no more than a possibility. Now it seemed the only answer to the Beatrice situation. If it were sold, she could buy her mother somewhere else to live . . .

"I don't know what I'm going to do," she said to Nick when the following week she had dinner with him in his apartment at Howldrevel. "I was in several minds about Lemorrick before

Beatrice turned up – still am, really! I change my mind about it a dozen times a day – but I'm damned if I'm going to let her waltz in and take possession. Nothing and nobody seems able to convince her that Verity didn't mean her to live there. She even told the solicitor he was talking nonsense."

Nick listened to this with amused disbelief. "But how on earth can she justify that? When Verity wrote her will, your mother presumably was perfectly happy in Majorca with no intention of coming home. She's just rewriting history to suit herself."

"I think she's always done that. She told me last night that it broke her heart to give me up when I was so young, and she never would have done so if I hadn't implored her to leave me with Verity."

"And that's not true?"

"Not at all! I didn't really know Verity then. I might well have implored her to leave me if I'd had any idea of the way things were going to turn out, but at the time I was terrified at being left in what was virtually a strange country, with someone I hardly knew."

"But you must have loved growing up at Lemorrick. I've always thought it would be a great place for kids."

"Yes." Remembering the fantasy she had indulged in the day of Beatrice's arrival, Clare felt suddenly and inexplicably shy, relieved when, at that moment, a waiter from the restaurant downstairs came to take away their empty plates. "That was absolutely delicious," she said.

"Coffee?" Nick asked. "Let's have it somewhere more comfortable, shall we?"

They moved to the settee in front of the fire and the waiter reappeared with a tray which he set down on the low table in front of them. Clare rested her head against the cushions feeling, suddenly, a great sense of peace, as if here she were insulated from all life's decisions and problems. But there was an edge of excitement, too, that she was unwilling to define. Because of Nick? Careful, she warned herself. Certainly it seemed natural to be with him again and conversation from the beginning had been easy, but to think that their old relationship could be revived was a step too far. Several steps, in fact.

They had talked of Nick's work: of the prize-winning marina he had seen in Cape Cod and his plans to take many of the same ideas to regenerate the old harbour at St Crispin, once a thriving little port, now nothing but a collection of boarded-up warehouses and a rotting wharf. They had talked of Beatrice and, yet again, of Lemorrick.

"You could be forgiven for thinking you don't owe your mother a lot," Nick said, returning to the subject of Beatrice as they sipped their coffee.

Clare nodded, agreeing with him. "That's true. But as Verity wrote in her last letter to me, I only have one mother. That implies a certain amount of responsibility – but oh, Nick! There's no way I can live with her."

"I can't imagine Verity would have expected you to. Even so, it seems a poor reason for selling Lemorrick."

"I know." She sighed. "It's not like me to shilly-shally like this. I'll have to come to some sort of decision before long." She put down the half-finished cup of coffee, frowning as if other issues had suddenly crowded in on her after all, disturbing the tranquillity of the evening. "I don't know what's wrong with me these days, Nick. I can't seem to make my mind up about anything. What's happened to me? I won't last five minutes in my job if I carry on like this."

"Maybe you need a holiday."

"I'm supposed to be having one! So far it doesn't seem to have had the right effect. To be honest, I really dread going back to work."

"Why go, then? Give it up."

"Have you any idea of the money I'm earning?"

"Probably not. But what does money matter if you're miserable?"

"You're right, of course. I know that perfectly well. Still—" She paused and sighed. "Let's face it, I haven't always been miserable. As a matter of fact, until just recently I've loved it, loved the cut and thrust and the intrigues and the element of gambling. But now—" She paused again, biting her lip. "Now, when I think of the enormous sums I'm responsible for, I'm overcome with terror."

He touched her shoulder in a comforting, concerned kind of way. "Hey, don't let it get to you. Give it up."

Suddenly it seemed to Clare the most desirable thing in the world to have someone to focus on her problems even to the point of telling her what to do with her life. And what about feminist principles, she asked herself derisively? Were they to be forgotten at the first whiff of Nick's expensive aftershave?

"And do what?" she said, pulling a little away from him.

"Well—" He paused a moment, brows drawn together, clearly giving the matter serious thought. "You could work from home, couldn't you? Work from Lemorrick? Who needs an office in London when you've got e-mail and the Internet?"

For a few seconds she looked at him without speaking. "I suppose it's a possibility," she said slowly. "I'd have to leave the bank, of course, and the moment I gave notice I'd be expected to clear my desk."

"So what? You'd find something else."

"I suppose I would."

"Of course you would! You must have thousands of contacts."

"A fair number. There could be consultancies, I imagine." She paused, the idea taking wing. It *was* a possibility! Why hadn't she thought of it for herself? Then she laughed. "That's really not at all a bad idea, Nick – and I have the feeling Verity would approve of it."

Nick look amused, but there was a rueful look in his eyes. "She's your reference for everything, isn't she?"

"No, not everything! I do miss talking things over with her, though. She wasn't infallible, but she was very wise. She'd had more experience of life than you might have imagined."

"Even though she was born at Lemorrick, and died there, too? What happened in between?"

"A lot. You'd be astonished. She left diaries—"

She stopped, surprised at herself, and a little annoyed if the truth were to be told. She hadn't intended to mention the diaries, had thought it would be bound to lead to discussion of Jeremy and of Nick's father's suspected part in his death; to all the unpleasant things, in fact, that had resulted in the disastrous quarrel between herself and Nick twenty years before.

"Dad had nothing to do with the little boy's death, you know," Nick said gently, as if reading her thoughts.

"I don't even want to think about that," she said quickly.

He looked at her quizzically, his mouth twisted a little.

"You really don't believe me, do you? What do the diaries say?"

"Nothing. Nothing conclusive, anyway. Nick—" For a moment

she hesitated, trying to read his expression. "We're never going to know the true story, are we? It was a tragedy. Let's just leave it at that."

"My father had nothing to do with it." His voice had hardened a little. "I just wish I could convince you."

"Nick, it doesn't matter—"

"But it *does*, Clare. It's always mattered to him. I asked him once, straight out, and he denied it absolutely. I know he was telling the truth. Listen to me—" He put his hands on her shoulders and turned her to face him. "My father had a lousy childhood. It made him what he is, stiff and shy and quite unable to let his hair down in any way. In fact I'd go so far as to say the term 'his own worst enemy' was made for him. I know him better now, but I was frightened to death of him when I was young and so were the girls. He was utterly unapproachable. Only my mother seemed able to bring out any lightness or playfulness in him. However, one thing I have always known about him." Clare could feel his fingers tighten a little on her shoulders, and sensed the strength of his feelings. "Dad's the soul of honour. If he gives his word about anything, then that's it. No power on earth will make him break it. He's been hard – even impossible – to live up to, sometimes, but that's the way he is. So if he says he wasn't involved in that accident that killed the little boy, then he wasn't. If he had been, he'd have said so. I haven't a single shred of doubt about that."

"That's a very impressive testimony," Clare said after a moment.

Nick looked into her face, then dropping his hands, he shrugged helplessly. "But I still haven't convinced you."

"Can't we just forget it, Nick? As I said, we're never going to know the full story. Whoever was to blame, it was an accident, not something that was done with malice aforethought. Oh, I wish I'd never mentioned the blasted diaries!"

"It's haunted Dad all his life. Imagine what it was like for him, what it's always been like, knowing that everyone suspects you're guilty of something, but thinks you don't have the guts to admit it. The death of a child – there's nothing more distressing or emotive, is there?"

Clare shook her head slowly, reliving Verity's account of the tragedy. "No. I can't imagine how Verity ever got over it. But Nick—" She broke off and for a moment he continued to look at her, the small, bitter smile still twisting his lips.

"I know what you're going to say. There was no one else who could have driven that car," he said. "Aren't I right?"

"I suppose so. And it's true, Nick! You can see how all the suspicion arose. But if it's any consolation, my mother was as guilty as whoever was at the wheel. She was there with Alan Truelove, doing heaven knows what while she was supposed to be looking after Jeremy. It's affected her, too, according to Verity. I suppose it was bound to. She said they heard the car accelerate away – but I expect you know all this."

"I've pieced it together. Read old newspaper reports. Heard what my father has to say about it."

"Oh, please let's forget it," Clare begged. "The whole wretched business has affected the lives of too many people as it is. Much as we might want to, we can't bring Jeremy back to life. Just accept that we'll never know exactly what happened."

"Maybe not," Nick admitted, regretfully. "But I can tell you, I'd give a lot to be able to relieve my father of this particular burden. It's one he doesn't deserve. Tell me," he went on, going off at something of a tangent, "does your mother know you've got Verity's diaries?"

Clare pulled a face. "No, she doesn't. I haven't told her, and I don't intend to. She'd only think she had a better right to them than I have."

"It might be a way of getting her to open up a bit more about what happened."

"You think there's more she could tell?"

"My father always thought so."

Clare considered the question, then shook her head. "I don't want her to see them," she said at last. "And I'm pretty sure Verity wouldn't have wanted it, either. She wasn't always very complimentary in what she wrote about her. But more than that, I have this gut feeling that somehow, however carefully I were to lock them away, Beatrice would get her hands on them and make sure they were never seen again. Certainly they'd be another bone of contention."

Nick reached to brush her cheek gently with the back of his forefinger. "And that you don't need. Hey—" His mood changed and, smiling, he got to his feet. "Remember this?" He crossed the room, sorted through some CDs and put one on the record player.

It was Rachmaninov's Second Piano Concerto, and as the strains of it filled the room Clare leaned her head back and laughed delightedly. She was transported immediately, as he must have known she would be, to a summer night under the stars when the two of them, on the deck of someone's yacht and wrapped in a single blanket, had listened in rapture. Twenty? It seemed like a hundred years ago; and, at the same time, like yesterday.

"You old softie," she said. "Of course I remember. How young and innocent we were."

"Some more innocent than others."

"Well, yes. Your dark desires are well documented. We'll say no more about them."

He came and sat beside her again.

"There's never been anyone like you, Clare. Never. Remember that night when we had dinner in London, after the party?"

"Very well."

"You'll never know what it took to walk away from you like that. In fact when I was half-way to the West End, I almost told the taxi driver to turn round and take me back to you."

And I would have welcomed you in, Clare thought, remembering. It was only the next day that she had persuaded herself that restraint was a commendable virtue.

"You were married to Lorraine then," she pointed out.

"Things were already falling apart. Had been for some time."

"This music—" Clare rested her head against the cushions again, distracted by its beauty. For several moments both were silent, then she gave a brief laugh. "I've – I've never been able to listen to it without remembering," she finished at last.

"I think we're a little young to live on memories, don't you?" There was amusement in Nick's voice as he turned, put an arm around her and pulled her closer. "Second chances aren't unknown, you know."

She felt his arms tighten round her and looked up at him.

"Nick—" she began, but got no further for his mouth was on hers and she could think of nothing except the pleasure of the moment and the way he excited her as he always had done, more than anyone before or since; and she knew, without doubt, that just like Verity, her first love was likely to be her last. But even then, even in the heat of the moment, the thought crossed her mind that as in Verity's case, this fact alone was no guarantee of eventual happiness.

Just enjoy the moment, she warned herself.

Sixteen

The two ladies who came to Lemorrick to help Minnie with the housework were Mrs Hollis and Mrs Treleaven. Mrs Hollis, a gaunt and rather severe woman, was a contemporary of Minnie's. She came on a Wednesday, and went about her work largely in silence and with an air of grim determination. No one, ever, called her anything but Mrs Hollis.

Peggy Treleaven, who came on Fridays, was quite a different proposition. She was twenty years younger and considerably more cheerful – fair, fat and forty, Clare thought, seeing her plump hindquarters encased in rather regrettable magenta leggings protruding from the cupboard in the kitchen from which she was extracting the tools of her trade.

"Hi, Peggy," she called as she crossed the room en route to rustling up some toast and coffee for her breakfast. "How are you today?"

"Fine, thanks." Armed with polish and duster, brush and dustpan, Peggy emerged pink in the face from her exertions. "You're looking very pleased with yourself," she said. "Won the lottery, have you?"

Clare grinned back at her. "I wish!"

"Then you must be in love."

Clare laughed, but neither confirmed nor denied it. That Peggy was right she had no doubt. She felt sixteen again – tremulous, full of hope, with a strange compulsion to smile at nothing.

Where it would all end she had no idea, but last night had surely been the beginning of something wonderful. She and Nick had talked for hours, the atmosphere one of increasing intimacy, but even so she had not given in to his proposal that she should stay the night.

"Let's take it a step at a time, Nick," she said when events seemed to be getting out of hand.

284

"Not still so coy?"

She'd laughed at that. "No, no! Not coy at all."

He'd laughed, too, and kissed her gently. "Whatever you want. I've learned patience with age, and in any case—" He paused and she looked at him quizzically. "It'll be fun, getting to know each other again, won't it?"

Peggy made another foray into the cupboard, emerging this time with the vacuum cleaner.

"How's madam?" she asked, jerking her head in an upward direction, presumably to indicate Beatrice's room. "Shall I leave hoovering the stairs and landing till she comes down? She gave me a proper mouthful last week because of the noise."

"You could make a start on the sitting room."

"OK, my love," Peggy said.

It wasn't, Clare reflected, the kind of response her mother would approve of any more than she approved of early-morning vacuuming; just as well, then, that she wasn't present to hear it – or to comment on her daughter's good spirits which Clare had no intention of explaining.

Being with Nick again had felt so good, and it was a remembered joy, feeling on the brink of things like this. She had no idea what the future would bring but there was a glow in her heart that seemed to say happiness was there for the asking, just over the horizon.

A step at a time, she reminded herself. Meantime she would think seriously about starting a career from home.

There had been no fixed plans to meet with Nick again, which had seemed, gratifyingly, a matter of great annoyance to him. A party of VIPs from all over the world, all of them engaged in the leisure industry, was about to descend on Howldrevel for a conference and fact-finding tour, and Nick had to be on hand, not only to greet them the following evening but to squire them around the Courtfield attractions in other areas of Cornwall. Free time would be at a premium the entire week, he'd said when they parted, but he would be in touch. He would ring her.

When – *when*? Clare longed to ask then and longed, still more, to ask now. She had said nothing, however. Play it cool, she had warned herself. Nick himself had said, that day they had met on the beach, that there should be no strings. That, of course, was before last night's events had brought them closer, but even so there was no need to rush fences or jump guns.

The kitchen door opened and Beatrice shuffled into the kitchen in dressing gown and feathered mules, her early-morning self almost unrecognisable to anyone more accustomed to seeing her clad in war paint and Gucci.

"I could hear that wretched woman through the ceiling," she grumbled. "I've never heard such a racket. What on earth does she think she's doing?"

Clare ignored this. "Shall I make you some toast?" she asked.

Beatrice shook her head. "No, nothing, thank you. And if you take my advice," she added tartly, looking at Clare's plate, "you shouldn't have it either, not at your age. You'll pay for it later on, you know. Weight gained at your time of life is hell to get rid of."

Clare opened her mouth to reply but was interrupted by the sound of the telephone and reached to answer it. "Hallo?"

"Clare? Hi!"

"Nick!" There was no disguising the pleasure in her voice. "Good morning."

"How are you?"

"Fine. I didn't expect—"

"Just wanted to say hallo and to say I've just seen my diary for the coming week. It's even more horrendous than I thought. Heaven knows when I'm going to be able to catch up with you again."

"Well, I'm not going anywhere." Clare kept her voice light and friendly and unconcerned. She glanced at Beatrice. She was sipping her coffee, watching her closely and making no attempt to disguise her interest in this conversation.

"I'm tied up for the next few days," he said, "then on Tuesday and Wednesday I'm down in Penzance showing off our Theme Park, after which we go to the Scillies. What a bloody awful week it's going to be!"

"It'll pass."

"But I don't want to spend my evenings with a crowd of strangers. I want to see you." There was a bleep at Nick's end of the phone, and he swore briefly. "Sorry! There's a call coming through from South Africa. I've been waiting for it for the last couple of hours and I've absolutely got to take it. Listen, I'll ring when I can, I promise."

"You do that."

"Talk to you soon."

She kept the non-committal smile on her face and returned to her toast, saying nothing. After a few moment's silence, Beatrice could restrain herself no longer.

"That was Nick Courtfield, I presume."

"You presume right," Clare said. "Are you sure you wouldn't like some toast? Or half a grapefruit? There's one in the fridge."

Beatrice ignored this. "He doesn't waste words, does he?" Her words carried an overtone of malicious amusement.

"He's in the office," Clare said lightly. "He's busy. An important call came through."

"Hm!" Beatrice raised her eyebrows and quirked her mouth as if she regarded this as no more than an empty excuse. "All I hope," she said, "is that you haven't let yourself fall for him."

"You sound like Minnie." Clare's voice was mild. "What's Nick ever done to you?"

"It's what his father did to little Jem. As you well know."

"As to that," Clare said after a moment. "Nobody actually *knows* anything, do they? Anyway, isn't it time we put all that ancient history behind us? After all, Nick wasn't even a gleam in his father's eye when Jeremy died, so you can hardly hold him responsible."

"I wouldn't trust any Courtfield further than I could throw him. Remember, I've known the family for ages. Seriously," Beatrice went on, "don't build your hopes up, will you? I'd hate you to get hurt."

"Nick and I are just good friends," Clare said, a note of finality in her voice. "Could we please now change the subject?"

For a moment Beatrice said nothing. She poured herself another coffee, lips pursed and a knowing look on her face. "A woman of your age is so vulnerable."

"Mother, please don't go on as if I'm completely over the hill! I may be all of thirty-six but I'm still sound in wind and limb."

Beatrice gave another derisive twist of her mouth. "You realise he wants Lemorrick, don't you? Everyone in the village knows it."

"Really?" Clare remained cool.

"You're simply asking for trouble if you think there's any more to it than that. He'll be hoping that a few kind words and the odd dinner will encourage you to let him have it for a knock-down price."

"Well, he'll be disappointed, then, won't he?" Clare, too, sipped her coffee, then very carefully put her cup down in its saucer. "Beatrice, I really don't want to pursue this any further. I've told you that Nick and I are friends and it happens to be the truth. Now please leave it at that."

Beatrice looked offended. "Well, the last thing I want to do is interfere, I assure you. I've never been that kind of mother – but you can't blame me for having your best interests at heart."

Clare was unable to hide her cynical amusement, but made no comment. There was silence between them for a few moments; then as if suddenly making up her mind, Clare took the bull by the horns, leaning forward, elbows on the table. "Beatrice—" Her voice was soft, inviting confidences. "Nick swears his father had nothing to do with Jeremy's death. I wish you'd tell me the whole story. I've never really heard it, you know."

"Nick knows nothing," Beatrice said tartly. "What could he possibly know?"

"Only what he's been told. You were there, though. Why are you so sure Hugh Courtfield was to blame?"

"Who else could it have been? The police found no evidence that anyone but Hugh had driven in or out of Howldrevel that day."

"Apparently they found no evidence that he was on the lower drive, either."

"You must think what you like." Beatrice shrugged her shoulders, as if dismissing the matter.

"You heard a car driving off. Did it sound like a sports car?"

Beatrice stared at her. "Who told you I heard anything?"

Careful, thought Clare. You'll be telling her about the diaries next. "I heard about it from Verity."

"She never forgave me for taking my eyes off Jem for five minutes, did she? Her little angel? Naturally I didn't want him to die, but believe me, he was the most pesky child, into everything. It took the patience of a saint to look after him."

"Why did you take him out with you, then?"

"Because—" Beatrice went no further, but pressed her lips

together as if refusing to say more. Eventually, however, she could not resist the opportunity to justify herself. When she spoke, her voice had a querulous note as if she was irritated by the world's inability to understand the way it was. "I was only young, a teenager, that's all. And you know what teenagers are like. I had this ridiculous crush on Alan Truelove – believe me, he was good-looking then, rather like a young Victor Mature, not the fat old soak he is now. You're too young to remember Victor Mature, of course, but he was a film star in my day and a real heart-throb."

"I've seen him on TV," Clare said, non-committally.

"Well, then, you know what I mean. We knew Verity wouldn't approve of us getting together – the class thing, you know. So Alan said taking Jem for walks would be a good excuse. We'd meet, sometimes, on the quay or in the field where the swings are."

"And sometimes in Howldrevel Woods?"

"Sometimes. It was all frightfully innocent. Just childish fun, really, though I don't suppose Vee thought so." Clare said nothing and the words seemed to hang in the air between them until even Beatrice looked a little shame-faced. "We couldn't possibly have known how it would all turn out," she said defensively. "I was devastated, just as devastated as Verity, but she never forgave me, you know. She pretended to, but she never did."

"You're wrong."

"No, I'm not. If she'd really forgiven and forgotten she would have left Lemorrick to me and I wouldn't be in the pickle I am now, with nowhere to lay my head."

Wearily, Clare sighed. "How you dramatise things," she said. "You have the villa, at least until it's sold, and you have a home here until we make other arrangements."

"Other arrangements?" Beatrice laughed shortly. "I can just imagine what's going through your mind. You think I can be shipped off somewhere, got rid of, so I'm out of sight and out of mind, while you sell the house and make a mint of money. Or do you imagine Nick Courtfield might marry you?" She laughed again. "Don't run away with that idea, darling. He might think it amusing to have a little dalliance with you, for old times' sake, but I was talking to someone who saw him in a restaurant in Truro with a ravishing redhead just a few weeks ago. No more than twenty, she said. Mark my words, that's the sort of girl he'll marry. After all, he's rich and he's good-looking and he could have anyone he chooses. Believe me, he's unlikely to choose a woman of your age, because another thing that everyone knows is that he's desperate for children."

"Just leave it, Mother." Clare was conscious of real anger now, fuelled in part by a terrible suspicion that there might be a grain of truth in Beatrice's words. "I must say," she went on, "considering how long it is since you set foot in Porthallic, it's odd you're so *au fait* with popular opinion."

"I ran into Maureen Smythe in the village yesterday. I've known her for years. She and I were at the same school in Truro when we were small and her husband worked for the Courtfield Corporation until he retired a few years ago, so he knows Nick quite well. We had quite a chat. Maureen says it's because Nick Courtfield's wife couldn't have children that his marriage broke up. It seems he's determined to have a son to carry on the family name."

Clare opened her eyes wide. "Wow! Like Henry the Eighth, you mean? Goodness me! How very fortunate for Lorraine that beheading went out of style!" She sighed. "Honestly, Mother, who knows what goes on in a marriage except the people involved? Which in this case, I presume, hardly included your old buddy Maureen."

"Just as you please." Beatrice gave a small, superior smile. "You know best, of course. You always do. Well, I'll go and got some clothes on—"

"Wait just a minute," Clare said. "Minnie's gone shopping and Peggy isn't likely to burst in, so while we have the kitchen to ourselves, could we just forget my future plans for a minute and talk about yours?"

Beatrice who had half-risen from her chair sat down again. "What is there to say?" she asked, a touch of wariness in her eyes.

Clare took a deep breath. "Just that whatever happens to Lemorrick, I'm afraid you're not going to be able to live here. Beatrice, please try to understand," she went on quickly, hoping to pre-empt the protests. "I might sell it or I might let it, or turn it into apartments. I just don't know yet, but whatever I do, I can't afford to pay for its upkeep without doing one or the other. It needs rewiring, a new boiler, the roof leaks, there's the insurance, the utilities, people to clean it, the chap who sees to the garden – you must see that it's a totally uneconomic proposition."

"I could chip in!"

"Chipping in isn't enough. It's not going to happen, Beatrice. What I will do is buy a flat for you, somewhere you'll enjoy. Somewhere with lots of nice shops. How about Exeter? Or Bath? London, even. Or – look, I can't help thinking about poor Gerald, all by himself in Barcelona. Suppose we found a little place for you there? It's a lovely city, chic and smart and cosmopolitan, and you're used to Spanish customs—"

"A little place?" Beatrice opened her eyes wide with horror. "I don't want a little place. I'm not used to little places. My surroundings mean a very great deal to me, Clare, and I simply cannot believe that Verity intended me to end my days in a 'little place'." She invested the words with such scorn that she might, Clare thought, have said "dog kennel". "Oh no," she went on. "I was brought up at Lemorrick and that's where I want to live. Among my own people. I'd *hate* to live in Barcelona!"

"Then think of somewhere else!" Clare was perilously near losing her temper. "Will you please get it into your head that you cannot live at Lemorrick? It simply isn't an option."

Beatrice got to her feet, pulling her dressing gown around her with tremulous fingers. "You're selfish," she hissed. "Utterly, utterly selfish." Her face was taut with rage, her mouth distorted, and she clenched her fists, raising them a little as if she would give much to be able to use them to batter her daughter. "Verity always indulged you far too much. You don't care who you trample underfoot so long as you get your own way! Well, we'll see." She seemed to invest the words with a wealth of meaning, as if she had untold powers at her disposal to force Clare to change her mind. "We'll see," she said again. And with that she slammed out of the kitchen.

Clare watched her go; then, as the door banged behind her she expelled her breath slowly, and put her head in her hands, elbows resting on the table. Had she said too much? On the whole, she didn't think so. It was time the exact position was spelled out, but even so she couldn't help feeling that she had somehow mishandled the situation. As Verity had pointed out, Beatrice was old now, and insecure.

But she was also extremely difficult. All that about Nick and Lorraine and his hopes for Lemorrick – it was all utter rubbish. Beatrice saw him as a threat, that was the truth of it, felt, somehow, that if he and Clare got together they would unite against her and she would never be able to regard Lemorrick as hers.

She was right in one respect, however. Being in love made any woman vulnerable, and Clare was no exception. It was so long since she had felt like this. There had been other men in the past twenty years, others for whom trumpets had sounded for a while, but she had met no one who had lasted, no man she could seriously commit to. None she could imagine living with for the rest of her life. Her feeling for Nick was different, but what was between them was so new, so fragile, that to listen to Beatrice's shrill little voice talking about him seemed like a kind of violation.

Later that morning she and Beatrice were due to go to coffee with Maggie Collins, who had phoned to invite them the previous day. Beatrice had seemed pleased at the time, but when Clare went upstairs to knock at her bedroom door to see if she were ready to walk the few hundred yards to the Collins's house, she found her still in a huff, barely able to speak to her.

"You've upset me," she snapped. "I've no wish to go anywhere in your company."

"Oh, come on, Beatrice! It was only sensible that I should spell out the situation. You have to accept it."

"I do not. I categorically refuse to. I'm staying right here until you come to your senses."

"So what am I to tell Maggie?"

"Tell her the truth. Tell her I'm upset because you're determined to turn your mother out of her home."

Clare turned round and left, exasperated to the point where she felt herself in danger of saying more than she should.

"It was good of you to ask her," she said to Maggie, when a little later she relaxed in the welcoming tranquillity of the Collins's sitting room. "Yesterday she was delighted at the thought of coming, but today she's staging a sit-in. I'm afraid she's furious with me."

Maggie, small and dark with a bright, intelligent face, was fully aware of the situation. "I can't imagine why she wants to stay in

Porthallic anyway," she said. "She's never made any secret of the fact that she loathes the British weather, and it's not as if she has any friends here, is it? Alex says she was always touchy and difficult."

"Well, it seems she's found one old friend. Someone called Maureen Smythe—"

"That old vixen? She's a well-known mischief-maker, best steered clear of."

"They sound a good couple." Clare sighed. "I'm pretty sure it's the status that makes Beatrice want to live at Lemorrick. She wants to take Verity's place as chatelaine. I don't know how I can convince her that it simply isn't going to happen."

"I hate the thought of the place being sold to a stranger."

"No more than I do, I promise you."

"I heard a rumour that Nick Courtfield wanted to buy it."

"He does. I said I'd give him first refusal, but he advised me to hang on to it."

"Did he now?" Maggie looked at her, her eyebrows raised. "Well, it's a big house for a man on his own. Not that I expect him to be on his own for very long."

"Not a case of once bitten?"

"I don't think so. Nick's the marrying sort and he'd love a family."

"Which is why, according to Mrs Smythe, that he divorced Lorraine. He wanted a son, and she couldn't produce one."

Clare was guiltily aware, even as she spoke, that gossip such as this might be said to put her in the same category as Mrs Smythe herself; she was glad, however, when Maggie laughed at this notion.

"Couldn't – wouldn't – I don't know. That might have contributed but it wasn't the real reason. Lorraine Courtfield was a floosie. No other word for it. No man was safe within a mile of her, I promise you. Nigel wouldn't so much as examine her little finger without the surgery nurse standing guard over him. To my certain knowledge Nick put up with an awful lot before she finally went off with the American oil man. Nick's a nice guy, Clare. He deserved better."

"I hope he finds it."

"Hey—" Maggie was smiling, looking at her quizzically, head on one side. "I've got a wonderful idea. You could sell Lemorrick to Nick, marry him and live happily ever after! Everyone's a winner. How about that?"

"How about it?" Clare countered. "Is life ever that neat?"

And that's enough, she thought. Maggie can dig as much as she likes, but I'm saying nothing.

She left shortly afterwards, arriving back at Lemorrick to find Minnie looking put out.

"Your mother's gone," she said. "Lord knows where. Went without a word, she did, and banged the door behind her."

"Probably down to the village."

"She's took your car. You left your keys on the side here. Careless, that was."

"Well, I never dreamed—" Clare broke off, feeling exasperated. She'd half intended to go to Truro that afternoon, but without a car it was out of the question. Beatrice could at least have waited to ask her if she needed it before helping herself.

"And if you ask me, she wasn't going down village," Minnie went on. "All dolled up, she was, in high heels and that new white sweater she bought the other day and the black coat with the fur collar. She don't wear that, going down village. 'Tis slacks and that shiny jacket, going down village."

She was right, Clare acknowledged. So where had Beatrice gone? She was intent, presumably, on demonstrating her annoyance. Well, it didn't matter too much. Her own particular errand in Truro wasn't urgent; another day would do if Beatrice didn't come back in time.

It was a dull day and darkness came early. By the time the lights were switched on in the village there was still no sign of her and Clare began to worry. Where on earth could she have gone? Plymouth, perhaps, drawn by bigger, if not better, shops than were to be found in Truro. Try as she might, Clare could think of no alternative. As far as she knew there were no old friends that her mother might suddenly have decided to look up. It crossed her mind that she might have gone house-hunting, but this she dismissed as nothing more than wishful thinking.

By seven o'clock, she felt much as a mother might feel at a child's prolonged absence – anxious but annoyed at one and the same time. Could something have happened to her? Beatrice had always been an erratic driver and her track record on Cornwall's narrow lanes was far from good. It was all too easy to imagine she could have crashed head on into a wall or an oncoming car.

Oh, stop it, she told herself angrily. She's simply staying away to annoy, to make a point; and with that she remembered the occasion detailed by Verity in her diary, the time when the whole household was out scouring the cliffs when all the time Beatrice was hiding nearby, laughing at them.

She hadn't changed. Not in sixty years. She still liked to think that she was the only person to be considered, that the world revolved around her wishes.

It was soon after eight-thirty when the phone rang. It was Greg Truelove, sounding a little tentative.

"We – er – have your mother down at the Lugger," he said. "I'm afraid she's a little – well, what they call tired and emotional, if you get my meaning. We're a bit worried about her. I said I'd call her a taxi, but she said no, she's got the car with her, but believe me, she's in no fit state to drive. I think she's been on a bit of a pub-crawl, to be honest."

Clare's heart sank. Beatrice, sober, was something of a loose cannon, likely to say the first thing that came into her head. Heaven alone knew what she would do when drunk.

"Thanks for letting me know, Greg," Clare said. "I'll come down to get her right away."

Her car was parked in a haphazard kind of way, straddling two of the few parking places provided on the quay. In the summer when the place was thronged with holidaymakers this would have caused mayhem, but on this misty autumnal night there were clearly few clients at the Lugger Inn to make any kind of complaint.

Clare went in under the slate-covered porch, and now she was closer she could hear voices and a burst of laughter from the public bar to the left. She opened the door and looked inside. Greg was there, pulling pints for a small group of venerable, blue-jerseyed fisherman clustered round the bar. Without pausing in his duties, he jerked his head to the rear, indicating the saloon bar.

Providentially, perhaps, this room was empty except for Beatrice, who was slumped on a high stool at the bar, and Alan Truelove, who was chatting to her in the over-cheerful, patronising voice more usually reserved for the aged or the insane.

"Here's your daughter, come to take you home," he said with obvious relief as he caught sight of Clare. He lifted the flap that enabled him to come round to the customer's side of the bar. "Come on, now, let's get you outside, there's a good girl—"

"Don't you good girl me," Beatrice said, shrugging away from him. "I'm not going anywhere." She rounded on Clare. "And what are you doing here? I'm *certainly* not going anywhere with you. Give me another little drinky, Alan." She was coyly flirtatious as she pushed her glass towards him. "Another one of those lovely ginnies-winnies, there's a dear."

"Now, I don't think that would be a good idea, do you?" Alan's voice was still in its emollient mode. "I think p'raps you've had enough, my love. Clare's going to drive you home."

At this, Beatrice sat up straighter and looked at him with extreme annoyance, on her dignity and clearly greatly offended.

"What do you mean, drive me home? I'll drive myself when I'm good and ready. I can drive! I'm perfectly comp— comp—" She gave up the struggle. "I can do it," she said angrily, banging her fist on the bar.

"Come on, Beatrice," Clare said coaxingly. "We'll be home in two shakes. You can have another drink there, if you like."

"We haven't any sloe gin at home. I like sloe gin." She was enunciating very carefully. "Give me another, Alan."

His eyes slid anxiously towards the door as a man and woman came into the bar, another more elderly couple hard on their heels, and he returned behind the bar to serve them. Clare continued, *sotto voce*, to urge her mother to leave without a fuss while Beatrice, equally determined, continued to resist.

"I can't give you another drink, my handsome," Alan said to Beatrice, his other customers having seated themselves at two of the tables round the side of the room. "'Twould be more than my licence is worth, and that's a fact. Now—" He lifted the flap once more and came to her side of the bar. "You be a good girl and let your daughter take you home."

"I don't need her! I can drive," Beatrice said again, more belligerently this time. "You know I can drive, Alan Truelove. It was you who taught me."

"Taught you?" Alan gave a short, dismissive, unamused grunt. "Tried to, maybe."

Beatrice swung her head towards Clare as if it had suddenly grown heavy.

"He did, you know. When I was just a girl. Very young," she elaborated. "Young and foolish." She turned towards Alan again and half-fell towards him, clinging to him, smiling up into his face. "Remember, Alan?"

"No." Alan extricated himself from her embrace and busied himself with a cloth, wiping the bar top.

"You do! You remember. You'd have done anything for me then."

"Beatrice—" Clare took her arm. "Let's go home. Dinner's ready."

Beatrice shook her off. "I don't want any dinner. I want another little ginnie-winnie." She reached for Alan again. "Don't be so mean, Alan." She swung her head towards Clare again. "I thought he was wonderful then – and he simply adored me, didn't you darling?" Flirtatiously, she pouted. "Now he won't even give me a little drinky for old time's sake."

"Go home, Beatrice. Go with your daughter."

Her mood changed and she became angry, her eyes glittering and her lips pressed together. Ineffectively she pushed at Alan.

"God, you're a bastard, Alan Truelove! When I *think* of what we went through together! You said you'd love me forever, that day in the woods."

"Go home," Alan said again, his voice hardly more than a whisper, his eyes suddenly wary. He flicked a glance over his shoulder to where his other customers were sitting, clearly fascinated and more than a little amused by what was going on at the bar. "Shut up and go home, Beatrice. There's no sense in dragging up the past."

Beatrice gave a bitter, unamused laugh. "You would say that, wouldn't you? You know it was all your fault. I was just a child, I wasn't re— re—" she fumbled over the word. "Sponsible," she said at last. "You shouted at me. Confused me. It was all your idea. I would never have *thought* of taking a car there. It wasn't my fault – it wasn't!" Her voice rose hysterically and she began to cry, tears running unchecked down her cheeks.

As if determined to end this confrontation once and for all,

Alan took a grip on her arm. "Come on," he said to Clare, "we can get her out between us."

"Don't you touch me!" Angry again, Beatrice reached for her handbag that lay on the bar beside her and gave him a swipe that was enough to make him recoil.

His face flushed with outrage. "You're going," he said menacingly. "You've said enough. Get out and don't come back. You're trouble; you always were."

"Trouble?" She laughed shrilly, though the tears still ran, causing her mascara to streak her face. "Me? Everything was your fault, I told you." She turned to Clare. "I told him," she said. "It wasn't my fault. He shouted at me. He came running out of the woods, shouting and swearing."

"Because, you silly bitch, you didn't know one gear from the next and you wouldn't be told, would you?" His voice was low, but he flicked another furtive glance over his shoulder as if afraid that others would hear him. "No one could ever tell you anything. Now that's enough. Let's get you out of here."

Clare, who had been following this exchange closely, put one arm around her mother. "Hang on a bit," she said, frowning, trying to make sense of it all. "What are we talking about here, Alan? When did you come running out of the woods, shouting at her?"

His face seemed to work for a moment before he spoke. "Forget it," he said at last. "It's all past history."

"What kind of past history? What does she mean? What was your fault?"

"I did nothing, except be fool enough to try to teach her to drive."

"I didn't mean to hurt anyone. I was confused! You were shouting! It wasn't my fault, Clare. He should have *seen* Jem there, but all he cared about was the car—"

For a moment nobody moved or spoke, not even Beatrice who, even in her drunken state, seemed suddenly aware that she had said too much. Still the tears flowed.

Clare found a tissue in her pocket and handed it to her. "Come," she said.

And now Beatrice offered no resistance as she was helped down from the stool, her knees buckling as her feet touched the ground.

"I can't manage on my own. You'll have to come too," Clare said to Alan. He did so, taking Beatrice's other arm, and in silence they supported her to the car and put her in the passenger seat.

"Now," Clare said, turning to Alan once she had closed the car door with Beatrice safely belted inside. "I have a pretty good idea what all that was about, but I want to hear it from you. What happened in the woods, when you shouted and Beatrice was confused? I must know," she added angrily as Alan said nothing.

For a few seconds more Alan Truelove was silent, then he gave a shuddering sigh and leant against the car, passing a hand across his face. "All these years," he said. "All these years. I still get nightmares—"

"About Jeremy Ashland? Was Beatrice right? Were you responsible for his death?"

"Oh, no. No, no—" Stung into animation, Alan stood up straight, shaking his head. "That's not true! I'm not having that! I wasn't even in the car. She was in the driving seat. We parked the car in the lower drive and went into the wood with the kid. We fooled about for a bit, then without any warning she ran out again saying she was going to try reversing. I knew she couldn't do it. I thought she'd end up running the car into a tree, or something, and then we'd have been for it. I didn't see the kid. I thought he was somewhere in the wood. He'd been playing there a minute before."

Clare felt hollow with the shock of it, yet there seemed, now that the words were spoken, as if there were a kind of inevitability about them. "Is that really the truth?" she asked faintly.

"I swear it," Alan said, more quietly. He seemed to swallow with difficulty, and once more passed his hand across his face. "'Tis something of a relief," he said. "'Twas like a bad dream and it's haunted me for years. That little tacker – dear little boy, he was."

"But I don't understand. You didn't have a car. You were only – what? Fifteen—?"

"I could drive, though. Dad used to take me up on the moor when I was only a little tacker myself. Mad about cars, he was, and so was I. Then Beatrice and I got talking to each other down here on the quay. Pretty maid she was then, and I fancied her. Wanted to show off, I suppose. She was the girl from the big house, see – and who was I? The local publican's son. 'Twasn't much, was it?"

"Go on," said Clare.

"We had a car, though. Not so many had cars in those days, and even fewer could get the petrol because of the war. Dad had contacts, though. Used to get some from one or two of the fishermen. Beer was short, too, so it was tit for tat, like." He paused and sighed. "Anyway, I said once I'd teach her to drive, just to look big, and she wouldn't let it rest. Kept on nagging at me. So I thought about the woods. They seemed a good place – off the road, where no one could see us. Nobody used that lower drive then, and it wasn't too far from the lock-up where we used to keep the car. Still do – well, not the same one, it's been rebuilt, but it's in the same place, right on the edge of the village. There's no space for a garage here, see?"

"But surely your father didn't agree—"

"Think I told him? 'Course I didn't! I pinched the spare key. It was easy – but mind you, I had to tell him after. . ." He hesitated. "It was dented, see, and scratched. I told him everything, and my Gor, he was some mad! He gave me a leathering, but he didn't want the police involved so he got the car fixed right away by a mate of his with a garage over to Wadebridge who owed him a favour. He knew everyone, did my Dad. Nobody round here twigged a thing, not even my mother."

"But how could he keep quiet about a thing like that? How could *you* keep quiet? And Beatrice—" The enormity of it took Clare's breath away.

"Least said, soonest mended, Dad thought. He kept his mouth shut and so did I. After all, 'twas a mistake when all was said and done, and nothing would bring the little tacker back. But whatever that bitch says, I'll deny I killed the kid, till my dying day. It was Beatrice in the driving seat."

"And Hugh Courtfield had nothing to do with it?"

"He was never anywhere near."

"But you let everyone think—" Clare stared at him. "*Beatrice* let everyone think—" She turned away, shaking her head in disbelief. Only that morning Beatrice had repeated the accusation. How could she? How *could* she?

"He was one of the nobs," Alan said, as if this excused all, made him invulnerable. "No one could touch him."

300

Clare looked at him. Would he believe her if she said he wasn't the only one who had been haunted by this tragedy? That Sir Hugh had been equally affected by it? That even people who lived in mansions had feelings and emotions? Something told her it would be a waste of breath even to suggest such a thing.

"We were only kids," he said again. "Frightened kids."

But cool customers, Clare thought. Cool and calculating. How could they have contrived to keep such a terrible secret?

"Old enough to know right from wrong," she said. "How could you have let an innocent man suffer like that?"

Alan stared into the distance for a moment without answering, then he pushed himself away from the car. "I've said my piece. I can't do more. God knows, I've suffered too. I've had nightmares about that day. You can say what you like, tell who you like, I don't care any more."

Clare watched him go. Thank God, she thought, that Verity never knew the extent of Beatrice's part in this. It could have been a blow from which even she would have found it hard to recover.

For herself, she felt in no hurry to get into the car to take her place beside her mother. She felt a cold anger, a distaste for so much duplicity that surely put the last nail in the coffin of any reconciliation between them.

There were bitter words on her lips as she belted herself into the driving seat, but they died unspoken as she looked at the small figure that was slumped beside her, fast asleep. In spite of her anger, she was overwhelmed by a reluctant pity. Beatrice had confronted the world with bravado and a string of lies, had neither confessed or professed penitence, but to assume that she had survived this tragedy unscathed was clearly mistaken. Guilt like that must surely be corrosive, corrupting and poisoning all it touched. It seemed, suddenly, to explain so much. Verity had been right in her assessment.

"Come on," she said wearily to the unconscious Beatrice. "Let's get you home."

Minnie helped her get Beatrice to bed, her disapproval filling the room like an ice-cold fog, though Clare said nothing about her mother's darker secrets.

"Never no better than she should be," Minnie muttered as she picked up Beatrice's clothes where they lay on the floor. "The sooner she goes the better, you ask me. She'll be nothing but a drag on you, mark my words."

"I imagine she'll sleep till morning," Clare said, making no direct reply to this.

"You ent had nothing to eat yet. I got your supper warming downstairs."

"Thank you."

Clare went to eat it, not because she was hungry but because Minnie would be put out if she did not. However she picked at the food without enthusiasm and finally pushed the plate away with half of it left.

"Sorry, Minnie," she said. "I'm just not hungry tonight."

"That's her fault, causing such an upset. Shall I make you a nice cup of cocoa?"

"No, but thanks for the thought. I think I might go to bed."

Minnie looked at her in astonishment for it was barely ten o'clock, but she said no more, merely folding her lips together and shaking her head, clearly holding Beatrice to blame for such unusual behaviour.

Clare poured herself a brandy and took it upstairs to her room. The windows were still uncurtained, and without turning on the light she went and stood looking out at the dark bulk of the hilly field that led towards the stile.

How was this latest revelation going to affect her relationship with Nick? What was between them was such a tender green shoot. Was this going to blight it for ever? He had left her last night in no doubt as to how the tragedy of Jeremy's death had scarred his father. Why she should feel personally guilty about Beatrice's part in this tragedy she couldn't quite make out; guilt was there, however, and shame and a mind-numbing sorrow that seemed to bring with it a dreary certainty that a happy ending for her and Nick was now probably out of the question. There was simply too much baggage, too much history to contend with. Also, she reminded herself, there was the matter of her own scepticism when he had assured her of his father's innocence. She'd maintained that it didn't matter, but of course it mattered! How could Nick forgive such a crass lack of trust on her part?

Sir Hugh would have to be told. By Beatrice? Clare gave a mirthless laugh. What a hope! She couldn't imagine such a happening, not in a million years.

She, Clare, would have to do it. Cravenly she thought of writing a letter, but dismissed the thought out of hand. That would be a shabby thing to do. But she had witnessed Sir Hugh in a rage once, years ago, when Nick had taken out a boat that his father had considered unseaworthy, and her heart quailed at the thought of confronting this choleric, unpredictable man with the truth about Jeremy's death.

Well, maybe it would resolve the dilemma concerning Lemorrick, she thought. It might be argued that the best thing she could do was to break all ties with Porthallic. She could sell the house, resume her career. After all, as she had told Nick, she had loved her work once and no doubt would again. And as for Nick – well, the way would be open for him to buy Lemorrick after all. She'd get used to the idea, eventually. People got used to all kinds of things. Perhaps at some future date its walls would resound to children's voices, just as she had imagined. The thought that they wouldn't be hers brought a pang of sadness, but she pushed it resolutely away. She would survive, she told herself.

This thing with Nick, it probably wouldn't have come to anything anyway. They barely knew each other, after all, not as adults. The whole brief episode had been something of a nostalgia trip for both of them, and she'd probably been a fool to treat it seriously, even for a moment.

Maybe, she thought, as eventually she lay sleepless in her bed, the ravishing redhead, so triumphantly described by Beatrice only that morning, would prove to be his choice. Perhaps she already was. Perhaps she was simply out of Cornwall for some reason and Nick had picked up the strands of their old friendship simply because he was at a loose end, bored with his own company.

Then she remembered how it had been, how easy they had been in each other's company, the laughter, the kisses and how they had stirred her. Was it only that morning she had been so euphoric, so certain that happiness was just within reach?

It seemed unbelievable, a million years away; and for a long time she stared into the darkness, feeling more alone than she had done for a long time.

Seventeen

At least the Courtfields' imminent departure from Porthallic with their group of foreign business men meant that she could postpone the dread task of facing Sir Hugh, though she was not sure that this was an unmitigated blessing. The thought of it haunted her all week and by Saturday morning she knew that if she were to get any peace at all, she would have to arrange a meeting with him at the earliest possible moment.

It wasn't easy to do so. She phoned the Courtfield Corporation's office in Truro to make an appointment, but though his secretary confirmed that he would be back in Porthallic that evening she was adamant that he could spare no time at all to see her. It was only by phoning the Dower House direct and appealing to Lady Courtfield, pleading an urgent need, that Clare had been granted an audience.

"Well, Clare, I'm afraid it will only be for a few minutes," Lady Courtfield said. "And you may have to wait while he showers and changes. He's down in the Scillies at the moment, you see. Indeed, he's been there for the past two days, but he'll be back this afternoon as we're holding a farewell party for the delegates over at the hotel this evening. Are you quite sure your business won't wait until tomorrow, when they'll all have gone?"

For a moment Clare hesitated. It was a temptation – but no, she had to see him, had to tell him in person before word of what had happened at the Lugger on the previous Friday evening filtered back to him.

"I'm awfully sorry," she said at last. "I really don't want to be a nuisance, but I'm going to London tomorrow and don't quite know when I'll be back. I really think I ought to speak to Sir Hugh before I go."

"Very well. If you come at six there should be time for a chat."

Clare had thanked her and had duly presented herself at the Dower House at the appointed time. A maid opened the door to her, but almost immediately she was greeted by Lady Courtfield who came from the drawing room, already dressed for cocktails in misty blue lace and numerous strings of pearls. She chatted pleasantly as she showed Clare into her husband's study, far too well-bred to give any hint of curiosity.

"You'll be more private here," she said. "Sit down and make yourself comfortable. Hugh shouldn't be long. Now, I must ask you to forgive me as Nick wants me to be on hand to make sure the delegates' wives are looked after so I'm going over to the hotel now and Hugh will join me later, when you've finished with him. I beg you not to keep him long!"

The study was a pleasant, rather masculine room, with framed studies of old sailing vessels on the walls and a massive, leather-topped desk set at an angle on the red Turkey carpet. Books lined one complete wall and opposite the window was a marble fireplace, a potted plant filling the otherwise empty grate. Above this was a portrait of an olive-skinned woman with a smile which, to Clare, looked every bit as enigmatic as that of the Mona Lisa. She had seen this picture before and knew that it was Hugh's mother and Verity's friend, Frances Wainright.

Having sat down, Clare rose to look at it once more feeling that she knew now what lay behind that wistful smile. Did Sir Hugh? Did he have any idea of the extent of his father's brutality? He'd had a rotten childhood, Nick had said, so perhaps he did.

When he finally entered the study, she saw nothing in his expression to make her think that the coming interview would be anything other than unpleasant. He was scowling ferociously, his furrowed, heavy-browed features looking like a series of darkly scored, downward-slanting lines, his thin lips clamped tight as a rat-trap. Her spirit, far from high to begin with, quailed still further but, forcing herself to appear bolder than she felt, she smiled and held out her hand. "It's good of you to see me, Sir Hugh. I'm grateful."

"Can't spare long," he said. He managed a grimace which she took for a smile, and shook the proffered hand. Not for the first time, Clare noticed his gawkiness, the awkwardness of his gestures, as if he had never grown out of his schoolboy shyne

"Busy week, this. Heard you were still at Lemorrick. Suppose there's a lot to do there."

"Yes, but I'm going up to London tomorrow."

"Really?" His eyebrows shot up as if he were surprised at this.

"I have to take my mother to Heathrow. She's decided to go back to Majorca."

He made a non-committal, harrumphing kind of noise at this and looked at his watch as if anxious to waste no more time. "Well, sit down, sit down. What can I do for you?" There was a touch of impatience in his voice as if his store of small-talk was exhausted. He sat in the chair beside the desk, angling it so that he faced her as she sat in one of the fireside chairs. Clare took a breath, unsure how to begin. "I'll have to hurry you," he added, like a TV quizmaster urging on a dilatory contestant. He turned away from her towards the desk, shuffling through some papers as if forced to fill every idle moment.

"It's – it's really about Beatrice – my mother – that I had to see you," Clare said hesitantly. "About – about Jeremy. You remember. Verity's little adopted son who was killed in the woods—"

The papers were stilled and for a moment he made no move. Then his head swivelled slowly to face her, his expression darker and more inimical than ever. "I have no wish to discuss that."

"I know! I know how you must feel. The thing is that I've found out the truth. I wanted you to know – wanted you to know how sorry my mother was ever to have involved you." This was not strictly true. Even knowing that Clare had been told the full story, Beatrice had uttered not one word of regret for Hugh Courtfield's anguish. It was the distressing knowledge that the story might become known to the village as a whole that caused her to make sudden plans to leave it.

"Go on." His voice sounded strange, strangled, and his eyes had become hard, like two dark, concentrated pinpoints.

Hesitantly, Clare told the story and having finished she braced herself for the outburst of rage that must surely come. But there was only silence. Sir Hugh turned away from her and lifted a shaking hand to his head before dropping it to the desk again. She was filled with pity for him. And yet, almost in spite of self, she was aware of pity for Beatrice, too.

"We – we have to remember how young she was," she said haltingly, as Sir Hugh continued to stay silent. "And I'm sure that she was never a happy child. Losing her parents as she did – it must have affected her. She craved love. Craved attention." Still Sir Hugh said nothing. "Believe me," Clare went on, "we are both sorry. So very sorry."

Sir Hugh remained silent, unmoving. His head was thrust forward, his hands flat on the desk, his breathing heavy. Then she heard a kind of guttural rumble coming from his throat as if he could think of no words to express his emotion, and pushing himself to his feet he strode agitatedly up and down the room, smacking the fist of one hand into the palm of the other, his shoulders hunched, his face contorted. Fearfully, Clare watched him, seeing his agitation, afraid that he might be on the point of some kind of seizure. Then at last he came to a halt in front of her.

"Empty-headed, meretricious little trollop. I always knew it. Always." Tears stood in his eyes and his mouth worked, and when he reached to steady himself by holding the mantelpiece, Clare saw that his hand was shaking. Anxiously she got up.

"Sir Hugh can I get you something? A drink, maybe?"

"Get out," he said thickly, turning his head away from her. Then, when still Clare hesitated, his voice rose to a roar. "Didn't you hear me? Get out of my sight. Never speak to me again. Get out, get out."

"I'm – I'm so sorry," she managed to say again, before turning to run from the room, closing the door behind her.

Once outside, she stood for a moment, her eyes closed, trying to regain some kind of equilibrium. She was more upset than she could have imagined by the way he had received her revelations and his loss of control had taken her by surprise. Poor man, she thought. Oh, the poor, poor man. Nick had been right, this terrible tragedy had blighted his life. Beatrice had blighted his life. Was it really any surprise that he had reacted so powerfully?

Pulling herself together she walked down the passage and into the hall. Lights were on in the drawing room to her left, but there seemed to be no one about, for which she was thankful. All she wanted now was to slip away, nurse her wounds and finish packing for the trip tomorrow. She'd intended leaving a letter of explanation for Nick, but now she wondered if there was any point. Like his father, he would probably want to forget that any branch of the Ashland family ever existed.

She had just reached the front door when she became conscious of movement behind her and realised that Sir Hugh was hurrying after her.

"Wait!" The words emerged as a kind of strangled cry. He still looked agitated, but perhaps less angry now. "Please wait," he said again, his tone more conciliatory. "I owe you an apology. I shouldn't have spoken to you as I did. A case of shooting the messenger – couldn't be more wrong. It was courageous of you to come and I should be grateful to you. Please – please, come into the drawing room and we'll both have a drink. We need to talk some more."

"Oh . . ." Bereft of words, Clare allowed herself to be ushered into the blue and gold sitting room and pressed into a chair. "I feel so inadequate," she said. "I really am so terribly sorry about all of this, but words are so – well, inadequate . . ."

"I'm about to give myself a restorative whisky and soda," Sir Hugh said, ignoring this. "What may I get for you?"

"Whisky sounds wonderful. Thank you." In truth she could marshal her thoughts to ask for nothing else. This sudden change of mood on his part had utterly confused her. A contrite Sir Hugh was something that she had never even imagined.

He left the room but returned moments later with the two glasses on a tray. "The maids are off," he said. "And my wife is over at the hotel—"

"Where you should be! I promised her I wouldn't keep you."

"Yes, well . . ." He harrumphed a little, raised his glass to her and took a sip. "I'm ashamed of myself," he muttered. "Shouldn't have taken it out on you. You were blameless."

"That's true, but I do understand how you feel. Nick told me—"

"Ah, Nick!" he said thoughtfully, and at this somewhat cryptic utterance, Clare looked at him questioningly. Sir Hugh frowned and cleared his throat and took a sip of his drink. "Now that's another thing," he said. "I'm – I'm very fond of my son, you know."

"He's fond of you, too."

"He's been hurt enough. His disastrous marriage – but you'll know all about that. No need to go into it. I don't want him to

308

suffer any more, if I can help it. When I behaved in such an ungentlemanly manner just now, I momentarily forgot Nick's interests."

Clare looked even more bewildered. "I'm sorry, I don't think I—"

"You said you were going away."

"To take my mother to the airport."

"But you'll be back? You see, Clare—" He hesitated and drew in his breath as if he found it difficult to frame his next words. "The past, all the injustice, is painful for me to contemplate, but that's of minor importance. It's the future that matters. Nick's future. If he thought that any words of mine drove you away, I'm not sure he would ever forgive me."

Clare's frown intensified. She found herself hardly daring to believe what he appeared to be implying. "I – I really don't know what I'm going to do," she said. "When I found out what Beatrice had done, I felt—" Helplessly she gestured as if the right word eluded her. "Angry, of course. Sickened. But one has to feel pity, too. She was young and mixed-up and felt deprived of love – mistakenly, of course, because Verity loved her, but at that age kids don't always think straight, do they? And Sir Hugh, you must believe me, she hasn't been unaffected by this. I think knowledge of what she did that day has haunted her, all her life."

Sir Hugh gave a bark of unamused laughter. "I'd be surprised if it hadn't. She should go down on her knees every day of her life and beg Almighty God to forgive her. I'm not sure that I ever can."

"So you see why I feel I must leave Porthallic?"

For a moment he looked at her and slowly his expression softened. "Not really," he said at last. "Why should this wretched business cause you to leave home if you don't want to? I know what Nick would say."

Clare drew in her breath, the question she hardly dared ask trembling on her lips. "Sir Hugh—" She dried up, licked her lips, and began again. "Sir Hugh, what exactly did you mean when you said that Nick wouldn't forgive you?"

He took a sip of his drink as if needing time to think out his reply. "As you probably know, we've been down in the Scillies," he said at last. "A lovely place. It was a calm, restful interlude in a fairly frantic week. One night – Thursday, it must have been – Nick came to my room for a nightcap and we sat talking for hours in a way and at a level we don't seem to have had time for lately."

"And?"

Again he hesitated, making Clare realise how difficult it was for this man, normally so stiff-necked and reserved, to find words for such intimate moments.

"Nick—" He paused. "Nick spoke of you," he said. His voice was gruff, a little embarrassed. "He spoke regretfully of the wasted years. I can't break his confidence to tell you all he said, but believe me, you mean a very great deal to him and it would be a great sadness to him if you were to leave Porthallic."

"But when he knows about my mother—"

"My dear child, what difference will that make to a man who feels as Nick does? He regrets all the wasted years – he told me so – so he won't want to waste any more. So put the past behind you. I never could, never did, and it coloured my life. Or rather, took the colour from it. That was my burden, rightly or wrongly, but I refuse to allow it to become Nick's. Your mother behaved abominably. No other word for it. Yes, yes, she was an unhappy child, I know all that, but I've no time for all that psychological clap-trap. I'm of the school that believes we are all ultimately responsible for our own misdeeds. Still, I daresay a close scrutiny of the history of the Courtfields would provide a few disreputable moments. We all have skeletons in our cupboards, you know."

Was he thinking of his violent rapist of a father? Or his mean-spirited grandmother who had wrecked Verity's early romance? It seemed, Clare thought, a strange twist of fate that it should be that same woman's descendant who was now asking her to stay. And what did he mean by the words "a man who feels as Nick does"? How, exactly, did Nick feel? A small shaft of happiness stirred inside her.

"I haven't finally decided what to do," she said.

"Then what shall I tell Nick?"

"Tell him—" She hesitated. "Just say I'll be back," she said.

"Good," Sir Hugh said; then he said it again. "Good. I'm glad.

He actually smiled quite broadly as he said it and his habitually dour expression was transformed. I do believe I could get quite fond of him, Clare thought, with some astonishment.

310

*   *   *

Clare and Beatrice made an early start the following day, in time for Beatrice to catch the three o'clock plane from Heathrow to Palma. It was, Beatrice told her daughter as they drove over the Tamar Bridge, entirely for Gerald's sake that she had decided to leave.

"I've been worried about the poor old boy," she said. "Couldn't sleep, night after night, for thinking about him. He's not happy in that home, you know. Now I've had time to think I can see that it's my duty to open up the villa and bring him back from Barcelona."

"I'm glad," Clare said. Adding, in case her mother thought she had only her own interests at heart, "He'll like that."

"Of course I would rather have stayed here," Beatrice went on, determined that her sacrifice in leaving Cornwall would not go unappreciated. "As you well know. But one has to think of one's duty."

These sentiments, couched in different words, were repeated numerous times during the journey and no mention was made of Alan Truelove, Sir Hugh Courtfield, or anything else connected with the long-ago tragedy that had robbed Verity of her son. She's air-brushed it out, Clare thought in astonishment. Somehow she truly sees herself as the devoted wife, leaving her ancestral home not because she was afraid of word of her past misdeeds becoming common currency but simply because her soft heart calls her to look after her ailing husband.

"Don't wait," Beatrice said once she had checked in at Heathrow. "I'll go straight through to the departure lounge."

They kissed briefly, meaninglessly, and she was gone. Clare stood for a moment, victim of conflicting emotions. Relief was there, of course; but regret, too, for she recognised that there would probably never be the rapprochement that Verity had so ardently wished. The pity she had felt for her mother immediately after Alan Truelove's revelations hadn't lasted. Who was it who said that the fault lay not in our stars but in ourselves? It was an aphorism that seemed more appropriate to Beatrice than to most.

Leaving Heathrow, she drove on into central London, finally arriving at her flat mid-afternoon. It seemed very cold, she thought; cold and over-tidy and rather alien, with its minimalist furnishings and pale curtains. Beautiful in its way, of course, for she had expended a lot of time and money in choosing the furniture and fixtures and it had seemed perfect then. Now, however, they were somehow out of tune with her present mood, as if they represented a phase of her life that had passed.

She made coffee and stood with the mug in her hand, looking out at the river. Then, and only then, did she allow herself to concentrate on the hints that Sir Hugh Courtfield had given her regarding Nick's feelings.

He wanted her to stay; would never forgive his father if his words were the cause of her leaving Porthallic; had spoken of the "wasted years" when they had been apart.

How could negative emotions such as regret or guilt even gain a foothold when she had such things to consider?

There were a number of loose ends to tie up before she went back to Lemorrick. She resigned her job, cleared her desk, met a few friends (Duncan, she was glad to learn, was enjoying a new relationship with a Polish flautist, but committed himself to throwing her way any freelance opportunities he might come across). She pursued a few other contacts who might be useful, put her flat on the market, took a quantity of unwanted clothes to Oxfam. She phoned Nick, too, and had a satisfying conversation with him, though she kept her own counsel regarding all that his father had said.

"Come home soon," he begged her.

"I will. I'll be there on Wednesday, all being well. About four, I should think."

"Then I'll be there at five past. Clare, it's great news about my father. Thank you for telling him."

"It was the least I could do." She gave a rueful little laugh. "Minnie knows, of course, which means everyone else will, too. Telling her anything is tantamount to putting a notice in the local paper."

"No one will blame you."

"No? Well, it's right the record should be put straight. I'll have to live with the consequences."

"There'll be talk, I suppose, but only until the next bit of gossip comes along."

"Which could well be when Minnie realises you are coming

to see me the moment I get home. What a tasty morsel that will be for her and her cronies to chew on!"

"So be it." Nick said, and she could tell from his voice that he was smiling.

The timing, it turned out, was slightly wrong. She arrived twenty minutes before four – which was, perhaps, a good thing as it gave her time to prepare Minnie for Nick's imminent arrival.

"Just as well I made a cake, then," Minnie said, leaving Clare to realise just how much the news of Beatrice's guilt had affected her and her attitude towards Nick and all the Courtfields. They had, it seemed, been rehabilitated in her eyes.

When Nick arrived, on the dot of five past four, they went into each other's arms as if somehow during their absence from each other and in spite of the fact that no far-reaching plans had been made, matters between them had nevertheless reached some kind of resolution.

Later she took him on a tour of the house, for he had never penetrated far and was curious to see what lay beyond the sitting room and dining room. He said very little as they went from boot room to kitchen to dining room and morning room, but clearly the patch of damp here and the fallen plaster there was not going unnoticed. Clare found his silence, his professional interest, a little disconcerting. What was he thinking? Surely Beatrice hadn't been right after all when she said that it was only the house he was interested in?

"And this was Verity's room," she said, having saved it till last, pausing for a moment with her hand on the doorknob as if, even now, there was a reluctance to invade this space – and, she thought, in the company of a Courtfield, too! What on earth would Verity have said?

But there was nothing to say, not now, except for regret for past suspicions. Verity, that most generous of women, would have done all in her power to make amends to the Courtfield family, of that Clare felt certain. If Nick did decide to buy Lemorrick, if – wondrous thought – they lived there together, there would be no need for Verity to turn in her grave.

Everything's going to be all right, Clare silently assured her as she opened the door. And when she saw the room bathed in the pale, diffused light that was somehow a reflection of the sea below, it seemed to her that for the first time there was an indefinable sense of abandonment about it, an expressionless air, as if all that was Verity had deserted it, quietly and peacefully taking its leave as if there were better places to go.

Nick took a step over the threshold and looked about him. "What a wonderful room," he said, making a subjective comment at last.

"I've always thought so. The sea gives it a special kind of light of its own – except when there's a gale blowing, of course. The wind seems to have a special kind of malevolence up here."

"I love it." He went to the window once more. "Imagine waking up to this." He turned and put an arm round her shoulders. "Ours?" he said softly, after a moment. "I think it has to be, don't you?"

Theirs? Hers and Nick's?

Yes, it had to be. Was written in the stars, you might say. It was the neat solution that Maggie had suggested, but now it didn't seem too neat to be true but simply right and inevitable. Even so, a certain perversity made her demur a little.

"We'll see," she said; but she smiled at him as she said it and it was a prevarication that fooled neither of them. Of course this room would be theirs, and in it they would wake up to many a new day together. She suddenly felt quite confident of it.

And there would be children; she felt sure of that, too. Lemorrick would come alive again, perhaps more alive than it had ever been, with love and laughter and the sound of young voices.

Verity would like that.